# LORD

†††††† OF ††††††

# ORDER

IMBRIFEX
BOOKS

*Also by Brett Riley*

The Subtle Dance of Impulse and Light

Comanche

# LORD

† † † † † † **OF** † † † † † †

# ORDER

IMBRIFEX BOOKS

IMBRIFEX BOOKS
8275 S. Eastern Avenue, Suite 200
Las Vegas, NV 89123
Imbrifex.com

IMBRIFEX.
BOOKS

*LORD OF ORDER: A Novel*

Library of Congress Cataloging-in-Publication Data

Names: Riley, Brett, 1970- author.
Title: Lord of order / Brett Riley.
Description: First Edition. | Las Vegas, NV : Imbrifex Books, 2021. |
Identifiers: LCCN 2020027324 (print) | LCCN 2020027325 (ebook) | ISBN 9781945501418 (hardcover) | ISBN 9781945501425 (epub) | ISBN 9781945501371 (e-book) | ISBN 9781945501326 (audiobook)
Subjects: GSAFD: Fantasy fiction.
Classification: LCC PS3618.I532724 L67 2021  (print) | LCC PS3618.I532724 (ebook) | DDC 813/.6--dc23
LC record available at https://lccn.loc.gov/2020027324
LC ebook record available at https://lccn.loc.gov/2020027325

Jacket design: Jason Heuer
Book design: Sue Campbell Book Design
Author photo: Benjamin Hager
Typeset in ITC Berkeley Oldstyle and Rockwell Extra Bold

Printed in the United States of America
Distributed by Publishers Group West
First Edition: April 2021

*This book is dedicated, as always, to Kalene (thanks for the suggestion about McClure), and to Shauna, John, Nova, Luna, Brendan, and Maya. To my God, without whom I am nothing. And to everyone who has suffered because of someone else's so-called morality, I see you. Never lose heart.*

# THE CEMETERY

The man stood on the crumbling road. Green grass grew through its many fissures. Old, faded symbols with long-forgotten meanings stretched into the distance down its center and near its edges. To the man's right, the boy rubbed his eyes, blond hair tousled and pillow-matted. He stood nearly as tall as the man, his father, though he had not yet seen twelve summers. To the left, the girl shielded her face against the rising sun, her curly red hair billowing in the breeze. Soon they would follow the road down the hill to the graveyard where, among monuments great and small, dew sparkled on the grass, though not for long; the air already felt warm. A scorching late June, portending a July that would fell strong men in their fields. But not yet. First came the telling.

The man embraced the children. The girl laid her head against him. Below them, the meticulous workers cropped the graveyard grass with handheld shears and their own sweat, dumping the detritus into cloth bags. When the sacks were filled to bursting, the landscapers tied them with heavy string and left them behind. Several dotted the ground like mottled warts.

Other workers scrubbed the monuments with horsehair brushes and water from barrels in horse-drawn carts. The clean stones marched outward in neat, straight rows. In some sections, marble gave way to wooden crosses. Unless the history books were wrong—always a possibility, given how long they had been banned, how nameless heroes hidden in darkness and damp had extended them with cramped and often near-illegible handwriting on flimsy parchment—the cemetery had once been reserved for the honored dead of a great army serving a country called the United States of America. Now, even the word *country* sounded archaic. Countries existed only in books and tales told around hearths. Generations ago, the Cult had risen, blasting old Earth and its ways into scree on which nothing could find purchase.

But all that was already known. The children had come to learn something both more and less than the wide world's story.

The girl fidgeted. Sweat gleamed on her freckled face. The boy stood as still as stone, but he was older. Only weeks ago, he had come to the man with questions about how things came to be. By custom, the man was bound to answer. So here they were.

We're looking for a grave in the very back, the man said. The workers won't reach it until dusk. Perhaps even tomorrow. Gather your packs and follow me.

He grabbed his poke from where it lay at their feet. Like his father before him, he had packed it with full canteens and jerky and a single blanket, the barest of provisions.

The boy and girl shouldered their own packs, and the three of them set out. Soon enough, they could not avoid stepping on graves, but they did so with their heads bowed, silent. Sooner or later, everyone returned to the earth.

They walked until the children's breath tore in and out of their lungs, until they grunted with every step, until sweat soaked their hair. The man seemed oblivious to their struggles. The children did not cry out or complain.

Finally, the man followed a row of sturdy white wooden crosses. The grass grew midcalf high. The cemetery's rear border was lined with thick foliage, as if it were the edge of the known world. Near that tree line, one cross stood three times as tall as the others. This grave had been tended even as the others grew their green beards. Surrounded by the lush blooming whites and purples of dogwood and crepe myrtles, the cross was made of polished stone the bleached color of desert sand. It had been festooned with flowers now in various stages of decay—red roses shriveling against the base, orchids and lilies lying wilted and desiccated. The man stopped before this monument.

He took off his pack and spread their blanket over the grave and sat cross-legged, back straight, the pack beside him. He motioned to the children. They unshouldered their burdens and sat, one near each of his knees in the shadows of the trees and the cross. The man closed his eyes for a moment and gathered his strength, knowing the tale would be long and the telling hard. But it was his duty, and he had never shirked duty in his life.

He opened his eyes and said, We come to celebrate what is and mourn what was. Here, we acknowledge the growth of your bodies and your minds. Here, you learn where you come from and who you are. You must remember what I tell you today for the rest of your lives. I'll not tell the tale again, and one day, you must come to this place and tell it to your own children. That is your charge. Take this greatest of all gifts—knowledge—and pass it on in your turn, and you will perpetuate all that is good in the world. You will stand vigil against the vile, the destructive, the cruel and merciless. There is nothing more at stake today, and nothing less. Do you understand?

The children nodded, solemn, eyes wide. Crickets struck up their low, buzzing orchestra. The sun trekked across the sky. The Earth turned. And the man began his story.

# ✤ 1 ✤

**G**abriel Troy crouched beside the blown-out windows as bullets whizzed by and pockmarked the wall. A double-barreled shotgun lay in the dirt and broken glass at his feet. His right hand clutched the .357, its barrel pointed up. He stuck his left index and middle fingers through the hole in his shirt and yanked, ripping most of the sleeve away. With the makeshift rag, he applied pressure where the bullet had gouged a shallow two-inch-long trench across his right shoulder. The wound bled and pulsed, but the arm seemed sound. Regardless, he could not stay put for long.

When the heretics had spotted him and opened fire, Troy had ducked into the Danna Student Center, a building where, if the histories told true, scholars had gathered for meals. Its windows had been shattered long ago, its walls vandalized with paint and edged weapons of who knew what kind or origin. Some of the graffiti looked old enough to have been written before the Purge. The floors were covered in dirt, broken plaster, shards of glass, animal droppings, and piles of rotting leaves.

Still, the façade seemed sturdy. *A few Troubler guns ain't gonna bring it down. If we live through this, I'll assign a renovation crew here. About time somebody did.*

The shells of old vehicles had, over the long years, been hauled away to the western dumping ground, most of the burned and ruined buildings repaired or razed, but some, like this one, had never been touched. Always too much to do, never enough time.

A rifle blast disintegrated part of the wall over Troy's head. *No time*

*for ruminations.* He grabbed his shotgun, stood, and ran, hurdling rubble and firing through the glassless windows. At the end of the hallway,
he ducked again, leaning the shotgun against the wall and pulling
the pack off his back. He dug through it and found some bullets and
reloaded his Magnum, listening in vain for cries from outside. *Reckon
I missed em all. Well, I was runnin and shootin blind.*

Scattered small-arms fire suggested the Troublers had hunkered
down in the Peace Quad, but at any moment, they might stop pressing
their luck and rabbit. If they crossed Broadway in Willa McClure's direction or headed back across Calhoun where old Ernie Tetweiller waited,
things might get sticky. The girl and the elder were mainly supposed
to be noisemakers, kicking up enough ruckus to herd the Troublers
toward Jack Hobbes or Gordy Boudreaux. If that failed, the Troublers
might duck into one of the unlocked buildings and turn this firefight
into a siege. *I gotta drive em toward St. Charles, and I gotta do it now.*

But even that presented risks. If the Troublers crossed St. Charles,
they would disappear amid the crops and trees in Audubon Park.
As directed, the field workers and foresters had slipped away as the
time for the raid drew near so no citizens would be harmed, but even
Santonio Ford would struggle to track the Troublers if they split up.
At best, pursuing them would mean a firefight on open ground or in a
wooded spot of the Troublers' choosing. Best if the battle ended here.

More shots—from Bobet or Marquette Hall? Those buildings had
been renovated during Tetweiller's tenure as lord. Troy had earmarked
them for storage and apprentice housing, but no one had moved in
yet, meaning their doors were bolted with heavy chains and padlocks,
the keys to which hung on a wall in Troy's office. Still, the Troublers
could perhaps break through the fortified windows. He could not let
that happen. To keep them in the open, he would have to show himself
without getting killed and then lead them across the horseshoe-shaped
drive facing St. Charles. If he could manage it, he and his crew could
neutralize the entire nest.

Another shot tore through the wall, showering him with dust. You had to laugh at the irony, or maybe cry—a gunfight in a place once called Peace Quad. He reached into his pack and pulled out six grenades, three smoke bombs and three concussives, and cradled them in his left arm as he closed his eyes. *Lord, keep me and mine safe. Guide my hand. And forgive me for the wrongs I've done.* Then he took a deep breath, selected a concussion grenade, and pulled the pin. He threw it out the window as hard as he could and crawfished back the way he had come, tossing grenades every few feet, alternating the concussions and the smokes. Halfway down the hall, the first grenade exploded. The roar echoed and amplified off the surrounding buildings. The student center shook. Chunks of earth and grass spattered the wall behind him. Dust and smoke blanketed the quad, and from somewhere in that miasma, human voices screamed.

Troy retrieved his shotgun and the Magnum. Then he kicked open the splintered door and dashed outside, firing into the gloom. They're hurt and blind, he shouted. Rip em to pieces.

*Let's hope they ain't figured out I'm talkin to myself.*

To his right, the sharp reports of a large-caliber pistol. That's gotta be Boudreaux, some unseen Troubler cried. Fall back.

Troy smiled. Willa McClure, the kid he had left on the other side of Broadway Avenue, had done her job, keeping the Troublers in the quad. He fired toward the voice. Someone grunted and fell. The flat crack of a rifle to his left. A Troubler hacked and coughed and started to sputter, like someone gargling heavy syrup.

Get the hell away from the street, said a woman Troy could not see. Hobbes must be over yonder.

They've got us on three sides, a man responded. Should we break into one of these goddam buildins or what? Where do we *go*?

Thataway, said the woman. Troy's comin, and I don't plan on waitin here until he shoves his shotgun up my ass.

Troy raised the shotgun and fired into the smoke, both barrels, but if he hit anyone, they kept quiet. He pressed forward as he reloaded, squinting against the smoke and gunpowder, stumbling over holes gouged in the grounds until he reached the back wall of Bobet Hall. Then he turned right and headed toward Broadway.

*I hope Willa don't shoot me. Still, better to take my chances there than on Calhoun. Ernie's got worse eyesight and a bigger gun.*

At the building's corner, a middle-aged Troubler crouched, trembling, a shotgun clutched in his dirty hands. He wore sweat- and mud-stained breeches and a ragged roughspun shirt. His eyes were closed, his lips moving. Troy crept up and shot him in the back of the head with the .357. The man slumped over, hindquarters in the air, blood and brains caking the brick. Troy stepped over the body and trotted toward St. Charles, leaving the Troubler's shotgun behind. He had no free hand to carry it.

Eight Troublers huddled up ahead. They spotted him and ran. Half of them broke south beyond Marquette Hall, heading for the horseshoe driveway and into the killing box. Boudreaux had hidden in the old Holy Name of Jesus Church, while Hobbes and his .30-06 lay somewhere in Thomas Hall. As soon as the Troublers entered the horseshoe, both deputies opened up, Boudreaux's shotgun blasting low peals of thunder, Hobbes's big rifle cracking. They fired three or four times each. All four Troublers skittered on the pavement, dead or dying.

Troy pursued the other four, one of them a woman. They had nearly reached St. Charles when someone in the brush across the street shot three times, and the male Troublers fell onto their faces. The woman ran ten more feet before she realized what had happened and stopped, her hands in the air.

Santonio Ford stepped out of the tree line, his long dreadlocks flowing behind him, his rifle pointed at the woman's head. Troy raised a hand. Ford nodded.

As Troy approached, the Troubler spat at Ford. You're a goddam ass licker, she said. Hope you enjoy them chains around your neck.

Ford watched her, impassive.

Troy kicked her in the back of her right knee. She grunted and fell, but she did not cry out. Her black hair hung in grungy strips, streaks of gray at her temples. Her green eyes blazed like twin emeralds in her ruddy face. Her lower lip was split open and bleeding, and when she smiled, her teeth shone bright red. She looked no more than five and a half feet, barely 120 pounds. And yet this woman had caused more trouble in the New Orleans principality than any other single person in the history of the Bright Crusade.

She spat blood onto Troy's boot and sneered. And look here. If it ain't the ass hisself.

Troy struck her in the head with his shotgun's stock. She fell over, unconscious, her left eyebrow split open, blood pooling beneath her.

Pleased to meet you, he said. Then he looked at Ford. Good shootin.

Ford began reloading his rifle with ammunition from the poke he carried over his shoulder. Thanks. Doubt I could have got all eight. You herded them other four thataway like cattle.

Cattle are smarter than this bunch.

Boudreaux stepped out of the church just as Willa McClure appeared, the Rottweiler that followed her everywhere at her heel. Her short blond hair looked as if she had cut it herself with a dull knife. Always clad in a hodgepodge wardrobe of whatever she could find, most often deerskin trousers and busted boots and roughspun or animal-skin shirts originally cut for some boy who apprenticed in a physical trade, usually as dirty as a swamp dweller and as ready to punch you in the privates as shake your hand, McClure now looked impassive, even bored.

Across the horseshoe driveway, Hobbes ambled toward them, rifle resting on his shoulder. Somewhere behind Hobbes, Ernie Tetweiller was almost certainly climbing down from whatever rooftop he had chosen. Hopefully, the old man would not fall and break his hip, or worse.

McClure walked up and stood over the woman. This her?

I'm pretty sure, yeah, said Troy.

She's got a nice ass, if you like em flat. Which I don't.

Willa.

Sorry, McClure said. She did not sound sincere.

Your information was good.

Course it was.

McClure always came through. She might have been only twelve, give or take a year, but she knew how to get and use information better than most adults. Troy clapped the kid on the shoulder as Hobbes joined them. In the distance, Tetweiller limped their way, favoring his right leg, as always.

Gordon Boudreaux, the youngest deputy, reached the group as Hobbes spat on the woman's head. Rest of em are dead, he said. Gotta say she don't look like much. Sure it's her?

Troy wiped sweat from his brow. It's Stransky, all right. I ain't never seen her before, but I heard her voice once, that time they tried to set fire to the Quarter. Still, don't you boys go thinkin the Troublers are done. Born fighters don't never stop.

He tried to sound firm and assured, but his traitor heart sang like the heavenly choirs themselves. They had smashed a major pocket of the resistance, and they had captured the leader of New Orleans's Troublers. All in all, the day was going well.

## ✤ 2 ✤

They walked their horses down St. Charles, through Lee Circle, and onto Camp Street, passing water bearers hauling barrels from the Mississippi and crews carrying fuel for the populace's stoves and lamps. Sanitation teams emptied chamber pots and drove wagons of sealed waste-filled barrels across the bridge and down Jean Lafitte Boulevard. There they would dump their casks into the canal, where the waters might lead to Mud Lake, Barataria Bay, the Gulf of Mexico.

When Troy's company turned onto Canal and then Decatur, Stransky stirred. Troy kicked Japeth, his gray, into a fast trot. The others followed, and when Stransky regained consciousness in the Quarter, her grunts as the animal's spine drove into her abdomen kept time with the hoofbeats. Near the Temple, they passed more and more armed guards.

*I wonder if it's time we made the Cabildo an armory,* Troy thought. *Seems a waste, makin all these folks take two extra trips every day, checkin out their weapons off-site and back in again eight hours later.*

As the officers of Order passed, the guards saluted, most of them eyeing Stransky with the kind of awe and horror usually reserved for gods or devils. Grown men and women scattered like chaff in the wind. Children ducked behind parents' legs or into the shadows of stoops. Soon enough, the company trotted through the gates of Jackson Square. They reined their horses and dismounted on the pristine grounds, tying their animals to the hitching posts erected around the statue depicting Jesus with outstretched arms.

Troy had searched the official histories and found no mention of any Jackson connected with New Orleans. His identity—indeed, his whole life—had blown away like dust before history's winds, like the origins of so many street names, bodies of water, whole territories. In any case, the square belonged to Jesus now, in fact if not in name.

Hobbes and Boudreaux untied Stransky and shoved her toward the High Temple as a groom scurried across the grounds. He saluted Troy. Your orders? he asked.

Rub em down and feed em.

Yes, sir. Should we shoot the infidel's mare?

No. That law's a relic. The animal ain't at fault for what her rider did.

The groom saluted again and turned to the horses. Ford and Tetweiller stood nearby. McClure had slipped away as soon as they had mounted up back at Loyola. She would reappear when she wanted. She had been living like that for years.

Troy first turned to Ford, the dreadlocked man with the muscular arms, the deerskin shirt, the alligator boots, the bear's teeth necklace. Ford had supervised the city's hunters for ten years, and though he was only thirty-seven, he had more experience spilling blood than even old Tetweiller, much of it from animals, fish, fowl. Today, as always, Ford had fought well and killed cleanly, but, as always, his eyes revealed his inner sadness. *In all the wide world's principalities,* Troy wondered, *is there another chief hunter who hates to kill?*

Couldn't have done it without you, Troy said, sticking out his hand.

Ford shook it. You hear anything else about the proposals?

The Dallas principality's high minister had recently and publicly urged Rook—the Supreme Crusader, who lived in Washington, D.C.— to legitimize Catholic rituals, arguing that a Christian was a Christian, no matter how the person got baptized or took the Lord's Supper. Troy liked the idea but doubted Rook would ever go that far.

Nothin, he said. I reckon we'll just have to keep prayin on it.

Ford looked as if he were about to say something, but then he saluted. Yes, sir.

Bag that. Old friends ain't gotta sir me.

Okay, Gabe.

Speak your mind, Santonio. Somethin's got you in its teeth.

Ford looked toward the river for a while. He seemed tired. Rook scares me, he said. From what I've heard, every suspicion in Washington turns into an accusation, and every accusation becomes truth. If that's how it is, we're buildin our house on sand.

Tetweiller, walking over and catching this last, said, And here I thought you always followed orders.

Ford frowned. I always have. Obedience is faith, right? But if Rook keeps takin the hardest line, we'll have a Stransky in every neighborhood. There's gotta be a middle ground. I think that's where most folks live.

Ain't you philosophical, Tetweiller said. Especially for a fella that won't have kids of his own to send into this future he's so worried about.

Ford looked as if he wanted to punch the old man. Instead, he turned away.

*Don't know why Ernie aimed so low with that comment, but he's right,* Troy thought. *We gave up any chance for kids and families when we took our vows. Just like the Catholic priests and nuns. Weird how the brass ain't ever seen that similarity.*

Still, Ford had a point, too. From what Troy had seen in his own life and gleaned from past lords' journals, the Crusade had grown more secular over time. Now Rook ruled in Washington, isolated, surrounded by acolytes, digging himself deeper and deeper into the old dogmas, pushing when the tides of most people's lives pulled. If those trends continued, revolution would be inevitable. If Rook had his way, they would all be wearing sackcloth and ashes by next year. Infertile ground in which to plant the future.

Still, Troy was a lord of order, not a theologian. He clapped Ford on the shoulder. That's a worry for another day. I gotta see to Stransky. Be well, my friend. After Ford had saddled up and trotted through the gates, Troy turned to Tetweiller. Thanks, Ernie. I don't know what we'd do without you.

The old man scoffed. Horseshit. You could have got anybody to lay on that roof and take potshots at them polecats. You're just too goddam sentimental to let me stay home and drink.

As always, Troy ignored the old man's salty tongue. You think Santonio's right?

Tetweiller's face was lined and creased, his eyes deep set, his bushy white eyebrows waving in the breeze like a crawdad's antennae. I ain't noticed much love for Matthew Rook, but we don't seem to be losin any folks to the Troublers. We might just need to hunker down and hope the next supreme's better.

Sometimes it seems like Santonio's travelin a dangerous road.

He's troubled, but he'll never turn Troubler. Still, the next time some Washington muckety-muck comes to town, you might wanna make sure he's gone fishin. Rook's people don't take kindly to talk about middle ground.

Troy considered this for a bit. Ford kept the city supplied with fresh meat, watched over the crops, drove away scavenging animals and Troublers. He had fought beside Troy countless times, had just helped him catch Lynn Stransky. If Rook were willing to toss aside such a loyal and valuable man simply for questioning methodology, then perhaps the Crusade really was losing its way.

Well, Troy said, I gotta figure out how to handle Stransky. You wanna come?

Naw. I'm old. It's almost time for my nap.

Time for your whiskey, you mean.

Tetweiller smiled. That, too.

The old man turned and ambled toward the gates. Troy wished he too could walk away from everything awaiting him in the Temple. His bones ached, as if he were closer to Tetweiller's age than Ford's. On some days, gunpowder seemed to make the world turn, to raise the crops. It wore on a man. He wanted to go home and soak in a cold bath, let today's deaths ebb out of his conscience like sweat from his pores. That house, that tub, the attendants who filled it at exactly the right times were part of the privileges that came with being the lord of order. He had earned them.

But duty came first. So despite his ringing ears and the will-sapping heat, he approached the Temple, which the ancients had called St. Louis Cathedral.

*Heavenly Father, give me the strength to get through this.*

Inside, Norville Unger manned the reception desk, as he did from dawn till dusk every day. Seventy years old, Unger lived in the prison out back and, in Troy's memory, had traveled no farther from his post than Jesus's statue, at least while on duty. He ate in his little cell and slept almost exactly eight hours a night. He took no days off. Though the guards outside searched all visitors, Unger searched them again. He interviewed them and determined their purpose, their politics, their faith. If someone made it past him, they had been deemed a loyal member of the Bright Crusade on urgent business. The only people who could enter the Temple without Unger's say-so were the lord of order, the deputy lords, and the city's most prominent, office-holding Crusaders like Ford and LaShanda Long, the chief weaponsmith.

The Temple's spires—seemingly ornamental when seen from the street—had been hollowed out and fortified. Inside the Temple, at the front of the sanctuary, entrances to each spire faced Unger's desk and opened onto narrow spiral staircases. No one except the lord of order was allowed in them without Unger's permission. Two floors above, twins of these doors separated Troy's office from the staircases. Only Troy and Unger possessed keys to these four doors, which proved how highly the lord esteemed his desk sergeant. Anyone climbing those staircases could move beyond Troy's third-floor office and up to the tiny cells at the terminus of either spiral staircase, though not even Norville Unger could open the cells' doors; the only keys sat in a locked drawer of Troy's desk. Only the Crusade's greatest enemies ever occupied the towers.

When Troy entered the sanctuary, Unger saluted. Congratulations on the arrest, the old man said.

Thanks, Troy said, returning the salute. The towers secure?

Unger frowned. Course they are.

Troy winked. I figured. They got the prisoner ready?

In your office now.

Okay. I'm headin up.

Beyond Unger's desk, pews bordered the long center aisle, which led to a raised platform where New Orleans's high minister—a pinch-faced, stoop-shouldered man named Jerold Babb, who was older than Tetweiller and wore isolated tufts of springy white hair like drifts of melting snow on his wrinkled and spotted pate—preached his sermons. Troy walked under ancient chandeliers hanging from long chains in the ceiling, their crystal globes holding thick candles, their glass fogged by time and soot and dust. The windows looking onto the alleys outside had once held stained glass, but it had been shattered during the Purge. In its place, smoked bulletproof glass had been installed, with thick iron bars bolted to the outer walls.

Despite these fortifications both within and without, the Temple's foundation had been sinking for centuries. Yet it still stood. Most New Orleanians believed this phenomenon proved their cause was just, though the secret histories revealed that some of the first Crusaders voiced outrage at how the bones of old Catholics had been disinterred and tossed in the great river back in the time of Jonas Strickland, the Crusade's founder. Strickland's forces had purified those early protestors through torture and confession, and the ancient Papists had gone unavenged.

But such unpleasantries had long since vanished from the Temple grounds. Now, in this place, the high commanders of the Bright Crusade's New Orleans chapter held their heavily guarded worship services every Sunday morning and evening. The gathered flock would file in, accompanied by the choir's a capella humming. Once everyone had found their seats, Jerold Babb led them in pledging allegiance to the Crusade. Two songs—one by the choir, one from the full congregation—preceded a prayer from the reigning lord of order. Next came testimony from any Crusader who had traveled beyond the principality's borders, followed by reaffirmations of faith and tributes to anyone who had distinguished themselves in the past week. These last parts were not repeated in the evening, which shortened the night service by as much as an hour. Then Jerold Babb would preach—though, these days, *wheeze* would have been more accurate—while drinking whole carafes of water and wiping his grizzled brow on the sleeves of his robes. His evening services seldom lasted more than an hour and a half and sometimes sputtered to a halt in half that time. After a final hymn and a brief benediction from Babb, the weary Crusaders would go forth into the city, there to fellowship and break bread. Once a month, Babb would deliver the Lord's Supper. No Crusader ever spoke the word *communion*.

Now, on a weekday, with the sanctuary mostly empty, Troy passed down the center aisle. Two more doors were set into the back wall. The left-hand one led to a short hallway, which opened into the prison out back. The jail, which had been built in Strickland's time, currently housed only twelve prisoners, most of them low-level Troublers. Troy passed through the right-hand exit, beyond which lay staircases any visitor allowed inside the sanctuary could use. They led to the second-floor offices of the deputy lords and to Troy's headquarters on the third floor. The first Crusaders had installed those rooms where once there had been only balconies. They reinforced the walls and mounted shatterproof windows every few feet so officials could look over the ground floor. Hobbes and Boudreaux shared the office on the right, their walls covered with city maps, sketches of possible Troubler positions in outlying areas, routes to Baton Rouge and Lafayette and the entire southern region, hand-drawn wanted posters, weather forecasts, personal notes. Both men used mahogany desks that were stacked high with government documents, political reports, crop and water information, pest control memoranda.

On the left side of the second story, in Babb's office, the minister's cedar desk, enscrolled with Bible verses in calligraphy, never held much besides an inkpot and quill, a sheaf of paper, the Jonas Strickland Bible, and an in-progress sermon. The walls were bare except for a few pinned-up notes near the desk. Babb kept no other furniture except an oil desk lamp, a rack for his heavy robes of office, and two hard straight-backed chairs for anyone in need of counsel. Deep, plush rugs meant to ease the pressure on Babb's creaky joints and spine covered most of the floor space. When the minister napped in his office, which was often, he slept on a rug, using his robes as a pillow. When he awoke, he would call out until Hobbes or Boudreaux or a passing Temple worker came and helped him up.

Babb met Troy as the lord reached the second-floor landing. The high minister's hands trembled, but his voice rang out strong and deep. Gabriel, he said. Congratulations. May you purify your prisoner and send her to meet the Lord's judgment scoured clean.

Troy touched a finger to his hat brim. Thank you, Jerold, he said, shouldering past the old man. Have a good evenin.

The lord of order's office was located in the hollowed-out and armored third floor. According to the histories, the front wall had once housed a huge clock face, but it had been replaced just after the Purge with an enormous stained-glass rendering of Jonas Strickland holding a Bible in one hand and a sword in the other. This glass was both bulletproof and one-way so Troy could look over the expanse of Jackson Square all the way to the river. Documents and maps annotated in Troy's neat and precise hand covered the office walls. His desk sat near the back wall, where visitors using the rear staircase could pass through the heavy oak door and pull up a chair. The lord kept his desk nearly bare; he liked to look his visitors in the eye, not barely glimpse them through mountains of reports.

Presently, Hobbes and Boudreaux sat on the desk, one at each corner. Lynn Stransky knelt before them, her head high, her greasy hair hanging like the strands of a wet mop. His padded straight-backed guest chairs had been pushed against a wall.

*Where should we put her when we're done here? The prison or a tower?*

Troy's humanity suggested the prison, but the cold and practical part of his mind already knew he would put Stransky in a tower. She was the kind of enemy of the state for which the place had been built.

Before that, though, she had to be interrogated.

*I ain't lookin forward to this. Shootin somebody in battle's one thing. This other, it never seems godly.*

The bare wooden floor creaked under Troy's feet as he crossed the room, sat behind his desk, and glanced at Hobbes, who shook his head, indicating Stransky had not spoken. Her eyes were open, their piercing green eerie in the dim room. Troy leaned back and crossed his arms over his chest.

Hobbes and Boudreaux took positions on either side of Stransky, facing Troy. Hobbes hooked his thumbs into his gun belt. Boudreaux tucked his hands into his pockets. Both men's faces were expressionless. Stransky stared at Troy's breastbone.

We know who you are, Troy said. We got your description from Willie Grout when we took him outta Armstrong Park two years ago. See? You're on my wall.

He cocked his thumb and indicated a wanted poster—painted, not sketched, and twice as big as the ones in the deputies' offices. Stransky glanced at it. One corner of her mouth twitched. Ain't that pretty, she said.

Troy cracked his knuckles. You can thank Willie if you ever see him again. That picture helped our source recognize you when you made your mistake.

What mistake?

Comin into my city without a mask.

Ain't you the shit.

Reckon you never saw our lookout when you rode outta the bayou, but he saw you. And he came a-runnin. Now your riders are dead, and you're all alone.

Stransky snorted. Boudreaux glanced at her and shifted his weight. Without looking at him, Stransky said, Don't get fidgety, boy. I ain't gonna bite your nuts off. Not today, anyway.

Boudreaux stilled, his face blank.

You've been spotted in a dozen different places over the last two months, Troy said. Sometimes in town, sometimes in the swamps. It ain't like you to be so visible. Makes us wonder what kind of Troubler business needs that much of your personal attention.

I reckon you can wonder your heart out.

Could be you're plannin an assault on this Temple. Could be somethin worse. Tell us what you're up to, or you're gonna wish you had.

Stransky grinned. Her teeth were white and straight, even though the rest of her looked like she had never seen a bathtub. I got the love of the true God on my side. You shitbirds don't scare me.

Hobbes backhanded her on her left temple, the sound flat and meaty. She grunted and fell against Boudreaux's legs. The younger deputy shoved her away, and when she regained her balance and looked at Troy again, the smile was gone.

Don't be bringin God into this, Troy said. I'm gonna ask you nice one more time. It's your last chance to leave here with all your teeth and both eyes. What are the Troublers plannin, and how many are comin? Where will they be?

Up your ass, Stransky said. She laughed, the sound like briars scraping broken glass.

Hobbes raised his hand again. Troy shook his head, and Hobbes hooked his thumb back in his gun belt. When Stransky's laughter subsided, Troy said, I gotta hand it to you. Ain't nobody ever laughed at me in this office before. Maybe out there in their little hidey-holes, but never where I can see em. Still, all them guts ain't gonna help you. These boys are losin patience.

Stransky spat.

Boudreaux grunted. Heathen, he hissed.

You ain't as smart as you look, Troy said, and you looked pretty dumb in the first place. Gentlemen?

Hobbes yanked Stransky to her feet. Boudreaux dragged one of the straight-backed chairs into the middle of the room, and Hobbes shoved Stransky into it. Go get them chains, Hobbes said to Boudreaux.

Boudreaux exited, his boots thundering down the stairs. Troy came around to the front of the desk and sat on its edge. He rested the toe of one boot on Stransky's knee. You people always gotta do things the hard way. But what good will that do? Even if you don't tell us nothin, we'll find out eventually. Look at how we found you.

Stransky cackled again. Hobbes punched her in the jaw. She crashed to the floor and lay there, still laughing. She spat blood. You think you know what's goin on in this city. In this *world*. But you don't know jack shit.

Hobbes raised his fist, but Troy waved him off. The lord of order bent and looked Stransky in the face. What's that mean? What can you and your godless scum friends know that we don't?

Stransky tried to sit up. Godless? We don't lick the boots of the bastards that killed billions of people. Them loony birds in Washington never had nothin to do with God. That was just a mask they wore so dumbasses like you would think you're on the right side. And look how well it worked.

Neither Troy nor Hobbes replied. Boudreaux was back on the stairs with the chains, thumping and rattling and creaking. Stransky held Troy's gaze. If she feared whatever was to come, she gave no sign.

Let's get back to the subject at hand, Troy said, and

remember—whether you'll be able to walk afterward depends on what you say. What are the Troublers up to, and where will they be?

Stransky looked into Troy's eyes, as intimate and serious as a lover. She moved as close to him as she could before Hobbes grabbed the back of her shirt. I won't tell you what or where, she said. But I'll tell you why.

Troy straightened and leaned against his desk. Boudreaux entered, thick chains hanging off one shoulder and dragging on the floor, the cuffs and locks clanking. After the young deputy stopped next to Hobbes, Troy said, I'm listenin.

Stransky turned her gaze on each of them, one at a time. I'm only tellin you because I hope you boys love this town. You can kill me, but I won't say shit else. You understand?

Get on with it, Troy said.

I've met with runners from our people in Washington. They've spent months confirmin rumors we've been hearin a long time.

What rumors?

She cleared her throat. Rook's gonna turn New Orleans into a city-sized prison for folks like me. But here's the *real* kicker. He's plannin a new Purge, and we're standin on ground zero.

Boudreaux gasped. Troy felt as if she had slapped him. He stared at her, silent.

But Hobbes scoffed. Garbage, he said. Y'all live hand to mouth out yonder in the muck. Don't need no Purge. Like usin a shotgun to kill a mosquito.

Stransky sneered. Your precious Crusade went and got secular in its old age. Rook believes most of y'all self-righteous jackoffs are headin for hell in the same handcart as us, and he wants to speed you along. He's gonna wipe out everybody but his own inner circle and some hand-picked brood mares with big tits and long legs.

Horse dung, Hobbes said.

And it all starts here.

No.

Prisoners from all over the continent are on the march. Everybody the other lords locked up, and everybody they can root out on the way. Guards are comin too. Scores of em.

But why would he drive all the Troublers here? asked Boudreaux.

To get us all in one place, dumbass, Stransky said. It'll be an event for the histories, the one that links Rook's name to Strickland's. He'll butcher us, and then, with nobody left to resist, he'll move on to the rest of the world. Kill off the wolves, and the sheep go easy.

She's crazy, said Hobbes. We're loyal. And saved.

In Rook's world, everybody's a Troubler except them that kiss his feet every day, said Stransky. And we're a long way from D.C.

Troy shook his head, frowning. I figured you for better than this. That's the most far-fetched lie I ever heard.

It ain't no bullshit. You'll see. Today we got word a rider's comin from the capital. Be here before you know it.

More lies, said Hobbes.

Stransky ignored him. This fella's gonna give you a new mission. He won't go into much detail, like about how Rook's ordered raids from ocean to ocean, or how the prisoners have been quarryin rock and fellin trees and forgin iron from Canada to Mississippi. But the orders will confirm what I'm sayin about New Orleans. They're gonna make it sound like you're bein done a favor, but once them prisoners show up, once they start droppin big-ass sections of fortified wall along the city perimeter, you'll believe. If you can't live with yourself at that point, come see me, and I'll tell you the rest.

She looked neither sardonic nor angry, even though they had beaten her and killed at least seven of her friends that very day. No, she looked *frightened*. Something about the bags under her eyes, the lilt in her voice. Troy had been trained to spot falsehood, and he saw no lie here. *She ain't scared of us. But she's scared all the same.* Something transferred from this woman to his spine and rattled his bones. *Why would anybody want another Purge? We're winnin the war. Her information's gotta be wrong.*

He crossed his arms and tried to keep the uncertainty out of his voice. Who told you all this?

Stransky grinned. I told you. A runner. Call him a little bird that flew into town today. And back out again. You didn't get us all, Gabe.

All right. Leave that for now. What do your people intend to do?

She looked at him as if he were mad. We're gonna fight. What the fuck do you *think* we're gonna do?

He waited, but she did not elaborate. He sighed and rubbed his temples. He had been chasing her for years, and now she knelt before him—Lynn Stransky, leader of the principality's Troublers, a terrorist and a heretic. He should have been lying in bed with an iced tea in one hand and the Jonas Strickland Bible in the other or indulging himself with a rare drink at Ernie Tetweiller's. Instead, he stood in his stuffy office, sweltering and uncertain. What if it were true? What if Matthew Rook had come to worship Jonas Strickland's acts more than God Himself? From the perspective of generations, the Purge seemed almost theoretical, abstract. The thought of it happening here, to people Troy knew, to his town—he could not force his mind to travel that road. It was the difference between watching lightning play over the horizon and being struck.

Boudreaux unfurled a length of chain. Its clinking disturbed Troy's contemplation. He shook his head. No. We won't need that. Take her to a tower cell. I ain't buyin your lies today, lady. Maybe you can peddle em some other time.

Boudreaux dragged Stransky to her feet and yanked her toward the door. She looked back at Troy. Like I said. Come see me when you learn who's really lyin.

They exited, thumping up the stairs. Stransky's cackles drifted down like the call of a carrion bird. Troy walked back behind his desk and sat in his chair. The day's weariness pulsed through his legs and lower back. Hobbes took a seat across from him. He removed his hat and fanned himself, looking worried. And something stirred in Troy's gut because Hobbes never worried.

So what do you think? Troy said.

Sounds like bull dung. But she believes it.

Troy nodded. I read it that way too.

Hobbes fanned himself a while. Troy stewed in his own sweat, thinking hard.

So what now? Hobbes said.

Troy took a deep breath. Go celebrate. We caught a big fish. Me, I'm gonna visit the sisters and sound them out. Maybe they've heard somethin.

And then?

Troy traced the loops and swirls of his desk's grain. If the sisters supported Stransky's story, things would change, irrevocably and fast.

If this rider don't show up, he said, then Stransky's a liar, and we can hang her. In public, where the rest of em can see. But if he's real, we're gonna listen close to what he says. If we don't like it, seems we'll have three choices. One, go along and let the city die. Either it'll be Purged, or the prisoners will raze it to the ground. Two, try to get our populace outta town and abandon the city. If there's enough guards comin, they might kill you and me and Gordy, but maybe we could save some of our people first.

When Troy fell back into silence, Hobbes said, And three?

Open rebellion.

Hobbes whistled, low and long. Rebellion's a mortal sin.

Yep.

Hobbes chewed on the possibilities. The weight of the conversation pressed on them, as omnipresent as the city's wet heat. A heap of bad choices, he said.

Yep. We gotta prepare for the worst.

How, without startin a panic? Don't reckon we can just ask folks to move outta the city for a month or two.

We should start small. You, me, and Gordy already know. Ernie and Santonio. LaShanda Long and Willa McClure. That would give us the folks in charge of order, food, and weaponry, plus Willa's information.

Anybody else?

Not till we get a better idea of what's true and how our group feels about the options.

Hobbes nodded and passed a hand over his face.

Troy got up and headed down the stairs. He needed a meal and a cool bath and a quiet house in which to think. Not for the first time, he wished Lynn Stransky damned to hell for what she had said and done.

**T**roy and Japeth clopped down Camp Street in fading amber light. The gray's hoofbeats echoed against the buildings. Two children dressed in deerskin sat on the walk, playing Go Fish. They glanced at Troy as he passed and then went back to their game. He had come here so many times that his presence no longer inspired awe, except when he shot somebody. Then, it seemed, everyone genuflected.

He reined up at the Church of the Sisters of Mercy and Grace, once known as St. Patrick's. Just after the Purge, Jonas Strickland had outlawed all non-Christian religions and sent his new lords of order to slay any adherents who survived the Purge. His new world church absorbed every Protestant denomination. He marginalized Catholicism but did not outlaw it, perhaps knowing only his most radical followers would countenance the extermination of Christian peoples. Thus, the Sisters still existed and performed their ancient rites. In his capacity as lord of order, Troy had long ago learned that some Troublers attended those services, but they never broke Crusade law during Mass. He respected the Church's status as a sanctuary, much to Jerold Babb's displeasure.

*It's part of your duty to stamp them out,* the old man was wont to say, jabbing a crooked, palsied finger at Troy. *They are heretics.*

*Not even Rook calls the Catholics heretics,* Troy usually replied. *I won't turn my gun on other Christians. And if we disrespect sanctuary, what's to stop some Catholic from bombin our services?*

Still, Babb lectured him about the Papists at least once a month.

The sisters' priest was an octogenarian who, except during Mass or confession, barely stayed sober long enough to string two sentences together. Troy had conversed with the man perhaps five times and could not remember when he had last seen the old rumpot. He might have left town or died. Sister Sarah Gonzales truly led the church. At forty-two, she was New Orleans's de facto Mother Superior, her elders having died or ridden away on missionary work. Sister Sarah's contacts with Troublers meant she held valuable information. The problem lay in how to get it out of her. She feared no earthly power, not even Matthew Rook. She could not be convinced the Crusade acted as God's earthly hand. She would not be tricked. One could only ask her what she knew and hope for the best.

Troy tied Japeth to a rusty metal post with a bulbous head, the previous function of which he could not fathom, and approached the church. He took off his hat, as he always did before entering, and glanced at the empty thoroughfare as a matter of habit, but the Troublers dealt their violence from the shadows, from around corners, from behind trees. They would not confront him in the open unless they could sneak a whole regiment onto Camp. And so, with no heretics to shoot, Troy pulled open the heavy doors and stepped inside.

Past the foyer and the swinging wooden doors leading to the sanctuary proper, darkness and the heat of closed spaces enveloped him. Up front, dozens of votive candles flickered on their bier. Weak sunlight filtered through the stained-glass windows. Dark lamps hung on the walls. The pews sat empty, the confessional doors open.

He took a deep breath. Hello! he cried.

His voice seemed to fade in the soupy heat before it could travel ten feet. Sweat poured down his face. He wiped it on his shirtsleeve and walked down the central aisle, pausing before the votives. They sat side by side on old chipped saucers marred by scattered blobs of wax. Perhaps three dozen flickered. Seventy or eighty more were dark. Apparently Sister Sarah's followers felt easy about their souls today. Often the altar appeared to be on fire. Troy passed his hand over the wicks. They flickered, though none went out. His shadow cavorted in the aisle, long and angular, somehow disturbing. No one answered him.

*Reckon I might as well go.* He thought of knocking on the closed door set into the back wall, but he had never been invited into the recesses of Sarah's church and probably never would be. He turned to leave, but the door opened on creaking hinges. When he looked back, Sarah Gonzales stood there, hand on the doorknob, her dusky face curtained in her black habit's coarse cloth. She held a lantern and wore a frown.

I've asked you a million times not to bring that gun in here, she said.

Troy looked down. He had slapped leather when she opened the door. He let his hand fall away from the weapon. And I've told you a million times, I don't take it off. I've been known to bathe with it.

The way she carried herself, her assurance, her dignity, her commitment to her work and her people—she was stronger and more beautiful than anyone he had ever known, even when she angered him. Perhaps he even loved her, despite knowing they could never be together. Neither nuns nor lords of order took spouses or consorts, married as they were to their churches, their duty.

How could she stand to wear that habit in such heat? Troy had never seen her hair, though Sister Jewel had told him it was black and curly and long enough to reach her hindquarters. Even in the shifting light, her almond-colored eyes, her full lips, and the sharp slope of her nose aroused him. Shame burned in his breast. She considered herself a bride of Christ. Even if he did not share that conviction, honor bound him to respect it.

She hung the lamp on a hook and sat on the altar, hands in her lap. Just remember this is God's house. Keep your fightin in the streets.

He sat on the nearest pew, facing her, elbows on his knees. I ain't lookin to fight. I need information.

You know I won't betray sanctuary or confession.

I caught my limit today. I reckon you heard we got Lynn Stransky.

Sister Sarah gestured dismissively. I doubt you're foolish enough to believe it'll change much. The rebellion is bigger than one person. Even her.

It's too hot in here to debate, Troy said. The lantern flickered, though the air seemed still and dead. Perhaps their breath troubled the flame. Its light danced across Sister Sarah's face, now revealing her eyes and mouth, now casting her in darkness. He looked away and waited for her to ask what he wanted, but she remained silent, as patient as time.

Stransky told us somethin that's got me a mite concerned, he finally said.

I doubt she'd tell you anything true.

It ain't her secrets she's tellin.

Sister Sarah might have raised her eyebrows. Perhaps her mouth opened, just a little. What, then?

She told us Washington's sendin riders here. They're bringin a load of prisoners. And they wanna turn New Orleans into a prison.

Troy waited, but Sister Sarah said nothing. She kept as still as the saints on the stained glass, kneeling or giving succor or dying forever in their frozen world.

Well? You heard anything like that?

She grunted. You've treated me and mine better than anybody else would have, Gabriel. But we can still barely show our faces in daylight. To us, this city, this *world* has been a prison since the days of Jonas Strickland. What's a few more inmates, a few more guards?

Troy rubbed his temples. A headache had formed behind his right eye, whether from heat exhaustion or stress he could not have said. Pain stabbed through his skull every time the lamp flickered. They sat for a while without any way to mark time. The world might have stopped turning.

You don't really believe that, he said.

Her tone softened. Yes and no. My people got quarantined

generations ago. That ain't right. But I've worked my whole life in this city. I wouldn't see it destroyed if I had a choice.

Sure sounds like you've heard somethin. You don't act surprised.

I'm not. More than one Catholic has passed through here tellin tales about mass arrests and chained laborers quarryin rock or choppin down whole forests. Somethin's goin on out yonder. It could all land here as easy as anywhere else.

Troy rubbed sweat from his eyes. He had soaked through his shirt. His behind felt damp. But if the heat bothered Sister Sarah, she gave no sign. Against her habit's black cloth and with the sanctuary's greater darkness, her face and hands seemed to float, disembodied, spectral. She seemed to be waiting for him to say something. But what? If Stransky were right, the Crusade had condemned New Orleans. Troy's people could never live inside the walls with the prisoners. It would mean fighting for their lives every moment of every day. And walled up in the city without supervision, the Troublers would drag the buildings down, set fire to the river, rip open the very sky. Their nature was destructive, their hearts vindictive.

If Stransky were lying, her fiction had taken root in the hearts of the Troublers themselves, so deeply that they lied to Sister Sarah with words that sounded like truth. Either way, the situation was as bad as he had ever seen.

Why didn't you tell me when you first heard? he asked.

I figured you already knew. And I had no proof. Besides, would you have believed me? You didn't believe Stransky.

I've always believed you. Some warnin would have been nice. Now I got no time to prepare.

Prepare for what? If you believe your cause is just, why are you worried? Sister Sarah stood, leaving the lantern on the altar. She patted him on the shoulder. He tried to ignore how his skin tingled beneath her hand. If all this comes to pass, these prisoners and their guards will trample your life's work to dust. Can you sit back and watch that happen? she asked.

The first words that came to Troy's mind would constitute treason: no, he could not watch it happen, would not let it happen, would die trying to stop it. He would ask Hobbes and the rest to stand with him, and if they would not, then he would fortify a position on the causeway and fight until the guards shot him dead or the marchers walked him down. He wanted to say he could not bear to see New Orleans ruined and forgotten, as if none of them had ever acted, loved, or died. But he could not say any of that. He had always served the Crusade, always believed. When he was with Sister Sarah, he often wished their lives had been different. But they had to live the lives God had given them. Those lives and no other.

I don't know what to say, he confessed.

Sister Sarah patted him again. You shouldn't be ashamed of strugglin. It only means you're human. You should only hang your head if you choose the wrong side.

And I reckon you think your side's the right one.

Sister Sarah picked up the lamp, shadows rolling in and retreating like tidewater. You've known me for twenty years. I'm happy here, at peace with my decisions. When everything's finished, I hope you can say the same.

She glided away as if she were standing on a moving track. For all Troy knew, she might have had wheels under those garments instead of legs. She passed beyond the door without looking back and shut it behind her.

Troy sat for a while, his thoughts following half a dozen paths through the history he shared with his companions. Before the boys could mark their ages in two numbers, Troubler ambushes had slaughtered Troy's and Hobbes's parents only weeks apart. They had been Crusaders, not Catholics, but the Troys had died on the steps of this very church, the same spot where, when he was twenty-two, Gabriel met Sister Sarah Gonzales. All part of God's design. Troy and Hobbes had apprenticed themselves to the office of order before they could understand what the word would mean in their lives, what it meant to New Orleans. Other orphans had, each in their own time, bound themselves to the principality and the Bright Crusade. They were tutored by citizens who spent their lives rearing and training future leaders—those who would keep order, those who would lead the hunts and coordinate the harvests. Ford and LaShanda Long apprenticed two or three years after Troy and Hobbes, Ford's parents and two siblings shot to pieces during a Troubler raid, Long's mother dead of disease. Her father fell from a roof and shattered himself on the road. Boudreaux joined much later, when Troy and Hobbes were deputies under Ernie Tetweiller.

*Without this city, who are we? Guardians of a cesspool. I reckon that's what prisons are. The places we dump our turds. The Troublers will defile everything we love. They'll stink and stain and offend.*

Troy stood and left the sanctuary, his head throbbing. Twilight had come, the buildings casting long, deep shadows over the streets. The tallest structures looked like great claws reaching for the moon. Most of the higher levels were empty and rotting, the city's population too small to need the living space, the stairs too old and dangerous to make the places useful for storage. If the city survived, those floors would need to be repaired or imploded. Already, debris sometimes fell, threatening to crush people on the streets. Why had no one ever fixed them? Why did it fall to Troy? And would there ever be time now, with the future bearing down on the city? In the darkness of a world without the fantastic machines of old, night made everything strange. You could stumble into the great river or collide with a building you passed every day of your life. Even the Bright Crusade's familiar shape had been distorted. Troy rubbed his eyes, wishing his headache gone. Perhaps he could find some medicine before he slept.

In his dreams, the history Troy had learned often came alive. *You must know the seed to understand the tree,* his teachers had said. *This is what we strive to preserve.* With words, they showed him the Crusade's genesis. He had never seen the kinds of machines he learned about; he had seen the ancient people only in paintings. But, slumbering, he floated backward through time, a ghost with eyes and ears but no voice.

It always started with a God's-eye view, the continent in all its vastness spreading before him. Then the distance narrowed until he stood on the streets of Washington, part of a crowd the scale of which he had never seen. Behind him, a rectangular pool stretched back and back. Despite the cold, many people stood knee-deep in its waters; to the pool's rear, a great monument pointed toward the sky like an arrow with its fletching buried in the planet. Far ahead, Jonas Strickland stood on a stage, his sand-colored hair blowing in the wind, his strange clothes formfitting. He shouted, red-faced, spittle flying, one fisted hand smacking into the other's open palm. Sometimes he raised both hands to the sky, and the people surrounding Troy would do likewise, moaning and lowing like cows in need of milking. Troy could never make out the words, but he had read the transcripts. Strickland spoke of a great country called the United States and how it had turned its back on Jesus Christ. Of how its people had devolved into gluttons who hoarded and strutted and fought each other over children's trinkets. Of how they coddled the slothful. Of how their nation's leaders had drifted from God's teachings, had even allowed worshippers of other deities to prosper—blasphemy masked as freedom. Of how their love of personal choice and legal equality amounted to nothing but hubris, a revision of God's true creation. Of how the nation needed a strong, godly hand to wipe away all that sin.

The scene changed. Strickland stood on another stage behind a lectern. Only feet away, another man behind another podium trembled with rage, shaking his head, his fists, as Strickland pointed a finger at him and preached. The winner of their argument would lead the nation. The words were muffled, but Troy had read these transcripts too. Strickland painted his opponent as a heathen who would bring more shame down on God's city on a hill. The Supremor's cadence peaked at just the right time, for Strickland was, at heart, a preacher. The opponent, whose name had been lost in history, could only weep. Troy had never been taught much about the people in those crowds, but in these dreams, some dressed in finery and wore precious jewels and scowled at the faceless masses supporting Strickland's opponent. Some hung on Strickland's every word, clutching their Bibles and weeping. And some were as red-faced as Strickland himself, screaming in triumph as he spoke.

And it came to pass that they chose Strickland as their leader, then called the president. He resided in the grand white mansion the Crusade's leaders had occupied ever since.

When Strickland stepped inside its doors, the building became a pale horse on which he rode, hair blowing in the wind, eyes blazing.

The horse faded, and Strickland stood in the great house's yard, watching a red-and-white-striped flag descend its pole. Two men wearing robes of crimson and white cast it on the ground and set it aflame. In its place, they raised the standard of the Bright Crusade, a simple white cross on a crimson field. When the new flag reached the pole's zenith, a great rumbling shook the earth. Strickland fell to his knees, head bowed, hands steepled together. From behind the mansion, long white tubes shot into the air, trailing fire, arcing across the sky, their screaming thunderous enough to rend the very air. The image came from one of the Bright Crusade's most famous paintings, titled *The Purge Begins*. The ancients had harnessed the unthinkable power of disease, the worst humanity had ever encountered, gases that melted organs and invisible creatures that ate flesh, sicknesses that cooked a person's brains or expelled blood through the eyes and nose and pores. Troy dreamed those tubes fell on the ancients' greatest cities and burst open, pestilence spilling from them and flowing over everything like black water. The fleeing hordes carried those illnesses into the countryside. Bodies fell everywhere. Pockets of survivors managed to escape and hide; some of these became the world's first Troublers. Strickland and his upper echelon watched it all from shelters secured against contagion. In every major city, handpicked Crusaders had somehow been protected, and in the wake of all that death, they swept over the lucky and the naturally immune, killing every potential Troubler they could find.

This was the Purge.

Then, as the last of the dying closed their eyes, one final tube shot skyward. It was bigger than the others, faster, and it did not arc over a city. It traveled far above Earth, into the darkness of space, and there it fired its payload, an energy wave that rippled through the nothingness and saturated the planet. The continents grew dark as all the ancients' mighty machines, all their sources of power, failed. Troy's teachers called this force the Godwave, and though none of them understood what it was or how it worked, every Crusader knew the result—the permanent crippling of technology, humanity's greatest affront to God's will. Flying carriages fell from the sky and burned, taking whole swaths of cities with them. In New Orleans, some struck the highest buildings and razed them, while others gouged enormous holes in the street, crushing people and animals and structures, burning and burning and burning. Strange smaller vehicles died on the roads. Ships on the oceans drifted until they capsized and disappeared or struck land.

The dead lay where they fell—families collapsed around their last meal, lone pedestrians sprawled on sidewalks—and rotted, their skin bloating and bursting or desiccating in the sun and collapsing, organs and blood spilling out or turning to dust. A motivated builder could have cobbled together great edifices from their bleached bones. The vermin came and feasted, the insects, the carrion creatures, bringing their own diseases to the scattered and desperate survivors who fought them tooth and claw, scrabbling out a life among the ruins.

But in their lairs, Strickland and his first Crusaders thrived, using their stores and whatever they wanted from the still and silent world they had made. They celebrated and sang and worshipped, so rapturous they lost track of the months and years, so even now, no one could have said when the Purge occurred or exactly how much time had passed since then.

Next came the emissaries, whom Strickland sent forth to preach the gospel of the Lord and the will of the Bright Crusade. They traveled to every city, every hamlet on the continent. They braved the wide and rolling oceans, bringing answers and certainty and the promise of order. The peoples of Earth flocked to them. Those who did not—those who saw Strickland as the architect of their misery or the prophet of a faith they would not, could not share—crept away to wring their subsistence from the land or conglomerated in hidden places, striking at the Crusaders with every available weapon. In Troy's dreams, they had always been faceless, but tonight they converged and collapsed into one body, a woman with stringy black hair and a smile born not of humor or happiness but sardonic hatred. Against this threat rose a tall and sturdy figure, androgynous, faceless, and shifting in hue and shape, wearing holstered guns and riding at the head of a small cadre. A lord of order, his deputies.

Here, as always, the dream faded. Troy lived the rest of the story every day. How the Crusade sliced the globe into principalities, each under a lord of order's rule. How each principality's rule of law functioned—the lords, their deputies, their chiefs who oversaw some vital profession, those chiefs' lieutenants, all the way down to the lowliest apprentice. How Strickland, upon his death, named a new supreme Crusader, and how that person followed suit. And so it went, all the way down to Matthew Rook.

Troy did not dream this progression. Instead, his sleeping mind turned to Sister Sarah Gonzales. Together, they sat on the Riverwalk, watching the water and talking of things he could not remember.

Troy awoke more enervated than if he had not slept at all. He lay in bed longer than he should have and thought about his office—how, by rights, he should still be Ernie Tetweiller's deputy, how the bitter cup Matthew Rook might be serving New Orleans should have passed to the old man with both more experience and more wisdom. But in his last days on duty, Tetweiller had grown disillusioned with the Crusade, with his job, with how nothing ever ended and no one ever won. Tetweiller had used his increasingly stiff leg as his reason for resigning. *I ain't in no shape to ride every day, much less jump outta the saddle and fight hand to hand,* he had said when he broke the news to Troy. Only the old man himself knew how much of that was truth and how much convenience. But it mattered little. New Orleans and its outlying areas fell to Troy now. So whatever came belonged to him too.

He sighed and got out of bed. The coming day would not dissipate just because he had no wish to face it.

That Sunday, Troy sat in the first row of the Temple's right-hand pews, listening to Jerold Babb preach. To Troy's right, Jack Hobbes flipped through his Bible to find the correct passages. Beside him sat Gordon Boudreaux, Santonio Ford, and LaShanda Long. No one occupied the pew across the aisle to their left; it was reserved for Babb himself, in the event of guest speakers, and outlander Crusader officials, none of whom were present in the city. Every other pew was jammed full of honored Temple workers and their families, along with high-ranking workers in the trades sitting with their kin and apprentices. They had sung and prayed together, and now they sat, mesmerized or half asleep, as Babb spoke in his old man's quaver, his text 1 Peter 3:12–17.

*Wonder what all my folks would think if they were privy to the title Peter held when he wrote it,* Troy thought. *Or that a high minister of the world's only sanctioned religion is preachin about persecution, like we're the ones confined to one building or a swamp.*

Still, the passages were beautiful, poetic, and, if you ignored the context, eerily prescient. *For the eyes of the Lord are over the righteous,* Babb intoned, *and his ears are open unto their prayers: but the face of the Lord is against them that do evil. And who is he that will harm you, if ye be followers of that which is good? But and if ye suffer for righteousness' sake, happy are ye: and be not afraid of their terror, neither be troubled.* Here, Peter assures every Crusader that our incomparable Father in heaven watches over us even in our darkest hours, when we feel most alone. When the temptations of the serpent himself hiss in our ears like the wind in the evening, and we are sorely tempted to listen. The Most High stands between us and the Troublers, between us and Satan, between us and utter destruction. And even when our pain seems unbearable, Peter says, we should rejoice. Suffering in God's name is no suffering at all. It is our pleasure, our purpose, the very meat that nourishes us.

Hobbes grunted. Troy could relate; it seemed pretty easy for a man like Babb, swaddled in the robes of his privilege and living a life under heavy guard, to call pain and suffering a kind of pleasure. To speak of suffering as virtue as long as the pain fell on somebody else. And would those words still hold true when *he that will harm you* referred to your own superiors, in whom you had been taught to trust without question or hesitation?

Troy glanced down the row. Boudreaux nodded along, rapt. Santonio Ford muttered amens as Babb spoke of the Lord's favor. LaShanda Long picked at a loose thread on her go-to-meeting blouse. Was she humming a nearly inaudible tune? What might she be thinking of?

The lord of order wondered where Willa McClure might be—fishing with a cane pole on the riverbank? Requisitioning vegetables from the fields? And Tetweiller—the old man likely lay under his backyard shade trees, sipping whiskey. Both of them probably felt little of the creeping uncertainty, the dread that weighed down Troy's soul that morning. He envied them, and then his face reddened with shame. Sinning on the front row, while Babb reminded them of the Lord's largesse.

In verse 17, Babb continued, Paul writes of our duty to the Most High. *For it is better, if the will of God be so, that ye suffer for well doing, than for evil doing.* Therefore, my friends, never lose heart. Always have faith. The worst moments of our short lives represent less than a passing instant to the eternal Father. Those moments have been decreed by Him from the beginning of time. Our smallest step on His unfathomable path. Even if we should fall into Troubler hands and find visited upon us the tortures of the damned, we go thence for His sake. His unblinking eye is ever on us. On the Bright Crusade. His face is our face. His strength, our strength. And though we sin and come short of the glory, He takes us in the palms of His hands and keeps us close. No darkness can quench the light of His love.

Someone in the back muttered an amen. Hobbes glanced back that way and then fell still. No one else moved, but despite how some congregants' attention might have wavered, the air in the sanctuary felt charged with joy. The untroubled spirits of the people found solace in Babb's words, in the Scriptures.

Troy wondered, though, if the Most High had put those verses in Babb's heart for a different reason. Maybe God was speaking to Troy through the minister: *Remember I am with you, though all the world abandon you.*

Or maybe thinking that way was vanity.

Babb preached on the same theme another forty minutes. When the gathered adherents rose for the final acts of the morning service, Troy prayed for clear vision and clearer thoughts in these, the most uncertain days of his life.

# ❖ 4 ❖

**T**wo weeks after his conversation with Sister Sarah, Troy reined up beside the Jesus statue and dismounted, tossing the reins to a groom. He had gone to the market on North Peters for dinner, but he still needed to peruse LaShanda Long's latest reports. The sun was disappearing, the river turning black.

Jack Hobbes galloped into the courtyard and hailed Troy. Hobbes reined up beside him, his face red, the horse blowing and sweating.

What's wrong? Troy said.

Been lookin for you, Hobbes said. He's here.

Who's here? Troy asked, knowing the answer.

Hobbes nodded at the Temple. The rider. The herald.

Troy took off his hat and fanned himself. *I really hoped Stransky was lyin.* Hobbes dismounted as the groom took his reins. Troy's gray nickered, as if he could sense tension the same way he could smell a coming storm. Perhaps he could. The groom struggled to hold both horses as Troy and Hobbes walked away, not speaking. On either side of the Temple's doors, burning torches had been thrust into brackets nailed into the wall. In the dusk and firelight, the men's shadows capered, goblins loosed from unimaginable subterranea.

Inside, they shielded their eyes. Every lantern and torch had been lit. The Temple workers stood at attention along the walls as Troy and Hobbes skirted the front desk and walked down the center aisle toward the three men standing near the stairway door. Jerold Babb wore his official robes, his shoulders slumping under their weight. Gordy Boudreaux's pistols were slung low on his hips. He held his hat and watched Troy and Hobbes, expressionless. The other man smiled, his eyes bright and intelligent. He was taller than everyone else in the room, and young too. Probably no more than twenty-eight, barely older than Boudreaux. His thick black hair spilled past his shoulders. Barrel chest, arms like a ship's anchor chain. He sported faded trousers, dusty boots, and a soiled white cotton shirt loose at the throat.

Big boy, ain't he? Hobbes muttered. About to bust outta that shirt.

Big don't say nothin about quality, Troy said. Don't let him scare you.

Ain't scared. Just wonderin how many times you'd have to shoot him before he'd fall down.

The stranger's smile widened, his teeth white and even. Unblemished tanned skin, layers of toned muscle over strong bones. *I reckon he's sent more than one Crusader to the prayer closet, askin forgiveness for lust. He's a fighter too. A good one.* Troy and Hobbes stopped an arm's length from the other three men. The herald's smile never reached his eyes, which were deep brown and full of intelligence. They bored into the New Orleanians, mining for what treasures Troy could not say.

Boudreaux saluted, then bowed. I hail my direct superior, New Orleans Lord of Order Gabriel Troy, and my senior partner, Deputy Lord Jack Hobbes. It's my honor to introduce Jevan Dwyer, herald of the honorable Matthew Rook. May the Bright Crusade endure forever.

Dwyer, Troy, and Hobbes saluted each other and then bowed, the tops of their heads nearly touching. Boudreaux cleared his throat. Sweat trickled from Troy's temple down to his neck. All this bowing and ritual—titles, fancy talk, old customs and traditions and rules. *Might as well let Sarah move her people into the Quarter and hold Mass right here. Can't say that to this fella, though.* Dwyer put out his hand. Troy shook it. The herald's hand was bigger, the grip strong. Troy squeezed back. They released each other, and Dwyer turned and shook hands with Hobbes, who grunted. The herald's eyes narrowed a bit.

All right, Troy said, now that we impressed each other and just about broke our ever-lovin hands, let's get outta this bonfire.

Dwyer threw back his head and laughed, hands on his hips. Babb smiled for perhaps two seconds before he seemed to remember how dour he was supposed to be. Boudreaux stood upright, like a plank someone had set on end, hands behind his back.

You can get the stick outta your hindquarters now, Gordy, said Hobbes.

Boudreaux turned red. Troy winked at him.

Deputy Hobbes, our guest, Babb scolded.

Please, Dwyer said. A little humor is welcome after my lonely trip. Lord Troy, can I trouble you for some water? The heat has parched me.

Jack, y'all get the staff to rustle up some refreshments and then meet us in my office, Troy said.

Yes, sir, said Hobbes, saluting.

He walked away, throwing an arm around Boudreaux and pulling him along. They motioned toward the staff members still standing at attention, and everyone followed them to the front desk, where Hobbes doled out orders.

Dwyer watched them. Your deputies seem well trained, and so far I've found your staff courteous and highly competent.

The crew ran in all directions. Hobbes laid one hand on Boudreaux's shoulder and spoke. The tension drained out of the junior deputy's face.

Yeah, said Troy. They're a good bunch. And I'd sure appreciate it if you'd call me Gabe. If I call you Herald Dwyer, folks around here's like to think your name's Harold.

Dwyer laughed again and clapped him on the shoulder. I like you, Gabe. I look forward to seeing your office.

Well, let's get to gettin.

Troy sat with his hands folded on his bare desk, his hat hanging on the corner rack. Dwyer had taken a visitor's chair and sat with his long legs crossed. He played with a coil of string, knitting it into geometric shapes, cat's cradles and multifaceted diamonds and near-perfect squares. Babb sat in the other straight-backed chair. His robes pooled over its back and behind him like a bridal train. Boudreaux stood to Troy's left, at ease, Hobbes to the right. Everyone seemed solemn except Dwyer. Troy waited, but the herald just sat there, playing with the string.

A tall pitcher of ice water sat on a side table someone had lugged up, which also meant somebody had visited the icehouse. The carafe was half full now; Dwyer had drunk the rest. Four glasses sat near the pitcher. Boudreaux harrumphed.

By all means, Deputy, have some water, Dwyer said. The trail dust gets to you, even in the city. Doesn't it?

Boudreaux looked at Troy, who nodded. The young deputy went to the table and poured himself a glass. Anybody else want some while I'm at it?

You heard our guest, Troy said. Trail dust and so forth. Pour em all.

Dwyer studied Troy's office as if it held the old world's lost treasures while Boudreaux handed the glasses around and refilled Dwyer's. Troy set his glass on the desk. Hobbes sipped from his and then held it in one hand, hooking his other thumb in his gun belt. Dwyer drank the water in one long gulp. He belched and placed the empty glass on the floor. Trying to keep up with the herald, Babb swallowed so much he choked and sputtered, droplets spewing onto his robes and Troy's desk.

No need to rush, Minister, Dwyer said. We have the night.

You had a long trip, I reckon, said Troy.

Not as long as some. I've ridden from Washington to California and back again. I've traveled from the tip of Florida to the northwestern point of Alaska.

You must get awful tired of the saddle.

I prefer the open road to the confines of cities. I assume you have remained within your borders since assuming your post?

Pretty much. Ain't got time for sightseein.

Of course not. We have heard great things about New Orleans, and about you. The Crusade intends to reward your service with a new position. A unique one.

Troy did not stir, but Boudreaux spilled water on his shirt. Troy knew how he felt. A new position made no sense; Troy had already reached the top. Either he was being demoted or transferred, which would trickle down to his subordinates, or else Dwyer was about to confirm Stransky's story. Bad news for the New Orleanians in the room, and everyone knew it.

*Except for Jerold. He looks like an angel just flew outta Dwyer's hindquarters.*

Dwyer made a circle with his string. I can sense your trepidation. Let me set you at ease. You are not moving, nor are you being demoted.

An icy finger stroked the base of Troy's spine, and despite the heat, his skin broke out in gooseflesh. *They're gonna make it sound like you're bein done a favor, but once them prisoners show up, once they start droppin big-ass sections of fortified wall along the city perimeter, you'll believe. If you can't live with yourself at that point, come see me, and I'll tell you the rest.*

Troy tried to read the herald's face, but Dwyer was all teeth.

What position? Troy asked.

Dwyer stood, his knees popping. He walked to the front window and looked out on the darkened city. Troy followed, Hobbes and Boudreaux flanking him. The square stretched toward the river, moonlight rippling across the water, shadowed buildings hulking in between. Here and there, people and horses moved about, their shapes little more than bits of concentrated shadow that occasionally solidified into recognizable figures as they passed under the streetlamps.

We are facing a great crisis, Dwyer said. Faithless wretches are abandoning the Crusade and joining the Troublers. In our major cities, you will find one corrupt and worldly grubber for every honest and righteous man. In their isolation, our rural citizens often backslide. The Troublers devastate righteousness and loyalty as the locust consumes fauna. Something must be done.

Yes, yes, Babb said, folding his hands and closing his eyes. Thank you, Lord, for Mister Rook's clarity of vision.

Troy glanced at Hobbes and Boudreaux. What's that got to do with us and our city?

Dwyer turned from the window. His grin had disappeared, as had his string. New Orleans is one of the few cities in which the Troubler threat remains mostly under control. We want your help with our problem at-large. We intend to turn New Orleans into the Crusade's prison. The city is to be walled off. Its people will be our permanent guards. And you are to be our warden.

Praise the Most High, Babb said, raising his hands.

Hobbes grunted. Boudreaux coughed. And Troy, who felt as if the herald had shot him in the guts, could not speak.

Their city. The only home they had ever known, where Troy had learned to ride and shoot. Where his parents had died and he had found his calling. He had swum in the great river, had sat among the old sarcophagi and pondered the people who had once walked the streets, had explored nearly every building. He had spilled blood in New Orleans's streets and chased Troublers through her French Quarter, her Central Business District, her Garden District, her wards. In the great storms that came almost every year, he had hauled sandbags and nailed windows shut and sat in rooms in the highest fortified buildings, listening to the wind rage and swirl. He had killed for New Orleans, had nearly died for her. And now they wanted to dump the country's scum here, as if she were no more than a landfill.

For the first time in his life when presented with an order, Troy dissented. No, he said.

Babb gasped, his eyes like saucers. Boudreaux cleared his throat. Hobbes watched.

Dwyer's face might have been carved out of marble. He did not even raise his eyebrows. Troy held his gaze.

When the herald spoke, his conversational voice shattered the silence as if he had shouted full throat. I'm not sure I understand you, Lord Troy. Are you refusing to follow an order from his holiness, Matthew Rook?

Of course not, Babb said. Are you, Gabriel?

I ain't refusin nothin. But I wouldn't be doin my job if I just up and agreed. We've all dedicated our lives to keepin this city safe. Now you're tellin me you want to turn it into a giant rat cage. And how are we supposed to guard a whole city full of heathens? They'll surely outnumber us.

Dwyer's eyes narrowed. His brow furrowed, giving his face a hawk-ish cast. He loomed over Troy, glaring, his open hands at his sides. Troy crossed his arms. *I could find out how good you are right now. If you're faster than me, I might die, but these boys behind me would make sure I didn't beat you to heaven by much.* The deputies fanned out, clearing their lines of vision. Babb scooted away.

If Boudreaux and Hobbes worried Dwyer, he gave no sign. Lord Troy, he said, the city of New Orleans does not belong to you. It belongs to the Bright Crusade, which liberated it from the sinners of the old world—the addicts, the whores, the murderers and molesters and thieves and pagans. The honorable Jonas Strickland and our Crusader ancestors did that work, not you. Matthew Rook is Strickland's recognized successor, our highest earthly authority. If he says this city is to be burned to the ground tonight, you should strike the first spark and fan the flames with your life's breath.

I'd burn down the city in a heartbeat if it would be the best thing for the citizens' lives, Troy said, his voice steady. Or their souls. That's my real charge. So I ask you again. How are we supposed to live under the conditions you named?

Dwyer glared a moment longer. Then he sighed. My apologies. In my zeal to serve our God and the Crusade, I often forget the niceties of human interaction. It makes my job rather difficult at times.

Troy exhaled and crossed the room again, taking a seat behind his desk while Hobbes and Boudreaux followed and leaned against the wall, still flanking him. Dwyer took his chair. Babb sat beside him.

And you got my apologies for any disrespect, Troy said.

Dwyer nodded and smiled, those teeth winking like somebody had stuck six or eight lit candles down his throat. As for your concerns, he said, you must make peace with the changes this directive will bring. The buildings, the parks, the streets you have so scrupulously maintained will undoubtedly suffer. If the prisoners are smart, they will maintain your crops and your buildings for themselves, but no one can guarantee what Troublers will do. For all that, I am sorry, and I am certain Matthew Rook shares those sentiments. As for your people, I am not privy to the Crusade's specific plan for their training or deployment. Still, the righteous always triumph, do they not? Your populace will find their way.

Yes, praise Jesus, said the high minister.

*If Dwyer said we should shove dynamite up our hindquarters and light the fuse, Jerold would praise Jesus and grab the matches.* Troy scratched his head. Look. We all understand the concept of the greater good. I don't know if lettin heretics wreck New Orleans is the best way to help the Crusade, but let's leave that point for now and stick with the people. Who decides who's righteous?

Dwyer looked apologetic. As I mentioned, I am not privy to those plans. But I have faith the Crusade will do what is right.

*Our ideas of what's right seem pretty far apart.* Let's hope so. Ain't no use in killin loyal folks.

I agree. Does this mean I can count on your compliance?

I've always done what was required of me. Don't aim to stop now.

Babb seemed relieved. Yes, he said. Gabriel has always been true.

Dwyer stood and held out his hand. Troy got up and shook it. The herald reached into his pocket and pulled out an envelope sealed with wax—the official seal of the Bright Crusade, a cross inside the sun, beams of light radiating outward. Dwyer handed the papers to Troy, who moved to break the seal.

The herald grabbed Troy's hands in one of his bearlike paws. No. You are to open this in solitude. Share the contents with no one, not even your deputies, not Minister Babb, until you receive further instructions. Is that clear?

Troy put the papers in his shirt pocket. Yeah.

Dwyer's grin returned. Now that we understand each other, can you point me to my quarters? I have ridden far and fast, and my bones are tired.

Troy nodded at Boudreaux, who bowed and gestured toward the door. Dwyer shook hands with Hobbes and Babb and exited. Boudreaux followed him, closing the door.

Babb turned to Troy. Are you insane? Questioning the will of the supreme Crusader? Worse, doing it in front of a Washington official?

Simmer down, Jerold.

I will not, said Babb, gathering his robes. Don't make me defend you, Gabriel. No one defies the will of God.

He stalked out, slamming the door behind him.

Well, that was fun, Troy said.

Hobbes walked around the desk and took one of the chairs. So. Gonna tell me what's in that packet?

Troy took his seat. When it seems safe. I get the feelin this herald will try to worm the orders out of y'all, just so he can say we disobeyed.

Your call. Hard to believe he don't know what they got planned, though.

In the big picture, he's a delivery boy. We're gonna have to take it up with the real authorities.

Hobbes took off his hat and ran a hand through his hair. Sweet Lord. Would have swore a Troubler wouldn't know truth if it walked up and shot em in the leg, but looks like Stransky was right.

Troy rubbed his eyes and winced. His head ached like the devil.

## ❧ 5 ❧

The cold stars glimmered as Troy rode to his house on Esplanade—two stories of red brick surrounded by shrubs and rich green grass, the interior painted in mild but exotic hues like dusty purple. The tiny bricked garden outside served well for springtime contemplations. But Troy had never cared much for the comforts his station afforded. If it was too good for the average citizen, it was too good for him. Jonas Strickland had decreed that lords should live in luxurious accommodations to underscore their position. Otherwise, Troy would have been happy sleeping in a stable. Strickland had also preached that with the greatest faith came the greatest privilege. It had always seemed contradictory—keep your eyes on heaven but your behind parked in the best house you can find. But what did Gabriel Troy know? He had never been much of a philosopher.

Now that Dwyer had come with his pronouncements and his envelopes, though, Troy had questions.

*Rode into New Orleans like he belongs. Marched into the High Temple as if God gave him leave, tried to bully me in my own office. And this envelope.* Open it alone and tell no one, *Dwyer said.* Might as well say, *Betray your people. Make em distrust you. Divide and conquer.*

Troy dismounted in the street and tied the horse to his fence. At the front door, he nodded to the two guards stationed there.

The big one with the broken nose saluted. Evenin, Lord Troy. Mr. Tetweiller's in yonder. Said he needed to speak with you, so we let him in.

That's fine, Silvanus. One of y'all run my mount over to the Cabrini Playground livery. Tell em I'll need him ready by dawn.

Yes, sir.

Y'all don't get too hot out here.

We'll be fine. It's so cool, you can't even fry an egg on the walk.

Troy laughed, just to be polite. He opened the front door. *I'd like to wring Silvanus Avishay's neck. My head hurts too bad for palaver.* But when Ernie Tetweiller came to talk this late, you would do well to listen.

Normally, Troy navigated the darkness by memory and touch until he found the oil lamp on the foyer's catch-all table. Then he would light the lantern with the matches he left next to it, toting it through the house as he ate or read or wrote letters until he fell into his feather bed, exhausted. But now the foyer lamp burned. Light spilled from other rooms. He walked into his den, where Ernie Tetweiller sat in his second-best chair, drinking bourbon from a flask and smoking a cigar. Troy took off his hat and dropped it onto an end table and sat.

Them fellas outside see that? he asked.

Tetweiller held up the flask. This? Naw. Want a belt?

You know better than that.

Yeah, well, an old fart like me needs a little help gettin to sleep of a night.

Troy rubbed his temples, squinting his eyes against the pain and Tetweiller's cigar smoke. I'm about wore out. What do you need?

Tetweiller drank again. You know damn well what I need. I seen that fancy-pants jackass ridin our roads like God put em there just for him. Bad news?

The envelope inside Troy's shirt felt heavy. He was probably sweating through it and ruining the orders. He pulled out the package and dropped it into his lap. Tetweiller glanced at it but said nothing, sipping his liquor.

Let's start with Stransky, Troy said. She claims Rook's plannin a new Purge, and he's startin it here.

Troy expected the old man to sputter, curse, stomp. Not long before Tetweiller resigned, he had started cracking Troubler skulls before asking them to talk. One day, he came to work drunk. He fell onto Norville Unger's desk in full view of the Temple staff. Troy and Hobbes had spent a few evenings in sweltering, darkened rooms like this one, speculating on what the Crusade would do with Tetweiller when word reached Washington. In the end, the old man had taken the decision out of their hands. Less than a week after the incident, he called Troy into his office and said it was time he spent his days gardening and reading old outlawed books confiscated from Troublers over the years. He had seemed relieved and happy. Troy believed the prospect of mass slaughter might drive the old man into such a rage he would need to be tackled.

Instead, Tetweiller took another sip and said, Huh.

Apparently that don't shock you much.

Tetweiller shrugged. Not much surprises me these days. It ain't like Matthew Rook's known for his mercy and love.

Troy got up and poured a glass of water. As he sat back down, he said, If a citizen said that to me, they'd be behind bars in about five minutes.

Well, hell. I reckon you better arrest me then. Tetweiller drank, his eyes red and watery. Shadows played across his face, an indigo mask that shifted and pulsed like oil on a river.

Just be careful who you talk to, Troy said.

I ain't talkin to nobody but you. Want some advice?

Troy had known this was coming as soon as he told Tetweiller about Stransky's claims. The old man was full of advice, most of it good, some of it foolhardy. Sometimes both at once. Of course, Troy said.

Think real careful about who you trust. You may have to choose between the Crusade and your friends.

Everything I ever done, I done in the Crusade's name. I can't just turn my back on it.

Tetweiller struggled out of the chair, wincing and holding his lower back. Troy stood and went to help, but Tetweiller waved him off and stretched. His old joints creaked. Tetweiller was on the north side of seventy and could barely get out of bed on some days, thanks to years of riding a horse over concrete and asphalt. Plus, there was the bum leg some Troubler's bullet had shattered, and the misery in his spine.

*He was so strong when I was a kid. I reckon I'm lookin at my own future, if I live so long.*

Finally, Tetweiller straightened. He put his hand on Troy's shoulder. Ain't nobody askin you to turn your back on nothin. I'm just tellin you to think for yourself. If Stransky's blowin smoke up your ass, I'll tie her noose myself. But if she's right, it's a different story.

You sayin you'd rebel?

Despite the booze on his breath, Tetweiller's eyes looked sober. If they mean to murder God knows how many folks and turn my city to dust, yeah. I'll stand against em. By myself if I have to.

After they had shaken hands, Tetweiller limped into the night, and Troy closed the door and turned the lock. His throat felt like a dirt road. He carried the lamp into the kitchen and poured a cool glass of water from the icebox. He drank it down and set the glass on the counter, where it would stay for perhaps ten hours until the cleaning crew arrived and washed, dried, and stored it. Most folks had to do their own dishes, but he and his officers never cleaned their own messes—although they were hardly ever home long enough to make any. Did the cleaning crews ever resent the lord's officers? Was resentment even possible when service had always been the watchword of your life? Troy picked up the lantern and walked down the hall and up the stairs to his bedroom, where he undressed in front of the open window, letting the light breeze play over him. He felt grimy, new sweat layering onto the old, mixing with the day's dust, forming a thin layer of mud that would stain his white sheets. But what of that? Amie Gerlach, who lived in an apartment barely bigger than Troy's den, changed his sheets every day. Power, spotlessness, an icebox that was always cold, sinners' lowered gazes, the big house, the respect of the men and women who followed him into combat, a sense of purpose and direction. The Crusade had given him everything. It had raised him to heights greater than he could ever deserve.

And now it was asking him to lead his people into devastation.

He had left the sealed orders and the lantern on his nightstand before undressing. Now he sat on the bed and took up the envelope and broke the seal. The orders were written in a neat, tight script.

> Lord Troy,
>
> I hope this letter finds you well. Please give my regards to your deputies, Jack Hobbes and Gordon Boudreaux, as well as your advisors and lieutenants. I know all their names and their occupations.
>
> To business—by this time, you will have spoken to my herald, Jevan Dwyer, who should have informed you of my decision to use your city as the Crusade's prison. Know that this decision was not made hastily. I have prayed and wept and sought counsel both heavenly and otherwise. New Orleans's unique geography makes it one of the best two choices for this undertaking, the other being Manhattan island in New York, which seemed much harder to oversee efficiently. I know this decision has and will cause you personal heartbreak and trauma. Please realize that your sacrifice serves the Crusade and its people.
>
> Prisoners are on the march, along with contingents of armed guards. Know I am also sending my representatives to oversee New Orleans's transition. You are to extend them every courtesy.
>
> Prior to their arrival, you will complete three tasks. First, you are to inventory the city's explosive ordnance, including the

*gunpowder reserved for your peacekeeping ammunition. Prepare a list and be ready to present it to my envoys. Second, you will record the type and location of every seaworthy contrivance—ship, boat, canoe, raft, anything that floats. Third, you are to quash any dissent with all available force. Any Troubler activity should be met with lethal force. Any citizen who protests should be silenced, by whatever means necessary. Make no exceptions.*

*My prayers will be with you. I look forward to meeting you personally and commending you for the fine work you always do.*

*Yours,*

*Matthew Rook*

Troy read the letter three times. Then he folded it and slipped it back into its envelope. He opened his closet and knelt in front of his safe, an old-fashioned gray monster with a rotary dial the size of an apple. He had no idea where it came from or which lord had installed it. He had inherited it, along with its combination and the rest of the house, from Ernie Tetweiller. Troy opened the safe, the hinges squeaking. He thrust the envelope inside and then shut the door. He highly doubted anyone would assault the house tonight, but with documents like these, he would take no chances.

He went to the bathroom and stared into the mirror for a long time—his olive complexion, brown eyes, straight dark hair, lines and wrinkles that had appeared in the last few years—and then cleaned his teeth. As usual, someone had filled his tub. The water crews hauled barrels and buckets all over the city every day, leaving every citizen a supply for drinking and bathing and cooking. Fuel crews replenished everyone's firewood and kindling and dry leaves and coal and whatever else they could find that might burn. But along with their other responsibilities, the cleaning crews lit the stoves and boiled water for the lord and their deputies. Everyone else had to do for themselves. Yet the fresh water in the tub was one privilege Troy truly enjoyed. He liked baths in the dark, even in the summer months, the time when, as children, he and his friends had nothing more pressing to do than skulk through the city and dunk each other in the Mississippi. Now he closed his eyes and sank into the water up to his chin.

Usually the tensions of the day would slip away in his tub, but tonight he found no peace. The talk with Tetweiller had given the water time to cool. And then there were questions. *What am I supposed to do now? I gotta tell Jack and Gordy. I know that much.* And what of Ford and Long—even McClure? It was their city too. *Gotta sleep, or tomorrow will crush me.*

Later, in bed, he closed his eyes and tried not to think. A guard's muffled cough drifted through the night.

The next day, Troy rode Japeth into the Temple's courtyard, the orders in his pocket. Hobbes and Boudreaux sat their horses near the statue, their guns holstered and tied down. The grooms stood nearby. Go on, fellas, Troy said to them. We got business.

The grooms saluted and walked toward the stables. When they had passed out of earshot, Hobbes turned to Troy. What's up?

Dwyer's probably watchin. Let's ride over to the river.

They ambled across the street, their horses sniffing air filled with the scent of cookfires. Around them, the city awakened. Workers milled along the sidewalks. Some rode horses or drove wagons, hauling hay and wood and cleaning supplies and food. Everyone nodded or waved or genuflected as Troy and the deputies passed. Troy nodded back and spoke to some, saluted others. Soon they reached the Riverwalk and looked out over the water stretching into the distance, light glistening on the surface. Here and there, a fish broke water in pursuit of bugs. A dozen turtles sunned themselves on a half-submerged log. A few citizens carrying fishing poles picked their way down the bank.

Troy pulled out the letter and passed it to Hobbes. Give it to Gordy when you're done. Don't make a show of it.

Hobbes took the paper and pressed it against his saddle and read. Then he folded it and handed it to Boudreaux. When he was done, Boudreaux passed it back to Troy, who returned it to his shirt pocket. A breeze rose off the water, cooling the sweat on their foreheads.

Thoughts? Troy asked.

Boudreaux looked sad. I don't know what I think.

Stinks like rotten fish, Hobbes growled. Askin us to give em our defenses and half our means of travel and feedin ourselves.

Troy spat. We need to think about our next move, but if we don't make these lists, we'll be hanged as heretics. So we're gonna start in the middle of town. You and Gordy go north. I'll head south. If we ain't figured out somethin by the time we hit the city limits, we deserve whatever happens to us.

Hang on, Boudreaux said. Are we talkin about buckin orders? Seriously?

Right now we're tryin to figure out how to take care of this city and follow orders at the same time, Troy said. If you can't handle that, tell me now.

Boudreaux looked at the ground. I just don't wanna go to hell.

Nobody's goin nowhere anytime soon. You two get started. I gotta run by Ernie's, and then I'll get goin on my end.

Ernie's in on this? Boudreaux asked.

Ain't nothin to be in on, said Hobbes. Not yet.

Boudreaux shook his head and shuddered.

Y'all swing by and talk to Santonio and LaShanda, Troy said. Tell em to be at Ernie's house at three this afternoon.

Hobbes nodded, and he and Boudreaux spurred their horses and trotted away.

Troy turned Japeth toward Ernie Tetweiller's place. The day felt hotter already.

## 6

**T**roy rode down the Pontchartrain Expressway and through the streets of Metairie. At Tetweiller's one-story white house on Elgin Street, he hitched Japeth to the post in the front yard. Then he walked up the driveway and knocked on the front door. No one answered, so he knocked harder. Still nothing. He turned the knob. The door was locked.

Back here, Tetweiller called.

In the back yard, the old man sprawled on a blanket in his oak tree's shade. Landscapers had recently trimmed the grass and the waist-high hedges ringing the house. Nearby lay the old swimming pool, empty and dull gray and cracked. Santonio Ford had offered a dozen times to fill it with soil and plant a small garden, but Tetweiller always refused. He seemed to like the emptiness.

Troy sat, crossed his legs, and wiped his brow with his shirtsleeve.

Tetweiller lay still, eyes closed. Mornin, he said.

Howdy, said Troy. He reached for the ice bucket Tetweiller had set against the tree trunk and removed the bottle of homemade wine chilling there. He shook his head and put the wine back, then selected a sliver of ice and popped it in his mouth. His teeth ached with the cold, but it eased his parched throat.

Tetweiller opened one eye. Help yourself.

I'll stick with ice. What are you doin out here?

I like to nap in the afternoons.

It's nine in the mornin.

I ain't no procrastinator. You think about what I said?

Troy pulled up some grass and let it drift through his fingers. They want a list of all our explosives. And our boats.

Tetweiller sat up and took the bottle from the bucket. He drank long and deep. Holding the bottle in one hand, he drew his knees up and rested his arms on them, grimacing. The two men sat in silence for a while. The temperature was already rising. Birds chirped in the trees. One defecated, the white droppings splattering the ground near Troy's outstretched hand.

Well, said Tetweiller. You gonna do it?

If we don't, they'll execute us right after Stransky.

Givin em somethin and givin em what they asked for ain't gotta be the same thing.

I've been thinkin about that. I got somethin for you to do.

Tetweiller drank again. He grinned at Troy, his eyes already blood-shot. The burst veins on his nose looked like splotches of bad sunburn. A little liquid courage, he said. Tell me.

Troy took another piece of ice. I'm sendin Santonio and LaShanda over here at three this afternoon. We need a plan—materials, execution, getaway routes, the whole shebang.

Tetweiller raised his gray eyebrows. A plan for what?

For Stransky. We need to bust her out and make it look like the Troublers did it.

Tetweiller looked at Troy for a long time. Damn, he said. You ain't fuckin around. Jack and Gordy know about this?

Not yet. Gordy's twitchy. I'm not sure he'd believe me if I told him I'm just keepin our options open while we figure things out.

We just caught that bitch.

She's got an intelligence network we need to access as long as the Crusade's playin fast and loose with our people's lives. They say we'll be guards, but they got no details, and when the brass keep secrets, it ain't good for those of us in the trenches. Stransky's pipeline may be all we got.

Tetweiller drank again and belched. I don't like it much. But I see your point. Still, if Jack and Gordy ain't on board, we'll end up in the towers anyway.

I'll tell em soon. I just want to give Gordy a day or two.

The old man nodded and held the bottle against his forehead. And what if Santonio and LaShanda get twitchy?

If they got doubts, that's natural. If they start hollerin for help, follow your conscience. Don't do nothin just for me.

Tetweiller put the bottle back in the bucket and stretched his legs. Hellfire, he muttered.

Troy hung his head and closed his eyes. Sweat rolled down his neck. He wanted nothing more than to lie on the grass beside Tetweiller and sleep, lose himself in darkness and dreams. But he could not. New Orleans and the Crusade, the dual landmarks by which he navigated this world, seemed to be collapsing toward each other, and he had no idea what to do.

Having managed to dodge Jerold Babb on the way up, Troy and Tetweiller stood in front of Stransky's cell. She sat cross-legged on her bunk. Her greasy hair looked like a fistful of dead snakes. In the stifling heat, her clothing clung to her like a second skin. Cold in the winter, an oven in summer, barely deep enough for the cot and bucket that were the only accommodations prisoners were afforded, the towers were a special kind of hell.

But if the conditions bothered Stransky, she gave no sign. I reckon you boys got some news you can't quite stomach, she said.

Ain't nobody said nothin about a Purge, Troy said.

Stransky laughed. Hell. You think they're just gonna ride in and admit it all? You ain't in their circle. You're too provincial.

Troy looked at Tetweiller, who shrugged. I think this salty bitch and Washington wouldn't know the truth if it bit em on the ass, said the old man.

Fuck off, you old fart, Stransky said, though she sounded almost affectionate. Then she turned to Troy. Those bastards are gonna murder hundreds of thousands of people. Again.

Troy wiped sweat on his shirtsleeve. He opened his canteen and drank. Stransky licked her lips but asked for nothing. You knew about the explosives cache at Loyola, didn't you? That's what y'all were after.

Stransky pushed her grimy hair out of her eyes. We need more ordnance if we're gonna stop their wall.

Why didn't you just come to us? Troy asked. We wouldn't have believed you, and you would have ended up here just the same, but your men might still be alive. You could have told your story.

Stransky took hold of the bars and looked Troy in the eye. Givin up ain't my nature, and I didn't trust you not to shoot me on sight.

How could you know about a new Purge? Even the herald don't know many details.

Could be he's lyin.

I looked in his eyes. I believe him.

Stransky groaned. You been lord of order here for years. I bet you got a hundred letters from some asshole in Washington worryin about leaks and spies and shit.

Troy grunted. He did not have a hundred such letters, but over the years he had gotten several, each warning him to watch for suspicious activities in even his most trusted associates.

What of it? he said.

They were right. We got people in high places, includin one in Rook's inner circle.

Bullshit, Tetweiller said. His face was red in the heat, his voice husky.

We need proof, Troy said.

Stransky sneered. What, like a signed confession? *Dear Local Asshole, I'm gonna destroy the world again.*

So I'm supposed to take your word for it.

We've heard rumors for months—mass arrests, mobile prison camps, scorched-earth policies, torture. We got the first tale from a river merchant, who heard it from a fella up in Illinois. We laughed it off. Third- and fourth-hand bullshit. Not even Rook's that crazy, right? Same shit you're probably sayin to yourself right now. We didn't believe the second report either, or the tenth. But once our inside man confirmed, we had to face some hard truths. Rook's grabbin folks from coast to coast, from upper Canada all the way to the Gulf. By the time you see it all for yourself, you'll be chokin on your own blood.

Tetweiller spat. Rook's enough of a hard case to do it.

The whole inner circle's hard cases, Stransky said. They branded crosses over their hearts. Not a tattoo. Not a cut with a little bitty knife. A brand. It's proof of who's committed. These folks are so fanatical, they make you boys look like alcoholic pederasts. Besides, let's say we're wrong about the Purge. The prison part's been confirmed, so this city's still dead. Can y'all live with that?

Tetweiller cleared his throat. Gabe, can I talk to you outside?

Stransky laughed and lay back on her cot. She shooed them away and closed her eyes. Troy watched her for a moment and then followed Tetweiller down the stairs and into his office. Tetweiller took a visitor's chair. Troy sat behind his desk and leaned back, propping his feet up. His dusty boots looked like a gun sight aimed at Tetweiller's head.

She's tellin the truth, the old man said.

Troy nodded. Or believes she is. When Santonio and LaShanda come by your place today, tell em about the prison part. If they get as nervous and mad as me and you, tell em everything and start makin them plans we talked about.

Tetweiller leaned forward and looked Troy in the eye. And if they wanna bend over for Washington?

Troy rubbed his temples. Another headache. Like I said. Follow
your conscience.

A white building at the intersection of Canal and South Carrollton
housed the first weapons cache on Troy's list. Crusade records indicated
the place had once served as a fresh market. Now it held gunpowder,
bullets, homemade plastique, and pipe bombs. Like all the armories,
it was guarded. Weapons troops had standing orders to destroy everything rather than let it fall into Troubler hands. In the Crusade's long
history, the rebels had successfully captured only one armory, and that
had happened in Seattle. New Orleans Troublers had come close once,
years before Tetweiller's time. The lord of order had detonated the
ordnance before they could overrun the place, taking himself, most of
the Troublers, and all the guards with it.

Six sentries were currently assigned to the white building's day
shift—two in the front, two in back, and two inside. The front-door
men saluted as Troy and Japeth ambled up. He saluted back with the
hand holding his reins. Then he dismounted and tied Japeth to the
hitching post and dug an inkwell, a quill, and a sheaf of blank paper
out of his saddlebags.

Howdy, Troy said to the men.

Lord Troy, said the shorter guard, Vu Dang, touching his hat brim.
Dang lived in the Eighth Ward, if memory served. He loved any dish
with crawfish. Sweat had plastered his black hair to his head. His
almond-colored eyes were sharp and clear, his gun hand steady. He had
won several shooting competitions over the years. At five feet, eight
inches and one hundred and thirty pounds, he did not look particularly
imposing—a mistake more than one dead Troubler had made.

Dang's taller, heavier, less-seasoned partner, Oswaldo Caskey,
hitched up his sagging britches and said, Hot enough for you? His fair

skin was flushed bright pink, perhaps burned. The long red hair on his head and chin waved in the breeze like Spanish moss.

Too hot, Troy said. I'm ordered to make an inventory. Probably gonna let the folks inside come out here with y'all for a spell. Conversation might make me lose count.

Yes, sir, said Caskey. Dang touched his hat brim again.

Inside, a thick smell of gunpowder. If anyone struck a match, the very air would ignite and send a city block to hell. The ordnance had been stacked on rusting metal shelves, remnants of the ancients. *Can't use those for a writin table. This pen has a metal tip. If it scrapes the shelf and sparks, I won't need to worry about Dwyer and Rook.* Pipe bombs lay side by side like enormous birthday candles, fuses poking from the tops. Boxes containing bricks of plastique were stacked five feet high on pallets. Guns of all kinds hung on hooks. Boxes of matching shells sat on more shelves. Crates of bladed weapons were stacked against the walls. Everything had been crafted by artisans like LaShanda Long, who could make a weapon out of nearly anything.

The nearest dynamite cache was located three blocks to the south. That would be Troy's next stop. If one of the dynamite huts ever exploded, the nearest weapons would hopefully survive, though no one alive had ever seen such a conflagration. Troy hoped Long's people had rotated out the older sticks recently. He had no desire to spend any time amid the nitroglycerin sweat of old dynamite.

Troy pulled out his pen and set the inkpot on a shelf full of pipe bombs. He straightened the sheaf of papers on a box top and tied his bandana around his nose and mouth. Then he started counting.

Tetweiller had drawn the hunter-green curtains he had chosen years ago, now thin enough to let in the light even when closed. He sat in his favorite chair, an oak straight-back with a soft cushion for his lower back, its arms covered in half-finished doodles he had carved with his pocketknives over the years as he pondered life's mysteries and frustrations. Tetweiller sipped from a glass of whiskey. LaShanda Long and Santonio Ford sat across from him on his couch's threadbare, forest-green down cushions. Ford was dressed in his usual deerskins, his dreadlocks hanging past his shoulders. Long wore a sundress, likely because of the heat, though in her forges, she wore skins or heavy cloth to protect her from sparks. Her hair fell to the middle of her back. When Tetweiller was lord and had access to the forbidden histories, he had read that before the Purge, two dark-skinned people sitting in an old white man's parlor would have been controversial, even unthinkable. *I ain't never understood that shit. Might as well shut out all the folks with blue eyes or red hair. Long's the best weaponsmith I've ever known, and Ford's the best hunter. Great fighters too. Always liked em. Hope we don't gotta kill each other.*

Long drank from the glass of ice water she had requested, her face blank. She had always been nearly impossible to read, even for an old law like Tetweiller.

Their glasses clinked on wood as they set them down, picked them up, set them down. No one, it seemed, wanted to start. Something in the kitchen creaked—old wood reshaping itself in the muggy Louisiana temperatures. Behind Long and Ford stood the entrance to the darkened hallway, which led back to the bedrooms and bathroom. It reminded the old man of his afternoon nap, which he was currently missing. Despite his bunched muscles, tensed against the potential confrontation, Tetweiller yawned.

Hands on his knees, Ford watched Tetweiller as if the old man were a buck slipping through the dawn forests. It's too hot to sit inside like this, he said. Why are we here?

Tetweiller sipped more whiskey. His mouth tingled; his throat burned. Gabe showed me them orders the herald brought. Washington's gonna wall off New Orleans and make it a prison.

What? said Long. She set her glass on the side table and narrowed her eyes.

You heard me, Tetweiller said. Ford and Long looked at each other, then back at him. Both seemed to be waiting for him to go on.

*Fuck it,* Tetweiller thought. *Time to find out which side of the bed they sleep on. If it's Dwyer's, maybe I can get one of em before they reach the door. The other one will get me, most likely. But I've fought beside em ever since they came of age. I owe em the first move.*

We've also heard Rook's plannin a new Purge. If that's true, the prison's just an excuse to get all the Troublers in one place. Our people will be here too. They ain't relocatin us.

Ford had leaned forward as Tetweiller talked. Now he fell back against the couch, eyes wide. Long looked stunned.

That's insane, she said.

I know it, Tetweiller said. But Stransky swears it's true.

Stransky? I trust her about as far as I can throw the Temple.

Me too. But she knew about Dwyer and what his orders would say. As for the Purge, they wouldn't write that kind of thing down and entrust it to one man. Not even that oak tree with arms.

Long shook her head. If this came from Willa McClure, I might believe it. But Stransky—

Stransky's crazier than a shithouse rat, Tetweiller said. But Gabe and me believe her. She says the prisoners and their guards are marchin on us now, and Rook's sendin envoys to take charge of New Orleans.

Ford stood and paced. Take charge. Like we ain't competent. Or don't they trust us?

Long studied Tetweiller. That ain't why we're here, Santonio. Ernie don't plan to go along.

Ford stopped pacing and goggled at the old man.

Look, said Tetweiller, ain't nobody sayin we should mount up and ambush the envoys. We're just sayin it's best to consider all our options. We might could live with seein our town ruined. But what if Washington plans to take the citizens with it? Do we let that happen?

We could get thrown in the towers just for talkin about this, Ford said.

The towers don't scare me, Tetweiller said. Not when you stack em against smashin our town and maybe slaughterin our people. This whole damn place will be one big tower, and we're all gonna be stuck in it for the rest of our short-ass lives.

He told them of how Rook had named Troy the warden, that Troy intended to show them the letter so they could see for themselves. As he spoke, the defiance and most of the disbelief drained from their faces.

Lord above, Ford said.

Here's the best-case scenario, Tetweiller said. Stransky's wrong about the Purge. You keep your positions. But we'll still be neck-deep in Troublers, and the main job's gonna be to make sure they don't escape. We'll swim in blood every day. Worst case? That fuckin harpy is right, and we're all on Rook's list. Me, I can't abide any of it.

It's insane, Long said again, her brow furrowed. We're faithful.

Tetweiller set the whiskey flask on his side table. He got up and poured himself a glass of water and sat again, sipping it. It ain't about our faith, he said. It's about Rook's fanaticism. Once the town's sealed in, everybody's dead.

Ford poured himself another glass. His hands trembled. I don't see how a wall can keep the Troublers in unless we rip out everything they could use to build ladders. Even then, they could find a way. The guards would have to outnumber the Troublers four to one or keep em chained forever.

And if you're gonna do that, Long said, why bother with a prison at all? Why not just execute em or chain em together limb to limb until they can't move? There must be a reason they want em all in one place, other than convenience.

It's symbolic, Ford said. So future generations will talk about New Orleans like we talk about Sodom and Gomorrah. Plus, you know how the Purge worked. Maybe Washington's got hold of them plagues like Jonas Strickland used. Could be New Orleans is the test case.

Tetweiller rubbed one hand on his face. It rasped against his gray stubble. He had already thought of all this. So had Troy. And that meant Rook had too. Every second they sat here debating brought the massed Troublers and armed Crusaders closer. Once that mob arrived, it would be much harder to plan and much more tempting to give in.

So it's over, Long said. We guard, or we die.

Tetweiller sipped again, for courage, and cleared his throat. Or it's like you said. We don't go along.

Long regarded him, her jaw set. Ford shook his head and slammed his fist on the wooden arm of the couch.

That's heresy, Long said.

Like I told you. We're just weighin all the options.

When can we see these orders? Ford asked.

When Gabe can talk to you without Dwyer lookin over his shoulder.

He could have left the orders here so we could see em now, Long said.

Tetweiller laughed. Sure. Pass around eyes-only documents. Good way to get hung.

You want us to talk heresy, but you don't trust us with the proof.

It ain't about trust, Tetweiller said. You think we'd be talkin at all if we didn't trust you?

*We. You*, Ford said. Sounds like two sides to me.

Only if you make it that way. You need to decide where you stand.

The men's gazes locked. Ford's hunting knife glistened in the dim light.

On the way over here, I passed one of our armories, Long said. I saw Jack and Gordy's horses outside.

Tetweiller watched Ford, the distance between the hunter's hand and the knife. More orders, the old man said. They're takin inventory of our explosives and our boats. Every .22 shell and leaky raft.

Ford and Long looked at each other, something passing between them.

Ford unsheathed the knife.

Tetweiller drew his gun, but Ford leaped from the couch and snatched it before he could fire.

*Shit. I was kiddin myself. I'm too old to get even one of em. Sorry, Gabe.*

Long drew her gun too.

Then Ford put one finger to his lips and handed the gun back to Tetweiller.

*What the fuck?*

The former lord of order listened. At first, nothing. Then, the soft sound of footfalls on the cracked and fractured concrete driveway, the click-click-click of spiked boots or claws. Someone was coming.

He signaled Ford and Long to hold their positions.

He turned and pointed his gun toward the entryway.

Someone knocked.

I think we know who it is, Tetweiller said, lowering his weapon.

He walked into the foyer, Long and Ford close behind. The old man opened the door. McClure stood on the front step, the Rottweiler at her heel. The dog's pink tongue lolled onto his black-and-brown fur. The girl was dressed in the same cotton shirt and soiled trousers she had worn during the raid. Her face was dirty, her blond hair greasy and askew. Everyone holstered their weapons.

We've missed y'all down at the forges, Long said.

Tetweiller raised his eyebrows. Is that where she stays nowadays?

Only sometimes, at suppertime, Long said, grinning at the girl. Where you been?

The child, tall for a twelve-year-old and lean, took off her hat and beat the dust from it. Here and there. I was with these fellas at Loyola.

Tetweiller smiled. You sure were. Come on in. We'll get y'all some water.

The adults stood aside. McClure headed for the kitchen as Tetweiller shut the door. They followed McClure as she sat at the table. Ford and Long joined her.

Gathered in a kitchen, chatting about their days, they could have been a normal family. *Ain't nothin normal about any of us, though.* When McClure was two years old, a Troubler bomb killed both her parents, along with dozens of other citizens. As the city mourned, the girl slept on a cot in the Temple prison. She stayed a few years until, one day, she simply wandered off. No one could find her, not even the lord's office. She had come back when she was good and ready, none the worse for wear and bearing news about a Troubler nest massing east of town. As everyone geared up, McClure wandered off again and set her life's pattern. In a sense, every Crusader in the city had adopted her. She slept in spare rooms and storage buildings and stables. She hid in places no one ever discovered. She ate out of people's gardens and from Ford's crops, at the table of whatever Crusader she happened to meet near mealtime. No one knew where she had found the dog. It seemed tame, but no one in the city recognized it. McClure had just walked into Jackson Square one day, a pup at her side. They had been together ever since. They bathed in the great river. The girl would not enter a dwelling where the dog was unwelcome, which is why she had not been inside the High Temple since adopting him. She would never reveal how she got so close to the Troublers without getting caught, but her information was always good.

Tetweiller set a water dish on the floor. Bandit lapped at it. The girl took her glass and drank.

You need a bath, Tetweiller said. You look like you been buried alive and dug up with a broke shovel.

McClure smiled. Ford winked at her. Ain't had time to bathe, she said. Been keepin watch since Loyola. Lotta crazy talk among the Troublers.

Ford's smile faded. Long glanced at Tetweiller. What kind of talk? Tetweiller asked.

Talk like this, the girl said. She took a folded piece of paper from her shirt pocket and tossed it onto the table. Tetweiller picked it up. A splotch of wax caked the top and bottom of the page. Two red finger-prints stained the front of the page, a similar thumbprint on the back.

That's blood, Ford said.

McClure shrugged. Fella didn't wanna give it to me. I persuaded him.

Tetweiller examined the seal and then showed it to Ford and Long. Long's eyes widened.

Rook, Ford said.

Tetweiller opened the paper and read. His throat went dry. *Left the goddam flask in the den.* Not even Lynn Stransky's damnable cackle had brought their situation home like this.

It's to Dwyer, he said.

Dwyer. Seen him when he rode in, McClure said. Prettiest man I ever laid eyes on. I could eat them arms for breakfast.

You're too young to talk like that, Tetweiller said.

If you ain't too old, I ain't too young.

How about we quit sinnin like devils and read the letter, said Long. So Tetweiller read.

> *To the Right Honorable Herald Jevan Dwyer:*
> *Greetings, and safe riding.*
> *Know you this: our reports indicate Gabriel Troy maintains strong loyalties to the citizens of New Orleans—much stronger than his dedication to the Bright Crusade. His most trusted subordinates— Deputy Lords John Hobbes and Gordon Boudreaux, Retired Lord of*

*Order Ernest Tetweiller, Chief Hunter and Gatherer Santonio Ford, and Chief Weaponsmith LaShanda Long—may have been similarly corrupted. Other highly placed sympathizers might exist. Troy seeks regular council from Sarah Gonzales, a Papist nun.*

*We do not know the extent to which Lord Troy and his subordinates would betray the Crusade. Perhaps our concerns are misplaced and Lord Troy will remember his first duty is to God. However, should he or any member of his staff attempt to hinder the Crusade's plans, deal with them using all necessary force. When my envoys arrive, share these orders with them. Under their command, New Orleans will be transformed and purged. Once they have read this document, destroy it. Share its contents with no one else.*

*Soon we will all be together in a new, purer world.*

*Love and Grace,*

*Matthew Rook*


The word *purged* suppurated in Tetweiller's mind, a leper's sore.

He threw the paper on the table. Ford picked it up and read it again. Then he handed it to Long. Tetweiller got up and poured himself a glass of whiskey. He intended to drink until he passed out. It might be the last chance he ever had.

The girl finished her water and regarded the grown-ups around the table. Sounds like a fight's comin. What's our play?

The adults looked at each other. At first no one said anything. The silence weighed on them like the heat, oppressive and thick.

Long dropped the paper on the table and said, I'll keep Gabriel's secret, Ernie—for now. And I'll help you because these orders don't sound godly to me. But this is our church. We gotta check our hearts and our consciences every single day. And if I think for one second we're wrong, I'll turn myself in and drag you to them towers myself. Or put a bullet in you.

Fair enough, Tetweiller said. *Ford looks like he's gonna puke. I reckon that's a natural reaction to learnin everything you ever worked for is diseased.*

Finally, though, Ford nodded and said, Yeah.

Tetweiller shook the hunter's hand, thinking, *Not exactly what I was hopin for, but better than I feared.* He turned to McClure and said, Tote that letter south. Look in every armory until you find Gabe. Then get him alone and give it to him.

McClure finished her glass of water and set it on the table. She seemed as calm as ever.

What are we supposed to do? Long asked. I don't know if I found my rope or lost my cow.

*Here we go.* Well, Tetweiller said, Gabe's got some ideas about that. We're gonna need information and warm bodies. Ladies and gents, how would you like to commit a jailbreak?

Again, no one said anything. On the floor, Bandit the Rottweiler had fallen asleep, as if nothing was wrong in the world.

## 7

**S**everal days later, just after dark, Troy and his deputies sat in the lord's office with Dwyer, going over fudged inventory numbers. Troy, Hobbes, and Boudreaux had gone back to every armory several times, ostensibly to double-check their figures, and had stolen weapons and ammo each time—explosives and handguns, edged weapons and shells—adjusting the reports and burning the originals. LaShanda Long had made that sure some supplies, including rifles and shotguns and longswords, never reached the armories in the first place. No guard would challenge or search the lord of order or his sworn representatives. Now Troy watched Dwyer for any sign of suspicion.

The herald played with his string as he listened, fashioning diamond shapes and hearts and cat's cradles. He seemed preoccupied. Any day now, outriders from cities like Atlanta would arrive and absorb the massed Troublers and guards from south Louisiana principalities like Baton Rouge and Lafayette.

Without Stransky or someone like her, all those Troublers would never work with a lord of order if it came to open rebellion. And so, somewhere out there, Tetweiller, Long, and Ford would be moving on the Temple, even as Dwyer sat there with that silly yarn of his. The plan was dangerous, especially for Jack Hobbes and Santonio Ford, and if Dwyer suspected a conspiracy for even a moment, they would have to kill him.

✤

The river's black water blended with the overcast sky. Only the Mississippi's undulations proved anything existed farther than ten feet away. Tetweiller wore dark clothing and two of his spare guns. In his right hand, he held a crude full-head mask with eyeholes, like those the Troublers sometimes used on their raids. Normally, he would have shot anyone carrying one. Now he had to wear it. *Shit. How did we not notice things had gotten this bad in Washington? Rook must have been goin insane for years, but we all* yes sir-ed *right along. Now we're starin mass murder in the face.* Crusaders had been taught from birth to think of the Purge as a sacrosanct *ur*-moment all citizens should honor, but Tetweiller had never been comfortable with slaughter on that level, no matter who wielded the weapon. It was much easier to glorify death if you had not tromped through the bone and gristle of it most of your life.

Light footfalls on the broken concrete behind him, the click of claws. You ain't comin, child, he said without turning. Ain't no way to disguise you, unless you can climb stairs on stilts.

McClure and Bandit appeared beside him. The dog sat near the girl's feet and bit at fleas on his hind legs. She knelt and scratched between his ears. Don't aim to come, the kid said. Just watch.

Then why bring that cannon under your shirt?

The girl's expression was inscrutable. She patted the lump beneath her left arm. Figure if one of you gets hit, I can cover.

If we get killed, we get killed. But Gabe will need you. You can go places we can't.

McClure said nothing. In the end, she would do what she wanted. The dog blended with the night. Somewhere nearby, a fish broke water with a flat clapping sound. The evening's warmth curled around them like a snug blanket.

*Hard to breathe already, and we still gotta put them goddam masks on.*

Long arrived dressed in black, her leather jerkin buttoned over a long-sleeved shirt. She wore wool pants, gloves, hair pinned tight against her skull. She carried a shotgun and a satchel, likely full of ammo and explosives paraphernalia. Protocol stated that all nearby guards and patrols, plus an official representative of the lord's office, had to investigate any attack within the Temple's general vicinity. That would leave a skeleton crew on high alert within the Temple proper, plus Jerold Babb, who would be in Troy's office or his home in the presbytère. Once Long's diversion began, the trick would be to get inside the Temple before the crew locked the place up like the fortress it was. Tetweiller and Ford would have only seconds. It was a risky plan, but better than assaulting a fully guarded Temple.

Ford emerged from the shadows wearing tight, dark clothing. His dreadlocks had been tucked into his shirt. He had been assigned the most difficult tasks of the evening—dealing with the guards and Jack Hobbes. Tetweiller could not read his face in the gloom.

They stood in a circle, four people and one dog. Tetweiller silently prayed for everyone's safety. The others were likely doing the same, except for the girl, who never prayed, and the dog, who was eating something she had given him.

Tetweiller took a deep breath. His heart was pounding, his mouth dry. It's about that time. If you want out, nobody will think less of you. What we're about to do can't be undone.

Long slung the satchel over her shoulder. Just remember what I said.

Tetweiller turned to the child. Go with LaShanda. Stay outta sight and follow her lead. Don't get shot. Don't even get *seen*.

They said their goodbyes, and Long and the girl walked away, the dog following. Ford wore his guns slung low on his hips. A mask was tucked into his waistband. He and Tetweiller stood at the river's edge and waited.

Later, on the shadowed steps of the Riverwalk across from the square, they pulled on their masks. The streetlamps near the closed gates spotlighted the two stationary guards. Others would be patrolling the perimeter in small groups, three clusters per street. To stay alert, they changed locations every hour. Because of the speed with which the Temple staff were likely to respond to the attack, Ford and Tetweiller needed to breach the square's perimeter before Long's diversion began; the trick would be to move during the rotation, hoping distance and dark and the laxity borne from years of unbroken security would prevent the guards on the front door from spotting them. Perhaps the Jesus statue would obscure some of what would happen. Still, even if the guards did not see and Dwyer did not pick the wrong moment to look out Troy's window, Tetweiller and Ford would have only seconds to get inside once everything started.

Soon, down the street and near the fence line, the perimeter patrol moved west, heading for St. Peter Street. The easternmost group filed past the gates, passing under the lamps, nodding to the guards, fading into darkness. When the last of them vanished, the footsteps of the St. Ann guards heading toward their Decatur shift were already audible.

Ford elbowed Tetweiller in the ribs. They stood, raised their pistols, and dashed across the street.

By the time the streetlamps revealed them, it was too late. The gate guards started to raise their rifles, but Tetweiller, his voice an octave lower than normal, growled, Put em down and keep your mouths shut, or you'll get to see what your guts look like.

The guards glanced at each other, looked for the foot patrols, saw no one close. They lowered their guns.

Tetweiller stepped up to the guard on the left, cocked his pistol, and put it to the boy's temple. The kid, no older than twenty-five, glared at him. Ford drew his knife and held it to the other guard's throat.

Troubler scum, Tetweiller's guard spat.

Yeah, yeah, Tetweiller said. Open the gate. Be quick about it.

Sure. You devils ain't never assaulted this place and lived to tell about it. It's okay with me if you go get killed.

The kid unlocked the gate and pushed it open. Ford and Tetweiller shoved the guards inside and shut the gate behind them. Ford reached through the bars and rewrapped the chains through them. Then he threaded the padlock back through the chains and clicked it shut.

When he was done, Tetweiller turned to the guards and said, On your knees.

The kid spat. His companion stared straight ahead, expressionless. Neither knelt.

*Good for you, boys,* thought Ford. *Sorry about this.* He stepped behind them and kicked them in the backs of their knees. They fell, and before they could speak, he bashed them in the head with his big hunting knife's handle. They slumped, one on top of the other. Ford and Tetweiller each grabbed a guard under the arms and dragged them into the bushes near the gate. They bound and hid the guards and then crept through the foliage until they were as close to the Temple as they could get.

Long, McClure, and Bandit skirted the streetlamps on Decatur until they reached the building nearest a lot where fishermen brought their daily hauls for cleaning and distribution. In the evenings, the lot was empty, so there would be no collateral damage except for some wooden stalls. The building itself had once served as a tavern. Now, Ford's workers used the old tankards to make and cask wine for the Lord's Supper. After hours, no one guarded it, for it had never been considered a strategic point, one reason Ford and Long had picked it. Folks could always crush grapes somewhere else.

McClure patted Bandit on the head and whispered something in his ear. The dog walked a block back the way they had come and lay down with his snout on his paws. The girl joined Long, who stood in the old brewery's doorway.

He minds you better than most kids mind their parents, Long whispered.

He's a good boy. What if somebody found your stash?

Pray they didn't.

Long pulled out her lock picks and opened the front doors in less than a minute. Then she and McClure circled to the back door.

Four casks stood underneath the tarp, where she and Ford had left them last night. Always thinking of what might happen if Troublers caught her unprepared anywhere in the city, Long had been stockpiling materials in hidden caches ever since she learned to make her first pipe bomb. These casks would not even put a dent in her personal stores, but rolling them through back alleys and from building to building, two at a time, while avoiding the roaming guards had been quite the chore. She and Ford had been up most of the night, and she had muddled through her daily tasks, telling her workers she might be coming down with a cold, her arms and legs aching.

She had no idea what story Ford had concocted or whether he had bothered. Few people questioned Santonio Ford. Only thirty years old and already the chief hunter, he could have been a deputy lord if he had wanted it. But Ford's first impulse had always been mercy. He would spend his days hunting human beings only when the Crusade required it.

*I would have been a good deputy lord too, but God had other plans.*

No one else had demonstrated her flair for weaponry and ammunition. And so the last primary law enforcement opening had gone to Gordy Boudreaux, who, except for his occasional naivety, made just as good a deputy as anyone would have been, and better than most. His heart was as gentle as Ford's, but he could harden it when he had to. Yet most times McClure seemed more world-wise than him. How would he survive in a cabal?

She and McClure started rolling and heaving the casks inside. As they wrestled the first one over the threshold, McClure asked, How unstable is this shit?

Long panted. It's dynamite, but it's new. We should be good. *And if we ain't, we won't find out till St. Peter tells us.*

So we're only half crazy.

Once they had gotten the casks inside, they rolled them into the four corners of the wine-making room, the old tankards looming above them. Long dug the fuses out of her satchel and moved from barrel to barrel, working by feel, prying off the tops with a small hatchet, attaching the fuses to a stick, running them to the center of the room, plaiting them into one.

When she was done, she said, We're late, so I can't run these outside. I want you gone before I light em. Meet me at the checkpoint. Don't dawdle, you hear?

That goes double for you, McClure said. Then she was gone.

*I hope three-minute fuses do the trick.* If they burned too slowly, Tetweiller and Ford would pay the price. If they burned too fast, nobody would ever find a trace of her.

She pulled a match out of her bag and lit it. Then she held its burning end to the four braided fuses in her hand. They caught, the fiery ends racing away. She dashed through the darkened building, praying she would not run face-first into something, wishing she could have risked a lantern.

The two guards on the Temple doors had not moved. The muted sound of their conversation drifted across the courtyard. Ford leaned in close to Tetweiller and whispered, We can't sit here all night.

Tetweiller grunted, his bent knees aching. You know LaShanda. She'll do her part.

Ford was right, though. Long had completed half a dozen practice runs from the Riverwalk to the target, but so much depended on timing her diversion with the guards' shift change, on her encountering no unexpected obstacles, on the casks still being where she and Ford had left them. If anything went wrong, Ford and Tetweiller would have to abort or shoot their way inside.

Ford tapped him on the shoulder and gestured toward the gate. Three guards armed with shotguns were gathered there, talking in whispers, looking about for the missing gatekeepers.

Damn it all, Tetweiller whispered. We can't wait. Let's go.

Then an explosion shook the ground and lit up the night sky, its roar deafening. Tetweiller barely kept his balance. The courtyard was bathed in light as a column of fire and smoke billowed several stories in the air.

Ford and Tetweiller ducked deeper into the foliage, covering their ears and waiting for the exodus.

Long sprinted out the brewery's back door, her upper right thigh and left elbow throbbing from crashing into shadowy objects. She ran around the corner and alongside the building and then across the street, the thick night air tearing in and out of her lungs. McClure waited for her in the shadowed doorway. Long stopped and dug through her satchel and found the cotton she had stored there. She handed some to the girl. They shoved it in their ears. Then she dragged the child into the alley and behind the building.

*Outta time.*

She pulled McClure close, covering the child's head with her arms. The brewery exploded.

The roar nearly burst her eardrums, despite the cotton. The whole edifice at their back shuddered. The night lit up as if a star had fallen onto Decatur, and even with a building between them and the heat wave, Long's skin went dry. Her mouth turned to sand. McClure struggled in Long's arms, so the weaponsmith shifted, afraid she was smothering the girl. Then the air turned too hot to breathe. Glass rained onto them. Long rolled them away from the building as fragments of brick and mortar smashed the ground. They stood, holding their shirts over their noses. McClure's left hand had sustained several scratches, and small fragments of glass stuck out of her palm. But overall, the damage seemed minimal. Good. Together they ran two blocks and into another alley. Long paused to dig the glass out of McClure's hand. The girl took off her shirt so Long could check her over. All the wounds looked superficial—a scrape here, a tiny puncture there.

I've imagined gettin naked with you, McClure said, a smile in her voice despite the pain. This ain't how I pictured it.

Quit it.

Pinpricks in Long's arms, thighs, torso—likely glass or debris picked up in the rolling. She and the girl would both need to clean those wounds well. Infections could kill.

McClure put her shirt back on, and they ran again, heading back toward Decatur and the rifles Long had hidden in the old café on the corner of Chartres and Pirate Alley.

Raised voices, pounding footsteps—Tetweiller and Ford had moved far enough along the tree line to hear it all as the Temple mobilized. Most of the staff would exit via the front doors at any moment. Then Ford and Tetweiller could make their move. They needed to get past the doors, reach Stransky's cell, and get back down without killing anyone.

*Lord,* thought Ford, *guide my hand, tonight of all nights.*

The guards stepped aside as the heavy doors swung open. Three dozen men and women carrying rifles and shotguns and pistols tromped out. Some would search for Troublers. Others would head for the fire stations and guard the water wagons. Gordy Boudreaux, who would lead the firefighting efforts and run interference for Long, left last. *Go with God.*

The door guards locked the Temple and resumed their positions as Boudreaux ran after the others. One of the patrollers unlocked the gate, and the little crowd that had gathered there merged with the Temple staff. No one hung back to look for the gate guards. When the crowd passed out of sight, Ford nodded to Tetweiller. They slipped through the foliage until they stood in the shadows of the Temple, Ford leading the way. They crouched low, hugging the wall, their guns drawn. When they were still ten yards from the doors, one of the guards turned, but when he saw Ford's pistol pointed at his head, he dropped his gun. The other man turned, surprised, and started to raise his shotgun.

Lowering his voice again, Tetweiller rasped, Drop it, or I put one in your brain. The guards glared at them with icy hate. The armed one did not move. Do it, or I'll gutshoot your friend, Tetweiller said. This time the guard complied.

Tetweiller covered them while Ford bound their wrists with rawhide thongs. *Hope it don't hurt you too bad, brothers,* the hunter thought.

One guard looked over his shoulder and said, Y'all won't make it out alive. If you're smart, you'll run while you still can. Otherwise, you better shoot us because if we get free, we're gonna—

Ford cuffed him upside the head, and the man fell to his knees. Lowering his voice as Tetweiller had done, Ford said, When I want your advice, I'll clout it outta you.

Ford and Tetweiller confiscated the guards' keys, gagged them, and bound the quiet one's feet. Ford burst through the door, guns drawn. Norville Unger's eyes widened as he staggered back from the desk, one hand going to his throat. He opened his mouth to shout a warning.

Ford cocked his pistols. Don't make me turn your skull into a planter. Get your hands up.

Unger shut his mouth and raised his hands. Tetweiller dragged the guards inside and locked the doors as Unger scowled.

Come out from behind that desk, Tetweiller said.

You ain't gonna find the lord of order, nor his deputies, Unger said. They headed out to see what you scum blew up.

We ain't here for them, Tetweiller growled.

Ford winced. Tetweiller sounded like someone *trying* to disguise his voice. A Troubler would not bother. What if Unger noticed?

They bound and gagged him, trying to be gentle. *I don't wanna do this. I wish I could tell you.* Troy had forbidden them from using the old man as a hostage, but they had to make certain he was out of the way. So, gritting his teeth and feeling awful, Ford pistol-whipped Unger. The old fellow fell beside the bound guard, whom Ford punched hard in the jaw. His eyelids fluttered and closed. The other guard mumbled something that sounded like a threat. He struggled, digging in his heels and twisting until Ford stepped in front of him and pointed the pistol right between his eyes. He stopped fighting.

This is the last time I'm gonna tell you, hissed Ford. Walk when we tell you, or you're dead. Now *get*.

Tetweiller shoved the guard toward a tower staircase and kicked him in the hindquarters. The man stumbled forward as Ford dug out Unger's keys. Moments later, they started up the stairs, Ford on point, thinking, *I hope you're watchin this fella, Ernie. If he decides to mule-kick you, I doubt you'll survive the tumble.* But the guard did nothing. They climbed toward Troy's office and the tower cell beyond.

Long pushed aside a trash bin in Pirate Alley. Behind it lay a rifle and a bag of ammunition. I didn't know you'd be here, she said, or I would have brought you a gun.

That's okay, said McClure, pulling the pistol out of her shirt.

Long hoisted the bag, and they trotted out of the alley and down Chartres until they turned left on Wilkinson Street. Soon they crossed Decatur and approached the building adjacent to the devastated brewery. Long wrapped her fist in her bandana and punched through a window. She and McClure climbed through. Outside, the conflagration raged, heating the already stuffy interior. On the upper floor, they set up at the window with the best line of sight. The fire's light revealed the bucket line stretching to the river. The last man in line would toss a pail of water on the fire and hand the empty to a runner, who took it to the shallows. But they were just marking time until the fire wagons arrived. No one showed signs of breaking off and heading back to the Temple.

*So far, so good. Let's hope it lasts long enough.*

As per protocol, the reinforced door between the tower staircase and Troy's office was closed and locked. On the narrow landing, Tetweiller stood behind the captive guard, one arm wrapped around his throat, holding a gun to his head. Ford pounded on the door. From within, muffled voices and someone's footsteps. Ford raised his pistol and pointed it at the door.

That you, Norville? Jack Hobbes called, following the script they had written after Boudreaux pointed out that they needed a reason for Unger to knock on the door and draw Hobbes close, rather than simply use his own keys.

Yes, sir, Tetweiller said.

Forgot your keys, I reckon, Hobbes teased as latches clicked and the door swung inward, hinges moaning. Keep tellin Gabe you're gettin old—

When he saw who waited on the landing, Hobbes's eyes widened theatrically. Ford struck him on the cheekbone with the pistol barrel. Hobbes grunted and fell back into the room, landing hard on his hindquarters, blood trickling down his cheek. Ford strode in, covering Hobbes. Across the room, Jerold Babb stood in the corner closest to Troy's desk, trying to press himself into the wall, his face red, hands shaking.

*Too yellow to run for the back door,* Tetweiller thought. *No surprise there.*

Troy had already drawn a pistol.

Uh-uh, Ford said. Throw em down, or this bootlicker dies. He waved the gun at Hobbes.

Jevan Dwyer sneered as Tetweiller pushed the guard into the room. The herald regarded them as a starving man might view a thick steak. His tongue snaked over his lips. He dropped his string on the desk. Lord Troy, he said, I was under the impression this Temple was secure, so I neglected to bring a firearm. Can you kill these pigs?

Troy laughed. Course I can.

Tetweiller pressed the barrel harder against the guard's head. The man winced. I got about three-quarters pressure on this trigger already. You can kill us, but I guarantee we'll take this fuckstick to the pearly gates.

The bootlicker goes, too, Ford said, again jabbing his barrel at Hobbes.

Troy's free hand hovered near his holsters, arm bent as if he were waiting for a clock to strike noon as it always did in the old, outlawed stories Tetweiller had heard from a thousand jailed Troublers over a thousand sleepless nights. Jack Hobbes got to one knee and then to his feet. If he felt nervous or frightened, he gave no sign. And Dwyer looked as if he would like to rip out Tetweiller's heart. He had drawn a hunting knife, ten inches long and razor sharp. When was the last time any of them had been in a knife fight? There was Ford's bloody duel with a Troubler in the swamps a year or so ago, but that peckerhead had been about as big as the herald's thigh.

*I hope you're watchin that big sumbitch, Santonio. If one of us has to go hand to hand with him, you'd last longer than I would.*

Gentlemen, Babb said, his voice quivering. No more violence need be done here.

Shut up, Dwyer hissed.

The old fart's right, Ford said. Give us your keys, and everybody goes home.

Dwyer's upper lip rose, as if he smelled something foul. Shoot them, Lord Troy.

Jerold Babb groaned.

Tetweiller shook his head. *I bet his bony-ass knees are knockin under them robes.*

You sure? Troy asked.

Do it now, Dwyer said.

Ford pivoted and fired, shooting Jack Hobbes just under his collarbone.

Blood spattered onto the floor, an abstract map of demon stars. Hobbes fell. Babb wailed and went to him. The old minister cradled Hobbes's head in his lap. The senior deputy lay there panting, one hand over the wound.

Ford pointed the gun at his head. Last chance.

The herald sputtered, glancing from Ford to Troy. I said *shoot* them.

No, Babb cried.

He's not the only fast gun here, Ford said. And he knows it.

Troy clenched his fists and tensed, as if he were about to draw. Tetweiller could not breathe. *Jesus, Gabe, back the fuck down.*

Then the lord of order raised his hands in the air, the pistol dangling from his index finger in the trigger guard. He's right. They'd put one in Jack's skull before I could get em both.

Thank the Most High, Babb whimpered.

Besides, Troy said, we'll run em down. Their kind always makes a mistake.

Do not let them leave this room, Dwyer spat.

I ain't lettin my friend die just because you're impatient.

Fine. I'll gut them myself. Dwyer moved forward.

Ford pivoted and aimed at him. Try it, and Rook's gonna need a new herald.

Just give them the keys, Babb cried. Jack needs help.

Hobbes had struggled into a sitting position, though he might not have been able to sustain it if Babb had not supported him. His shirt was soaked with blood. He was the color of old cheese. Still holding his hands up, Troy approached Hobbes, knelt, and pulled the deputy's shirt aside. The bullet wound was a blackish-red hole. Blood steadily dribbled from it. Troy tore off a piece of his own shirt and pressed it against the wound. Hobbes moaned.

Tetweiller gritted his teeth.

All right, said Ford. Skin them guns off and kick em over here. Don't forget the bootlicker's.

Troy took out his other pistol, placed them both on the floor, and slid them to Ford. Then he did the same with Hobbes's. Ford booted them past Tetweiller and out the door.

Now the keys, said Tetweiller. He turned to Dwyer. And that knife, big fella, before you hurt somebody. *And let's hope you don't prefer death to surrender. If you do, I'll burn you down and figure out how to explain it to the goddam envoys later.*

But Dwyer tossed his knife underhand. Tetweiller let it sail past him and clatter across the floor. Ford kicked it into the stairwell. Then he pulled more rawhide out of his satchel. Soon Dwyer lay on the floor near Hobbes, hogtied. The blood pooling under Hobbes edged toward him.

Troy and Babb were still applying pressure on Hobbes's wound. The heavy fabric was almost soaked through. Troy looked at Ford, his eyes grave. We gotta get help, he said.

Not our problem, Ford said.

Give them the keys and let them go, Gabriel, Babb said. He turned to Ford and Tetweiller. And may the Most High forgive you.

*From your lips to His ear*, thought Tetweiller.

Hobbes had dropped the keyring when he fell. Troy slid them across to Ford and then resumed helping Babb with Hobbes's wound.

Tetweiller looked at Ford, keeping his voice loud enough for Dwyer to hear. Didn't expect the herald to be here. We ain't got enough rawhide for the rest of em.

Ford scratched his head as if he were puzzled. What do you wanna do?

Better get to gettin. I'll watch em.

Ford nodded and backed out of the room. Tetweiller kept his gun trained on Gabriel Troy, as anyone would expect him to.

*Hurry, Santonio.*

The guard stared at him, eyes bright with hate.

Ford took the stairs two at a time, flipping through Troy's master key ring as he climbed. From below, Dwyer shouted at Troy to kill that Troubler, to free him, to stop those heretics. Troy said something about keeping Hobbes stable. Ford found the right key just before he reached the narrow landing outside Stransky's cell. No one guarded her. There was no need. Troublers had never assaulted the towers, much less broken someone out.

Stransky was sitting up. She looked Ford up and down and threw back her head and laughed, her greasy hair dangling down her back. What are you supposed to be? A highwayman? A bank robber? A cowpuncher?

Ford ignored her. The key was an old and heavy brass number that might have been forged two hundred years before the Purge. He jammed it in the lock and turned it. The tumblers clicked. Stransky stood and grasped the cell bars. Well, she said. Sounds like trouble below. Better hurry.

Ford swung the door open and grabbed Stransky by the hair, yanking her toward him, their faces inches apart. You better hold up your end, or I'll skin you alive. You hear me?

Stransky's wild green eyes sparkled. She puckered her lips and then flicked her tongue. You keep talkin like that, and you're gonna have to send me flowers.

Ford let her go. Come on, he said, before I change my mind.

They descended. One floor below, they entered Troy's office. Troy and Babb had laid Hobbes on the floor. The pool of blood beneath the senior deputy had spread. Troy had ripped off another piece of his shirt. He continued to apply pressure to Hobbes's wound. The herald and the guard lay in the same position, though Dwyer's face had turned beet red as he strained against his bonds. Through the stained glass, the light of the fire flickered as if the night were winking at them, eternal, amused at humanity's follies.

Ford locked the stairwell door and nodded at Tetweiller. They went over and cut the rawhide binding the guard's feet and pulled him up. Then Ford motioned for Stransky to lead the way, toward the entrance near Troy's desk. He shoved the guard after her, Tetweiller bringing up the rear.

As they passed, Dwyer stopped straining and glared at them, his expression wolfish, savage. I name you cowards, he hissed. Cut these bonds and face me. Let the Most High judge us.

Nah, said Tetweiller.

He's a big un, Stransky said. I bet his horse rides him.

They crossed the room and exited into the back stairwell.

❖

Ford found the right key and locked the office. Then the four of them headed down the stairwell, Tetweiller's gun jammed into the guard's back. Halfway down, a tremendous crash. Tetweiller turned. Dust wafted from the doorframe. *Hell,* Tetweiller thought. *Dwyer's already loose. Or maybe Jack's lost too much blood, and that's Gabe tryin to bust out. Either way, we gotta move.* He turned, refusing to look back, though more crashes, metronomic and almost certainly Dwyer given the sheer force, followed them. The herald seemed made of steel.

He seems a mite outta sorts, Stransky said.

Hellfire, Tetweiller muttered. *If that damn door opened outward, he'd be on us already.*

They reached the ground floor without incident. The Temple was empty, except for Norville Unger and the other guard, who had both awakened and lay struggling with their bonds. Ford was already searching through the keys for the one that would open the door leading to the prison.

So we're leavin one prison and walkin straight into another one, Stransky said. Great.

If you don't like it, Tetweiller said, you can go back to the tower.

Stransky threw her head back and cackled, hands on her hips.

*Sweet Jesus, I wish I could just shoot her.*

Ford got the door open and led them through. They walked down an aisle between five-by-ten cells, most empty except for cots and chamber pots, others peopled by scruffy-looking Troublers sitting among their soiled supper dishes. The prisoners leaped to their feet, hooting and shouting as the masked men led Stransky toward the rear. She waved to them. Don't worry, y'all. Freedom's comin. The prisoners hallooed. One of them tried to reach through the bars and punch the guard.

*Tomorrow I think I'll come back and crack that asshole's skull for him,*

Tetweiller thought. *It's a bonus that he'll wonder why I did it for the rest of his life.*

Near the back, they had to pass through a final gate. Ford worked the keys again, jamming one into the lock, yanking it out, trying the next one. After ten or twelve tries, the lock turned, and he swung the heavy gate open, the old hinges screaming. Behind them, the prisoners cheered. Stransky's grin widened.

Watch out the top of your head don't fall off, Tetweiller said.

She walked through. The rest of them followed. They passed the empty guard posts and sleeping quarters until they reached the doors leading to the street. Ford unlocked them and then tossed Unger's and Troy's key rings onto a nearby desk.

Tetweiller turned to the others. Should just be a couple guards out there, he said. Then he looked at their hostage. Let's hope they like you, boy.

He turned the knob and cracked open the door.

Two guards, just as planned, but the men heard the door creak, turned, and drew their weapons.

*They're well trained, anyhow.*

You in there, one shouted. Come on out.

Tetweiller dragged their hostage forward. The man tried to scream something defiant, but the gag rendered it muffled gibberish. Tetweiller opened the door and positioned the guard between him and the men outside. We're comin, he called. And you're gonna let us.

The men glanced at each other. For a moment, no one said anything; then something seemed to pass between them. Let him go and surrender, in the name of the Bright Crusade, the spokesman said.

Counteroffer, Tetweiller said, still using his stage voice. Throw them pistols away and let us pass, or your buddy here dies first. If I don't kill him, you will because he's walkin point.

The guards looked at each other again. The quiet one started to lower his weapon, but the spokesman cocked his gun. Then come on out and let's get it done, he said.

*Hell.*

They had to talk the guard down, or else they would have to kill innocent men right there in the High Temple.

Long and McClure peered through the windows, the weaponsmith's scope trained on the water haulers. Three fire wagons were parked on Decatur, the horses stamping the pavement as the brigade pumped water onto the brewery. Gordy Boudreaux barked orders from atop one of the wagons. The building looked to be a total loss, but the workers' efforts, combined with Long's strategic placing of the explosives, had contained the blaze. The city was safe.

Long leaned over and whispered, You okay? I'm about to melt.

Yeah, McClure whispered back. Then she sat straighter and pointed to the street. That fella's about to make a move.

Two men conversed near the fire wagons, one of them gesticulating in the direction of the Temple. The second man kept looking back and nodding. Boudreaux was herding a half dozen Crusaders toward the river and did not see them.

Long sighed. *I can't let him leave. Santonio and Ernie need all the time we can give. Plus, if even a single guard outflanks us when we rabbit, somebody'll die.* She nudged McClure and backed away from the window. The girl followed, keeping low.

When they reached the ground floor, they crab-walked to the street-side windows. Long peeked out. The man who had been gesturing toward the Temple had vanished, but his subordinate was unhitching a horse.

Long turned to the girl and whispered, He's mountin up. Head around back. Stay in the shadows. Fire on anybody that makes a move toward you, but don't shoot em if you can help it. And if you can't, then—

Wing em, McClure interrupted. Flesh wounds only. I got it.

Then she was gone. Long rested her rifle's barrel on the windowsill. *Lord, I hate givin up the high ground, but once they spot me, I'll need that back door close.* Outside, the rider hooked his left foot into his stirrup and grabbed his saddle horn.

Long fired, the bullet crashing through the window and striking the pavement near the man's feet. The horse let out a long, ululating whinny and reared, throwing the Crusader onto the pavement, and then it took off, the staccato clops of its hooves on pavement audible over the firefighters' shouts. The dazed man sat up. He shook his head, feeling the back of his skull with one hand. Then he looked about, trying to find the source of the shot he must have heard.

*If he sees the broken window, he'll come after me.*

But Boudreaux ran over and spoke to the man, pointing in a different direction.

Long backed away. Nobody had spotted McClure. She would have heard gunfire if they had. *I hope the kid remembered to bring a mask.* She took hers from the satchel and pulled it over her head. Then she slipped out the door.

The fire lit up the night. She watched the brigade work. *I don't know how those folks stand it. It's hot enough to burn a polar bear's butt.*

She circumnavigated the building until she reached the northeast corner. The man she had fired on had disappeared, but those working the fire wagons shouted to each other and pointed at the building Long had vacated. She ducked back behind the wall. *Gordy will have to check this building, or they'll wonder why he didn't. Jesus, help me get through this without killin anybody.*

She dashed across Decatur and dove behind the Templeside Café. She had eaten there thousands of times. Now she was using it as cover to hide from, perhaps shoot at, her friends and colleagues. She bit her lip.

McClure's pistol cracked once, twice, three times. Someone yelped and returned fire. Crusaders shouted and scrambled for cover or weapons or both. Some ran, while five others, Boudreaux included, sprinted to the building in which Long and McClure had first hidden. The figures flattened themselves against its wall.

One of them crouched under the window from which Long had fired. She put a slug through the remaining glass over his head. They all hit the ground. More troops would arrive soon, probably armed with something more powerful and accurate than sidearms. McClure was still shooting from somewhere on the river side. Someone cried out.

*Two more minutes. Then we can fall back. I hope everybody's still alive.*

Behind the Temple, the guards tensed, preparing to rush.

*We gotta move first,* Tetweiller thought.

Stransky pinned their hostage to the wall and patted him on the cheek. Then she kissed him full on the mouth. The guard sputtered as Tetweiller drew his other pistol. Ford opened the door and flattened himself to one side as Tetweiller burst out, firing low, striking both guards in the kneecaps. Screaming, the men fell and dropped their weapons. One pistol must have been cocked. It went off as it hit the ground. Tetweiller jerked and dropped his left-hand gun, his upper arm on fire. He bent and tried to pick up the weapon, but his fingers would not close. Stransky darted forward, bumping him aside to grab it. She grinned. Tetweiller could do nothing. If the downed guards saw a masked Troubler and Stransky pointing pistols at each other, it would raise too many questions.

*Santonio better put a bullet in her brain if she shoots me.*

She cackled at the groaning, writhing guards. You boys take a load off your feet.

Ford dragged the captive guard outside and shoved him to the ground next to his fellows. Let's get outta here, he said, his voice flat. We got what we came for.

Stransky blew him a kiss. You damn sure did.

Blood had soaked through Tetweiller's shirtsleeve and dripped from his elbow, but the ex-lord did not complain. Ford led them down Royal, away from the fire. They got as far as St. Phillip before stopping in the mouth of an alley. They stayed put a while, hands on knees, breathing hard. Soon, the slap of boot heels on pavement, the click of too-long toenails. McClure and Bandit ambled down St. Phillip, the girl with her hands in her pockets. When she reached them, she crouched beside Tetweiller. The dog sat at the girl's heel, looking sleepy.

Stransky watched the child, some emotion playing across her face—anger? I reckon you're Troy's ghost, she said.

McClure glanced at her. Hey, Flat Ass.

Stransky laughed. Then she started to walk away.

Ford grabbed her shoulder. Where do you think you're goin?

She cocked her head and looked at him as if he were a dullard. Back to my people. Or maybe you busted me out just to haul me around like that little girl's dog?

Who's little? McClure said.

We're takin you to a friend of ours. You'll be safe until we can establish some protocols.

No thanks.

Tetweiller moved behind her and stuck his gun barrel on the base of her skull. He cocked the pistol. We insist, he said. And while we're at it, give me back the gun I gave you.

Stransky never blinked, but she held the pistol out. Tetweiller holstered it, disregarding the blood dripping onto it.

Ten minutes later, Long sprinted up the street, glancing over her shoulder, satchel bouncing against her ribs. She ducked into the alley and sat, taking out her canteen and gulping water.

You're gonna cramp up, Ford said.

She capped the canteen and stored it. Then she took a deep breath and stood, stretching her legs, knees popping. We need to go, she said, still panting. You'll have to circle around to the sisters'. I led as many of em toward the river as I could, but some fanned out near the Temple.

Where's Gordy? Ford asked.

Leadin a party in the wrong direction.

We gotta get back to our houses before any runners come to fetch us, Tetweiller said. They'll go to Gabe and Jack first, but when they find out somebody hit the Temple, we'll be their next stop.

Ford took Stransky's elbow. She looked perturbed but did not pull away. Y'all go home, he said. If a runner's waitin, tell em you heard the boom and went out to secure your neighborhood. And if they start firin questions, remind em who's in charge. Questions?

No one had any.

Camp Street was deserted. Still, Ford and Stransky darted from building to building toward the sisters', avoiding the cones of light under the streetlamps. Ford hoped Sister Sarah Gonzales would be receptive. If not, he would have to leave Stransky in somebody's basement or set her loose and hope for the best. Of course, once she was out of his sight, she could waltz off anytime she pleased, but the patrols they had dodged on the way over should have convinced her that trying to navigate the city on her own would be madness.

They crept to the entrance, which would be unlocked, as always, for anyone who needed sanctuary or a place to pray. Stransky followed Ford inside, where the warm night became a steaming tropical misery as they felt their way along the foyer and through the swinging double doors into the sanctuary proper. The darkness was nearly impenetrable. Stransky walked into a pew and grumbled. Ford grinned. He had spent a lot of time hunting in darkness, so his eyes adjusted well, but even so, the room seemed filled with amorphous blobs. He walked with his hands extended until he found the altar. Then he took some matches from his pocket and lit a votive. Its pitiful light made the darkness seem heavier, but now his visibility extended a couple of feet. He picked up the candle as Stransky slipped her hand into his belt just over his buttocks. He stiffened.

She leaned close, her lips at his ear. Don't flatter yourself. I just don't feature breakin my hips on these pews.

Keep your hands above the waist.

He edged his way to the door leading to the living quarters beyond the sanctuary and rapped twice, paused a few seconds, then knocked four more times.

Secret knocks and everything, Stransky said. Y'all took to this shit fast.

Someone rustled behind the door. Then it opened inward. Sister Sarah Gonzales stood there, holding a lantern. Ford squinted and shaded his eyes with his hand.

Hello, Santonio, said Sister Sarah. It's late.

Ford pulled Stransky into the light. Sister Sarah Gonzales, he said, meet Lynn Stransky. She needs sanctuary.

Sister Sarah's eyes widened. She looked at the Troubler for a long time. If she wants it, she has to ask for it. Does Gabriel know she's with you?

I'm right here, Stransky offered. You can ask me.

I'm here on Gabe's orders, Ford said. He'll explain when he can.

Right now, all I got time to say is we busted her outta the tower, and she needs a place to hide.

You busted her out? As in you and Gabriel?

And some others. He'll explain, but I gotta go. Can she stay?

She's gotta ask. Those are the rules.

Stransky laughed and opened her mouth, probably to say something that would ruin the whole deal. So Ford took her by the shoulders and squeezed. You saw the patrols. Everybody's after you. There's no leverage here.

Stransky pulled free, all her humor gone. She stared a hole in him. Then, her jaw set, she turned to Sister Sarah, who stood her ground. They looked as if they might throw punches.

Ford wanted to slap the Troubler upside her head. *Don't mess this up.*

Finally, Stransky said, I hope you don't expect me to confess and all that bullshit.

Sister Sarah's gaze was as cold as her voice. You don't have to convert. But you'll respect us and our ways. Otherwise, you can take your chances on the street.

The Troubler frowned. Ford inched closer, ready to intervene. *It kills Stransky to ask for anything.*

But then she shrugged. Fine. I ask sanctuary. Until I can get back to my people.

Sister Sarah nodded, her mouth a thin line. She glanced at Ford and then turned. I'll fix you a bed, she said. Then she disappeared, taking her lantern. The darkness swooped in and nearly drowned them.

Stransky's voice floated out of the darkness. So what's the deal?

Your network tells you what the Crusade's up to. You tell us. We help you stop em.

That's puttin a gauze bandage on a broken arm. The Crusade's gotta die.

All we want is to save New Orleans and our people. You're askin too much.

No. I'm askin just enough. Your precious Crusade ain't about God no more, if it ever was. It's about Matthew Rook tryin to *be* God. If you don't see that yet, you will. I guarantee it.

Ford said nothing. There was nothing to say. If Stransky were wrong, it would not matter. They would use her until she had nothing left to give, and then she would hang. And if she were right, then she would find plenty of opportunities to crow about it later.

## 8

**T**roy had assumed that, after the returning Temple personnel had carried Hobbes away, Dwyer would snort and bellow and demand action. But he had not.

The masks trouble me, he had said.

No tellin what a Troubler's thinkin, Troy said. Maybe they heard about you and didn't cotton to bumpin into you when they ain't already drawn their guns.

Dwyer thought about that for a minute. Then he nodded. Let me know when you have some idea of who attacked us and where they took the prisoner, he said. He left, threading his string around his fingers as he walked.

The runners Troy had sent for his lieutenants reported rousting Long from bed. Tetweiller and Ford had returned to their houses to find messengers waiting. Tetweiller claimed he had gone out to secure the neighborhood. Everyone knew Ford often checked his traps in the middle of the night, fished and hunted before dawn, slept little, and answered to no one but Troy.

Jack Hobbes lay in the prison infirmary, pale and wasted.

He had volunteered to be wounded so the breakout would seem real, and as planned, Ford's bullet had missed his major organs, but he had lost a lot of blood. The doctors transfused him and gave him the most comfortable bed in the prison and ordered him not to leave it for at least a few days. The wound had turned an ugly blue-black, and Hobbes had reported some numbness in his upper arm. Troy could barely look at him. *If Jack loses any mobility, I'll never forgive myself.*

Someone rapped on the office door. It's open, Troy said.

Ford walked in and closed the door behind him. He glanced around. Where's Dwyer?

He left. Ain't said boo to a goose. Ford pulled up a chair and sat across from Troy. He looked tired. You get any sleep? Troy asked.

Not much, but I'm used to that. It's Jack that's buggin me.

I gave the order. Whatever happens is on me.

Ford did not look convinced. Stransky's at the sisters'. If she's got sense enough to stay there, she'll be fine.

Troy grunted and yawned. He had slept only an hour and dreaded working with Stransky after spending so many years shooting at her. *Nothin makes sense anymore. It's like we've built our church on sand.*

Dwyer's gonna be watchin us till things die down, he said. So let's stay away from the sisters' until them prisoners get closer. Maybe she'll know somethin new by then.

All right, Ford said.

Over his shoulder, dawn's light sparkled on the river. A handful of fishing skiffs cut through the ripples like bullets through flesh.

Dwyer reappeared later that day. He knocked three times and entered Troy's office without waiting for an answer. He took one of Troy's straight-backed chairs, settled his thick frame into it, and took out his string.

Good morning, he said. What have you discovered about our egregious security breach?

Troy picked up his mug of coffee and blew on it, eyeing Dwyer over the rim. The herald's face was impassive. *You'd make a fine cardsharp, if anybody but Troublers gambled.*

We got men combin the streets, Troy said. Nothin so far, but Stransky's always been good at goin to ground. As for the others, you saw em. With them masks, there ain't no way to find em unless we catch a prisoner that'll talk.

Dwyer nodded, as if he had expected precisely this answer. The string skittered back and forth, hypnotic. Yes, he said. I've dealt with their ilk before.

I reckon Washington's got it worse than we do. I feel for y'all.

My thanks. What else?

We doubled the guard and the street patrols with orders to engage and capture. If anybody even thinks wrong, we'll get em.

Dwyer said nothing. The string metamorphosed into starbursts, a series of parallel lines, a circled letter A. Then he stood and went to the window and looked out. Troy fidgeted and sipped his coffee. He did not like the way Dwyer contemplated the water. If the herald discovered Troy and the others had met down there mere hours before the Temple assault, they might have to kill him.

Troy cleared his throat and said, I got some new munitions figures. We're about sixty percent done with the inventory.

Dwyer turned back to him. The string had stopped moving, covering half his fingers like threadbare gloves. You'll need to hurry. I expect the first arrivals in a day, perhaps two.

That soon?

Not soon enough. I have not seen your high minister. Dwyer glanced around the room as if Babb, heretofore invisible, might reveal himself.

Jerold seemed half dead this mornin, so I sent him home. He's old, and he ain't used to lookin down the business end of a pistol.

I hope he is well. I shall check back soon. Dwyer pocketed his string and offered Troy his hand. Troy stood and shook it. The herald started to leave, but he paused in the doorway and looked back. There is something to consider. You might ask your citizens about Stransky's escape.

Troy frowned. Why would I ask them? What good would it do?

Because somewhere out there, in your city or beyond, someone knows. And because ferreting out a traitor might be worth the trouble of asking—harshly.

Harshly. Troy crossed his arms. I don't know what you mean.

After a moment, Dwyer smiled. Never mind, he said.

When Dwyer was gone, Troy sat and closed his eyes. He sighed and opened his drawers. He took out the maps of the armories and spent the next hour calculating how long they could delay the final accounting. When he finished, he got up and walked to the window. The day was bright, the azure sky spotted with clouds. On the square, people came and went, oblivious, blind.

Troy drank the rest of his coffee and set the cup on the windowsill. Outriders in New Orleans as early as tomorrow. A demand for the inventory lists. He needed to speak with Lynn Stransky sooner than planned.

Sister Sarah met Troy at the entrance, her habit soaked with sweat. She looked up and down the street. Then she led Troy into the vestibule. Sunspots played across his vision like fireworks. A figure sat on the first pew.

That Crusader you're babysittin better not have followed you, Sister Sarah said. I'll burn this house down before I let him take it.

This ain't my first picnic.

She turned and hugged him. He would not have been more surprised if she had sprouted wings. I'm glad you made it through that madness, she said.

Troy barely heard her. *What would her hair look like, spillin over her shoulders?* Her slim and graceful throat, her skin—but no. Sinful thoughts, more so because she believed herself wed to Christ Himself.

*If she wasn't, I would have started somethin that would have damned us both a long time ago.*

He wriggled out of her arms, feeling his face redden. Thank goodness she could not see it. She clasped her hands at her waist while he pulled out a soggy handkerchief and mopped his brow, leaving both his forehead and the cloth wetter than before. He lifted his chin in Stransky's direction. She drivin you crazy?

Nothin we can't handle. She had a visitor this mornin, so I expect she'll have news. He was a dirty fella who looked like he needed a month of good meals.

Someone had lit the wall lamps. Votives burned on the altar, casting globular and shifting pools of light onto Stransky. She gazed at the hanging wooden cross, her head cocked to one side, her hair askew. Drop her into any other church in any other city and you might mistake her for a Christian. Just a good woman sitting on a strong pew, heart right with God and soul unstained with curses and thefts and bloody murders.

Troy and Sister Sarah stepped in front of Stransky. I was just admirin your decorations, Sister, the Troubler said. Fancy as shit. Oak?

Sister Sarah scowled. This is the last time I'm warnin you about your language. From now on, you can use it out yonder. In the light of day.

Stransky laughed. Don't get your panties in a bunch. Say, do you wear panties under that getup?

Troy took Sister Sarah's arm, pulling her closer to the altar. She looked like something out of a painting—unwrinkled, cherubic, her complexion like strong coffee shot with milk. He squeezed her upper arm, liking the feel of the hard muscle there, the strength.

I really appreciate you lettin her stay, he said.

Sarah lifted her hand to his face, her fingers rasping through his stubble, and said, If she can help New Orleans, she's a friend. Even if she acts like a five-year-old.

They looked into each other's eyes for a moment, still touching, a foot apart. Such a short distance, and such an impossible journey. Like stepping outside your door and onto the moon.

Then Stransky chuckled. Sister Sarah's hand dropped. Troy backed away.

Awww, Stransky said. Y'all are so cute.

And you've got a hole where your heart should be, Sister Sarah said. You don't know nothin about me.

Then it seems we're both ignorant. Sister Sarah turned back to Troy. Watch your back.

Always.

She walked to the back door and put her hand on the knob. Hurt him, Sarah said, and I may forget my vows long enough to scratch your eyes out. Bible study's in one hour. Don't be late.

Stransky cackled.

If only Troy could disappear into the bowels of the nunnery until whatever was coming had passed by or conquered. He felt bone-weary. A lifetime of battle and responsibility had settled deep into him like sickness. On most days, the faces of the citizens kept him going. But now everything seemed to be crumbling. The Crusade had betrayed them, but Matthew Rook ruled the world. What could he do against that?

Well, well. Looks like you're human after all. Stransky tittered.

He tucked his thumbs into his gun belt. No idea what you're bab-blin about.

You and Sister Tightpants there. You got the hots for each other. You in love, or does she just make your pecker stand up and salute?

Troy knotted his hands into Stransky's shirt and yanked her upright, his face two inches from hers. Don't talk about her. Not ever. Or I'll put a bullet in your gut.

You need me.

Not that bad.

Stransky laughed again. Troy shoved her back onto the pew.

Oh sure, she said. You're just friends.

Troy gritted his teeth. You had a visitor. Tell me about that before I kick your teeth in.

Stransky patted the pew. Troy sat, keeping distance between them. He checked his pistols, making sure they were tied down. Sometimes the hand moved without the brain's leave. Stransky faced him, tucking her legs beneath her.

Fella was one of my runners, she said. He brought news from our man inside Rook's inner circle.

Am I supposed to guess what he told you?

First off, he passed the marchers' vanguard. They're a day out, two at the most.

That's what Dwyer said. We ain't nowhere near ready.

That ain't the biggest problem.

What's worse than that?

Rook plans to use bioweapons again, just like the first Purge.

Troy's mouth fell open. What?

Stransky grinned. She seemed to enjoy his discomfort. Yep. They ain't got enough left for the whole world, though, so they're plannin to use topography wherever they can. Settin wildfires in California. Confiscatin winter fuel up in Canada and Minnesota. They're gonna do somethin like that here. I reckon we should thank God we'll miss the plagues.

Troy and his lieutenants had debated the purpose of the explosives inventory. Now one of their theories seemed likely.

They're gonna blow up the levees and drown us, he said.

That's what I figured too. Then they'll get in your boats and pick off any survivors. Starvation and thirst will take care of anybody they miss.

Troy's stomach fluttered. His hands shook as he mopped his brow again. Lord help us all.

Stransky leaned toward him. How's it feel knowin you been killin the wrong folks all these years?

Troy said nothing. He could think of no adequate reply.

That night, Troy visited the Riverwalk. Patrols rode by Jackson Square, twice as many mounted guards circulating through the Quarter twice as often. *I hope it helps folks sleep better. I wish I could tell em this is the first time the Temple's been completely safe from the Troublers.* He found his favorite bench and sat. The overcast sky merged with the black water, an abyss where nothing could live and no one could hear his prayers. He offered one up anyway, the same one he had said a hundred times since they captured Stransky: *Please help me do right.*

He could not get the blasphemous, impure thoughts about Sarah Gonzales out of his head. *Father, forgive me my weakness.* But forgiveness seemed as cold and dead as the starlight he could not even see. He fanned himself with his hat and waited.

Soon they materialized from the dark: Long, Ford, and Tetweiller ambled in from different directions. Boudreaux jogged up moments later, probably straight from the prison infirmary where he had been spending every free minute with Jack Hobbes. McClure and Bandit padded up from the water's edge or, for all Troy knew, the river itself, two creatures from some other age whose comings and goings no person of aging flesh could understand. They fanned out in front of Troy, even Bandit, who sat between McClure and Tetweiller. The old lord knelt and scratched the dog's ears.

Stransky's got news, Troy said, keeping his voice low. The first prisoners will be here tomorrow, the day after at the latest.

Hell, Tetweiller said.

The dog yawned.

That ain't all. They're gonna use biologicals. Not here, but wherever they can, until their supply runs out.

Tetweiller spat. Son of a bitch.

What else? Long asked.

Stransky and me agree about what they're gonna do in New Orleans. They're gonna wall us in and blow the levees. Drown us like rats.

Sweet Father, Ford muttered.

Y'all been stockpilin supplies and ordnance?

Yes, sir, said Boudreaux.

We all have, said Tetweiller.

They sounded angry and nervous. Drawn faces, darting eyes, hunched postures that suggested stomachs crawling into throats. The rope they had fashioned to pull themselves out of sin's deepest pit had knotted itself into a noose and was now draped around their throats.

Look, Troy said, we're all scared. But we gotta keep it together. Our people are countin on us, even if they don't know it. So are the Troublers. Ain't no way we can convert em if they're all dead.

McClure tittered. The child did not believe. She had seen too much blood on the streets and had turned harder than the cracked pavement on which they walked. McClure felt you could not embrace sinners when you held a loaded gun to their heads. You had to choose, the open hand or the pistol.

Hush up, Tetweiller said to her.

She's earned the right to believe what she wants, Troy said. Willa, once the soldiers get here, I'll need regular reports about the levees.

McClure's voice floated out of the darkness. Sure.

The rest of you, keep on filchin. We're gonna need as much ammo as we can get. Let's grab tools too. Lord knows what all we'll need. Ernie, I want a list of every place the Crusade might wire. I doubt they'll bother with every foot of the floodwalls. Too much to guard.

Got it, said Tetweiller.

Boudreaux stepped closer. What about me?

We're the ones workin closest to Dwyer, and he'll be watchin, Troy said. You're gonna watch him back. If he moves against us, we'll cut him down. The lord of order stood and shook all their hands. I wish this had fallen to somebody else, but I couldn't ask for a better crew. LaShanda, would you like to lead us in prayer?

See y'all later, McClure said. A stirring in the night, and she was gone.

The others bowed their heads. Troy closed his eyes out of habit.

Lord Father, Long said, we know it's always darkest before the dawn, but sunrise seems a year away. Lead us down the path of righteousness for Your name's sake. Let Your light guide us. Give us understanding and clarity, Father. Help us serve Your will. And if the devil drags us down and yokes us to his wagon, bury us under the mountains, Lord. We're nothin if we ain't your servants, and we want to be good ones. Your will be done, forever and ever. Amen.

Amen, Troy said. I love every one of you. You'll do this city proud. Now go get some sleep. Company's comin.

They melted into the shadows, except for Boudreaux. Neither he nor Troy spoke until the sounds of the others' leaving had faded. The hoofbeats of another patrol grew louder, clopped by, faded.

Can we really find a way through this? Boudreaux asked.

I'm prayin every five minutes, Troy said. He listened to the guards' passing conversations. Soon all those voices might be raised against him or stilled forever. Despite the heat, he shivered.

# ♣ 9 ♣

**T**roy sat his horse facing the Lake Pontchartrain Causeway. It stretched across the water and disappeared into the horizon, two parallel trails of concrete and steel that time and weather had eroded but not crumbled. To Troy's left, Dwyer worked his string in the saddle. To the right, Gordy Boudreaux chewed jerky and patted his horse's neck every few minutes. Behind them, Jerold Babb sat in the two-horse wain he had driven, sweating through his robes of office, his wispy hair plastered to his head. He had drunk one canteen dry and had started on a second. *He's gonna have to relieve himself every five minutes on the way home.*

Hobbes had left the infirmary, but when he tried to saddle up and join them that morning, Troy had denied him.

I can ride, Hobbes had said.

Troy patted his good shoulder. I know it. But we don't want them stitches bustin open. Take her easy till they come out.

Hobbes had ridden home in a wagon's shotgun seat, glaring whenever the boy Troy had conscripted to drive it tried to speak.

Now Troy pulled his hat low. The rising sun sparkled off calm water in dazzling crystal facets. A cool breeze blew over the lake, the horses' manes fluttering. Boudreaux snuffled, hawked, and spat a wad of phlegm onto the road. Troy glanced at him. Boudreaux shook his head.

*If he gets a fever, he'll keep pushin until it burns him down or we have to shoot him too. Mostly because he'll know we can't afford to lose somebody else.*

Dwyer slipped the string into his saddlebag and dismounted. Then he walked to the edge of the causeway, where he stopped and stretched, his palms flat against his lower back. He groaned as the vertebrae popped. What a sight, he said. So many of the ancients were heathens, blasphemers, and adulterers, but when they put their minds to it, they built their structures to last.

Troy knew what Dwyer meant. He had read the church's secret history of this city and the journals of past lords. The causeway had nearly been destroyed in some of the hurricanes that often skirted the city's edge, and once a storm called Katrina had nearly wrecked it in a matter of hours. Sometime later, when Hurricane Melvin overwhelmed the improved levees and flooded the city again, killing nearly fifty percent of the population, a quarter-mile section of the causeway had sunk into the lake. Troy had always taken those events as proof that the ancients, for all their ingenuity, learned their lessons slowly. Like the builders of Babel, so sure they could master God Himself until His mighty hand showed them their folly. After Melvin, the levees had been raised another fifteen feet and reinforced yet again, the causeway restored and buttressed. It had been spot repaired many times since, the basic structure and design never changing. In his lifetime, Troy had never even seen it damaged. It had most recently survived Hurricane Oscar, which had flooded lower-lying streets, taken off roofs, shattered windows. The levees held that day too, despite storm surges and heavy rains swelling the lake like the fat gray ticks that plagued dogs in summer.

Troy dismounted and stood beside the herald, thumbs tucked into his gun belt. What time you reckon they'll make it? he asked.

Dwyer's white teeth practically sparkled. I have no idea. They're riding herd on the biggest prisoner migration in history, all those Troublers chained together at the ankles and walking in lockstep. You can imagine the delays that would result from even one child tripping over its own feet.

Troy whistled long and low. A tangle of arms and legs and heads, each Troubler landing on someone else, only to be landed upon a second later. The screams, the broken bones, the deep and hopeless sobs. It had probably happened more than once, especially to those who came from far up north. The first arrivals would be contingents from Baton Rouge and Lafayette, Shreveport and Monroe, Natchez and Jackson, which had been absorbed into the larger forces from Atlanta and Houston. Soon enough, prisoners from New York, California, Washington State, and Canada would walk the twin roads built over all that water. Thousands upon thousands of Troublers and enough chain to wrap around the globe bearing down on New Orleans.

But Troy could not give voice to recriminations in Dwyer's presence. I reckon it would take an age to walk just fifty or sixty miles.

Dwyer nodded. Indeed. I imagine many have died on the road. They will be cut loose or dragged to pieces. More time lost.

Boudreaux sat in his saddle, expressionless. Babb had nodded off, his chin resting on his chest. Troy got back on his horse. Whatever came down the causeway, he would meet it mounted and proud.

After a while, thudding, rhythmic footsteps drifted to them like thunder rumbling through distant mountains. Dwyer stayed afoot another ten minutes, watching through his spyglass. Then he remounted and sat straight, his long hair cascading over his shoulders, his hand shielding his eyes against the glare of the sunlight reflecting off the water. When the rumble got loud enough, Babb woke up and yawned. Boudreaux adjusted his hat and spat again. They waited until the first prisoners came into sight, inched toward them, and finally stepped off the causeway onto Metairie soil.

They walked in ten single-file lines, each chained to whoever walked in front and behind, the tintinnabulation of their steel almost musical. When the guards called halt, the arresting of their motion created an illusion of movement, a wave that seemed to ripple northward along the causeway, taking with it the thuds and the clinks in ever-fading contrapuntal clamors. Looking at the mass of men, women, and children standing in torn and soiled clothes, at feet clad in scuffed boots or fraying shoes or nothing but blood and grime, Troy thought it seemed a miracle they had come so far without trampling each other into bloody paste, without overlapping their chains and tying themselves into knots. They were hungry and exhausted. Only their guards, mounted and bearing the sigil of the Crusade on their shirts, looked fresh. They sat their horses with heads held high, their rifles and shotguns scabbarded, their loaded pistols tied down in their holsters.

*Any of em might be the one that kills me,* thought Troy. *And half of me believes I deserve it.*

One of the guards rode up and saluted. Dwyer and Troy returned it. What news? the herald asked.

Our prisoners walked from Lafayette, Breaux Bridge, Baton Rouge, and St. Francisville, sir, said the guard. Plus a hundred other towns. Behind us, they're from Vidalia and Woodville, Mississippi, even Natchez. Behind them, who knows? This here's a motley lot. I'm glad I didn't have to bring em no farther than I did.

Before them, men and women, children and the elderly, the healthy and the sick. The fierce light of hatred or determination in some eyes, terror in the rest. No food in sight, no water, though every prisoner looked parched, the harbingers of a cruelty that would sweep the earth before it.

Where are the envoys? Troy asked.

They'll be along directly, said the guard. They was still sittin off a ways and cookin breakfast when we broke camp. I reckon they're takin their time.

Dwyer turned to Troy. We should square away these heathens. Where do you suggest we direct them?

Troy took off his hat and scratched his head. Probably best just to march em all the way to the southernmost point and stack em up anyplace our citizens ain't usin. Ernie Tetweiller's waitin on the road back yonder a piece. He'll lead em in.

You want me to help him? Boudreaux asked.

No. Escort Jerold home, and check on Jack. He's itchin to mount up and shoot at somebody. Tie him down if you have to.

Eyeing the massed Troublers, Boudreaux saluted and turned his horse. So much humanity, stretching past the horizon—once they all arrived, New Orleans would look as it must have before the Purge, a great anthill, its catacombs aswarm, the inhabitants walking on top of each other. And if Troy and his friends—who had begun to think of themselves as Conspirators, rather than Crusaders or Troublers—were right, the bodies of the dead would soon choke waterlogged streets and spill into the great river. They would pile against buildings and bloat and rot and burst. No one could live in New Orleans after that, not for decades. The diseases from all those bodies would kill any flood survivors just as efficiently and perhaps more terribly. Then the coming of vermin and carrion animals.

*That ain't God's work. It just can't be. And I gotta save em all because how could I know whose soul is innocent and whose is stained? How was I ever supposed to know? And why did I never think to ask until my own neck was in the noose?*

The guards whistled and shouted commands, and the weary prisoners trudged forward again, finding that same rhythm and cadence. Many eyes met Troy's, holding his gaze as they passed. But as before, most looked frightened, pleading, despairing.

Soon he and Dwyer left. Troy would meet the envoys in his office, as befitted a lord of order.

Troy, Dwyer, and Babb had made a table of the lord's desk as they ate their beefsteak and boiled potatoes. Juice dribbled down Babb's chin. One of Tetweiller's runners had just left after bringing the latest news: Incoming Troublers had reached the city's southern borders and were spreading east and west and back again, wrapping the avenues in limbs and chains. They sat on bare concrete walks, on streets, on grass in front of uninhabited houses and apartment complexes and buildings whose ancient purposes no one understood. Would the Crusaders leave the Troublers chained together when the floodwaters came? Each prisoner acting as the next one's anchor. Hundreds of children had already trooped by, emaciated babes with dirty faces and hollow eyes. How could they all be hardened, fanatical Troublers?

*If we got any chance to save em, we should try. Christ said to suffer the little children and let em come unto him. I don't think he meant kill em to get em there faster. Or maybe this is just my moment in the Garden, and I ain't got the courage to drink from the cup.*

Troy had spent most of the morning thinking about impossible logistics: how to shelter and feed so many, how to help the sick, how his tiny band of Conspirators—Hobbes, Boudreaux, Tetweiller, Long, Ford, McClure, and whomever they could recruit between now and the end—could stop the Crusade. There was still time to abort, to fall in line like the good soldier he had always been, to trust his superiors and reject the evidence he had already seen. It was tempting beyond words. To fight the Crusade would put his soul at hazard, and his friends'.

No good answers, no rest. He had slept less than four hours a stretch since the day they took Stransky. Now he could barely keep his eyes open.

Dwyer ate his bloody steak, the rich red juices pooling on his plate. When he smiled, his teeth were pinkish, the incisors sharp. The sheer carnivorous pleasure of a man built to rend flesh.

Someone knocked. Door's open, Troy called.

Boudreaux entered and bowed. The traditional genuflections for Dwyer's benefit. Troy wiped his hands and mouth on his napkin and stood. Dwyer and Babb did the same.

I bid you greetings, Deputy Lord, Troy said. The formal words felt odd, like a misaligned jaw.

Boudreaux straightened. Greetings to you, Lord Troy. From his grace, Matthew Rook, I present the Crusade's envoy, Lisander Royster.

A scarecrow walked in, so tall he had to duck under the doorframe, nearly as thin as the Troublers clanking down the streets. His nose looked long and sharp enough to chisel stone, his Adam's apple like a small goiter. He was dressed in the long purple robes of Rook's inner council and bore the Crusade's sigil on both sleeves.

Royster bowed, his robes and loose undershirt falling open so Troy could see the brand of the cross on his chest. Greetings to you, Gabriel Troy, New Orleans lord of order.

Troy bowed. Royster's deep green eyes shone even with his back to the sunlight streaming through the stained glass.

Troy had heard of Lisander Royster, who oversaw the Crusade's darkest business—state executions, exterminating whole Troubler communities in the countryside. If the Crusade had ever christened a national lord of order, it would have been Royster, though he had never personally done any fighting. He was said to be naturally distrustful and without mercy.

I present the herald of Matthew Rook, Jevan Dwyer, said Boudreaux.

Dwyer and Royster bowed. Then they smiled and shook hands.

It's good to see you again, Mister Dwyer, said Royster.

And you, sir, said the herald.

Boudreaux cleared his throat. I present the high minister of the New Orleans principality, Jerold Babb.

Babb and Royster bowed.

Welcome, said Babb. We're honored to host such august presences. Whatever you need, just ask.

Royster laid a hand on Babb's shoulder. My thanks, High Minister.

Babb shivered, perhaps in ecstasy.

Royster moved to the side, and Boudreaux said, Deputy Envoy Benn.

The man who entered was a foot and a half shorter than Royster. Built like a child's kickball, Benn wore wool pants, scuffed boots, and a coarse and sweat-stained work shirt. His broad chest expanded with every breath, so much that Troy half expected the buttons to pop right off his shirt. His arms and legs looked thick and powerful. He bowed to Troy, an action that shortened him only marginally, and greeted the lord of order.

Troy bowed. Greetings to you, Deputy.

Benn shook hands with Babb and Dwyer. When he took his place beside Royster, Boudreaux announced, Deputy Envoy Clemens.

The last person to enter stood perhaps six feet tall. He was of average build. His thinning brown hair, gray at the temples, reached his shoulders. Like Benn, he dressed for work, not ceremony, which would have told any fool which envoy gave the orders and who actually labored. *I don't even have to see the brand to know they got it. I bet if Royster cut off his ear, they'd do it too.* Clemens said his how-dos as Boudreaux hauled in three more chairs. Everyone sat except Boudreaux, who walked around the desk and stood beside Troy, hands clasped.

Gentlemen, Troy said, welcome to New Orleans.

Thank you, said Royster. His voice was deep for such a skinny man. He probably sang bass. For the duration of our stay here, we'll need offices.

Troy gestured round about. Figured you'd want ours.

That would do nicely, but we don't want to put you out.

*Uh-huh. You'd dump us all in the river if it made your hindquarters a little more comfortable.* No trouble. This is our hub. I reckoned you'd wanna stick close.

And you won't have to travel for Sunday services, said Babb.

Many thanks, Royster said. Now. We are naturally prepared to answer your questions in the name of Matthew Rook. We know this is a traumatic time. Gentlemen?

Benn and Clemens nodded.

Troy had told Boudreaux to say as little as possible. That way, if any enmity resulted, it would fall on Troy alone. Besides, if Boudreaux spoke out of turn, the envoys would assume Troy could not control his people.

Well, said Troy, I admit we're concerned. We grew up here. Good people have died for this town. Now we're makin it a dump for Troublers. Kinda makes you feel like you wasted your life.

Benn narrowed his eyes. When my duty called me here, I left my wife and two children, but I thanked my Maker for the chance. If you've spent your life serving God, how could you consider that a waste under any circumstances?

Mister Benn is right, said Babb, shaking his finger at Troy. Gentlemen, I apologize. Lord Troy has never raised these objections to me, or I would have advised him to keep still.

Troy ignored Babb. Servin God wasn't the waste. Keepin this city safe and clean was. We could have relocated our populace years ago.

Gabriel—Babb began, but Royster held up a hand. Babb's mouth snapped shut fast enough to catch flies.

Your city's geography suits our purposes, the envoy said. The preponderance of nearby waters. How the town sits in a bowl of sorts, below sea level. The causeway and the bridges. Few locations of comparable size and circumstances exist on this continent. Our other choices had far greater population densities. For all these reasons, it had to be New Orleans. But, of course, the greatest reason is that God has willed it so, and He revealed this plan to Matthew only recently. Our lives march to His beat.

Babb nodded, his eyes closed. Yes, Father.

Troy resisted the urge to groan. You said *Matthew*. First-name basis, huh?

Royster smiled. The expression's sharklike qualities made Dwyer's seem warm and wholesome. Indeed. We have been close since our seminary days.

Yet he sent you along with the riffraff.

Royster started.

*Gabriel*, Babb hissed.

Leave off, Jerold. I don't need you bird-doggin my every word.

Royster recovered himself. Yes. Matthew believes my talents will be useful here. I sense hostility, Lord Troy. Toward me, if not our plans.

Boudreaux shifted his weight.

*We're talkin about Gordy's fate too, but he's expected to stand there and shut up. A hard task, especially for a youngster.*

It's this bit about leavin my people here that really worries me, Troy said. Makin em start over out in the muck like the folks they've always fought. We're gonna lose our crops, our shelter. Only the Lord knows how many diseases we'll face.

For the first time, the man named Clemens spoke, his voice dripping with insolence. That's your problem. You aren't the lord of hot meals and afternoon naps.

Despite himself, Troy's temper blazed. Ain't you a peach. You gents sure this fella's Christian?

Clemens started to rise.

Gentlemen, please, Babb said, sounding strangled.

Royster stood. Deputy Envoy Clemens, he bellowed. Clemens froze. You will address Lord Troy by his title, and you will show him respect. Do you understand?

Clemens sat, but he stared at Troy like a wild dog eyeing a lamb. Yes, sir. Forgive me, Lord Troy. His tone could have cut throats.

Troy said nothing. Babb mopped his brow with a handkerchief. After a moment, he took his seat.

You must overlook Mister Clemens's lack of manners, Royster said.

The road has been long and stressful. As for your concerns, I understand them, but we have our orders.

When are we supposed to evacuate?

I see no reason to displace anyone yet.

Ain't that sweet.

Your people will not be abandoned. And neither will you.

Royster's eyes flicked to the left as he spoke. Twice.

*Liar.* Boudreaux shifted again. *Gordy saw it too. Good.*

If that is all for now, Royster said, please describe how you've divided the city's responsibilities. And then, considering how tired and dirty we are, perhaps someone could show us to our quarters.

All right, Troy said.

Mister Benn, take notes, please.

Benn pulled a sheaf of papers and a chewed-up pencil from his back pocket. He scooted up to Troy's desk and smoothed out the wrinkled paper.

Okay, said Troy. I reckon our day-to-day work ain't much different than what you'd find anywhere. I got the final say in everything except Jerold's ministrations, but my deputies and officials run most everything in my name. Their subordinates oversee specific neighborhoods and jobs—the plantin and reapin of a certain crop, the manufacture of a particular weapon, and so forth. Anything you say to me, I can relay to my people, and they'll relay it to theirs, all the way down the line.

Royster nodded. Yes, it sounds as if you follow protocols.

Of course we do, Babb said.

Troy frowned at the high minister. If Babb bent over any further for the envoy, he might fall over.

As for peacekeepin, Gordy runs everything south of the river. It's a lot of territory, but he's the youngest and most energetic. Benn wrote it all down. After a bit, Royster whirled a finger in the air, a *please continue* gesture, so Troy said, I personally oversee the Vieux Carré.

Very good, said Royster. The lord of order belongs near the High Temple.

Troy opened a drawer. He pulled out a city map and spread it over the desk. Royster got up and leaned over it. Benn kept writing, sweat pouring off his brow.

This here's the river, Troy said, tracing a blue squiggle with his finger. My territory stretches north from the river to Rampart, and from Canal Street to Esplanade Avenue.

Ah, yes, Royster said. Benn sketched a crude map on his own paper.

LaShanda Long's in charge east of Esplanade and Wisner Boulevard, includin the neighborhoods of Faubourg Marigny, Treme, and Mid-City. She's our weaponsmith and ammo expert.

And where is her main forge?

Troy pointed at the map. Here. The ancients called it the Lakefront Arena. Now, Jack Hobbes runs everything west of Esplanade all the way to North Causeway Boulevard. That includes the Central Business District, the Arts District, and Lakeview.

Royster concentrated, as if he planned to memorize everything. Why did he bother with having Benn take notes? Continue, he said, whirling his finger again.

Everything west of the causeway is Santonio Ford's territory. He's our chief hunter and gatherer, and he also runs the parks and waterways. Anyplace you can plant a crop or hunt or fish, we defer to him.

And what of Mr. Tetweiller?

Retired. He lives over in Metairie, not too far from where you hit town. That's in Ford's territory. Sometimes Ernie helps us out, but he ain't in charge of nothin but his own self.

Very well. Tell me, what do you think of Jonas Strickland's decision to continue using the ancients' names for things? Our streets, our parks? Our histories tell us he did it to help the Great Purge's survivors feel more at ease with the new world, but it seems odd.

*A clumsy test, Envoy.* I reckon he knew what he was doin.

Of course he did.

Benn wrote, drew, annotated. Finally, he finished his notes and sat back, wiping sweat from his face. Dark stains had spread from his armpits to his chest and back. He huffed in the hot, still air.

What else? Troy asked.

That will do for now. Royster stuck out his hand. Thank you, Lord Troy.

Troy shook with him. We'll have the offices ready by tomorrow. Gordy?

Boudreaux took the three men downstairs. Troy sat and rubbed his temples. Another headache had begun to throb behind his left eye. He had hoped the Crusade would make at least some pretense of relocating the population, but Royster's flickering eyes said no.

Stransky had been right. About everything.

Chain gangs trooped across the causeway and through the city ceaselessly, the reverberations of their footfalls shaking jars off shelves and pounding into dreams. All those people moving at once suggested months, perhaps years, of planning, which belied Royster's claim about the recency of Rook's vision. Did the envoy think no one would realize that, or did he not care? Guards poured into town on horseback, on foot, in supply wagons. Shots had been fired eight or ten times already. The first time, when Troy tried to dash out of the office, Royster assured him some Troubler had gotten too uppity or had attempted escape, an unfortunate but inevitable occurrence. Troy stayed.

Boudreaux and Ford had joined Tetweiller in directing the prisoners as far south as Estelle and Woodmere. No one had indicated whether the Crusade planned to let the southern bogs function as a natural border or wall them off or drain the swamps and raze the whole place. Troy had chased Troublers out there for years, running them to ground and dragging the survivors back to the city in chains. The dead he left for the gators and insects. Now, if he returned to the bogs, he would likely do so as an outcast, as much a traitor as those whose bones he would tread on, because where else was there to hide?

He managed to get away from Royster around five o'clock. The sounds of the march drummed against his temples as he and Japeth rode through town. The buildings' shadows stretched like the talons of some unimaginable prey bird. Every glance at the prisoners yielded a fresh crop of expressionless faces and bobbing greasy heads. The deep suspiration of thousands of lungs created its own breeze, fetid and swampy. Troy rode among his own people, going to or coming from work, their faces wan, their bodies hunched. They looked to him as he passed, and the hope in their expressions broke his heart, for what was hope in the face of genocide?

Later, on empty thoroughfares, solitary in the gloaming, Troy ambled toward Sister Sarah's, and then, thinking better of it, turned for home, his new office, a token of both his authority and the loss of it.

*I've probably used my Temple office for the last time.* His eyes stung with the salt of unfamiliar tears.

Jack Hobbes sat on the front steps, his saddled roan tethered to the hitching post near the street. Troy dismounted and hitched Japeth. Then he walked up and sat next to Hobbes, who was wearing a sling, the poultice and bandages hunched beneath his shirt. The men sat in silence for a bit, listening. Hobbes smelled of mustard.

Racket got old real quick, the senior deputy said.

Troy laughed, humorless and bitter. How's the collarbone?

Arm's stiff, but I'll live. Been workin the shoulder as much as I can without poppin the stitches. What's our next move?

We need to talk about that. All of us, includin Willa. Everybody should get a say.

Hobbes nodded. Seen LaShanda today. A guard told her the wall's already built. They got the Troublers draggin it here in sections.

Troy spat. I knew Royster lied. He knows exactly what's comin.

Whole thing ain't seemed real till now. But it is. They're gonna turn New Orleans into a lake, with us still in it.

When we meet, Stransky's gotta be there.

And if one of us decides their salvation depends on killin the rest? I reckon somebody will die.

The horses shifted. What moon and stars there were rode between cloud banks pendulous and jagged. Up and down the avenues, candlelight flickered in windows. Gray smoke from cookfires drifted along the blue-black horizon. *It would be nice to live in a peaceful world where a man could stretch out on his porch and sleep in the drowsy heat, but the world ain't never been peaceful and never will be. All my life I've fought to keep order, but if it ain't the Troublers, it's men like Rook. I might as well try to sop up the ocean with a bath towel.*

They sat for a while longer, and then Troy invited Jack Hobbes inside, where they talked long into the night.

During Sunday morning services, the envoys sat in the front row on the left-hand side of the Temple. Royster sang bass, Benn tenor. Clemens sounded more like a cat somebody had stepped on, but none could say he had not made his joyful noise. When Babb took the podium and spoke for an hour and a half on I John 3:4, *Whosoever committeth sin transgresseth also the law: for sin is the transgression of the law,* Royster amened so loudly that he sounded as if the Holy Spirit had overcome him, making him forget the august dignity of his office.

Ford cut his eyes at Troy. The lord of order's jaw was set, his right fist clenched, but his face betrayed nothing. Nor did Jack Hobbes's or LaShanda Long's. Perhaps they agreed with Babb in their hearts. Perhaps they kept still through sheer will, like Troy.

*I don't know how them folks in the back can even hear Jerold, what with all that noise from the city.*

The Office of Order had never been able to afford taking the Sabbath off, as the rest of the professions did. Neither, it seemed, would the emigration. Night or day, Sunday or not, the prisoners marched.

And so I beseech you, Babb cried, as if he had read Ford's thoughts. Turn your eyes and ears to God. Trouble yourselves not, for our Father stands with us. His greatest earthly servant, Matthew Rook, has sent us three men to lead us into our new life. Trust in them, for to do so is to trust in the Most High.

*Is Jerold right, Father God? Or has the adversary laid a finger on his heart? Oh, dear Father, has the devil touched mine?*

After the service, Royster, Benn, and Clemens stood beside Babb at the front doors, shaking hands as the congregants exited the Temple. Ford embraced all four men, but even as he passed into the day's dull heat, he shivered.

roy sat in his saddle and glared at the Crusade guard standing before him. To Troy's right, Jack Hobbes's jaw clenched hard enough to shatter his teeth. To the left, Gordy Boudreaux's eyes narrowed. The guard white-knuckled a shotgun. He glanced over his shoulder at the troops lined across the bridge thirty yards away. They stood at ease, but if anything happened, they would cut down everyone in their path, even this guard, who had positioned Tetweiller between himself and the lords, a human shield. All of this before anyone had said a word. For the hundredth time since they had captured Lynn Stransky, Troy wondered how moments like this were possible, how the Crusade had changed so much without his noticing it.

*Or maybe it never changed, and I've just been blind my whole life.*

Blushing, Tetweiller sputtered, It's a damn outrage. Gabriel, you better straighten out this young pup before I pistol-whip him and kick his damn teeth in.

The guard's shotgun moved upward two inches, as if he were about to jab the barrel into Tetweiller's back, but Troy said, You don't wanna do that, son.

The guard froze.

Ernie, come on over here with us, Hobbes said.

Tetweiller approached and put a hand on Troy's saddle. They say we ain't allowed across the river no more. And they requisitioned my horse. My *horse.*

No wonder the old man had lost his temper. When outsiders took over your hometown, you tended to take it personally, especially when they also commandeered your mount.

They had me leadin em street to street, droppin Troublers and guards every few feet, and then this whippersnapper asks if I can dismount and show him a good fallback point in case we got attacked, Tetweiller said, spittle flying. When we come back, Pete was gone, and they drug me all the way here, tellin me Royster ordered it all. I'd of busted his head open, but you see how I'm outnumbered. All them jackasses back there for one old man. They didn't even have the balls to tell me about Pete until they got me on the north side of the water.

Tetweiller had ridden Pete for ten years. Tears welled in the old man's eyes.

Troy's stomach roiled. *These devils. I reckon it's good they took Pete behind Ernie's back, or else he wouldn't be standin here right now, and at least a dozen outlanders would never see another sunrise.* Troy took a deep breath and tried to calm himself. A shootout would help no one. He looked at the guard. I want to talk with your bosses right away, he said. If you see em before I do, tell em. As for this mess, Ernie Tetweiller is a retired lord of order. Pete better be back at his house by dark, or you and me will have this little chat again. Not Royster. Not you and thirty guards against one old man. Just me and you. We clear?

The young guard glanced over his shoulder. His fellows on the bridge had not moved.

Don't look at them, Troy said. Look at me.

The guard swallowed hard. He could not have been older than twenty, and he was caught between a furious lord and the specter of the envoys. But it was not Troy's business to make the guard's life easier. Perhaps this was a test to see how far they could push him before he pushed back, but either way, his course was set.

I'll see what I can do, sir, the guard said. But I'll have to ask Mr. Royster for permission to release the horse.

Troy pulled on the reins. Japeth turned. Troy helped Ernie Tetweiller into the saddle behind him. Go ahead. But if you don't get the okay, you better bring Pete home anyhow.

He spurred Japeth and trotted away. Hobbes and Boudreaux followed. Troy did not have to look to know the young guard had turned and sprinted back toward his comrades.

Boudreaux had an armory to inventory, so he took his leave. Troy dropped Tetweiller at his house to wait for Pete. Afterward, Hobbes rode home with him. They hitched their horses and went inside. McClure and Bandit waited in the den. The girl had helped herself to some tea and a bowl of water for the dog. Troy and Hobbes took off their hats and gun belts, hanging them on the rack near the window. McClure still wore hers.

*Have I ever seen her without em? Not that I recall.*

Troy nodded at the girl. How are you today?

Fair to middlin. You seen what's goin on across the river?

Hobbes sat on the sofa. Troy joined him and said, What do you know?

It was full daylight, so I couldn't get too close. They got every man, woman, and child just sittin in the streets, with the guards marchin up and down like the whole bunch might stand up at once and make a break for it.

Hobbes grunted. In this heat, they're more likely to die.

Yep, said McClure. There's somethin goin on down at the river too. I couldn't get close enough to see. I'll try again after dark.

If there's time, Troy said. First, I need you to set up a meetin with Stransky.

For when?

Tomorrow night, or the day after. She says she's got friends in Washington. I want to test that one more time, right now, before we go too far. If you can find out what they're doin at the river, we can compare it to what she says.

She knows about Willa, Hobbes said. Might tell us the truth about this just because she knows we can double-check her.

As long as she's alive, we'll have to watch our backs. But if she's stupid enough to lie, we can put her behind us for good. You took a bullet to get her outta the tower. If the time comes, you'll be first in line to put one in her brain.

Hobbes said nothing. He looked troubled.

*Could be he's lost his taste for that kind of justice. And I can't blame him, now that we're on the other end of it. Or maybe it's the whole shebang—Rook, Royster, the uncertainty. That last part should work itself out soon enough.*

Troy planned to ask the envoys about the confrontation on the bridge, and that conversation would tell him much he needed to know.

McClure had already faded into the gathering shadows when Troy and Hobbes untied their horses and rode back toward the Temple.

May have to fracture somebody's skull if they try to pull rank, Hobbes said as the church loomed ahead.

When they entered the building minutes later, the personnel milling about quieted and turned to watch them. He and Hobbes nodded at the staff and tipped their hats. Everyone looked pale and nervous. No eye contact. Shifting from foot to foot. Forced smiles on reddened faces.

Like horses just before a big storm hits, Hobbes muttered.

They climbed the back stairs and found Troy's office door open. Royster sat behind the desk. Clemens and Benn had taken the straight-backs. Dwyer stood at ease behind the deputy envoys, while Jerold Babb flitted at Royster's right hand. As Troy and Hobbes entered, Royster looked up and smiled. Troy and Hobbes positioned themselves to Clemens's left, thumbs in their gun belts. Intensity boiled off the deputy envoy, despite his blank face.

*He's the most dangerous,* Troy thought. *Even if we killed every Crusader who outranked him, he'd hound us to the ends of the earth.*

I'm happy you're here, said Royster. I was going to send for you.

Glad we could spare you some trouble, Troy said. We need to talk about Ernie Tetweiller's horse.

Royster chuckled and flapped his hand. The animal in question has been returned.

Troy gritted his teeth. He wanted to nail that flapping hand to the desk. That's all well and good, as long as you understand that my people should be treated with respect.

As Babb's face reddened and he began to sputter, Clemens snorted and stood. He tried to edge past Hobbes, who stood his ground. Over Hobbes's shoulder, Clemens said, Are you giving orders to Matthew Rook's envoy? Because if you are—

Oh, sit down, Aloysius, said Royster. This isn't a schoolyard game of King of the Mountain.

Hobbes coughed and cleared his throat. Aloysius?

Clemens sat, his face red.

Royster sighed. I apologize for Mr. Clemens's temper. It is, perhaps, his least admirable quality, though I have found it useful on occasion. I assume *you* meant no disrespect to *us.*

Troy looked him in the eye. None. I just want to make sure it goes both ways.

Gabriel, for heaven's sake, Babb said.

Pipe down, Jerold. This ain't your department.

Clemens sat stone-faced, staring straight ahead. Benn had regained his composure. Dwyer, monolithic, stood with his arms crossed. The Crusade's rules of order dictated only Troy and Royster should speak, given their ranks. The others should have remained silent and still, like children in church, unless called on. Clemens had broken that rule and would probably pay for it somewhere down the line. Royster did not strike Troy as a man who would forgive any sin, even a political one. *And if he decides to gut-shoot Clemens and dump him in the landfill, I bet folks will line up for the privilege of pullin that trigger.*

Royster held his hands out, palms up. Respect earned is respect given, he said. I assure you both I and my men will treat you and yours as your position and service merit.

That's good. For starters, you can leave our mounts alone.

New Orleans is full of horses. Why, we could slaughter half of them to feed our prisoners, and you'd still have more than enough.

*Is that a threat?* Troy studied Royster a moment. Folks earn their horses here. Takin em ain't any way to repay loyalty.

Royster laughed and slapped the desk. Oh, Lord Troy, you look so *serious.* Such concern for beasts of burden. I'm afraid the best I can do is pledge to disrupt your people's lives as little as possible. Though under the circumstances, *little* is a truly relative term.

A generous pledge, Babb said, giving Troy the stink eye.

Troy shrugged. A pledge was not a vow or a promise. Royster had chosen his words carefully so he could renege without sinning. Not a good sign, but exactly what Troy had come to expect. *Now for the real test.*

I reckon that'll have to do for now. But since we're talkin about my people and their lives, maybe you can tell me what's goin on across the river. I hear you got the Troublers sittin in the streets. You plan to keep em there?

Royster's smile faded. He sat back and folded his hands across his abdomen, looking from Troy to Hobbes. He even glanced at his deputies and Dwyer for a moment, a sure sign he expected trouble.

I should like very much to know the name of the person you talked with, he said.

Don't recall, Troy said.

Babb clucked his tongue and wrung his hands as Royster frowned.

My orders come from Matthew Rook himself, the envoy said. The Troublers will remain where they are until more troops arrive. At that time, we will begin sequestering the prisoners in existing edifices and erecting the prison walls.

Which edifices? And what happens when the Troublers start spillin into areas where my people live and work?

Now Royster's expression hardened. When he spoke, his voice was toneless. We are in control of this situation. We will tell you what you need to know. Beyond that, you must have faith. Those without faith die a thousand deaths in times like these. Do we understand each other, Lord Troy?

The envoy never blinked, nor did he look away. Babb looked constipated. The deputies sat as still as stone.

Yeah, Troy said. We understand each other just fine.

McClure and Bandit waited in Troy's living room again, the girl sitting on the couch with her boots on the coffee table. She was reading Troy's copy of Jonas Strickland's *The Unbelievers*. Troy had read it a dozen times. Strickland's sharp suggestions for rooting out heathens had always inspired him, despite the near-extinction of humanity, which had seemed so remote and abstract. Whenever Troy executed Troublers, he drew comfort knowing he would never have to kill on that scale. He would never doom billions to death and hell. Still, what had Strickland felt before giving the order to Purge? Had he known faith could not exist without disbelief, life without death, salvation without damnation? Had he felt comfortable choosing who would see the new world and whose bones would bleach in the sun?

*I hold thousands of lives in my hands now. Enough to make ghosts for a hundred boneyards. How far can a man carry that much failure? And where on God's Earth could he set it down and rest?*

His bleary eyes stung.

McClure put the book on the end table. She sat up, boots clumping the floor, and nodded at Troy, who nodded back. Troy took the chair nearest the couch and removed his hat, beating its dust onto his rug. What's doin over yonder? he asked.

McClure scratched Bandit's head. Long lines of Troublers chained together on the streets, she said. One guard for every ten or twelve prisoners. A third of the troops mounted. Most of em armed, though I only saw the mounted ones packin guns. Lotta knives, clubs, and so forth. A few swords.

Huh.

Yeah. Why so few guns?

Can't know for sure, but generally speakin, when you know people can't trust you, then you don't tend to trust them either. Or maybe Rook figured the chains and the starvation and walkin unarmed with your family would keep the prisoners in line, and not havin guns or horses would keep the guards from gettin soft-hearted. Just a guess.

Troy sat for a while, sipping water and calculating. The girl and her dog waited, ever patient.

*Unless we can harness a load of our folks and all of Stransky's Troublers, or some of the guards spontaneously combust, our chances of savin this city are slim. My bunch could probably shoot our own way out. Any operation this big will have weak points. But we can't just leave everybody else to die.*

How fucked are we? McClure asked.

Very. So they're just droppin folks in the street, like Ernie said?

Yep. Minimum rations, doled out every six or eight hours.

Good Lord. The sun will kill a passel before the flood gets a chance.

I heard a couple guards talkin about that near the privies.

Troy leaned forward. Tell me. Word for word.

McClure closed her eyes. Well, one of em said, *I almost feel sorry for these folks. It's a rough way to go.* And the second one said, *They're Troublers. They deserve it.* Then the first guy said, *Yeah, but some of em's* kids. But the other one laughed. *If you came across a litter of wolf pups, would you want them to grow up? These kids, they're liable to shoot you one day. I really wish I was on the wall crew. Then we'd see em put to good use before they die.* After that, they left.

Anything else?

One of em had a dingus as long as my forearm. Looked like a dead king snake.

Willa.

Only noteworthy thing about em.

Troy had just been thinking of mass death. These guards made killing children sound as upsetting as taking out garbage.

Did you set that meetin with Stransky? he asked, shaking his head.

The sister said to come tomorrow night. I'd go after dark if I was you.

Troy walked to the nearest window and pulled back the curtain. Another humid night had settled over the city. Lightning bugs zipped over the street like shooting stars. Bats flapped in and out of the streetlamps' glow. Somewhere out there, the builders drew closer, bearing their tools and arms and Crusade flags. Some might already be here. Explosives were being confiscated from New Orleans's armories. Beyond that, he knew very little to compare with whatever Stransky would tell him. *I reckon I gotta trust her. She's been straighter with me than the envoys. And if she's leadin me astray, Lord, please know I'm doin my best.*

McClure stood, Bandit at heel, and joined Troy at the window. So. How do we get outta this?

Troy clapped her on the shoulder. You ever wanted to be a Troubler?

She snorted. Hell. Why not?

Twenty hours later, as Troy traveled on foot, the sun hung bright and bloody on the cloudless western horizon. Beneath the usual smells of cookfires drifted the sour scents of the march, unwashed flesh and sweat and illness. The walkers moved from causeway to city streets to bridge, their tread like some great beast's heartbeat. A low buzzing from south of the river—nonstop movement and conversations, the hum of populace, a microcosmic version of what the city must have sounded like in the time before. It felt both familiar and disquieting, as if Troy had stepped through a hole in his own life and fallen into his city's past.

*Or its future. If there was ever a time when Christians sent so many into bondage and death, our historians didn't write about it. The south-side streets will probably fill in another day or two. Then we'll be trippin over prisoners every time we move.*

Troy saluted patrolling guards and stopped to chat with some workers on their way home. To make sure he was noticed, he paused for an hour at the river, alone on his bench. Citizens trudged past and greeted him. Near dusk, he eased through the shadows, street by street, toward the Church of the Sisters of Mercy and Grace. When he came upon the unbroken south-moving line of Troublers and guards, he pulled his hat low, turned up his collar, and stepped over the chains between two prisoners. No one hailed him. These new guards would not know his face, even if they could see it in the gloom. He hoped he would have the same luck getting back. Likely the guards would be too focused on their charges to worry much about a citizen.

Camp Street was mostly deserted, as usual. The few people who lived there kept strict hours so they could attend Mass. *I bet Royster's not gonna be happy with the size of our Catholic population. Maybe that's another reason they picked New Orleans—the chance to drown so many Papists at once. Just one more bit of wrong in a great big pile of awful.*

He slipped inside the church. Stransky waited on the front pew, staring into the votives' light. She did not turn to greet him, even when the floorboards creaked. Her eyes were closed, as if in prayer. Troy crossed in front of her and took a seat to her right. She had bathed since he saw her last. The oil had been washed from her freshly combed hair, which hung straight down to her shoulders. She had scrubbed the dirt and grime from her face and arms. In her clean deerskin clothes, Stransky almost looked like a citizen.

She kept still for perhaps two minutes. Then she turned to him. Welcome back, partner, she said.

I can't believe you got the gall to pray, after all you done.

Stransky laughed and slapped her knee. Then she stood and placed her hands in the small of her back, arching her spine. It crackled; she grunted. Not that it's any of your goddam business, but I pray. I got my own religion, taught to me by my daddy and my granddaddy before him, until your buddy Ernie Tetweiller shot em down in the streets like dogs.

Troublers don't care nothin for God.

Stransky looked as if she had been sprayed by a skunk. We don't care nothin for the Crusade. There's a big difference, in case you hadn't noticed.

Troy shook his head. It wasn't always like this.

She grinned. Wasn't it?

She sat and faced him, crossing her legs beneath her as before. The deerskin hung from her body. Even though her face seemed fuller than it had in the tower, she still looked like a famine victim. Perhaps she was. Troy had spent much of his life guarding Crusade supplies from Troubler theft, damning the guerillas every time one of them stole food or water or weapons. Had their actions been just, Troy's wrong? How could starving someone serve God?

Still, the woman had murdered.

Don't talk to me about my own church, he said.

We got a Bible at our headquarters. It's been passed down from ancient times, dog-eared and flimsy, disintegratin every day. It's the real thing, not that cherry-picked piece of shit Strickland gave y'all. You should read it sometime. It might open your eyes.

I told you. I ain't gonna debate my religion with a heretic.

You brought it up.

Troy took a deep breath. *Don't let her get to you.* He exhaled. We got bigger problems. South of the river's stuffed with prisoners and guards, and they're bringin in the wall already built. I asked Royster about it. He clammed up.

Uh-huh. What do you plan to do about it?

Troy hated what he was about to say. Stransky watched him, expressionless. *She's lovin this.* He sighed. We've been recruitin. Hidin as much explosives and ammo as we can. But we're still gonna be outnumbered. The outlanders will have enough ordnance to blow those levees five times over.

She studied her nails as if they were discussing how best to mend a cuticle. And? she said.

And we need to get you back to your people. We need supplies. Combustibles, weapons, food stores, manpower.

Stransky smiled. Live together or die alone, huh?

Somethin like that.

They sat for a bit, watching the candles. When the sanctuary looked like this—no lamps, only the votives' finicky light—it always seemed solemn and spooky, like a graveyard by moonlight. Yet the combination of comfort and fear could be useful. Safety and ease felt good, but fright kept your guard up. Soon, if they failed, the sisters' steeple would thrust from murky water like a grasping hand.

She's sweet on you, Stransky said.

Troy started. Huh? Who?

Stransky grinned. Sarah. I mean, the first time I said somethin, I was just ribbin you, but it's true. She's got enough nun in her to hide it, but it's there. If you pushed her just a bit, I bet you could find out what's under that habit.

Troy shoved Stransky onto her back and jammed his bent knee between her breasts, one hand on her throat, the other cocking a pistol, pressing the barrel against her forehead. You ever speak of her like that again, he said through clenched teeth, and I'll blow your brains out.

Stransky cackled and flicked her tongue. Troy pressed the barrel harder, as if he meant to punch it through her skull. His grip on her throat tightened. Her face reddened. Bits of spittle flew from her lips. Yet still she laughed.

Then a voice broke through his anger. Gabriel Troy. You know I won't have violence here.

Sister Sarah stood near the back door, blending into the shadows.

Stransky's laughter had weakened. Saliva flecked her lips.

*If I squeeze a little more, she'll die laughin.*

Instead, he uncocked his gun and holstered it. The barrel left a red O in Stransky's skin. He let go of her neck and got off her.

She sat up, coughing and rubbing her throat, still grinning. Her eyes sparkled with glee and madness. Now I trust you'll fight to your dyin breath, she croaked, nodding at Sister Sarah. You got somethin precious to lose.

I always did, he said. All my people are precious to me.

She cackled again and scooted away. Some more than others.

*I want to put her down like the rabid animal she is. But if I do, Sarah will never let me cross this threshold again. And I'd be handin New Orleans to Royster.*

Sister Sarah began to come forward, but Stransky held up her hand. Hang on, Sister. Me and Gabe got a little more jawin to do. Better if you don't hear. That way, if anybody ever asks, you ain't gotta lie.

Behave yourselves, Sister Sarah said. Both of you.

She backed out of the room, glaring at them, a mother leaving her petulant children alone in a room full of glassware.

Troy leaned against the pew. The votives flickered and wavered. *I wish I could ask Sarah to light one for me. Any shelter in a hurricane, right? But I've burdened her too much already.*

Stransky edged close to him. Now that we know where we stand, I got a condition.

You ain't in no position to bargain.

Neither are you. Right now, we got a common enemy. It don't matter if we don't like each other much. Until that enemy's gone, I need your solemn promise before God, here in this house of worship, that you won't betray me and mine. That you won't sell us out to those outlander fucks. Can you do that?

Troy examined his hands. They had done so much violence, first in his days as a deputy and then during his tour as lord of order. He had killed and tortured. He had shot men, women, children barely big enough to hold a gun. Just now he had nearly strangled a woman with one hand and shot her with the other. And he had done it all because he believed it was right, commensurate with the Crusade's teachings and the will of the one true God. Now he could no longer reconcile the Crusade's orders with his own heart. Perhaps in disobeying his church, he was damning himself. Or maybe he had been damned for years, following Rook and his ilk straight to hell. Troy did not know how you could try so hard to do right and still lose your soul, but that contradiction now seemed truer than any of the easy certainties he had always known. Against such a backdrop, why not promise Stransky whatever she needed to hear? What more harm could he do? Besides, no one knew what tomorrow would bring. Perhaps he would get to keep his word.

He looked her in the eye. You got my word before God that I won't turn on you or yours, at least not till the city's safe.

Stransky smiled again. I reckon that'll do. We can sort each other out later, if it comes to that. And hell, Gabe. We might even be real friends by then. She stood without another word and walked to the door. When she opened it, Sister Sarah was on the other side, her hands clasped, as patient and immobile as a statue. He's all yours, Sister. I think this went pretty good, don't you?

Stransky disappeared into the sanctuary's recesses, slapping Sister Sarah on the buttocks as she passed. Sister Sarah shrieked. She scowled as she entered and closed the door behind her. As she strode to Troy, her habit swished against her legs as a horse's tail shoos away flies. Taking a seat beside him, she winced and rubbed the back of her neck. The dark bags under her eyes seemed more pronounced. *Stransky's doin? Or Royster's? Or mine?* Troy took her hand. It was almost as rough and calloused as his, a fragile link in a world fraught with peril and pain. Too fragile. He was stained with Troubler blood. She believed she had married Christ Himself. Who could compete with such a suitor? Sorrow clenched Troy in its fist. *Even when we stand at the edge of eternity, watchin the days march past any known measurement of time or distance, I could never walk with her. All I can do is try to save her life here and now.*

She squeezed his hand. You look tireder than I feel. When was the last time you slept through the night?

I ain't got time these days. Is Stransky drivin you batty?

She's a challenge. It's like she's addicted to heresy. If she weren't such a religious fanatic, I'd call her an atheist.

Troy frowned. She just shined me on about her faith, but I ain't never met a Troubler with any religion, much less fanaticism.

Sarah looked at him as if he might be stupid or a little deranged. You ought to know better than that. Some Troublers believe in nothin but food and guns, but most of em are Protestants. Around here, anyway.

The Crusade supplanted all the Protestant sects after the Purge.

No. They only drove the loyal believers underground. The Troublers practice a kind of hybrid religion. Immersion baptism, individual prayer by a congregant like the old Baptists used, the pew-jumpin ecstasy of the Assembly and the Pentecostal, the Amen corners and call-and-response you'd see in black churches.

What's a black church?

In the ancients' time, folks with white skin, like you, went to different churches than dark-skinned folks like Ford. Or me.

Troy blinked. Why?

Different traditions, different dogmas, sometimes plain old hatred.

I never knew that.

There's a lot the Crusader Bible and the histories leave out. Even the forbidden ones.

How do you know all this, and why didn't you ever tell me?

I know because I've talked with the Troublers and read their books. Plus, us Catholics got our own histories, not all of em written down. As for why I didn't tell you? Because you would have used it against em. Same reason I don't tell them what you say when we talk. I won't help y'all kill each other.

Troy removed his hat and scratched his head. We do a good enough job without any help.

Yeah. They've always seen you lords as cold-blooded killers and tyrants.

You don't believe that, I hope.

I believe every religion in history has committed atrocities in the name of God. Includin mine. Maybe, when all this is over, I'll tell you about the Inquisition.

But somebody's gotta be right, don't they?

I hope to God. Otherwise, nobody'll make it outta this world alive.

They sat in silence for a while. Sister Sarah's hand grew damp in his own, but neither let go. *There's a whole life I'll never see on the other side of moments like this. Skin on skin. Body heat. Love.*

Finally, she pulled her hand away. Your ache's like a scent. I feel it too.

Troy's heart hammered. Sarah, do you ever wonder—

If I was somethin other than what I am, you might not love me at all.

Do you love me back? Can you tell me that much at least?

She closed her eyes. Of course I love you. Why do you think I always run off so soon? I can't afford to be tempted. Too many people depend on me.

He nodded and passed a hand over his face, feeling himself tremble. They had never spoken of their feelings aloud until now. Hearing they were doomed pained him more than he would have believed. A funereal wail emanated from the deepest parts of himself. Yet no matter what happened, he would face it knowing someone loved him, not as a brother-in-arms or as a Christian, but as a man. And how could love ever be wrong?

He cleared his throat and willed his runaway pulse to slow. I reckon Stransky's told you what the Crusade's plannin.

Yes, but she says a lot. I don't know what to believe.

As far as we can tell, she's shootin straight. They're dumpin Troublers on the streets. The wall's comin, and they're confiscatin our explosives.

Sister Sarah's mouth pressed into a bloodless line. She looked away and shuddered. How long will it take to build this wall?

It'd take months, maybe years, if they were startin from scratch, but it's just gonna be a matter of placin the sections and securin em together. I figure we've got a few weeks at most.

Sarah looked to the votives and crossed herself. Then I gotta get my people out of town.

Or you could join up with us.

Tears glistened on her cheeks. There's more of us here than in most places, but that ain't sayin much. Some of us might wanna stay, but if even one goes, I have to shepherd. It's my callin.

I know, he said.

Troy put his arm around her. They sat in the dark and the heat for another twenty minutes, listening to each other breathe, feeling each other's touch through three layers of cloth, which, together, made only one of the many barriers separating them.

## 11

Lisander Royster watched the flickering streetlamps down on Decatur and thought about change.

*Some Troubler in Miami has mucked about with forbidden technology advanced enough to light streets and houses. At least these provincials, doomed though they are, scurry about in the dark, as is proper.*

Bits of tech had popped up in recent years. Someone in New York had gotten an old underground train running and caused a riot. The local lord of order had been forced to cleanse the entire area, Troubler and Crusader alike, to keep it quiet. A now-dead Troubler in Detroit had managed to start three automobiles, which meant they had also managed to find a more or less intact chassis, locate and refine crude oil, make those alien rubber wheels, and a hundred other impossibilities. Those rebels had been found and crushed, the technology destroyed, but if one Troubler could make something work, another might take up their mantle. Matthew Rook himself had come to Royster and explained it all—how the world Jonas Strickland created for the faithful was fading, how the Troublers grew stronger even as the Crusaders' wills waned every year. The only way to stem the blasphemous tide would be the old way—a Purge that would destroy even the double agents, who did much worse damage than the herds of Troublers roaming the world's ruins.

Though New Orleans seemed like a true Crusade stronghold, it was, in fact, a breeding ground for sin and insurrectionists. Rook had proven it by showing Royster the journals of Jonas Strickland. Rook had brought Royster into his study and opened Strickland's election-year journal, directing Royster's attention to one passage.

*Of all the areas in this country that must feel the strong right hand of God, New Orleans is perhaps the worst. The city is a wretched cesspool of sin—prostitution, homosexuality, voodoo, fornication and adultery, public nudity and micturition, murder, rape, graft. Its officials are liars, its people decadent, even worse than those in Las Vegas. The hurricanes failed to wipe New Orleans from the face of the earth, but when I am President, that city will be a priority. She will learn to fear God, or she will burn.*

As in other cities, much of New Orleans *had* burned when Jonas Strickland activated the Godwave. Metal wagons called trolleys crushed panicked pedestrians. Flying machines fell from the sky and exploded, destroying buildings and foliage and people. Had it not been for a resourceful citizenry and some unfortunately timed rainstorms, the whole town might have turned to ash. But New Orleans had survived, and so the armies of Jonas Strickland had descended on her like God's own wrath, slaughtering heathens, driving those who escaped into the dank and pestilential swamps. As generations passed, the rubble had been cleared away, the wreckage hauled to designated sites and buried or burned or melted down in the forges, most of the ruined areas rebuilt. So it was across the world. Travel to any major city and you might not know any disaster had befallen, thanks to the hard work of Crusaders and the labor of captured Troublers, those terrorists who never seemed to agree on what they wanted. They might set a fire and burn down whole neighborhoods. But let the Crusade start any improvement project—which, of course, always had to begin with destruction of some kind, a fire or a building demolition—and the Troublers would drive off the workers. *They want whatever seems dia-metrically opposed to the Crusade. They are that simple and that tenacious. Watching them drown will be like standing at the pearly gates as the wicked are cast into the lake of fire. Their screams will be music, their deaths a balm for this world's soul. And if Lord Troy keeps asking the wrong questions and making demands, Mister Clemens will be happy to slip a knife between his ribs ahead of schedule.*

From below came the sound of many boots on the stairs. So Clemens had found everyone. Royster crossed quickly to Troy's desk— *his* desk now—and sat. He folded his hands and smiled. And when the door opened and Clemens ushered in Santonio Ford, LaShanda Long, and Gordon Boudreaux, Royster clapped his hands together like a child who has been given a rare treat.

Boudreaux and Ford flanked LaShanda Long. Benn brought in a steaming kettle of tea and poured it into chipped cups and handed them out. Boudreaux sipped, squinting against the steam.

Royster looked them over. You three are the youngest of Lord Troy's lieutenants.

As the senior official present, Ford would do the talking, so Boudreaux looked to him. Yes, sir, the hunter said.

Good, good. Tell me, young men and lady. Are you loyal to the Bright Crusade or to your lord of order?

Boudreaux clenched his jaw. *Here it comes.*

But if the question bothered Ford, he gave no sign. Instead, he took what struck Boudreaux as the most practical course—feigned ignorance. I don't get your meanin, sir. Is there a difference?

In theory, there shouldn't be, but for the moment, let us consider the possibility. What would you do if Gabriel Troy tried to hinder the Crusade's goals and Matthew Rook's written orders?

*Sweet Father. He expects us to cast Gabe out just like that, after all these years.*

Can't imagine that, Ford said, his face expressionless. The Crusade's his whole life.

Of course. I am simply asking if you would side with the Crusade against *all* enemies, regardless of who they might be.

Ford never blinked. We do what's right around here. Always have. Always will.

Royster smiled, put one hand over his heart, bowed his head a moment. Splendid. That will be all for now. We shall call on you again, should the need arise. He stood up and stuck out his hand.

Ford shook it, looking Royster in the eye. Anytime.

Benn and Clemens herded them toward the door.

*Don't look back,* Boudreaux thought. *Don't give him a reason to wonder about you too.*

The deputy envoys escorted them outside the Temple and shut the doors without so much as a good evening. Boudreaux opened his mouth, but Long put her hand on his shoulder and cut her eyes toward the guards, and he shut it again.

After dark, under an overcast sky as black as coal, Ford met Troy on the bench by the river.

I told Sister Sarah what Royster's plannin, Troy said as Ford sat. She wants to get her people out.

Ford scratched his head. If all the Catholics leave, Royster will know somebody talked. He might figure it was you.

I reckon he might.

We can't do this without you. I don't know if we can do it at all.

You can. If a Troubler had shot me in the back last month, you or Jack would be in charge anyway. What happened at your meetin?

Royster asked what we'd do if you turned traitor. If I'd have answered wrong, there'd be three bodies in the river right now. Theirs or ours.

Troy turned to the water. Ford let him ponder for a while. *The*

*Crusade lied to us,* the hunter thought. *By omission and by outright deception. Now we're lyin to help people, but also to stay alive. Sin for sin, we're matchin each other.*

So, Troy said. He thinks me, Jack, and Ernie are too far gone to reach.

I ain't much of an expert on what Royster thinks. But that seems about right.

And y'all said what?

That we'd do our duty.

Good. That should keep y'all outta the towers. If you hear anything we can use, stop by my house for dinner or invite me out for some night fishin. In the meantime, we better get back.

He patted Ford on the shoulder, stood, and slipped away into the darkness.

Ford bowed his head. *Father God, keep us strong and on Your path. Give each of us the wisdom to know what's right and the strength to act on it.*

When he left, he took a different route, just in case.

# ✤ 12 ✤

The Westbank Expressway's pavement crumbled under Royster's horse's hooves. Troublers knotted the roads and sidewalks. Chained together at the ankles, they sat or walked in sunburnt, mosquito-stung misery, dragged along by those in front of them, kicked by those behind. At night, they slept shoulder to shoulder and in great stinking piles. Soon their decamping in the city proper would begin. The great wall grew daily, the sections thirty-five feet high by thirty feet long by ten feet deep, wood reinforced with iron, snaking around the city as crews worked both ends. When head finally met tail and every Troubler had been herded inside, Royster's task would be complete, and he could return to Washington.

Clemens trotted up on a jet-black mare with rippling muscles, its sheen so dark it looked wet. The deputy reined in beside Royster and fanned himself with his hat, wiping his sweating forehead on his shirtsleeve. He nodded at the masses stomping and clanking away on the roads.

It's like the Sermon on the Mount, he said. Nothing but sinners as far as the eye can see.

Royster smiled. It's quite a sight.

So what's next?

The envoy grunted. *What next, indeed? On the surface, everything proceeds apace. Even if Gabriel Troy and his lieutenants prove false, we have the guns and the numbers. Our faithful are planting the charges that will flood this city. Lynn Stransky remains in exile. The common people are sheep. So far, only Troy has questioned us. Soon I will test him further. Jack Hobbes and Ernest Tetweiller as well.*

He turned to Clemens. We should inform Lord Troy and his colleagues that we need no assistance from them. All local officials are to remain with their populace, quelling fears and eliminating dissent as the prisoners begin to settle north of the river.

What if they balk?

Frankly, I expect them to. If I am right, we'll lock them in the towers. I doubt any masked bandits will liberate them.

Clemens grinned, showing uneven white teeth. I'll hunt them down myself, if it comes to that. He saluted and turned his horse, clopping back the way he had come.

Royster frowned. Clemens had always been useful, but something about this mission had made him reckless and prideful. And Mister Rook had been clear: Only the most faithful, pure, loyal Crusaders were to survive the coming Purge. Clemens seemed too wild a card to keep in play for long.

Benn would put a bullet in his head, should it become necessary. Like Lisander Royster himself, Benn had always followed orders. His soul was safe.

## 13

Clemens found Troy with Tetweiller and Hobbes on Dauphine Street, where a short, bald man appeared to be suffering a panic attack. Troy and Hobbes held his arms while Tetweiller spoke to him. Clemens dismounted and approached.

I just don't think I can take much more, fellas, the diminutive citizen said. All that clankin, day and night. All these bad seeds movin in. I feel like I'm bein punished when I ain't did nothin wrong.

Well, you can't go around yellin your fool head off, Tetweiller said. Everybody's on edge as it is. Now. If we turn you loose, you gonna keep calm?

The little man swallowed hard and nodded. Troy and Hobbes let go and stepped back. They looked ready to tackle him at the first sign of trouble.

Clemens cleared his throat. What's happening here?

Troy glanced at Clemens. Nothin much. Billy's just got a case of the nerves. He's okay.

*The lord of order doesn't much like me,* Clemens thought. *And I don't like any of these yokels.* He *better* be okay. Only Troublers incite panic.

Billy's eyes widened. Now wait a minute—

Troy shoved Billy away. You get along home.

Billy walked off, glancing back at Clemens, nearly plowing into a rusty street sign. Troy watched him go until he rounded the corner. Then he turned to Clemens. When we need your help with our people, we'll ask. Until that day, stay away from em, or you and me's gonna have a problem.

Clemens's eye twitched. *I'd love to headbutt him right in the nose and blow that hardcase expression right off his face.* But orders were to speak, not act, and Clemens had no intention of crossing Royster. He stepped back. Tetweiller and Hobbes relaxed. *Mister Royster's right. Those two believe in Troy, not the Crusade. If I'd made a move, they would have burned me down.*

I was just trying to help drive home your point, he said. Speaking of which, I've got one of my own. Straight from Mister Royster.

Troy held Clemens's gaze. Clemens kept his hands clear of his gun belt. *That old fart Tetweiller's staring a hole in me. As if such a dried-up husk could stand against one of Matthew Rook's chosen. And look how calm Hobbes is. He might as well be sitting in church or watching the grass grow. Better be careful with him.*

Let's hear it, Troy said.

You've got far too much on your plate these days, what with your populace's penchant for coming down with—what did you call it?—a case of the nerves. Mr. Royster says to stay out of the areas where the Troublers are being kept. See to your own people.

The old man spat. So Royster's tellin us where we can and can't ride in our own city.

Ernie, Troy said.

Clemens scowled. Yes, he is. He outranks us all. If he orders you to hop on one leg right into the lake, you should do it. Assuming you're loyal.

The old man stepped forward and opened his mouth to say something, but Troy put a hand on his chest. Hobbes took Tetweiller by the arm. None of them had taken their eyes off Clemens.

Mister Royster's right, Troy said. We got plenty to do. Don't we, fellas?

Hobbes nodded, unblinking and cold. Tetweiller did not acknowledge that anyone had spoken.

*We'd be well served to see them in chains, squatting on the streets and urinating in the gutters like the Troublers they are. No telling how deeply their sin has wormed into the general population.*

At least one of them knew where Lynn Stransky was hiding. Clemens would have bet his life on it.

Well, if we all understand each other, he said, I'll leave you to your duties. Gentlemen. The last word dripped with sarcasm.

No one replied. They might have been statues.

*I'm going to enjoy blowing Tetweiller's brains out, if he has any. With Hobbes, I might start with a gutshot, just to see if he can be that stoic with his innards hanging to his knees.*

Clemens mounted up, turned his horse south, and rode away. Their stares made the back of his neck itch. He grinned, a savage expression men like Gabriel Troy would have recognized.

## 14

**H**orses and heretics surged against chains and ropes, dragging the wall segment toward an angled trench ten feet deep along its terminus. More Troublers pushed against the back side, muscles straining. Soon the segment thudded into the trench. When the dust settled, the section leaned outward a bit, so Melton, the foreman on duty, directed the workers and animals as they pushed and tugged it straight. More workers shoveled and packed the loose dirt in, leaving twenty-five feet of wall above ground. Then they nailed prepared wooden braces to the wall on the city side. Another group mounted ladders near the seam and hammered supporting planks onto the two sections, shoring up the connections. Finally they painted the wall with pitch, waterproofing it. Yet another bunch was already digging a trench for the next section, their bodies lean and filthy and glistening with sweat.

Benn sat his horse nearby, eating a slice of jerky. *I hate to see these wretches loosed from their rightful places on the street, even for a work detail. But Mister Rook insisted the Troublers erect the wall themselves. And I admit it feels right.*

Melton rode his dust-colored stallion and signaled to the field bosses, who turned to the Troublers, shouting orders that were met with groans and a grudging increase in effort.

Benn rode up beside Melton. Mr. Royster sent me to check your progress.

Melton hawked and spat a thick greenish blob that Benn looked at with distaste. I don't know how Glau's doing, but we're on schedule. Maybe even a little ahead.

Glau was Melton's counterpart at the other end of the wall. When the two crews met, the Crusaders would march the Troublers inside and erect the last section themselves. The heathens would await the flood they did not even know was coming while the Lord's own celebrated, rested, and put this godforsaken piece of swamp behind them.

I visited Glau earlier, Benn said. He's ahead of schedule.

Thank the Most High. This humidity is killing me. I feel like I'm trying to breathe soup.

Benn chuckled, but Melton was right. The air was thick and oppressive. It had gotten progressively worse as the herd of prisoners had trudged ever southward; since leaving Washington, Benn had seen upward of two dozen Troublers collapse, their filthy bodies dragged hither and yon by their mates still chained to them at the ankles. Now, more from the work crews fell every day, and anytime the Troublers stopped to help a fellow who had collapsed, the field bosses laid into them until they went back to work. *It hardly seems charitable, but Mister Rook is closer to God than anyone. Gabriel Troy might be stupid enough to question his orders, but I'm not. I plan to kiss my wife and daughters again, and that right soon.*

Mister Royster will be pleased, he said to Melton. Do you need anything?

Melton indicated the crew. Replacements. These rogues are almost played out.

I'll make it happen. In the meantime, if these ask for a bath, give it to them. They stink worse than hell itself.

He spurred his horse and headed back toward the Temple.

# ✤ 15 ✤

That night, Jack Hobbes slipped through the clanking Troublers. He went afoot, just as Troy had ordered, his injured arm held tightly against his body. Later, he would hoof it back home or, if that seemed too risky, spend the night in the church. He was not worried about anyone asking why he looked so tired. No one slept well these days. Too much noise and too many problems.

Still, Hobbes dreaded the rendezvous with Stransky. She just plain bugged him, what with her looking at a man like she planned to fornicate with him and then bite off his head. She had looked at *him* that way, at least, both when they caught her and as they broke her out of the tower.

*Well, we all got our crosses to bear. Ain't never shirked mine.*

The sisters' spire rose against the half-moon sky. It had always seemed sinister, housing all those popish ceremonies and nuns' cold faces. *Would have run em out long ago if it had been my call. But I would have been wrong. They're useful. Besides, Gabe and Sister Sarah are sweet on each other. Foolish, but when did love ever make sense?*

Hobbes scanned the road, the outlying buildings, even the rooftops. He could not afford for anyone to see a deputy lord visiting the Catholics this late. If someone did, he would have to kill them, and he did not want murder on his conscience.

*Unless it's Benn or Clemens. Could shoot them bootlickers, dump em in the river, and sleep like a babe.*

Nothing moved, so Hobbes sprinted down the street, up the steps, and through the double doors. The air in the sanctum was so hot it smelled burnt. Sarah was absent, but a bareheaded woman sat on the front pew, a lamp on the altar bathing her in a pool of muted light. He barely recognized her. Dark hair, clean and silky, spilled to her shoulders. Before, it had looked like a wet skunk pelt. With his good hand, Hobbes untied the rawhide holding down his gun. He did not like the thought of killing inside a house of worship, but he would do as he must.

He stepped on a creaky floorboard. She stood and turned to him, her face lost in the gloom.

Jacky, Stransky said as he walked up the aisle, cute as ever.

Hobbes scoffed. Might as well bury that bone. Got nothin to say about it.

She shrugged. Fine. Pull up a pew, asshole.

Stransky sat. She wore a pair of deerskin pants and a cotton top. Her face looked fuller. The sisters had been feeding her. Her skin was ruddy but clean. If she had been anyone else and they had been anywhere besides a church, Hobbes might have found her fetching.

He looked away. *Remember she's a rattlesnake.*

She patted the pew and grinned. Hobbes cleared his throat and sat a good five feet away.

Ain't much to tell, he said. But he told it anyway.

My people's been watchin them prisoners and talkin to em all casual like, she said when he had finished. Most of em seem like what you Crusaders would call upright citizens. I think your boy Rook's gettin a jump on the Purge by sendin a shitload of regular folks down here to drown.

Hobbes wiped sweat from his brow. *Only got her word on this, but don't see no sign of falsehood. Or maybe I just wanna believe her because she's been straighter with me than my own superiors.* Regular folks, he said.

I know you'd like proof, Stransky said. But all you're gonna get is somebody's word. Mine, whatever prisoner you talk to, or Royster's.

The sooner y'all figure out we're in the same boat, the better chance we'll have.

The scorched air hurt to breathe. Was this what drowning would feel like once the levees were gone? Would your body float? For how long? Would it bloat and rot? Would some river creature consume your dead flesh? Would it rip you apart or take you a bite at a time?

Hobbes's hands shook. *Calm down. Don't show weakness.*

Be in touch, he said.

Don't take too long. From what I'm told, that wall's growin fast.

Hobbes inhaled, held in the hot air, let it out. He hoped his face betrayed nothing, least of all the unmooring of his courage, however brief. The lamp burned the oil Ford's workers had rendered from animal fat, the greasy, smoky flame spilling its dirty light into the room.

Stransky watched him from behind the curtain of her hair.

Somethin else on your mind? he said.

She put a hand on his knee. You took a bullet gettin me out, and you're a damn sight handsomer than most of the lapdogs I met. Maybe you and me can have some fun some time.

Her touch sent a chill up his spine. His engorged pecker pressed against his trousers. Hobbes took her hand in his good one and closed his eyes for a moment. Then he opened them again and pushed her away.

You're talkin fornication. You look a load better with clean clothes and that rat nest off the top of your head, but I took vows. Aim to keep em.

Stransky laughed. Vows. Like one of Sarah's priests. You ever wonder why they made you do it? What harm havin a family would have done you?

Ain't got time to ponder it.

He stood and put his hat back on. Her laughter floated down the aisle behind him as he left.

Next time, sexy, she called.

He poked his head out the door and saw nothing, so he jogged across the thoroughfare and into the shadows beyond the streetlights.

As he reached the alley, a voice drifted out of the darkness. So how'd it go?

He whipped around and drew. Come on out. Slow.

A short, misshapen shadow ambled toward him, breaking into two as it got closer, and Hobbes uncocked and holstered his gun. McClure and Bandit, silent as death. The girl must have clipped the dog's nails.

Willa, said Hobbes. Almost blew your head off.

The child's voice suggested a smile. You was aimin too high. You might have knocked off my hat, though.

What's your purpose?

Just wondered if you had any news.

A bit. Hobbes wiped the sweat out of his eyes with his shirtsleeve. He told McClure what Stransky had said.

When he finished, the girl said, It sounds like somethin the Crusade would do. Efficient and cold, just like Royster. Just like Rook.

*She's never loved the Crusade.*

Confirm it if you can. Gotta get home before somebody figures out I ain't in bed.

That's why it helps not to have a house.

She melted into the darkness, the dog on her heel. Hobbes headed home.

## 16

**A**day later in Troy's den, the lord of order and Hobbes rested their feet on the coffee table and held glasses of tepid water while McClure reported. She had slipped across the river and had spoken to a dozen prisoners. Two had been openly hostile to the Crusade. The rest were bewildered, depressed, and despairing, but they expressed none of the naked disloyalty or heresy that generally marked a Troubler.

You're convinced they was tellin the truth? Troy asked.

McClure shrugged. One man told me if I was born from a Crusader, I could go fuck myself and die. Another said he'd just as soon set a Bible on fire as bow before Matthew Rook. The rest of em all sounded alike. *Why am I here? I ain't done nothin. Mr. Rook must have made a mistake.*

Troy looked at Hobbes, who seemed ready to spit. *Good. He's been distracted all day. I better find out what's eatin him.* We thank you, Troy said. You're one of the best we got, even if you ain't grown yet.

McClure settled into the chair. You got anything else for me? I got nothin better to do.

Can you sniff out the ordnance Royster's confiscated? You ain't gotta try to get it back. Just bring us a list of what's where.

Hell, Gabe, I thought you might have wanted somethin hard. I can tell you right now they've roped bundles of dynamite to all the river bridges' piers and abutments.

Troy passed a hand over his eyes. We was afraid of that. Get back to us with the rest as soon as you can.

McClure stood. The men followed suit and shook hands with the girl. She tipped her hat. Then she turned and went out, clucking her tongue. Bandit had been asleep in the sunlight filtering through a window. Now he woke, scrambled to his feet, and trotted across the room after McClure, glancing at Troy and Hobbes as if to say, *See you later.*

The men took their seats after the door closed. Troy sipped water. Hobbes put his glass on the coffee table and rubbed his temples. The heat was beginning to radiate through the house. Soon Troy would have to open the windows or cook like a pig in a roasting pit.

Okay, he said. You been somewhere else half the mornin. What's up?

Hobbes grimaced. Been thinkin about Stransky. That meetin with her—it kindly shook me up.

Troy frowned. Shook you up how? You don't scare easy.

Never feared anybody walkin the earth. Not even you. Reckon I can fear this woman, though.

She can't outdraw you.

Ain't that kind of scared. She touched me last night. Propositioned me. All clean and soft lookin. I wanted her. God forgive me. Wanted to take her right there in that church.

Troy felt as if someone had kicked him in the gut. If Hobbes had ever been interested in romance, or sex, he had kept it well hidden. And now this, at all times, and Stransky, of all people. Better if Hobbes had confessed lust for Bandit.

I know better than most how the heart wants what the brain tells you might be crazy or dangerous, Troy said. And with what's goin on here, it's easy to question our vows. All I can tell you is follow your conscience. But be careful. If Stransky guts you, don't let it be in bed.

Hobbes looked tired and wasted. Don't know why she gets to me like this when nobody else ever has.

Love makes us all stupid. So does lust. After the city's safe, maybe we can look at Stransky and everything else with some perspective.

Hobbes looked out the window again. Somewhere out there the other Conspirators toiled at their jobs. Maybe they were recruiting.

Lynn Stransky was hiding wherever the sisters kept her, probably in the nuns' living quarters, though now that Sister Sarah had started sending her fellow brides of Christ and her parishioners away, perhaps they had moved the Troubler. *Lord help us, I ought to know.* Perhaps Troy suffered from the same illness that had struck Hobbes. Maybe he just wanted another excuse to see Sarah. Half of him was glad she was leaving. The other half wished she would stay.

He and Hobbes talked as the temperature soared, as the guilty and innocent tramped into their city, as the sun rose on another day in the long, slow flow of time's river. They talked of lust and ammunition, women and plastic explosive, love and hatred and death. And when they finally went out for grub, they had resolved absolutely nothing regarding Lynn Stransky, Sister Sarah Gonzales, or the confines of their own hearts.

Troy, Hobbes, Ford, McClure, Boudreaux, and Long met after dark and sat on Boudreaux's back porch, shooing away mosquitoes and drinking warm lemonade as Bandit lay at their feet, enticing each of them to scratch his belly. His muscles rippled. He had been eating well. *I wish I knew how Willa does it,* Troy thought. *Her and that dog always seem fit and fine, and whenever they ain't right in front of you, it's like they cease to exist.* No one ever saw the kid or the dog meandering about the city.

They've set charges on the bridges and the first fifty yards of the causeway, the girl said. They got caches on the 17th Street Canal too. I ain't checked em all yet, but I figure they plan to blow every canal and levee, plus any roads outta town. Wouldn't be surprised if they hit the highest-populated areas too.

They've started confiscatin our boats, said Ford.

What? said Troy. I thought they just wanted an inventory.

Not as of this mornin. A tenth of my fisherfolk are already down to rods and reels and cane poles.

Everyone let that information sink in. The undertows and currents and sheer effort it took to swim the river made using it to get out of town without a boat potentially, even probably, fatal. Santonio Ford's recruits had started building rafts and canoes and hiding them in every conceivable nook and cranny, but they were making beds in a burning house.

Okay, said Troy, leaning forward, elbows on his knees. We can't move the explosives, or else Royster will know somethin's up, and then he'll turn this town upside down. Probably throw the lot of us in jail. LaShanda, can you disarm the charges without makin em *look* disarmed?

Long scoffed. Who you talkin to? Anything they can cobble together, I can take apart. Problem is findin em all and gettin close enough.

McClure scratched Bandit's ears. Findin em's my job. Gettin close, that's somethin else. Just to look, you'd think they ain't nobody guardin the goods, but when you study the situation for a spell, you see three or four folks millin near every location. They act like they're just walkin by, but they don't go far. We're gonna have to slip past em, distract em, or kill em. I got no preference.

If we kill guards at every cache, Troy said, they'll figure out what's goin on long before we finish.

Long nodded. Even if we can get close enough to disarm the caches, we'll still have to stop em from detonatin the ordnance manually, come the day.

We'll cross that bridge when we come to it, Troy said. Y'all get any assignments yet?

Ford and Long shook their heads.

So far, it's all hypotheticals and business as usual, Boudreaux said. I'm supposed to go on some errand with Benn and Clemens tomorrow, though.

Be careful, said Troy. Them boys are snakes.

They lapsed into silence, swatting bugs and watching the sun set. It shone through the clouds and over the lake's killing water, turning the sky blood red. On the porch, Bandit's legs twitched as he dreamed his canine dreams.

## 17

**T**he next morning, Gordy Boudreaux walked through the High Temple, trying not to look as nervous as he felt. A kind of creeping dread had shrunk his scrotum. A lump of wet paper settled in his throat, even as his mouth filled with spit. *I'm ridin with men who want to kill everybody I've ever known and loved, but I can't show fear. For all I know, Benn and Clemens are gonna take me to the swamps and shoot me. And for all I know, they're right and just, and I'm damned for thinkin we should stand against em. What in the name of the Most High am I supposed to do?*

He passed through the sanctuary and mounted the stairs to Troy's office, wondering if it were for the last time.

*Yea, though I walk through the valley of the shadow.*

Upstairs, Royster was absent, but Clemens and Benn stood near Troy's desk, Clemens inspecting his weapons.

You're early, Benn said. I like that. Let's get going.

Where we headed? Boudreaux asked.

Clemens slapped him on the back. Pest control mission. You'll love it.

Benn led them downstairs. The morning cleaners dusted and swept, raising small clouds that hung in the air. Several said hello. Boudreaux nodded and tipped his hat. Benn and Clemens ignored them. When the three men passed the front desk, Norville Unger saluted. Neither Benn nor Clemens so much as glanced at him. He scowled and seemed about to speak. Boudreaux shook his head, and Unger's mouth snapped shut. The old desk sergeant would make a loyal addition to whichever side he chose. Troy's Conspiracy grew by twos and threes every day.

Had Unger already been approached? Boudreaux wished all of them could share their lists of loyalists. But then, if someone were captured or turned, everyone else would be at hazard.

*And the worst part? That might be best. A man could go mad tryin to figure this out. Maybe that's why Royster met with me and LaShanda and Santonio—not because we're valuable, but because we're uncertain.*

The sky was overcast and gray, with clouds hanging so low it seemed you could stand on your tiptoes and touch them. To the west, they grew darker. A cool wind blew, carrying the promise of rain. *Should have brought my duster.* Boudreaux's horse waited next to the Jesus statue. The animal smelled the air and shifted from foot to foot as grooms led the envoys' horses across the square. Benn and Clemens took their reins without a word, Benn patting his horse and rubbing its muzzle. They saddled up and rode out of the square.

Boudreaux could feel Clemens staring at his back.

They rode through the Lower Garden District and across the expressway. Boudreaux broke into gooseflesh, and not just because of the breeze. They had crossed into the regions from which locals had been forbidden. Perhaps the deputy envoys planned to initiate him into their inner circle. Or maybe his old jurisdiction would be his dying ground. He knew where they were going. Not far from a bend in the great river lay an old base that had once lodged part of the ancients' armies. Since the Purge, it had held enormous stores of weapons and gunpowder, dynamite and plastic explosives, guard quarters. With Dwyer's arrival, the Conspirators had managed, with the help of a few sympathizers, to move some of the stores and alter the records, but the place still housed plenty of goods.

Perhaps Benn and Clemens planned to interrogate him about the missing ordnance. Or maybe they wanted him to confirm the records' accuracy.

All around them, prisoners baked in the morning sun. Whenever one dared look at the passing figures, a Crusader lashed them until they screamed and fell, pulling their fellows down with them. *Sweet Lord, how do they relieve themselves? How do they sleep?* The whole area stank of human waste and rotting food, both of which littered the streets. Gulls and crows swirled overhead and pecked at the refuse. Adults moaned and children cried, their lamentations mixing with the calls of the great flock. Would bigger animals maraud among the Troublers at night? Would the guards drive predators away? Or would the wildlife take as it pleased, human flesh or otherwise? The whole cityscape south of the river suppurated like hell itself. *At this rate, they won't even need the flood to kill everybody.*

Soon enough, Boudreaux, Benn, and Clemens entered the base proper. The last time Boudreaux had visited, it had teemed with life— the guards, their families, their pets. Now it was nearly empty. Strangers manned the gates and towers. All New Orleans natives had been relocated into the city as if the generations who had lived and died on these blocks had been stricken from the cosmic record. The world had fallen into slippage, schism, dissolution.

Boudreaux and the deputy envoys reined up and hitched their horses in front of a drab two-story bunkhouse. The sky had gone a deeper gray. Thunder muttered in the distance.

They walked inside. The bunks and furniture had been ripped out. Iron-barred doors had replaced the wooden ones. The inmates, filthy and malnourished and broken, watched the floor as Boudreaux and the envoys passed. Some wept. More than a few had deep, dark patches on their skin, bleeding gums, bulging eyes, distended bellies. *My Lord, they're malnourished and scurvied worse than I've ever seen. Ain't we even feedin these wretches?* Down the corridor in the kitchen, an enormous wood stove sat against the back wall, but someone had boarded up the heat vents and installed chains and cuffs on each corner of the island. Chairs were nailed to the floor. The double sink against one wall had also been fitted with restraints on either side. The back door was barricaded, the inner door barred.

*It's a torture room. Sweet Jesus.*

Benn and Clemens looked at him as one might inspect sides of beef. *Somethin's about to happen.*

He eased his hands near his holsters.

*They might kill me, but they won't torture me. I can do that much.*

Footsteps in the hall. Boudreaux turned. A guard was shoving an emaciated, grimy thing toward the room, its long greasy hair hanging over a face like a gutshot, filthy rags billowing around stick limbs. The figure stumbled and fell, coughing. Through that veil of hair, a hint of beard—a man. The guard kicked him in the hindquarters, sending him sprawling on his face. A bloody tooth skittered across the floor.

Get up, pond scum, the guard barked.

As the man struggled to comply, his hair parted enough to reveal bleeding gums and bulging insectile eyes. Boudreaux did not recognize him. He regained his feet and started toward the chamber again, the guard prodding him in the back every few steps. The prisoner whimpered like a whipped puppy. He could have been anyone, a long-time preacher of the Word who had spoken to the wrong person, a hunter who had demonstrated too much skill and not enough lock-step dogmatism, a deputy lord who had followed orders right into the jailhouse. He could have been Jack Hobbes or Santonio Ford. Even Gabriel Troy. Might still be, before all was said and done.

Boudreaux's stomach roiled.

The guard pushed the prisoner through the door and pulled it shut. Then, taking a key ring the size of a mushmelon out of his satchel, Clemens locked them all in. The Troubler stood before them, stinking, palsied.

Mister Kouf, said Benn. Welcome.

Clemens grabbed Kouf by the neck and dragged him to the island. Benn drew his gun and covered them while Clemens wiped his hand on his pants, scowling as if he had just handled rotten meat. Perhaps he had.

Climb up on this block, if you please, said Benn, his voice conversational.

Kouf leaned against the island, palms on its surface, one finger tracing a deep groove left by someone's knife or bone saw. When he spoke, his whisper sounded as scratchy as sandpaper on coarse wood. I haven't done anything, sirs. Please let my family go. We have always been loyal.

Benn backhanded the prisoner with his gun barrel, knocking Kouf to the floor. He lay there, moaning. Benn and Clemens looked at Boudreaux.

Well, don't just stand there, Deputy, said Clemens, grinning. Get this trash on the block.

Benn's face was impassive. The envoys waited to see what Boudreaux would do.

*They got me two to one. I'm deep in their territory, surrounded by armed guards. If I draw, I'll have to fight my way outta the room, through the building, and across the river, where the first Crusader I see will probably shoot me. And for all I know, Kouf's guilty. Nobody's shown any evidence either way. Won't it be better to play along until I know for sure?*

Boudreaux gritted his teeth.

Well? said Benn.

Boudreaux swallowed hard. His hands twitched near his guns.

Then he grasped Kouf by the wrists and hauled him to his feet. Best you get up, mister. They ain't gonna stop until you do.

Don't you mean *we* won't stop? asked Benn.

Boudreaux held Benn's gaze. That's right. *We* won't stop.

Kouf tried to climb onto the island, his scabbed feet kicking for purchase. Boudreaux boosted him up and rolled him onto his back. Kouf was a sack of dry leaves. He grimaced in pain, his teeth yellow and red, the gums receded down to the roots. A deep bruise in the shape of Boudreaux's hand was already forming where he had gripped the man, the skin still sunken in. *No elasticity. It's like they plucked him off a ship that had been becalmed for months.*

Benn yanked Kouf's arms upward and shackled his wrists in the corner restraints, while Clemens did the same to his ankles. Spread-eagled, Kouf lay there, panting. He could barely raise his head. Where had he found the strength to walk down the corridor?

Kouf looked at Boudreaux, desperation in his eyes. Please, sir. My wife and daughter.

Clemens punched him in the mouth. Blood dribbled from his lips and onto the island. He opened his mouth to groan, revealing the jagged stumps of three teeth, the remnants on his tongue. Kouf spat them out.

I have a wife and two daughters as well, Benn said, his voice cold. They have never stolen so much as a crumb. Besides, we aren't here to talk about the traitor you married or the one you sired. We're here for you. If we were popish, you might call us your confessors. Answer us truthfully, and you can go to God with a clean conscience. Wouldn't you like that? To stand before the Almighty's throne, shining white like the angels' very wings?

Kouf drooled blood. Boudreaux moved closer to the wall, watching Kouf and Benn as the one glanced about, goggling like a frightened horse, and the other leaned on the island, studying his fingernails. Clemens stood nearby, fists clenched, ready to strike again. A creeping sense of dread settled in Boudreaux's stomach, turning fiery and climbing up his throat like heartburn.

*Two to one, then out the building and across the river.*

Kouf groaned. I've nothing to confess.

Benn stroked the man's oily hair. Nothing? Are you without sin, as only the Son of God ever was? Blasphemy, sir.

Clemens struck Kouf again, this time on the cheekbone. Clemens grinned, shaking out his hand. Ow, he laughed.

No, you are just another sinner, Benn said, as if he had not noticed the interruption. We're aware that, on your march here, you stole several strips of jerky and a canteen from a sleeping guard. The very Commandments condemn you, sir. Would you go against Matthew Rook and the Bible in the same breath?

Kouf looked from Clemens to Benn and back again, despair in his eyes. He burst into tears, his flesh torn and bloody where Clemens had punched him.

Clemens strode to the other side of the room and grabbed a covered rolling cart. He pulled it over to the island and yanked off the cloth. On the cart's surface, a set of tools, some brand new and recently forged, others so rusty they might have been produced in the ancients' time. Two hammers, two chisels, a handsaw, a bone saw. Two knives, one serrated. A long, hooked implement Boudreaux had never seen before.

Clemens unhooked and brought over a wall lantern. He held it over the instruments. Kouf saw them and blubbered like a child.

Benn selected the serrated knife. He held it to the lamplight. Dried blood coated its teeth. Benn turned it this way and that, as if inspecting it for flaws. Kouf struggled against his bonds, yanking, grunting like a pig.

Now, now, Benn said. None of that.

Clemens grabbed Kouf's head, wrapping his fingers in the greasy hair, and held it still while Benn stuck the knife into Kouf's nostril and yanked upward. The blade ripped through flesh and cartilage, blood splattering Clemens's face. Kouf howled, his nose laid opened on its right side from tip to bridge. Cilia and blood and snot wiggled when he breathed.

Benn slit the other nostril.

Kouf babbled as Boudreaux started toward the table, hand dropping to his gun.

By the time he touched it, Benn had drawn his, the barrel pointing straight at Boudreaux's head, the knife in his other hand.

I assume you're stepping up to help us get this Troubler's confession, he said. Because if you make one move to stop us, I'll gutshoot you and let you take his place.

Boudreaux's hand fell away from the gun. He raised both hands, palms out, trying hard to keep his face expressionless.

*Not even outta the room.*

Do something, said Clemens. Or don't.

Boudreaux's mouth had gone dry. *Lord, forgive me. He's got me dead to rights. If they get me on that table, they'll work me till I betray everybody. No matter what else I do, I can't be the engine of their destruction. I just can't. Forgive me. Forgive me.*

He cleared his throat. I was just thinkin maybe you should ease up. Look at him. He'd blow away in a strong wind. He said his family was starvin. You really plan to torture him for tryin to save em?

Clemens sneered. We don't make the rules, boy. We just enforce them. Mr. Rook says sinners have to pay for their crimes. It's that simple.

Boudreaux said nothing. He felt his face redden. He was no good to anyone dead, no good to Kouf alive. Shame burned through him like fever.

Benn turned back to Kouf. This gentleman could probably explain the economics of thievery, Deputy Boudreaux. When one man steals and gets away with it, he licenses every other thief. That way lies chaos. And then there is the matter of the sin. We must make him repent, or else it will weigh his soul down and sink it into the fiery pit. Just as the darkest sin can shine in our flawed vision like diamonds, so is salvation often jagged and ugly, like this knife's blade. That is the way of things. Even if we wish it otherwise.

Benn holstered his weapon and stuck the point of the knife on Kouf's torso, just below the breastbone.

*PLEASE!* Kouf wailed.

Benn flicked his wrist, opening a two-inch vertical incision. Blood pooled out of it and ran down Kouf's sides in rivulets. He shrieked, sucked in air, shrieked again. Blood dripped onto the floor. Boudreaux felt his gorge rise and struggled to stop it. He burped. Clemens grinned and let go of Kouf's hair. Benn tossed him the knife. He dropped it on the cart and picked up the hook, handing it to Benn, who let Kouf contemplate it. The man whimpered again.

Benn shoved the hook into the incision with a sound like a man walking in water-logged boots. Kouf screamed again. Hot, acidic bile rose into Boudreaux's throat. He held his hand over his mouth but did not turn away. Clemens watched him as Kouf's head thrashed from side to side, lips pulled back in a grimace, rotting teeth clenched and splintering. Benn rotated the hook and then pulled it out, dragging with it a link of bluish intestine.

This ain't right, Boudreaux croaked. It's sick.

Clemens's sardonic grin disappeared. We've been killing Troublers since before you were born, son. It's about time you bayou rats caught up to the times. Now get over here and help hold him down.

Boudreaux retched. No. I'm gettin outta here.

Clemens drew his weapon. We've been over this. Come hold his head still before he beats his own brains out. Or you can be next.

Boudreaux stared down the gun's barrel. Then he turned to Kouf, who still thrashed, his screams now little more than hoarse whispers, his hands hooked into claws. Benn looked serene as he yanked the intestines out. He might have been alone in his kitchen, stirring a pot of soup. His eyes met Boudreaux's. The deputy lord saw no fear or uncertainty there, only conviction.

Forgive me, Boudreaux said. He did not know if he were speaking to Kouf or to God.

He grabbed Kouf's head with both hands and held on with all his might, the cords in his neck standing out. Clemens holstered his weapon and moved to Boudreaux's left, placing his palms on Kouf's shoulders, pushing down as Benn yanked the hook upward again. A good two feet of Kouf's insides now hung in the air between implement and wound.

Kouf could no longer scream. He moaned instead. Then he moved his lips.

*He's prayin.*

Benn lowered the bloody, gut-wrapped hook and laid the whole mess on the island. You want to be very still, Mr. Kouf, he said. If you jerk, you'll knock that hook onto the floor, and Mr. Clemens will likely kick it across the room, taking your innards with it. Do you understand?

Kouf's face had turned fish-belly white. His eyelids fluttered as if he might pass out. Benn slapped him. He still did not answer, but he seemed more present.

Good enough, Clemens asked, or should I pull out an eye?

Good enough, Benn said. Now, Mr. Kouf, I'm going to ask you again, and before you answer, you should remember you'll die here either way. Your only choice lies in how you'll face God. Are you ready?

Yes, Kouf rasped.

On the march, did you or did you not steal your guard's supplies?

Kouf swallowed hard several times and closed his eyes. His lips moved again.

I took some jerky and water, he whispered. My wife and daughter were starving. I begged the guards for water, just enough for my girl, but they laughed at me.

Clemens grinned. Safer not to have a family, he said to Boudreaux. Like me. Like you. We're free in a way this Troubler never was, even before somebody put him in chains.

Benn frowned. Family is strength, Mister Clemens. Unless you yourself are weak. He pushed the sweaty, greasy hair away from Kouf's face. Only one more question, and then you can rest. Do you admit your disloyalty to the Crusade?

Kouf never blinked. His voice seemed stronger now. No. I love my God and my church. As do my wife and daughter.

Kouf had barely finished speaking when Benn grabbed the hook and yanked, dragging out more intestine. Kouf's hoarse, cracking cry filled the room. Clemens chuckled.

*Clemens is crazy. They both are, and damned too. So what does that make me?*

Benn yanked. Kouf whimpered.

Benn rolled the loose intestines around the hook's handle and yanked again.

Sweet God, Kouf cried.

Do it again, Clemens said, breathy and flushed.

*No.*

Boudreaux let go of Kouf and elbowed Clemens in the face. Clemens stumbled over his own feet and fell. Boudreaux whirled and shoved Benn with both hands, sending him flailing toward the wall, still holding the hook, yanking Kouf's guts with him like a fish unspooling line.

Gordy Boudreaux drew his gun. He jammed the barrel against the top of Kouf's skull. And then he pulled the trigger.

Blood and brains spattered Kouf's wasted body, which jerked hard, just once, then stilled. Boudreaux's ears rang like a struck bell.

Benn regained his balance and drew his gun while Clemens scrambled to his feet. Boudreaux holstered his pistol, tears and sweat stinging his eyes. He felt as if he had been hollowed out and filled with sewage.

Benn watched him for a second. Then he holstered his weapon and looked at Clemens, shrugging.

Huh, said Clemens. Killing him with sin still on his conscience. That's cold, son. Colder than me even. Maybe you have what it takes after all.

Benn walked away, flinging Kouf's blood and sweat from his hands. He left the hook on the floor, the guts trailing across the room. Clemens uncuffed Kouf's body. And Boudreaux watched, feeling filthy and sick.

⚜

Boudreaux and Clemens dragged Kouf's body into the hall, leaving a long bloody smear on the floor, and dropped it there. Kouf's ruined head oozed. They had wrapped his intestines around his torso like macabre chains.

In their cells, the emaciated prisoners did not react, but they watched. A guard stepped forward to take the body, but Benn said, No. Let the rest of them look on their futures, should they refuse to confess and die in peace.

In their cells, the prisoners—men, women, even a few children— were already drifting back into themselves.

*There ain't no lesson here. Folks only fear you when they still have hope.* Benn and Clemens walked outside. Boudreaux lingered, still nauseous. *This man stole water and jerky for a child. If that's sin, what about what I just did? I snuffed out Kouf's life like a candle in a drafty room. I did it for mercy, but only after I stood by while they butchered him. Just one more Troubler I've killed, and for all I know, every one of em had a starvin kid. Lord above, were we ever right about anything?*

The world seemed awash in guilt and gore. Lightning flashed through the barred cell windows. Thunder crashed overhead like gunshots.

Boudreaux looked at Kouf one last time, and then he followed Benn and Clemens into the storm.

Later, sodden and alone, Boudreaux rode down Pelican Avenue toward his house, a modest one-story wooden structure. A yard and a columned porch surrounded it. An ancient magnolia towered near the street. Seeing the house's shape in the gloom of an evening had always helped ease the day's burdens. But now, with Kouf's blood stuck under his fingernails, Boudreaux thought the place looked like a wart-infested toad squashed on the road. Rainwater puddled in his yard and dripped off the magnolia's leaves. The wind had shaken loose a mess of white petals that now lay clumped around the trunk. They would be shriveled and brown before the landscapers came back around.

He dismounted and hitched the horse and entered the house and locked the front door. Then he crossed the foyer by feel until he reached the great room, where he stumbled over the boots he had left out last night. He found matches and a lamp on a side table, the same lamp he had lit almost every night since Troy had given him the house. The place suited him. It stood outside the city's most populated areas and faced east. Gordy Boudreaux was responsible for meeting attacks from that direction and holding the line until reinforcements arrived. The obligation had never weighed on him. It had seemed like a portent of his great destiny as a defender of the faith.

What hogwash.

Kouf's death played on a loop in his mind. Each time, he thought of a new way he might have stopped Benn. Yes, the deputy envoys had been armed, and yes, Clemens had gotten the drop on Boudreaux. Yet with time for reflection, it seemed better to have died fighting than to live as a coward and a failure.

Boudreaux turned up the wick all the way, driving the shadows into the corners. Near his foyer hung an old silver mirror with ornate metalwork framing the glass. He had found it in the rubble of a Metairie building the Troublers had burned down years ago. The silverwork reminded him of what he had read of the old times, of great machines that barreled down roads faster than horses and ripped up the earth and knocked down buildings and flew through the sky. He had never been able to imagine what it must have been like to soar above the clouds like an angel. Now he could not stop thinking of the ancients' efficient and terrible weapons. Guns that could pepper every inch of a city block in seconds. Flying bombs that could cross oceans and vaporize entire cities. A wealth of devastation.

Once, this very city had been pockmarked with rusting hulks, scarred by the destruction their crashing had caused: burned and smashed buildings, torn-up streets, acres of wood splintered in long trenched paths as if God's own finger had written *death* in some unimaginable language. Over time, the Crusaders had cleared it all away, rebuilt, replanted. He had played a small part in all that.

Now Boudreaux had obliterated all his good deeds. What could put it all aright?

In his mirror, haunted eyes stared back at him. A corpse's face, unspeakably old and ruined, a shattered, tangled mass good only for dumping in a landfill.

He set the lamp on the floor, drew his gun, and smashed its butt into the mirror.

In the shattered glass, his face looked misshapen and demonic. *Ugly inside and out. If Lake Pontchartrain or the Mississippi swallows me up, it's no more than I deserve. Or maybe I belong with Royster and Benn and Clemens. One more devil walkin the earth until it's time to burn beside Judas Iscariot and all the other betrayers. If the Lord feels merciful, Kouf will hear me scream.*

After a while, Boudreaux turned away from the mirror and took up the lamp. In his bedroom, he stripped off his clothes and snuffed the lantern and wept for Kouf, who had looked for compassion and found only pain.

## 18

**B**efore LaShanda Long could leave home in the early morning, a messenger appeared—a dark-haired boy no older than seventeen, his shirt bearing the Crusade insignia over his heart. He watched her read the note he had brought before turning on his heel and mounting his skinny paint. After he rode away, Long shut her door and read the message twice more.

A meeting in the lord of order's office that evening, agenda unknown.

She spent the day inspecting her forges, trying not to think of how you could barely turn around inside a tower cell, how you could hear the wind but never feel it, how no sunlight penetrated the walls. Almost as bad as a coffin.

When she entered the office that evening, Ford stood at ease, watching Benn and Clemens. The deputy envoys looked upon the courtyard from the massive window. Long raised her eyebrows. Ford shrugged. Outside the sun was setting, the river shadowed. Five straight-backed chairs sat in a half circle near the desk.

Gordy Boudreaux walked in. Stubble covered his cheeks and chin. His eyes were dark and swollen. When he said hello, Long would have sworn she smelled hard liquor on his breath. Like most of them, he had never drunk a drop in his life. He slouched to a chair and fell into it without anyone's leave.

*What in the world?*

Soon Royster arrived, his open-throated shirt billowing as he walked, revealing his pale and wiry frame. The brand over his heart was gnarled and purple. Royster sat behind the desk. Long, Ford, and

Boudreaux faced him—Long and Ford on their feet, Boudreaux slumping in the chair, his head hanging. Benn and Clemens joined them and
stood to Ford's right.

Good evening, the envoy said. I apologize for my tardiness. I've
been meeting with our search parties. No one has seen or heard from
Lynn Stransky since her escape. Misters Ford and Boudreaux, Ms.
Long—do any of you find that strange?

That's the Troublers' way, Ford said. They're guerillas. They hit us
and disappear.

Royster put his elbows on the desk and brought his hands together,
fingertips touching. True, but given present events, she could be ready-
ing a major offensive.

Maybe, but I'd reckon she rabbited, what with all the guards comin
to town. If she's got any sense, that is. I think she does.

Nonetheless, we must remain vigilant.

Yes, sir, Benn and Clemens said.

Yes, sir, said Long.

I reckon so, Ford said.

Boudreaux nodded. Then he looked away.

Against *all* enemies, Royster said, glancing at Boudreaux. Even
those whom we have long believed our closest friends. He folded his
hands and smiled.

Long shivered. The expression looked as genuine as a wooden
bullet.

You got somebody particular in mind? Ford asked.

I do, said Royster. What I am about to say must not leave this room.
Know I take no pleasure in it.

*Sure you don't. That's why you look like the cat that ate the canary.*

Benn stepped forward. It's our honor to serve, sir.

Royster leaned back and sighed. Very well. I fear Gabriel Troy loves
this city more than our church. I believe he plots betrayal. If so, he must
be stopped, by any means necessary, along with all who stand with him.

I know where my deputies' loyalty lies. What of you three? Will you stand with the Crusade, though your enemy be Gabriel Troy himself?

Again, they all answered in unison, like good soldiers—aye. But in her heart, LaShanda Long felt cold. *He knows. Somehow he knows about Gabe, which means he probably suspects us all.* She glanced at Ford and Boudreaux. They had not moved, had not altered their expressions.

Royster gestured to the empty seats. Please, he said.

They all sat. From the stairwell, the sound of many feet. Long's heart raced. Perhaps Royster had summoned his guards to haul them to the towers, the gulags south of the river, or even the Big Muddy itself. Bodies disappeared into its waters like the stones children sometimes threw.

Several servers entered the room, carrying dishes on trays. Two more brought a folding table into the office and placed it against a wall. Then the dish carriers set their burdens down and removed the lids. The smells of roasted chicken and grilled vegetables—squash, turnips, cauliflower, potatoes—filled the room, and despite herself, Long's mouth watered. She had barely eaten all day.

Royster looked to the servers. Thank you. That will be all. As the Temple personnel left, Royster opened his palms to those who remained. Gentlemen and lady, please join me in the breaking of bread.

He did not have to ask anyone twice. They ate more than the prisoners had seen since the shackles first closed.

Afterward, as Ford sipped the last of his water, Royster turned to Boudreaux. Mr. Benn and Mr. Clemens must check the wall's progress. You will accompany them.

Eyes reddened and moist, Boudreaux turned to the envoy. Now?
Yes.

Boudreaux got up and set his plate in a bin filled with soiled dishes.

*He barely touched his food. Maybe he's sick. All these lies and half-truths could do that to a fella.* Soon Ford and Long were alone with Royster. The envoy's empty plate was piled high with chicken bones and the skin of two potatoes. *Did you eat like that in front of all them starvin kids out yonder? I bet you did. I'd like to shove my fist down your throat and pull your stomach out by the roots.*

We have another matter to discuss, Royster said. I was loath to speak of it in front of Gordon. He is still so young, you see, and would likely find this conversation distressing. He might even try to stop us.

Stop us doin what? Ford asked.

As I said before, Lord Gabriel Troy is fomenting rebellion.

Ford's heart trip-hammered. He would not have been surprised if Royster could hear it. I've known Gabe all my life. I've bled with him. I can't believe he'd stand on the wrong side.

The smile disappeared. Troy's betrayal has been revealed to Mister Rook in his meditations. Would you question his divine vision? Or God's word? The same word that set orphans like you on high?

I'm just sayin Gabe's always done right.

Ah, but that is the root of it. Lord Troy believes we are wrong, that he knows the Most High's will better than the Crusade.

Ford looked at Long. She gripped her chair's armrests with both hands, but she said nothing. He turned back to Royster. Let me talk to him.

No, said Royster. He is condemned. What you do now determines your own fate. Do what I ask and prove your loyalty. Refuse, and we must assume you stand with Troy.

Ford scowled. I don't much like tests. We've done everything you've said since you got here. How did we buy this trouble?

You hesitated. Royster leaned forward, his brow furrowed, his jaw clenched. Make your decision, Chief Hunter. Do your duty, or sit beside your Troubler lord in the towers.

Ford clenched his fists. *If I crush his throat, maybe we can slip outside before anybody knows what's happened.*

Then Long laid a hand on his arm and squeezed. He looked at her, but she was watching Royster. Why us? she asked.

Royster turned to her and seemed to relax, despite the breach in protocol. If Misters Benn and Clemens arrest Troy, I believe the populace would revolt. And Gordon, already being so upset, cannot handle him.

Gabe won't come easy, even for us, Ford said.

Royster's eyes were ice. As I said before, you are authorized to use all necessary force.

Sweat broke out on Ford's back, his brow. Royster had reached into his heart and poked the exact spot where his deepest, most conflicted feelings lived—his gratitude for his position and his ability to make a difference in people's lives, as well as his ambivalence about why he deserved it. His loyalty to Gabriel Troy, who had named him chief hunter, struggled hand to hand with his lifelong service to God.

*It's Gabe or us. Hell and damnation. So this is what fear feels like.*

Royster watched him, implacable, tireless, demanding.

I'll do what's required of me, Ford said, like I always have.

Royster turned to Long. And you, Madam Weaponsmith?

Long's lower lip trembled. She did not look at Ford. I stand with the Crusade, sir. But I'm strugglin.

Was she being truthful? How much did she doubt? Repudiating a lifetime's devotion—to the Crusade, to Troy—should not be as easy as shucking off an old, frayed shirt.

Or maybe she was just shining Royster on, waiting for the moment when she could slip a knife in his back.

Had the Crusade never set our current course, I believe Gabriel Troy would have died an old, revered Crusader, Royster said. But Mister Rook has been watching him a long time, ever since the plan for this city was first revealed to him. He was afraid Troy's passion for New

Orleans would prove his undoing. And so it has come to pass. As for you two, Mister Rook values your loyalty, your skills. He wants to raise you even higher. Now is your moment. Can I count on you?

Long sighed. A tear slipped down her cheek. Yes, sir, she whispered.

Royster stood, holding out his hand. Ford and Long rose and shook it. Until it is time to act, he said, keep this between us.

Yes, sir, Ford said.

You may go. I have much work to do.

He took up a stack of papers. At least some of them were marked-up city maps. *I could steal those and smuggle em to Gabe. Or I could show Royster where we've stored our weapons and food caches. Really come clean. Get right with the faith again.* Royster's and Troy's voices shouted in Ford's head, advocating their moralities and plans. *Hell and damnation.*

Minutes later, Ford and Long walked out of the office and down the stairs in silence, caught between two causes like ships struggling through a wind-tossed channel full of jagged rocks.

Long followed Ford to the hitching post. Their saddled animals stood side by side, freshly brushed coats gleaming. Ford's long rifle hung in its scabbard. Long's saddlebags bulged with tools. Canteens had been strung from their pommels. Long took her reins and thanked the groom, a pale boy of fifteen. The other groom was a girl, age indeterminate. She had blond hair and a round, dirty face. *If they choose the wrong side, I may have to kill em myself,* Long thought. *Or maybe they'll drown. Would that be better or worse than me shootin em to pieces? Gators and gulls will eat their bodies.*

She put her foot in the stirrup and hauled herself into the saddle. Ford mounted up. They turned their horses toward Canal, riding close while the grass muffled their hoofbeats.

The endgame's closer than we thought, Ford said as they passed out of sight of the Temple.

Long looked around. No one was within earshot. You think he knows about Stransky?

He might suspect, but if he knew, we'd be dead.

Did you mean what you said? About killin Gabe?

Ford rode in silence for a long time. I don't know that I got the heart, he finally said. There's a special place in hell for betrayers. But if we don't, it's heresy. Seems like we're damned either way.

From somewhere in the city, the flat clap of a rifle, the roar of a shotgun, screams.

So, Long said. We kill Gabe, or we keep on doin what we've been doin.

Can't do nothin right now. We've had tails since we left the Temple.

Long knew better than to look back. I don't know about you, but I'm as skittish as a cat on hot bricks.

When they reached Canal Street, they turned their horses in opposite directions without saying another word.

## 19

**J**ust before sunrise, someone knocked. Troy opened his door, pistol in hand, but when he saw Mordecai Jones on his stoop, he holstered it. Jones shook Troy's hand and took off his hat. His long, sand-colored hair hung about his face in damp strips. Even his beard looked wet. *Lord help. By noon, the Troublers' brains will cook. Their tongues will darken and swell. Their lips will split open, and they'll lick their own blood just because it's wet.*

Troy stood aside. Jones, nearly six and a half feet tall, ducked as he stepped across the threshold. Troy led him to the kitchen and took a pitcher of water from the icebox and poured them a couple of glasses. Jones took his and drained half of it, smacking and wiping his mouth on his shirtsleeve. He had fought with Troy back to back in the Seventh Ward uprising ten years ago, had dug ditches and mended streets and corralled neighbors in dispute. Always faithful, a fine man, fair and honest and hardworking.

*Do you feel it, Mordecai? Do you sense this moment determines the rest of your life?*

Jones had always been sharp, strong, clever with angles and leverage. Before Dwyer came, Troy had intended to nominate him for the next available administrative position, perhaps even create one just for him—special deputy, downtown section. But time had slipped through Troy's fingers like sand.

I appreciate the drink, Jones said, but I don't reckon you called me over here just to dirty a glass.

Troy sipped his water. Had Jones noticed his unstrapped pistol?

Probably so. Not much had ever escaped the man. He had come unarmed, of course. Crusade law forbade anyone but lords and deputies from carrying firearms without permission. Even Santonio Ford's hunters checked out their weapons in the mornings and turned them in at day's end. If you could not prove Troy or Ford had given you leave to carry, you were probably a Troubler. Still, Jones would have plenty of opportunity to fight, if it came to that. The kitchen was chock-full of bladed and blunt weapons. Troy meant to give Jones every chance to live, no matter the cost. He owed the man.

We need to talk, Troy said. It ain't good.

Jones drank the rest of his water, watching Troy. He set his glass on the counter and boosted himself up, sitting on the edge, feet dangling like a child dipping his toes in the river from a dock, his right hand only a foot away from the knife block, his left six inches from a cast-iron skillet.

Could be you're thinkin about them chained-up folks out yonder, Jones said. And maybe about the folks bringin em in too.

Could be. Got an opinion?

I ain't never questioned my orders or my faith. But—and I hope you won't gun me down for sayin so—well, I don't get what we're doin.

Troy crossed his arms. Go on.

Jones scratched his head. Folks starvin and dyin of thirst. Grown men blubberin like babies. All of em eatin maggoty meat and wilted greens a starvin rabbit wouldn't touch. I've shot men and women by your side, Gabriel. A couple of teenagers too. But we always took prisoners when the Troublers gave us a choice. We fed em and sheltered em and tried to convert em. What's happenin here, it's pure torture with no clear aim. I don't see the right of it.

Troy studied Jones's face. So your heart's troubled.

I reckon so. You gonna cuff me now?

The two men looked at each other for a moment. Something

seemed to hang in the air, a tension, as if the world waited for the shooting to start.

*If I can't trust this man, I might as well let him brain me with that skillet.*

Mordecai, Troy said, that's exactly how I see it.

It's a dangerous time to be us, the big man said, wiping his brow again. He went to Troy's icebox and got the pitcher and poured himself another glass. Glad to know I'm not alone, at least. Lands, it's hot.

And apt to get hotter. Anybody else feel this way?

Tommy Gautreaux. Antoine Baptiste. Laura Derosier. A dozen others, at least. They can't even look at them prisoners. Might be more. I don't know. We've all been too fidgety to talk much.

Troy clapped Jones on the shoulder. Well, we need to *start* talkin. But this ain't no small thing. We're puttin our lives at hazard. Maybe our souls too.

Jones laughed, but it sounded more like a groan. How'd we come to this sorry state?

Troy refilled his own glass, and they retired to his living room, where he opened the shades to the sun. The two of them talked well into the morning.

At dusk the next evening, Troy walked through the French Market, ruffling children's hair and speaking to citizens picking up their daily quotas of fish and meat and vegetables, new wares from Long's forges, extra rations, or equipment for special occasions. Soon the stalls would close for the night. Nearby a woman Troy could not place asked for extra vegetables, now that she had another baby to feed.

*I should know her name. And her kids'. We should know she needs more.* Soon she and her children could be floating down Poydras or St. Charles.

Troy walked down the road, stifling a yawn. He had barely slept in three days, and never peacefully since capturing Lynn Stransky.

Reaching the steps leading to the river, Troy paused. Citizens headed home for the night passed and waved, saluted, tipped their hats. He acknowledged them all.

*I hope this wasn't a stupid idea. Is it more suspicious if we're seen socializin or if we ain't?*

He sat on his favorite bench and watched the river winding toward the Gulf. The water had always soothed him. They rode upon it, fished in it, washed in it, drank from it. Crusade histories taught how the ancients had dumped waste into their waters until no one could drink without risking disease and death. Troy thanked God those days had passed. But lately he wondered how much of the histories was true.

*Did the Purge really cleanse this world, or drown it in blood? Did the first Troublers worship their dead machines? Were they all wicked? Or were they just mad with grief for all they had lost?* Accounts of the Purge were vague, but he had always taken them on faith. *Was I a fool? Is Rook the only madman we've served, or were they all this way?*

Long ambled up the walkway to his right, her lengthy stride and strong shoulders distinguishing her even in the gathering shadows. McClure and Bandit climbed the steps from the riverside. They reached Troy first. The girl touched her hat brim and then pointed behind Troy, who turned. From the direction of the Quarter, Tetweiller and Hobbes walked together in silence. McClure sat beside Troy on the bench, Bandit lying at their feet and pricking his ears as the others neared. Troy could barely see their faces in the gloaming.

No one heard or saw Ford coming. One moment he was absent; the next, he stood beside Tetweiller, thumbs tucked into his belt.

Anybody close? Troy asked.

Just a few folks on the streets, Hobbes said.

Can they hear us?

Not unless they're bats, Ford said.

All right. Report.

South of the bridge, some of the Troublers are dyin, said McClure. Mostly the real old and kids under five. The guards just unchain em and toss em on a pyre or dump em in the river.

Jesus *Christ*, Tetweiller muttered. I wondered where that smoke and the goddam stink came from.

Christ ain't got nothin to do with it, said Troy. I'm more certain of that than ever. How about the rest of you? Any progress?

I've got two dozen folks I can trust, Ford said.

LaShanda?

So far, about thirty, Long said. Every one of em knows others who can't stomach this. If we had enough time, we could probably turn near everybody. But with things as they are, I'm as nervous as a long-tailed cat in a room full of rockin chairs.

Ernie? Troy said.

I've talked with twenty-five, thirty people who sounded ready to carve out Rook's gizzard with a rusty spoon. I've been askin folks, real casual like, *So what do you think about this here situation?* And most of em answer. I reckon they figure they can be honest with an old man who drinks and cusses more than Stransky. Short answer—they're pissed and scared.

We can work with that, said Troy. Jack?

Talked to half a dozen that seemed solid, but they weren't sure they could get anybody else. Be proud of their loyalty any other time.

Troy pondered the information. It sounded like a good start, but who knew how things would play out. Once the shooting began, men and women who seemed brave might cower or throw down their weapons and beg for mercy. Or the meekest child might slaughter a dozen Crusaders with a shotgun or a hunting knife.

Well, he said, it won't be just us at least. Keep your people recruitin, but only when they're *sure*. I'd rather err on the side of caution than trust the wrong person and get us all killed. Jack, how about Gordy?

Hobbes hesitated. Don't know. Been keepin to himself since he took that trip across the bridge with yon envoys.

You think he's sidin with Royster? asked Long. Every time I see him, he's with Benn or Clemens.

Can't believe that, said Hobbes. Do my heart good to know what's wrong, though.

*Even if Gordy won't fight, he'd never give us up. He just wouldn't.* Keep an eye on him, and let somebody know if there's any change, Troy said.

There's a question nobody's askin, McClure said. Couldn't we just kill Royster and them? Then blow that wall to hell and gone?

Wouldn't do no good, Tetweiller said.

Why not?

Lots of reasons. One, Rook would just send some other assholes to finish what Royster started. And next time they'd bring an army. Trained fighters, not guards.

But we'd have time to get ready.

Ford put a hand on the girl's shoulder. Ain't enough folks in this town to fight the whole Crusade, nor even stand em off. Not without defenses, which we don't have the time or labor to build.

Right now Rook's got a lot on his plate, Long said. But if we kill his envoys, he'll be on us like stink on manure.

Well, we'll have to kill em sooner or later, won't we? McClure asked.

Uh huh, said Hobbes. Afterward.

The child knelt and scratched her dog's ears. After what?

Me and Jack think the best way to handle this is to let em build their wall, Troy said. And then take it from em.

For a moment, no one spoke. Then everyone talked at once.

Hold on now, Long said. We're gonna let em wall us in with a whole city of Troublers? That's crazy.

Damn crazy, said Tetweiller. Once that wall's in place, we better be outside it, or we're fucked.

Not if we move at just the right time, said Troy. If we can keep

Royster's folks too busy to evacuate, maybe they won't blow the levees. And while they're fightin their way out, we can free the prisoners and take the city back.

That's a big *if*, said Long. Tryin to get that many people movin just right at the same time's gonna be like herdin cats.

Especially when they're Troublers, Ford said. We never could turn our backs on em.

Now hang on, Troy barked. They all fell silent. I know how you feel. But look at our options. Let Royster kill everybody? I can't do it. Fight em right now? We got maybe a hundred people on our side against all them guards. Burn the wall and kill the envoys? It's like Ernie said. That's just a delay. But if we use all our time to recruit and hide supplies and plan, we got a better chance.

The armies will come anyway, Tetweiller said. Once Royster's dead.

Odds will be better by then, Hobbes said. Hunt and fish and gather and harvest and forge until this whole city's one big fortress.

Huh, Ford said. The wall's just the kind of defense we can't build ourselves in the time we got. Lord above, Gabe, it's risky, but if we could pull it off—

We might be safe for the duration, Troy said.

No one spoke for a time. Something big splashed in the river. From the streets, guards' voices drifted on the breeze as they talked of aching lower backs, the temperaments of the new arrivals, the weather, food. Crickets chirped. Bandit scratched himself. The girl rubbed the dog's belly.

Well, I'm on pins and needles, Long said.

As are we all, Hobbes muttered.

There's somethin else, Ford said. I can't speak for y'all, but my conscience—it's still eatin at me. What we're doin now—we've always called it treason and heresy.

Lord, yes, Long said.

Everything feels wrong, Troy said. I can't say it don't. But we swore to protect our people. I can't let Rook murder em.

The lesser of two evils, Long whispered. She turned to the water.

Yes, said Troy. That's the best I can give you.

Ford spat and ran a hand over his face. He exhaled. There ain't no best, he said. It's all just one big heap of awful.

They fell silent again. The river gurgled.

Finally, Tetweiller sighed. Fuck it. I'm in.

Troy stood and shook his hand. Thank you, my good friend.

I'll do my part, Ford said. Lord forgive me.

So will I, Long said. But it took her a moment.

Troy shook their hands. A great weight lifted from his chest. Okay, listen up. After tomorrow, we can't meet like this anymore. Not all of us.

What's happenin tomorrow? asked McClure.

Never you mind. It'll look better if y'all don't know.

My ass, Ernie Tetweiller said. Spill.

Just keep in mind, it's all part of the plan, unless Royster hangs my body from the Temple walls. Keep doin what you're doin. And have faith. Believe in our God and in each other.

God's all well and good, McClure said. But I'll put my faith in us.

LaShanda, if you and Santonio could hang back a spell, I'd appreciate it.

Soon everyone else dispersed. Troy gazed across the river's dark expanse. *After tomorrow, I might never see you again. Or you might be my grave. Well, I reckon I could do worse. Mother Muddy.* His heart pounded. His throat had gone dry. *Help me, Father. I can't afford to be scared. I just can't.*

He turned to his chief hunter and his master smith. I got a task for y'all, he said.

❖

Moonlight still streamed through his bedroom window when Troy woke. He rubbed the sleep from his eyes and went to the kitchen, boiled coffee, and drank three cups, the steam and aroma driving away the fog in his mind. Back in his bedroom, he threw open the curtains to the rising sun and checked his spare six-guns and ammo. Four pistols lay scattered about the house with just enough shells to look suspicious. His clothes, his spare hat, even his father's Bible remained where he had left them. When the Crusaders searched his house, it had to look as if he had planned to come back.

The supplies he had packed in his poke seemed pitiful, a piece of gauze on an amputated limb. *If they find the caches I've been buryin, I'll have to depend on Stransky. She'll love that.*

In the foyer, he looked back. His comfortable old furniture sat in mute witness to his departure as dust motes drifted through the air. Countless friends and visiting officials had sat on that couch, in those chairs. Life and memory as indelibly imprinted in the walls as the wood's very grain. *I'm probably never gonna see this place again. It's been a good home.* Tears blurred his vision. He wiped them away. He gritted his teeth and slapped himself on the cheek. *Quit it. You ain't got the luxury.*

He turned, opened the door, and stepped outside.

The red mare with the white heart-shaped splotch on her hindquarters had been saddled and hitched. A good horse that might have grown to excellence, given more time, but the mare's hourglass had emptied too. Troy wished he could have chosen an old warhorse with one foot in the grave, a good soldier ready for one last chase, like Japeth. But he needed something fast and lithe. *Besides, Japeth deserves a better ride than we'll get today.*

He untied the mare. She snorted as he saddled up. They ambled along the streets, greeting citizens and the few outlander guards who bothered saluting. Most did not. Why bother? The town was theirs. Locals, even Troy, were blue ticks waiting to be picked off and squeezed to death.

The smells of beignets and croissants and fresh butter and jam rode the breeze. New Orleans culture you could eat. Troy rode to Roddy Trahan's little cafe on Chartres and ate eggs and andouille and buttered croissants. A few tables away sat Jones, along with Tommy Gautreaux, a big-bellied fiftyish man who split his time between lamplighting and fishing for Ford; the Temple guard Antoine Baptiste, eating sausage and biscuits by the fistful, fuel for his dusky, powerful frame; Laura Derosier, the lanky forger of handheld bladed weapons, her sandy hair pulled back, her swan's neck nearly as thin and corded as her arms. Before Troy left, he stopped by their table. They spoke of banalities, but Derosier winked at him, and Baptiste made a point of shaking his hand, not just saluting. They were finishing their last cups of coffee when he put on his hat and exited.

He rode toward the Temple and listened to his city—clinking and shuffling, the low sounds of construction from the wall, horses' hooves on pavement, children running to their lessons or apprenticeships. He lingered in the old wards and the Central Business District, the Quarter, Treme, Lakeside. The sites of his birth, his raising, his life. Despite hurricanes and the blood that had soaked the ground, he loved these streets. The rich stores of grain and barrels of wine and canned preserves in New Orleans's storehouses; the way the river chopped and thrashed in a storm; the landfill, with the rubble from the old times buried under its refuse, the twisted and rusting metal skeletons of strange machines, the crumbling mortar of once mighty buildings. Many times he had stood high on rooftops and tried to imagine New Orleans during the great burning—flying machines falling from the heavens, explosions rising ten stories high and spurting steel and human shrapnel in all directions, unimaginable ships stalling on the waters until their crews died of thirst or while careening rudderless onto shore, crushing all in their paths. Troy had helped build and repair dwellings and forges and tabernacles before he had ever picked up a gun. He had defended the city from Troublers and slept in her embrace almost every night of his life.

Now it was over.

At the river, he hitched the mare and sent a passing boy to procure a feedbag. The river glittered like a field of diamonds. No canoes or rafts or fishing boats, only a few Crusade patrol crafts gliding along, their lookouts armed with shotguns. Troy smelled gumbo and jambalaya, red beans and rice. His stomach ached with wanting. He tried not to think about what he might be forced to eat in the coming days.

He sat on his bench near the river until the sun rode low in the west. Day workers headed home, passing the night watch and the lamplighters and the bearers of water barrels and fuel, fellow nodding to fellow, some pausing to shake a hand or speak to a neighbor. Sheep living among wolves none of them could even smell.

Troy got up and walked back to the mare and unhitched her. Then he mounted up, rode over to Decatur, and waited.

Soon enough, Ford and Long rounded the corner. He waved. Long pointed at him. They reined their horses thirty yards away.

*Lord, help us,* Troy prayed.

Everybody clear the street, Santonio Ford shouted.

People stopped in their tracks and gawked. Ford sat his roan with a rifle across his lap. LaShanda Long rode her favorite paint, a six-gun drawn.

He means *now,* she cried.

The crowd scattered, many glancing at Troy, confused. Seconds later, faces appeared in every window.

*Good. I hope they can hear us.*

Gabriel Troy, Ford said. Throw down your weapons in the name of Matthew Rook and the Bright Crusade.

The mare nickered. Troy patted her neck. On what charge?

Sedition. Mister Royster knows your heart.

Does he now?

Gabriel, please, Long said. If we don't bring you in, somebody else will.

Dead or alive?

We'd prefer alive, said Ford. But it's up to you.

You got your duty, Troy said. I got mine.

And with that, he drew his guns.

Muffled screams from the closed-up buildings as Troy fired high over Ford's head. Long's and Ford's horses reared up. Ford was nearly thrown. He saved himself by wrapping the reins around one arm and grasping the pommel with his other hand. The rifle struck the pavement. Troy turned the mare toward Poydras and spurred it. Ford's rifle bellowed. He had recovered even faster than expected. The slug whizzed past Troy's right ear, close enough to trim his hair. Long's six-gun boomed, and a piece of pavement just under Troy's mare's back hoof disintegrated.

Citizens hugged walls and dove into open doors as Troy rode past. He turned in the saddle and fired again, aiming down and to Long's left. *Father, please don't let me hurt somebody.*

Long glared, her teeth set in a snarl. She fired again, and Troy's hat flew off his head. His scalp burned. Something warm trickled over his ears. *Heaven above, LaShanda.*

He turned. Several lengths back, Ford steadied the rifle on his forearm, the reins gathered in his trigger hand. Troy faced forward as he reached Claiborne Avenue and yanked his own reins, peeling west just as the rifle crashed again.

*They're cuttin it too close. Maybe Royster got his hooks into em after all.*

Ford shouted for everyone to clear the streets, watch out, *get outta the way.*

On the walk ahead, a mother covered her children's bodies with her own. A father grabbed a toddler before she could blunder into the mare's path. When Troy passed, the adults picked up the children and ran for the nearest doorway.

Troy tied the reins around his left hand and turned again, aiming for Ford's center mass. His finger tightened on the trigger.

*Dang it, Santonio, are y'all still with me or not?*

Ford veered his horse onto the far sidewalk, scattering citizens. A girl of no more than eight crouched in his path, hands over her head, screaming. The hunter sawed his reins again, and the horse careened back onto the street, missing the girl by inches.

Long fired, the bullet whinging by Troy's face. He spurred the mare harder and harder, the buildings and citizens no more than a blur. Bullets whizzed by every few seconds as they passed south of Tulane.

*I'll do my part*, Ford had said.

*So will I*, Long had added.

But what had they meant?

Wagons on the road ahead. Troy weaved between them, the drivers shouting in surprise, the harnessed horses nickering. Had his own mount left swatches of hair on the boards, the nail heads?

*Santonio and LaShanda can't fire with all these folks here. But if a wagon drifts at the wrong time, they won't need to.*

Ford and Long were still shouting for him to stop in the name of Royster and Matthew Rook and the Crusade. And if he could hear it, so could all these citizens, who would spread the word, as people do. Perhaps, if this chase accomplished nothing else, it would measure the city's true temperature.

Troy passed a wagon on his left, avoiding another collision by a hair. Behind him, a crash and a startled cry. He turned. Ford was riding sidesaddle and struggling to throw his leg back over and into the stirrup as the wagon spilled its contents through a hole in its side. Ford's roan bled from its flanks. The hunter had almost crippled himself, had nearly killed his horse. He regained his saddle and aimed, fired. The round whined past Troy. Ford reloaded.

They approached the Huey P. Long Bridge. The river flowed below it, patrol boats maneuvering around floating bodies as if they were logs. A handful of citizens bathed near the water's edge, despite the corpses. They heard the shots and looked up as Troy galloped onto the bridge, leading Ford and Long by perhaps forty yards.

Troy reined up, and the horse skidded to a halt, blowing hard, its sides slick with sweat. He leaned over and whispered into her ear. Good luck, girl. This ain't your fault or your fight.

As Ford and Long reached the foot of the bridge, Troy dismounted, drew, and fired on them. Their animals bucked as his bullets zinged off the pavement. Then they dismounted and pulled their horses to the ground, taking refuge behind them. Whinnying in protest, the animals tried to raise their heads. Long reloaded as Ford talked to his horse, probably trying to calm it, and propped his rifle on the animal's side.

Give it up, Long shouted. You got nowhere to go.

Troy fired, the round striking the pavement between their horses. Then he swatted the mare's hindquarters. It charged Ford and Long's position, and in the moment that it blocked their view, Troy stepped over the side of the bridge and jumped.

He kicked and flailed, unable to stop himself, the river rushing up to meet him, its waters frothing. Wind tore past him and into his nose, inflating his lungs until they felt ready to burst. His stomach rose into his throat. A young guard stood up in his skiff and watched Troy plunge. For a moment, they seemed to lock eyes.

*Close your mouth, kid. You could catch a ten-pound bass in there.*

Then he hit the water. The impact smashed the sense out of him. Something in his knee popped. Cold water rushed over him. He expelled half his breath in the shock. Bullets cut the water all around him, their sound like someone's palm striking the surface.

His satchel, still tied to his back, pulled him down and down.

❖

Three hours later, from the foot of the bridge, Ford and Long watched the search parties' torches sweeping the banks, the nearby streets, the river itself, these latter lights bobbing with the currents. Royster stood nearby, giddy. He even clapped Ford and Long on their backs and congratulated them. Benn sat his horse behind them, directing the searchers. Clemens was out there somewhere, his guns unstrapped, ready to burn Troy down if the lord of order should be found alive. No sign of Tetweiller or Hobbes. Long had barely seen Boudreaux in days, and what she had seen, she had not liked. He had looked gaunt, haunted, older. He still refused to discuss what had happened across the river. Long prayed for him every night and morning.

You think we hit him? Ford said. His expression was blank, but his voice quavered, just a little.

Long watched the search a while longer. I know I grazed him, and I'm pretty sure you did too. But once he hit the water? No way to know.

Royster approached. He put a hand on each of their shoulders. You have done us all a great service, he said. The Crusade thanks you. But now I must leave you. Much is left to do. He turned to the nearest Crusader. Kill that red mare. Then take a detail to Lord Troy's house and burn it. I want no trace of that traitor to remain by morning.

A Crusader grabbed the mare's reins. The gathering crowd buzzed. It stretched back two blocks. On the front line, Mordecai Jones stood with his arms folded, his hat tipped back. Long did not like the look in his eyes—baleful, like a hungry wolf's. Even from a distance, tension radiated off him like heat. Tommy Gautreaux held vigil at Jones's left, his salt-and-pepper beard hanging halfway down his chest, his prodigious gut puddling over his belt, his thumbs tucked into his pockets. To Gautreaux's right, Antoine Baptiste sneered, his skin glistening with sweat. His shirt, open at the throat, revealed his thick neck and powerful pectorals. He looked as if he wondered how Long's bones might taste. On the other side of Jones, tall, beanpole-thin Laura Derosier's face was expressionless, her straight brown hair blowing in the wind.

Long turned away. Down on the banks, no one hailed them. No shots were fired. No one hallooed. For the moment, Gabriel Troy had disappeared.

Downriver, the lord of order dragged himself out of the water near Evangeline Road. A mounted figure waited on the pitch-black street. *If he's hostile,* Troy thought, *I reckon I'm done.* Something had torn in his right knee, and the scrapes on his scalp and arm oozed. Every muscle ached. He had never been so tired in his life.

The figure trotted forward, face obscured by a bandana and a hat pulled low. Troy bent over, both hands on his good knee, breathing hard. The rider shook his head. Then he pulled off his bandana, revealing a weathered, sun-blasted face, wrinkles like cracked earth, a scruffy white beard.

You look like ten pounds of shit in a five-pound bag, Ernie Tetweiller said.

Troy coughed and sputtered and vomited river water. In the distance, the glow of many torches shimmered faint and ephemeral like a veiled lantern. You got the rest of my stuff? Troy croaked, wiping puke from his mouth with his shirtsleeve.

Right here, the old man said. He squinted at Troy. Sweet Lord above. Did somebody actually shoot you?

Troy winced. A hive of angry bees swarmed in his knee. His lower leg felt cold and numb, yet his scalp and arm were afire. They grazed me a couple times, he said. Plus, I think I ripped up my knee. Maybe worse. Got no idea how I'm gonna make it all the way to the sisters' on foot.

Tetweiller dismounted and took Troy's arm, leading him to the horse. Here's how.

Troy did not protest. Tetweiller was old and limped worse every day, but Troy had seen him walk across the city in July, gunning down Troublers while his left leg pile-drove the ground. He could manage a few miles.

Troy grabbed the pommel. How'd you get this horse around the Troubler line?

Tetweiller got behind Troy and pushed him into the saddle. Stole him from a house down the road a piece. When you get to the sisters', let him go. He'll find his way home, if some fool guard don't shoot him.

Together they clopped off, two half-lame men and a stolen horse.

Near the sisters', Hobbes walked out of a shadowed doorway, holstering his pistols. He saw Troy and grunted. Gonna punch Santonio Ford in the throat.

He helped Troy off the horse. Troy tried not to moan too much. They did the best they could, Troy said through gritted teeth. We were ridin hard over uneven ground.

Hobbes scoffed. Tenderized you like a steak, didn't they?

They could have shot me in the back. They didn't.

Hobbes grumbled as he took the reins. Troy limped toward the entrance. When Hobbes started to hitch the horse, Troy said, Ernie stole him. Just turn him loose.

Hobbes led the animal away from the post and slapped it on the hindquarters. The horse whinnied and broke into a trot, heading back the way they had come. Hobbes walked over and draped Troy's arm around his neck. Together they ascended the steps and opened the doors. Inside, Sister Jewel, Sarah Gonzales's right hand, scurried up and washed the blood from Troy's face with a rag, walking backward and never missing a step. She even turned at the altar as if she could see it through the back of her head. Hobbes helped Troy sit while the nun ministrated, keeper of a dim and smoky temple to a God of mystery and ritual, her face lined with care and sun, her age indeterminate, her movements quick and economical, dabbing blood and dirt from flesh as a chick pecks feed from the ground. She stepped out for a moment. When she came back, she carried a basin and bandages, a wet rag draped on her shoulder. Hobbes helped Troy remove his shirt. Sister Jewel cleaned the shoulder wound, a two-inch gouge, dark about the edges with crusted blood. She poulticed and dressed it as well as any physician Troy had ever known. Then she went to work on his head.

Troy looked at Hobbes, who stood by the flickering votives, and raised his eyebrows. Hobbes nodded.

*We've long suspected the sisters have been patchin up Troublers. Jewel's good enough to support that theory. Not that it matters anymore.*

Sister Jewel knotted the bandage. Skin off them britches, she said.

Groaning and moving as if he were a hundred years old, Troy unbuttoned his pants. Sister Jewel pulled them down, easing them over his knee. It already looked as big as a mushmelon. As she wrapped the knee, the back door opened again. Sister Sarah Gonzales entered, holding folded clothes. Lynn Stransky followed, her hair and clothes freshly washed. She winked at Hobbes, who turned from her, stone-faced.

Troy smiled. *She really does get to him. In another world, they might have made a good couple. Who knows? Maybe they still can.* The future was unspooling before them like a night highway, twists and turns and precipices and dead ends.

Troy wanted to cover himself, but if Sister Sarah felt uncomfortable, she gave no sign. She handed him the clothes and inspected Sister Jewel's work.

Stransky peered over Sarah's shoulder and whistled. Nice legs, she said.

Then she threw her arm around Hobbes, who stiffened and

clenched his jaw. Troy could not be sure in the dim light, but he would have sworn Hobbes was blushing. *Probably the first time a woman's touched him that way. If we had all just been born other people or in some other world. That's all it would have taken—for every single thing in our lives to have been different.*

Sorry about all this, he said to Sarah. I know it's a risk.

She glanced at him and then turned away. We risk ourselves every time we open these doors.

When they were done, Troy pushed himself off the pew, setting his jaw against the stiffness in his violated limbs, and managed to put on the fresh clothes without aid, though he could barely get the pants over his knee.

Thank you, he said. These fit right fine.

Sister Sarah nodded. I had to guess your size.

Troy squeezed her shoulder. Then Sister Sarah put her arms around him. He embraced her. Her heartbeat thumped against his chest, her breath on his neck, the tips of her fingers tracing his ribs. He tried to think of the habit's coarse fabric rather than the way her breasts pressed against his chest, how her cheek felt on his shoulder.

After a moment, they let go. She stroked his cheek with the back of her hand, her breath quickening. Her eyes fluttered as she blinked away tears. She looked away. Vaya con Dios, Gabriel.

Troy nodded. His throat felt like he had swallowed raw cotton.

Sister Sarah helped Sister Jewel gather their materials and his ruined clothes. Together, without another word, the nuns exited through the back door.

No one spoke for a moment. Then Stransky sighed. You're both damn fools.

Troy turned back to Hobbes. They'll be watchin you and Ernie even closer now. Assume somebody's tailin you every second. Tell Ernie the same.

Hobbes frowned. Ain't gonna be able to squirrel away a single bullet. Might as well come with you.

Troy shook his head. Conviction's more dangerous than bullets. Spread the word. Be watchful. And be ready.

One thing we ain't established. How will we know when to make our move?

It's best if we don't get too particular. But believe me—everybody in town will know when it's time.

Hobbes stuck out his hand. Troy shook it. Stransky hugged Hobbes again. Troy wondered if the deputy would break her jaw. Instead, after a moment's hesitation, Hobbes hugged her back.

*If that don't beat all.* It looked about as natural as a bear riding a horse.

Hobbes caught him looking and pulled away, clearing his throat. Stransky patted the deputy lord's cheek, grinning.

You better get back before they notice you're gone, Troy said.

Okay, Hobbes said. He tipped his hat. Ma'am.

Troy watched him go. *I hope I see you again this side of heaven, my friend.*

Stransky shook her head. Ma'am, he called me. Jesus Christ. She turned to Troy. You ready for this?

Ain't got no choice.

If you're playin me, my people will rip you apart.

I'd expect nothin less.

She clapped him on the shoulder—his wounded arm. He winced. Okay, then, she said. Let's go get ready to pick a fight.

## 20

**B**oudreaux tried to ignore the prisoners' moans, the stink of their fouled garments, the drone of flies buzzing over buckets of human waste. On the table before him lay an emaciated wretch. But for a few scraggly patches, the man's hair had fallen out. His limbs were pine straw. The roots of his eight or ten remaining teeth showed. The rest lay on an old steel tray flecked with blood and rust. Boudreaux gripped the pliers hard, hoping they would break, but LaShanda Long's smiths had made them well. *Damn her for that. Damn her smiths. Damn me too. Me most of all.*

Clemens whispered in Boudreaux's ear. Don't stop now. You're getting to the good part.

*This is hell, all right.*

On the march, a guard's canteen had disappeared. It had fallen to Boudreaux and Clemens to interrogate certain prisoners who had been chained in the vicinity. Of course, Clemens had only the guard's word that the canteen had even existed. Perhaps the man had lost it or even thrown it away so someone would end up in a place such as this, facing someone like Boudreaux. For all anyone knew, the guard held some personal grudge against certain prisoners. Or perhaps he was just sadistic. Yet his word had been enough.

*This man was somebody's precious babe once. And now he's here. His whole life led him to me, his destiny so certain it might have been prophesied in the Testaments. What kind of plan is that, and what kind of abominable god would conceive it?*

The skeleton strapped to the torture table knew nothing about the canteen. That had been clear as soon as they had dragged him in by his wrists and thrown him on the table like a cut of meat. Yet there lay the man's teeth, and here were the pliers, in Boudreaux's hand. Because you had to ask. And ask. And ask again, each question punctuated with misery, until you heard the answer you wanted to hear. That was Boudreaux's job now.

Once, he would have laughed at the very idea of a Crusader thief. Why steal when everybody had plenty? The notion would have seemed as foreign and exotic as a mountain in the Quarter. But now, after so many trips to this blight of a room, he could believe anything about anyone. Especially himself. He no longer recognized the face in his mirror—the hollow eyes, the gaunt cheeks, the oily and unkempt hair. The things he had done had poisoned his dreams, his faith. *No love or charity here. No godliness, unless God's insane. If this is justice, it's sick and perverted. So are my friends, who passed me this cup. None of them so sick as me.* Boudreaux had fallen to his knees night after night, begging God to give him a sign, to strike him down rather than let him hurt another person. Yet God had been silent, and for the first time in his life, Gordon Boudreaux could not accept the mystery. He had no one to lean on, no one to share his pain with. It seemed to matter little whether the Crusade drowned New Orleans or if Troy succeeded. Everyone was vile. Everything was senseless.

He isn't going to tell us anything, Clemens said, if you plan to bore him to death.

Boudreaux clenched his teeth and managed not to twist Clemens's nose off with the pliers like one might yank a bent nail out of a wall. Instead, he grabbed the man's face and held the pliers an inch from his eyes. What was the prisoner's name again? It had seemed so important before they—*he*—began pulling teeth. He searched his memory and finally found it.

Mister Potrello, he said. You can make it stop. Just tell us. Did you steal that canteen, or do you know who did? It's one or the other, sir. You were chained right there.

The man tried to speak, but the words caught in his throat. He rasped and stared at Boudreaux without really seeing. Gah, he said. Gah. God.

*He has no energy. They've starved him for weeks.* Boudreaux leaned closer, caressing Potrello's cheek. If you tell me, I'll see you're fed and given plenty of water. Come on now.

The man gargled and gagged and spat red-flecked white foam. His teeth yanked out, yet he barely bled. He was desiccating like a grape in July. Boudreaux looked in his eyes and saw in them all the universe's despair, the cold cruelty that sistered imagination. In the end, Potrello only whined.

Clemens nudged Boudreaux. Get on with it. It's the only way we can save his thieving soul from hellfire. Besides, he stinks. I want out of this room.

Boudreaux looked back at Clemens. *I can jam these pliers through his eyeball. And then I can stab Mister Benn in the throat. The guards will get me, but the deputy envoys will die first. Maybe that's the answer I should have given when they first brought me here. There's no future for me. No old age. But maybe if I kill these cockroaches, I can save my soul. If I can't, at least they'll be in hell a few minutes longer than me.*

He raised the pliers.

But Clemens caught his hand. No. We're done with teeth.

Boudreaux tensed. His free hand balled into a fist.

A knock at the door. Benn opened it. Half a dozen armed guards stood in the hall.

Despair clenched Boudreaux's guts with icy claws. Too many guns to assure the deputy envoys died. Surely even his godforsaken life was worth more than a half sacrifice.

His fist unballed.

Yes? Benn said to the guards.

Message from Mister Royster, said the leader, a man of medium build and middle age and a scarred, weather-beaten face. After you're done here, you're to ride straight to his office for debriefing. No stops.

Certainly, Benn said. Have you gentlemen ever seen an interrogation like this?

No, sir.

Well, come and watch. You may need to perform one someday.

The guards entered and crowded around the island. Their body heat, their sour sweat wafted in the close quarters. Half of them grinned. The others showed no emotion at all.

Watch this, said Clemens. He bent over the table and unbuttoned Potrello's pants and yanked them down, exposing the man's genitals, which looked as shriveled as the rest of him, the scrotum retreating into a patchy nest of pubic hair, the penis a dead worm on a hot thoroughfare. Clemens grabbed Boudreaux's hand and fit the pliers around Potrello's scrotum. Then the deputy envoy stepped back. *Now* we'll see how badly he wants to hold on to his sin.

Potrello stared at the ceiling, eyes sunken. His mouth worked as if he were gumming a piece of steak. Perhaps he prayed.

A tear slid down Boudreaux's cheek.

Potrello found the strength to scream again after all.

## 21

In the square, the sun blazed on grooms and landscapers, guards and pedestrians ambulating through their prosaic lives. Lisander Royster watched them all through his window. Sweat covered every inch of the envoy's body, but he had never felt more refreshed. Foul Troubler pollution poured into New Orleans, which would soon become the world's grandest chamber pot. Moreover, according to Mister Clemens, Gordon Boudreaux had made great strides as an interrogator. *When Troublers raise their filthy heads from the globe's gutters after the coming Purge, Mister Rook will have another loyal man who can make anyone talk or send them to hell knowing what pain really means.* Ford and Long had proven their loyalty. Benn had found Troy's blood at the spot where he jumped. Half the town had seen him run to ground. The other half had no doubt heard of it. Another blow to the Troubler cause, another demonstration of the Crusade's might. The only danger lay in those who might see the lord of order as a martyr.

*We will not make that mistake with Hobbes and Tetweiller. We needed the symbolic value of disgracing Troy publicly, and he took advantage of that, perhaps salvaging some measure of dignity in death. We will neutralize the others quietly and without violence. They can roast in this hellish heat and then drown with their fellows. New Orleans belongs to the Crusade.*

The plan for the new Purge had, at first, seemed dangerous, perhaps even insane. Even God Himself had destroyed the world only once. The Scriptures spelled that out, even the ones deemed safe for public study. The original Purge had been the global catastrophe prophesied in John's great Revelation. Jonas Strickland had simply given the apocalypse a little nudge. Ever since, the Crusade had controlled the earth in God's name. The Troublers had been marginalized, hunted, purified through pain. Why did the world require a third cleansing? Royster had prayed about it, meditated, consulted the Crusade's histories and the Scriptures. In the end, he had come to realize what he should have known all along—that Matthew Rook had been chosen for a reason. His will was commensurate with God's. Questioning him was heresy. Royster had spent three days fasting in his chambers, scourging himself, and praying for forgiveness. And when he emerged, he had been broken anew on the wheel of the Lord's pleasure.

Now he watched the blessed and the doomed milling together. *Father, I pray their hearts are right with You, because most of them will face Your judgment right soon. I will send them to You myself, in Your name and in the name of Matthew Rook.*

Had Gabriel Troy faced a similar crisis of conscience? Probably, but he had failed his test. He had pretended to serve the Crusade, but he had loved this city more. Now he almost certainly lay at the bottom of the river, food for fish, flotsam in the currents. Good riddance.

Benn entered. Report, Royster said.

Yes, sir. The crews have completed approximately sixty percent of the wall. Lord Rook was wise to have ordered the sections constructed all those months ago.

Of course he was. What else?

The rest of the Troublers and their guards will arrive as scheduled. No one reports any significant obstacles or delays.

Good. And Hobbes? The old man?

Within the hour, they will be neutralized.

Royster smiled.

Boudreaux stumbled out of the interrogation chamber and through the holding facility. Prisoners jeered or begged for release or simply lay staring at the walls and moaning. Outside, the sky clear and beautiful, the young deputy lord ran to the side of the building and vomited a ghastly stew of bile and water and half-dissolved bread. Then he straightened and stumbled to the hitching post, wiping his mouth on his sleeve. He untied his horse and saddled up and rode through the streets, ignoring everyone who spoke or saluted or threatened to kill him *if I ever get outta these goddam chains*. The horse carried him home through a city buzzing with miserable, gibbering half-life. As the sun set, they reached his yard, where he unsaddled the horse and hitched it. The saddle he dumped on the porch, waving the grooms away. It could sit there all night. Who would dare take it?

He left the door open and walked into the dim living room, unbuckling the gun belt and tossing it on the couch, weapons and all. Since assuming his post, he had never taken off his guns unless he was going to bed or taking a bath, and even then, he kept them nearby. Now, that seemed as pointless as everything else. Screams echoed in his mind. How many emaciated wrecks like Kouf and Potrello were scattered about the city?

Boudreaux passed through the kitchen, shedding clothes, first his hat and shirt, then his boots and socks and pants. Naked, he entered his back yard, his stark white torso and legs juxtaposed with the deep tan of his face and hands. A child's half-finished finger painting.

He walked to the middle of the yard and fell to his knees, craned his head back, and howled.

Lights flickered in nearby houses. Faces appeared in windows and just as quickly vanished, the lights extinguished. Crickets chirped. Mosquitoes buzzed. Summer heat lay on him like a damp quilt.

What did I do to deserve this? he cried, tears on his cheeks. Where are You? When no one answered, he said, Then kill me. If I'm so worthless in Your sight, just strike me down and be done with it. *Don't let em use me like this.*

Again, no answer, save for the buzzing insects.

Boudreaux's chin dropped to his chest. He stayed on his knees, sobbing, for some time. When he finally stood, nothing had changed. Ephemeral grief, invisible pain, a wind made of razors. The night sounds seemed like a curtain that parted as he walked and closed behind him again, unaffected. As if he had never been there at all.

Gordon Boudreaux walked inside. Lantern light flickered in his bedroom window most of the night.

That same evening, Jack Hobbes found Clemens and a dozen Crusaders on his porch. The guards sipped from their canteens and looked at Hobbes as if he were a skunk that had just sprayed their mothers. Clemens had been squatting on his heels. Seeing Hobbes ride up, he straightened to his full height and spat.

Hobbes's hands twitched. *Might be worth dyin just to see the hole between his eyes.*

Instead, he dismounted. A guard with a handlebar mustache and a black wart on his neck stepped off the porch and came down the walk. Hobbes handed the reins to the man, whom he did not recognize. Take him to the livery, Hobbes said. He needs a rubdown and a feed bucket.

I don't take orders from you, the man said.

Better make it there unharmed too. Otherwise, I'll find you. Same goes for the saddle and bags.

The Crusader tensed. Hobbes stroked the handles of his pistols with his fingers and smiled.

Do it, Clemens barked, irritable. I have places to be.

The guard cleared his throat and snatched the reins without looking at Hobbes and led the horse away.

*Reckon I can kiss the ammo in them bags goodbye.*

The other Crusaders stepped into the yard and surrounded him, hands on their sidearms. Hobbes scoffed. Nobody better not shoot, or you'll kill each other.

Clemens met him in the middle, expressionless but for his eyes, which sparkled with madness. Jack Hobbes, for suspicion of treason against Lord Matthew Rook and the Bright Crusade, you're under arrest.

Hobbes looked at the sky as if checking for rain. His fingers stroked his grips again. Got proof of this here treason?

Clemens stepped closer, practically daring Hobbes to make a move. You're a long-time associate of the cowardly traitor, Gabriel Troy.

Hobbes locked eyes with the deputy envoy. If Gabe Troy was a traitor, so's your mother.

Clemens looked as if he wanted to eat Hobbes's kidneys in a pie, but he made no move. Troy's gone, he said. Your friends Ford, Long, and Boudreaux have proven their loyalty—to the Crusade. You haven't.

Sure their mommas would be right proud, except they're dead. Supposed to take me to the towers?

If it were up to me, we'd nail you to your roof and let your brain cook like bacon. But Mister Royster wants you confined to your house until further notice.

Ain't that lovely.

Sweat fell into Clemens's eyes. He wiped it away as if he wanted to kill it too. Hand over your weapons and go inside, or we'll cut you to pieces.

Hobbes looked at each guard as he spoke. Don't know when the Crusade started eatin its own. Wonder what happens when somebody decides y'all ain't loyal enough?

The guards said nothing, though he fancied one or two might have glanced away.

You have ten seconds to surrender those guns, Clemens said. Starting now.

Hobbes stroked the grips one more time, slowly, his index fingers easing toward the trigger guards. Clemens's jaw tightened.

Then Hobbes unbuckled his gun belt and held it out to the deputy envoy. Here, boy. Try not to scuff em.

Clemens took the weapons. Too bad. I was hoping you'd fight.

Hobbes tipped his hat. Sure you did. Maybe one day we can see how tough you are without all this backup. He walked toward the house, shouldering Clemens hard as he passed. The guards followed him, breaking into groups and surrounding the house. At the door, Hobbes glanced back over his shoulder. This ain't over.

Yes, Clemens said. It is. For you, and for all Troublers.

The two remaining guards positioned themselves on either side of the door and waited, watching, their bodies humming with tension, perhaps fear.

Across the street, Mordecai Jones and Tommy Gautreaux observed the proceedings. Gautreaux's white shirt clung to his corpulent body like skin. He spat black tobacco juice and nodded. Jones touched a finger to his hat brim.

Hobbes tilted his chin upward an inch.

Jones and Gautreaux walked away. Clemens turned, but there was nothing to see except the sweaty backs of two men who might have been anybody.

Hobbes opened his door and went inside.

Ernie Tetweiller sat on his couch, windows closed, curtains pulled, doors locked. A lit lantern sat next to him on an end table; in his lap, a bottle of moonshine confiscated from a Troubler nest no more than a month before Jevan Dwyer arrived. Tetweiller took out the cork and swigged. The liquor burned his throat and set fire to his stomach. He should not have been drinking. His guts often pained him and sometimes sent a little blood to garnish his stool. He needed a stiff belt, though. It had taken all his self-control not to shoot Benn when the son of a bitch showed up with a cadre of guards and demanded Tetweiller's sidearms.

If you was a man, you would have come by yourself, Tetweiller had said.

Benn's face had been blank, his round body soaked in sweat. I don't have to prove anything to you, old man. Turn those pistols over or draw them. Let's have done with this.

Benn had not particularly seemed to enjoy the duty. If he had, Tetweiller probably would have drawn and gotten himself killed. He did not like the deputy envoy, but Benn was better than the other one, that Clemens. *Solid as a cypress stump, Benn is. Might be he ain't the worst swingin dick the Crusade could have sent, but it don't stop him from lickin Royster's boots like a trained dog.*

When Benn held out his hand, the ex-lord turned over his guns and came inside, wondering if anyone would notice how the pistols looked a bit too old, too worn. *If they got an eye for such things and they ain't too full of their own hot air, they might wonder. But I think they're pretty damn sure they got us right where they want us. Why pay close attention to bugs you done squished?* The guns he surrendered had been his worst pair, confiscated from his first-ever arrested Troubler nearly fifty years ago, and they had been in pretty poor shape even then. *That Troubler lived in a drainage culvert. The only thing wetter and rustier than them guns was the man himself.*

Tetweiller had cached most of his weapons around the city, along with his share of the other supplies they had prepared in anticipation of Royster's arrival. He had kept one extra pair of six-guns, his favorites, and a good supply of ammo hidden beneath the floorboards under his bed. Even if the Crusade quartered as many as three guards in the house, he believed he could take them out and fetch those guns, for he knew the layout even in pitch darkness, the location of every object he might weaponize. He knew where he might hide for a few moments and where he would be vulnerable.

*Jack ain't part of Royster's little circle either. I wonder what's happened to him. If they try to arrest him, will he let em? Are they crazy enough to gun him down in front of God and everybody? Maybe they'll take him—us— across the river, like they did with Gordy. And Gordy came back different.*

Then there was Laura Derosier and Antoine Baptiste. Troy had said those two were recruiting for the Conspiracy. Had they just happened to be walking across the street when Benn showed up, or had they come to witness? Derosier had not made eye contact. She just passed by, head bobbing on the end of that long neck like a pigeon's, but Tetweiller had seen the bulges in her pockets and under her shirt. She probably had more knives on her than a porcupine had quills. Baptiste had nodded to Tetweiller as they passed.

The old man took another drink of the moonshine and grimaced. It was powerful stuff, even to someone more used to alcohol than any Crusader should have been. *Maybe I should save the four bottles stashed in the icebox. They'll make fine incendiaries if it comes to that. I'd hate to burn this house down, though. Too many good memories.* He thought of Gabriel Troy, whose own house had been burned to the ground on Royster's orders. Tetweiller had gone to see it and came home to find Benn and his lackeys. *Where you at tonight, Gabriel? Did that bitch Stransky shoot you in the goddam back as soon as you cleared the city, or did she really show you her nest?* So much was uncertain. Stuck here, he might know nothing until the floodwaters came or the guards out front burst in and shot him.

He took one more drink and recorked the bottle. Then he set it on the end table beside the lamp and settled back, feeling the alcohol work its magic. Perhaps in the light of morning, things would seem clearer.

## 22

**B**efore dawn, Santonio Ford rode to the sisters', hoping for a word with Sarah Gonzales. *Gabe always seemed more at peace after talkin with her. Maybe she can do somethin for me.* But when he arrived, the sanctuary doors were locked. That had never happened before. He knocked four or five times. No one answered. He circled around and tried the back door. It was locked too. Ford waited until the sun came up, but no one stirred. He mounted up and rode through the neighborhood, stopping at Catholic residences. No one answered. They had cleared out overnight.

Later, as Ford tended his crops, the sun shone brighter than it had any right to, given the suffering under it. *At least we'll die on full stomachs.* The work helped him focus on what had happened during that chase. Troy in his sights, the old thrill of the hunt, his blood singing, a perfect clarity of mind and senses, the exhilaration when he aimed, the triumph when his bullet grazed one of his oldest friends. He had shown more loyalty to Gabriel Troy than to any other earthly man, but hunting him had still been hunting, what he had been made for, what he loved.

Until that moment, he had known in his heart that Troy was right. He still wanted to believe it. He intended to meet his trusted lieutenants, to have them recruit. He even planned to reach out to Hobbes's and Tetweiller's people, now that the men had been arrested. But was he doing all that to help Troy or to compile information for Royster?

Dangerous avenues, doubt on all sides. And in a situation like this, doubt could get you killed.

As Ford hoed a row of carrots, Benn rode up on old Paladin, the horse Jack Hobbes had been using. Everyone's best mounts, a whole remuda, had been corralled in the wetlands. Ford had not told the envoys about those horses. That had to mean something.

Paladin had been Hobbes's best horse once, but he had long since been put out to stud. Until pressed back into service after Dwyer's arrival, he had capered about wherever the stable workers let him and took long naps in the sun. When Hobbes rode him again for the first time, he seemed changed—better posture, greater energy, even what appeared to be a more serious expression. Paladin had, in other words, acted like a soldier brought out of retirement. Now he had been confiscated. If the Most High was feeling merciful, the horse would not understand what was happening.

You're ridin my friend's horse, Ford said. It sounded like an accusation.

Benn spat. Jack Hobbes is no friend to any loyal Crusader. We suspect he and that old man have been conspiring with Gabriel Troy.

Ford dropped the hoe. *Suspect* ain't the same thing as *prove*.

Benn smiled, though his eyes were humorless and cold. You know better than that.

Yeah, Ford sighed. I reckon I do. But I've known them men all my life. I ain't never seen em do anything but what would keep this town safe and righteous.

But you can't watch them all the time, can you? Not even a lord of order can do that, which is why the Troublers have been so—well, troublesome.

I reckon so.

Benn dismounted. He knelt and gathered a fistful of rich black soil. He let it fall through his fingers and dusted his hand on his pants. Mister Royster wants to name you the new lord of order.

Ford had been drinking from his canteen. Now he almost choked. He wiped his mouth on the back of his hand. *Gotta be careful here. Showin weakness in front of this man is the same as doin it before Royster.* Benn was shorter than Ford and seemed to be all but melting in the heat, but he radiated confidence. *If we stay on this path, one of us will have to deal with him. I think I can take him hand to hand, but it ain't guaranteed. I get the feelin that big belly hides some muscle.*

Gabriel Troy was the best lord of order this town's ever had, Ford said. I know. I've studied the histories. Him turnin Troubler's got nothin to do with his faith and everything to do with his love for New Orleans. He knew it better than any of us and loved it more. I can't match that.

Mister Royster thinks you can.

I got too much on me already. Crops to work, traps to check, hunts to organize, the killin and the cleanin and the saltin and the smokin and the storin. If this was winter, I might be able to delegate the crops, but it ain't winter. Find somebody else.

Benn looked at him for a long time. Ford looked right back, eyes open and steady. The afternoon went silent around them. Even the birds held their tongues.

Mister Royster will be disappointed, Benn said.

I reckon he'll understand. Somebody's gotta feed all these folks y'all are bringin in.

If Benn felt any true displeasure, he gave no sign. I'll deliver your sentiments. Keep up the good work, Mister Ford.

Ford drank again. Benn climbed back into the saddle—also one of Jack Hobbes's old ones—and turned Paladin toward the road. After the deputy envoy ambled out of sight, Ford picked up the hoe and attacked the rows again, his back muscles aching. Later he would have to find his lieutenants and warn them to expect a new lord of order. The burgeoning prison would soon have its warden, one more step toward whatever fate awaited them all.

## ✤ 23 ✤

**L**aShanda Long handed her reins to a night groom in the Temple courtyard. It was nearly dark—time for her appointment with Royster. She looked up at the stained-glass window. Gabriel Troy no longer worked up there, probably never would again. She sighed. *I've come to hate this place worse than sin. Ever since Dwyer rode into town, it's brought us all nothin but pain.*

Earlier, she had been washing up after a day's forging, every muscle aching, her right arm numb. Over and over in her mind, Troy fell from the bridge and disappeared. She imagined him washed up on shore, head split open, or floating far downriver, one of her own bullets lodged in his heart. She had tried to beat those images out of her head, the red-hot metal under her hammer shaping what would be a broadsword. It would stand nearly as tall as she did, too cumbersome for most people to wield, though Jevan Dwyer could do it.

But then—*speak of the devil, and he shall appear*—a figure in the doorway blocked out the sunlight. Even with his features backlit, Dwyer was unmistakable—that muscular build, the long and flowing hair, the upright stance, legs shoulder-width apart, arms folded.

Her hammer lay nearby. The partially finished sword rested on an anvil. Soot caked her arms and face. Her long hair was pinned back, the open-throated shirt revealing more of herself than Dwyer likely cared to see.

She straightened and wiped her hands on her dirty pants. Not the best image for meeting someone high-level, but it would have to do. Royster had accepted her. The herald could take her or leave her.

Dwyer stepped inside. Good day, Madame Weaponsmith. I hope you are well.

She sat on a stool and drank from her canteen. I reckon I can't complain. Yourself?

Dwyer smiled, though he seemed rather sad. He pulled up another stool and sat. Then he took his multicolored string out of his pocket and knitted shapes and swirls and loops, his fingers like a pianist's.

I had hoped, once I delivered my message, that Mister Royster would allow me to aid his mission or leave, he said. Instead, I have sat mostly idle. I've ridden through this city three times over. It truly is a beautiful place.

Yeah. Too bad it won't last a month under prison conditions.

But ours is not to reason why, is it? We serve at the pleasure of our God and our divinely appointed leaders. And they have decided. I wish it weren't so, but it is. As well try to stop the tides.

*He really does seem sad. There's humanity in those eyes. For a fella used to ridin the roads, stickin in one place makes this town his prison too. I could almost feel sorry for him. Almost.*

His pectorals rippled under his tunic. Veins and tendons road-mapped his exposed forearms. He would have made a fine smith.

What's your business? she asked. I'm about ready to drop.

Dwyer stood and put away his string. He bowed like a man asking for the next dance. Mister Royster still finds me useful as a messenger, it seems. He requires your presence in his office. Come at nightfall.

She raised her eyebrows. What for?

That, the envoy did not confide.

All right. I'll be there.

Dwyer looked at the sword, his eyes bright and dazzling in the forge's glow. Is this to be a broadsword?

That's right.

I have always wanted one. I love the tales of the original Crusaders, who ventured deep into heathen lands and fought the devil's spawn in their own streets. Perhaps one day you could make such a weapon for me.

I reckon anything's possible.

Soon enough Dwyer excused himself, and Long spent the rest of the afternoon on the sword, trying not to think of Troy. Then she rode to her two-story wooden home on Esplanade's 1900 block, her mind awash with images—Dwyer and Royster standing together before the Crusade flag, Bibles in hand; Troy's body floating through the murk, neck broken, legs smashed; her heart and soul pulled in separate directions like the rope in tug-of-war. She hitched her horse to the gate standing in the shadow of the house's beautiful design—white columns on the porch and second-floor balcony. The upstairs balustrade. The small flower garden near the walk, the cypress tree just off the street. Too much house for her. She had not wanted it. But Troy had convinced her to take it, knowing she often brought her work home, that she would need space to lay out the arrows and bows she hand-carved, the old guns she took apart and cleaned and oiled and reassembled while others spent their evenings with friends. Despite her initial reticence, she had been happy here. Now the cypress limbs shuddering in the breeze looked like Troy's, flapping as he fell.

She washed up and rode to the Temple, thinking of conscience and duty.

The towers loomed, monuments to God's strength and the Crusade's mission. They were Royster's, like the rest of New Orleans, the familiar made alien. A church from which even God had fled. She did not want to go in there. But when duty called, she had ever answered.

Long walked toward the front doors, wondering whether the guards would look her in the face.

They did. They even saluted. One of them opened the doors. At the front desk, Norville Unger stopped shuffling his ever-present papers and bowed.

*Now what's got into that old fool?*

Near the back stairs, the personnel had lined up against the walls. They held stiff salutes. What to make of it all? Perhaps Royster had ordered them to observe all the niceties, another sign of Troy's absence.

She took the stairs two at a time, ready to start the meeting so it could end. *This place is so different. It might as well be on the moon.* When she reached Troy's office, Benn and Clemens stood on either side of the closed door, thumbs tucked into their gun belts.

Benn stepped forward. Good evening, Deputy Long. I hope your day went well. He stuck out his hand.

She shook it. Benn's grip strength rivaled Santonio Ford's. He might have been fat, but he was strong. That depends on what's waitin in yonder, she said. You gonna let me in?

Certainly.

Benn backed away. Clemens had not moved. Their faces were fresh sheets stretched across a bed. She took a deep breath and stepped inside before she could change her mind. No one followed her.

Royster sat at Troy's desk and grinned, as he had done so often since his arrival. Clad in his robes of office, Jerold Babb stood to Royster's left, liver-spotted hands clasped at his waist.

Royster gestured to one of Troy's straight-backed chairs. Long took it.

Good evening, the envoy said. I trust our Father has blessed you today.

I think that depends on what happens here, Long said for the second time in less than a minute.

Royster picked up a steaming mug of coffee and sipped it, watching her over the rim, eyes gleaming like a clever animal's in torchlight.

When he put his cup down, he said, Weaponsmith Long, can the Bright Crusade lean on your strength and depend on your heart? Or does the city of New Orleans hold sway over you, as it did Gabriel Troy?

Long clenched her teeth. *What do I have to do, have a first-born child and sacrifice it on a stone altar?* She breathed, exhaled, breathed, exhaled. I showed you where I stand when I chased my lord of order off a bridge, she said. And before that, I shot him.

LaShanda, Babb scolded. Haven't we had enough bickering? Do you want Mister Royster to believe we are all malcontents?

Royster sipped coffee and watched her.

Long wanted to slap the mug out of his hand and scream. No, that was not true. She wanted to shoot him and toss Babb through the window. Royster had ridden into her city and filled it with so-called Troublers, many of whom seemed about as dangerous as a dead fly on a windowsill. He had driven Troy away. He had made her doubt her faith, the state of her soul. Babb had watched it all, approved it. He had taken his morning toast and tea with the scent of starving children's rabbitlike turds in his nostrils. And now they wanted more. *Well, I'm done. Let em lock me in the tower. Somebody else will have to kill Jack or Ernie or whoever they're scared of now.* She looked Royster in the eye but said nothing else.

You speak true, Madame Weaponsmith, the envoy said. But your work is not yet done.

So what's next? she asked. *When you name another one of my friends, I'll spit in your eye.*

The city still needs a lord of order, Royster said. Troy was unfit, and Santonio Ford has refused the office. Thus, this cup passes to you.

Royster was still smiling that shark's smile, his hands folded on the desk. Even Babb grinned, revealing his crooked yellow old man's teeth. Long sat in her chair, thunderstruck. She had expected another arrest order or even an assassination, but in some ways, Royster had named an even worse fate.

I don't know what to say. My duties—

City records indicate you have often spent days at a time scouring the city and outlying areas for Troubler nests, which proves you are already familiar with strategy and procedure. It also indicates you can delegate. I assure you that you may continue to inspect your forges at will.

I just don't know—

LaShanda, Babb said, we raised you better than this. The Most High's will—

Royster held up a hand, frowning. Babb shut up.

Let me be frank, the envoy said. This is not a request. Mister Ford has refused, claiming he must concentrate on feeding the populace. Perhaps his people are not as well trained as yours. We cannot give the position to Mister Boudreaux. We are grooming him for different work.

What about Jack Hobbes or Ernie Tetweiller? They've both got seniority.

Babb looked away. Royster stopped smiling. Misters Hobbes and Tetweiller are no longer available.

Long's stomach knotted. Her hands trembled. *Are Jack and Ernie dead? And what's this other work they got Gordy doin? He's been scarce as hen's teeth lately.*

Can I ask what *no longer available* means?

Royster's voice was flat and even. They have been placed under house arrest.

On what charge?

Sedition.

*Not dead, thank God. Not dead.* She did not know whether she could bear losing another close friend. I just can't see that, she said.

Has everyone in this city lost their minds? Babb cried. We do not question the church's edicts.

Please, Minister, Royster said, the edge in his voice belying the words. Madame, your faith in your friends is the reason you were not tasked with their arrest. But their taking office is out of the question.

And Troy is dead. I could name someone new to the city, but I believe New Orleans's citizens need continuity in leadership. Don't you?

He smiled again.

Not for the first time, Long wondered whether she had ever seen an expression so insincere, so cold. He was thrusting this position at her as if it were fire and his own hair was catching. Who knew what might happen if she refused? House arrest at best, the towers or a bullet in the brain at worst. *No choice. Some of us gotta stay free, don't we? Or is that the devil talkin? Lord, it's gettin so I can barely remember not bein all at sea.*

Royster was waiting.

I reckon I accept, she sighed.

Finally, some sense, Babb said, raising his hands, eyes closed. Thank You, Lord.

Royster's grin widened. He stood and stuck out his hand. Long got to her feet and shook it. Congratulations, Lord Long. May you smite the Troubler scourge wherever you find it.

I'll do my best to serve with honor. But you'll have to pardon me if I don't thank you.

Royster let go of her hand and indicated her chair. They took their seats again. Royster patted his chest where he had been branded. Once our new prison is complete, you and Misters Ford and Boudreaux will take on the symbol of your earthly ascension so you may ride back to Washington marked as one of God's greatest servants. As for tonight, we must discuss the city's transition. Minister Babb, you may go.

The high minister bowed and shuffled out, leaving Long to wonder what she might be called to do in the coming days.

As she left the office, Benn and Clemens snapped to attention and saluted. Long returned the gesture but did not linger. She walked downstairs, thinking. Royster had not told her everything, of course.

She would probably have to execute Hobbes or Tetweiller to earn that much confidence, which she would not do, no matter what. Still, the envoy had said enough. The Crusade's great wall would be completed sooner than anyone had suspected. The combination of careful planning and nearly unlimited prisoner labor had expedited it. After its raising, she would take control of the prison, which meant supervising her guards as they shot anyone who tried to scale the wall or tunnel under it or blow it up or use the river as egress. But as brutal as that task seemed, it was illusory, for Royster had also confirmed that charges had been set at key waterways across the city. The envoy claimed they were a fail-safe in case of a full-scale revolt. That sounded plausible, but thanks to Lynn Stransky, Long knew better. That ordnance would bring the killing waters down on the damned and the saved alike. And with everyone dead, what need would the Crusade have for a lord of order? Or a warden? Or her colleagues?

*If that's the Crusade's will, I should bow to it. Every lesson I was ever taught says so. Maybe that's why I wounded Gabe. But a Purge. It's one thing to read about the first one. It's another to know I'm helpin kill tens of thousands of people, many of em the Lord's own. How can that be right?*

She entered the sanctuary. The Temple workers stood at attention against the walls. They saluted in unison, eyes forward. She had never seen them act with such military precision. *Sweet Lord. Somehow, somewhere, Royster must have started drillin em. Why? Temple personnel almost never fight.*

Maybe he was just keeping them busy, passing the time before their own sentences were carried out.

They were still holding the salute when she passed through the Temple doors and into the courtyard. The guards outside saluted too. When she reached the hitching post, the grooms would likely follow suit. Word was spreading. A new lord of order reigned for the first time in years.

## ✤ **24** ✤

**N**ight fell. The cold stars shone—ageless, indifferent to New Orleans and humanity and the turning Earth. Humidity hung heavy on the city. Sweat soaked Santonio Ford's body as he sat his black mare with the gray socks, the only truly strong horse he had kept out of the remuda. The envoys seemed unlikely to confiscate it as long as Ford worked for them.

The woman was late, and Ford had no idea who she was, beyond the fact that she was a Hobbes subordinate. How could you know you were being set up when you did not even know whom to look for?

Willa McClure had arranged the meeting for three hours after sunset, plenty of time to get home and settled, to sneak out. Plenty of time for the heat to enervate the night guards. Yet the woman had not arrived. *If she got captured or just changed her mind and stayed home, I don't know what I'll do. But I don't know what I'll do if she shows up either. I'm goin through the motions in two different worlds, servin both the Crusade and the Conspiracy with half conviction.*

This meeting would be the forge in which he would craft his future.

He hoped the woman's appearance would coincide with some affirmation of what was right, but so far, hidden deep in the shadows under Armstrong Park's trees, he had seen nothing unusual. The incoming Troublers had not yet reached the park, but they would soon. Every waterway would be guarded, each sentry ready to kill any citizen who tried to leave. Except for the rare diplomatic trip to Baton Rouge or Lafayette, Ford had never traveled more than twenty miles from the city's borders. Now he probably never would. The wall inched farther around New Orleans every day, like a great snake ready to squeeze the life from them all. Once it was completed, either the Troublers would slaughter everyone or Royster's guards would.

All the Troublers Ford had seen—the ones he had killed, the countless numbers who had lived since the ancients' time—surely some of them had envisioned grander acts than stealing a bushel of grain or blowing up a building or assassinating an official. An end to the Crusade itself, the establishment of a Troubler nation, a new world religion. Yet the Crusade endured. Was that the sign Ford needed? Or was the Troublers' undying opposition the true signal?

Approaching hoofbeats—a shadowed figure ambled toward him. He gripped the crossbow across his lap. If the rider were an unknown Crusader, Ford would have no excuse for sitting in the dark, alone and long past curfew. He would have to put a bolt through the person's throat before they could cry out. His heart beat heavily in his chest.

*Forgive me, Father God. This is what we've come to. Murder from ambush. None of us justified.*

But as the rider drew closer, Ford recognized the way she sat her horse, the outline of her body—Nella Charters. Hobbes had handpicked her to ride with them on several raids of suspected Troubler nests in his territory. *Good in the saddle. A fine shot. Brave and true.* Still, with so much at stake, Ford kept one hand on the crossbow. If she made a move, he would get only one chance.

She reined her horse next to Ford's and whispered, That Clemens fella picked tonight to ride through our neighborhoods. Took me a while to slip through, but I don't think he saw me.

And what if he did?

Charters pulled her shirt away from her body and flapped it and fanned herself with her other hand. I reckon I'd be under arrest, she said. We'd know by now if they followed me.

Ford's mare nickered and sniffed the new arrivals. He patted her neck. I reckon so. How's your husband and them?

Ready to spit nails. Some outlanders came by and told us we'd have to move. We knew it was comin, but Lars near about throttled a guard anyway. It's the only home we've ever known.

And your young uns?

We're tryin to keep em in good spirits, but it's hard, lyin to em.

Sometimes lies are necessary, Ford said and hated himself for it. *Forgive me my own lies, Father God. Help me find the kind of surety Ernie and Jack and the envoys have.* He could see the fruit his actions bore as if with two sets of eyes—Royster's face, blood dripping from a bullet hole in the forehead; Gabriel Troy's body floating out to sea, nibbled by sharks and gulls.

Charters watched him. Where y'at?

Fine.

She seemed about to press the matter, but she let it drop. So Jack's stuck in his house. What now?

*That's the question of a lifetime.* We keep on goin and hope things turn out right. What can you tell me about y'all's operation?

Jack contacted around a dozen of us, and each of us found half a dozen more. I'm estimatin, you understand. Everybody's been goin down the line like that. I'm hopin we'll have time to turn half our people before the end. We'll have to hope the rest throw in with us once the shootin starts.

Or that they sit it out at least.

Yep. Speakin of that, some folks are just gone.

Gone?

Charters's horse snorted. She patted its neck and whispered to it. As in disappeared. No idea if the guards took em or if they just snuck out after dark. Most of their stuff's still in their houses.

Ford pondered that. If Royster were winnowing down New

Orleans's population in secret, time was even shorter than Ford had believed. He had seen no New Orleanians in chains, but they could have been taken over the bridge in the night, one family at a time. Or they might have ducked into the bayous to join the Troublers. Fled to Mississippi or Texas or across the ocean.

*Ain't no way this is good. Every day we find out we know even less than we thought.*

From a few blocks over, raised voices. Ford and Charters fell silent. He could not tell whether they came from the Quarter or deeper in Treme. A gunshot echoed through the streets, then a scream, more shouts, an angry chorus. Definitely Treme.

The guards just shot somebody, Charters said. And the prisoners ain't happy about it. We better get on.

Let's meet back here in three days, Ford said. Keep doin what you're doin. Bring me some solid numbers if you can, and any news. If you can't come, send Lars.

Will do. You heard anything about Troy? Is he dead or alive?

Ford said nothing for a moment. Then, his voice barely audible even in the close quarters, he said, Ernie was supposed to meet him after the bridge, but then Ernie got arrested. So I don't know. None of us do.

Three nights later, Ford was back in Armstrong Park. He had gone to the stables to get the mare, but once he saw her, he stared at her for a long time and moved on. Instead, he had picked Thessalonians, his oldest horse that could still bear a rider. Thess and Ford had ridden down rabbits, deer, Troublers. Once they had even brought down a bear, Thess charging the creature against all instinct and sense. They had watched sunrises and sunsets, stood in knee-deep grassy meadows, warmed themselves by the same fires.

Still, if someone had asked Ford why he took Thess instead of the mare, he would not have been able to explain. His gut told him Thess was right for this job, and his gut had seen him through a lifetime of blood fighting. Good to hear it talking again.

From somewhere nearby, the acrid smell of burned meat, a scent that stuck in the back of your throat. Frogs and crickets sang nocturnes while squirrels and cats and raccoons chased each other through the shadows.

It was an hour past the meeting time, and no sign of Charters.

*Somethin's wrong.*

Ford gathered his reins.

But before he could spur, someone came running down the street, crouching low and hugging the shadows. Ford reached into his saddle-bags and took out the pistol fitted with the suppressor. He could have brought the crossbow again, but when he had reached for it, he had picked up the pistol instead. Faster firing, faster reloading. He had no reason to think he would need such a weapon, but his gut had insisted.

Still, shooting human beings, even the vilest Troubler, had always made him feel dirty, especially from ambush. *And then I was justified, or believed I was. I beseech you again for clarity, Father God.* The running figure was closer now, a distinct outline instead of a moving glob. The body, the hair, the gait seemed both familiar and female. *Gotta be Charters. She's afoot. That's bad.* He laid the pistol across his saddle. Then he folded his hands across the pommel and waited.

Charters spotted him and trotted over, panting and sweaty, her long brown hair matted against her skull.

So, Ford said. How was your day?

She bent over, hands on her knees. They know, she croaked.

Know what?

That somebody turned. They're lookin hard at all of us.

It felt as if Thess had kicked Ford in the guts. No one had mentioned any new suspicions. What had happened over the last three days?

How do you know they know? he asked.

They doubled our guards and took some folks away for interrogation. Everybody's scared to death.

*Is this your answer, Father God?* The Conspirators had calculated the most likely times when a guard's back might be turned, when the noise of the prisoners would drown the sounds of whispered conversation, but in Hobbes's territory, it had come to naught.

Who slipped up? Ford asked.

I don't know. Charters panted and gasped. She tried to spit, but the saliva was too thick and stuck to her chin. She wiped it away.

Well, who did they take?

A whole passel of folks.

Who, blast it?

Charters stood upright and glanced over her shoulder. Tommy Gautreaux's cousin Lorne. And his wife. And their boys.

Even the children.

Yeah. Even them.

Do the envoys have our names?

No.

Thank the Father. I—

Coldness engulfed his innards.

Charters looked toward the street again. Then she turned back to him, wiping sweat from her brow. Even in the dark, she seemed to sense his apprehension. What? she said.

How could you know?

Know what?

That they ain't got our names?

She hesitated. Because if they knew about us, we'd be dead or in chains.

Charters's clothes stuck to her as if they had been tarred there. Yet she trembled—just barely, but noticeable to Ford's hunter's eye. And she kept looking at the street, as if she expected Matthew Rook himself to pop out from behind the park's gates.

What's wrong with you? Ford asked. You're skittish as a doe.

I just told you, she said, still looking away. They're watchin us.

The coldness spread through Ford's chest and down to his testicles. Something was happening here.

Then how'd you get away at all? he asked.

I fell in with a bunch of em headin for chow. They never noticed when I slipped away.

Just because I ain't Jack Hobbes don't mean you can lie to me.

She said nothing for a moment. Then she sighed. I told em it would never work.

Ford went for the silenced pistol, but her arm flashed out, and hot pain ripped across the back of his hand. He jerked back, knocking the gun off the saddle. Warm blood splashed onto his pants, his horse. Thess whinnied and backed away.

Charters held a butcher's knife, her legs shoulder-width apart and bent at the knees. She stood perhaps four feet away.

Ford cradled his injured hand against his chest. How long you been with em?

Charters stepped closer. Thess nickered and danced back, as if the woman were a rattlesnake. I ain't with em, she said. Not in my heart. But the other night, a patrol caught me comin home. They took Lars. They took my *kids*.

Despair hammered Ford's chest like physical blows. Where?

To the old compound across the river. Stuck em in a cell with one bunk and one chamber pot, no food or water.

Bright red arrows of pain shot from Ford's hand all the way to his neck. And this is how you get em out.

Charters slid closer. Thess backed away.

Part of you wants to get caught, she said, sounding sad and resigned.
I've heard it in your voice. You got doubts.

Don't presume to know my heart.

She tossed the knife from hand to hand. All right. But I ain't goin
back without you.

He scanned the shapeless ground for the pistol. If he lived through
this, he could not leave it.

*Keep her talking.* And what if you do? he asked.

They chain my kids together and toss em in the river. While they're
still alive. Then they send me Lars's head.

*There it is. I was selfish enough to ask for a sign, and now Nella's payin
the price. The Crusade eats its young.* I'll ask you again. You owe it to Jack
to tell the truth. Do they know our names?

Not from me. The deal is, I give em my contact in the park. I didn't
even tell em who you was. Like you said. I owe Jack.

You really think they'll honor the bargain? Ford asked. On the
ground, a shape that might have been his pistol. They'll kill your family
and torture you until you give up every name you know.

Maybe. But if there's a chance to save my kids, I'm takin it. Get off
the horse.

She stepped forward. Thess backed away.

Give me a day, Ford said. I'll figure out a way to save your family.

You couldn't even save Troy, and he wasn't in no fortress. She continued to toss the knife back and forth, easing closer, closer. We were
fools to think we could beat em, Santonio. Just give up. Maybe we can
save our souls.

Thess circled away from her. Ford tried to keep track of that shape
on the ground. Don't do this, he said. I can just leave. Tell em I never
showed.

I told you. I can't go back empty-handed. Now get down from there.

Ford looked past her. I reckon they followed you.

They're hangin back. I convinced em you'd hear em all comin, so they gave me ten minutes to bring you in. Or gut you. Now it's almost up. Get off that horse before I hamstring you where you sit.

Ford dismounted. His six-guns bounced against his thigh. He hoped he could draw faster than she could close the distance. There's gotta be a way outta this. For both of us.

She moved past a break in the trees, revealing herself in the moonlight. She was weeping. This is the best I can do—this knife. I told em I was better with a blade than a gun, so you got a fair chance. If I get you, maybe it saves my family. If you get me, they can't say I didn't try. Maybe they'll pity my kids.

She came forward and slashed at him. Ford dodged.

If they had pity, he said, they wouldn't do this to you in the first place.

Shoot me or die, Santonio. Right now.

She leaped forward, thrusting the blade at him. It missed his throat by millimeters.

From the south, a dull glow—torches, a couple of dozen at least. Charters turned the knife over in her hand, the blade pointed at her elbow.

Ford did not draw.

Charters bared her teeth, raised the knife over her head, and lunged, arcing it down. He grabbed her wrist with his injured hand. She punched him in the jaw. He kneed her in the gut and then let go of her and kicked her in the sternum. She crashed against a tree and groaned. The moonlight filtering through the trees cast abstract patterns on her upturned face. She leaned there for a moment, looking at him. The stamp of horses' hooves grew closer.

Damn you, she spat. This ain't no schoolyard dustup. Get serious.

Nella, he said. Come with me. I'll hide you. I promise you we'll find a way to get your family out.

She watched him a moment. Then she pushed away from the tree, the knife pointing at his heart. What would Gabe Troy say about your promises? You say you're on his side, but you ran him right off that bridge. How are you better than Clemens?

There's things you don't know.

She laughed. It was bitter, like citrus peel or wild chicory. I wanted to fight you toe to toe and let God decide who goes home. But I can see your heart ain't in it. She turned and ran toward the glow and the hoofbeats, cupping her hands to her mouth, shouting, He's over here, in the park. It's Sant—

Ford shot her in the back. The report echoed off the buildings.

He looked at the pistol in his hand. He did not remember drawing.

Charters grunted and fell to one knee.

In the muzzle flash, he had seen the other pistol. He hunted around until his hand closed on it. He holstered his six-gun, stuck the silenced one in his belt, and ran to Charters.

Shouts from the south, louder hoofbeats. The torches' glow had doubled in size.

Here, she cried, holding one hand to her back.

Shut up, Ford hissed. Just hush. He tried to help her up.

She threw her body weight against him. He fell onto his hind-quarters. Charters landed in his lap, bleeding all over him, soaking his clothes. She was trying to scream again, but she had lost her wind, her voice little louder than a rasp. Over here. Ford's over here.

The torch glow broke into individual points, the sounds of shod hooves thundering on the ground. Charters kept trying to scream.

Ford took the knife from her loose grip and cut her throat.

He pushed her away. She rolled onto her back, blood misting upward, spilling out of the wound in a torrent, pooling beneath her. Her eyes bugged out, and she sputtered, grasping at her neck. More blood spurted with each heartbeat. Ford stood, but not before it seeped into his pants from the knees down. His hair dripped with it. His shirt was soaked through. Charters spasmed, clawed the ground, gurgled.

Ford knelt beside her and leaned close. Charters looked at him, her throat grinning. When she exhaled, red mist blew from her mouth and nostrils.

Nella, he whispered. Has anybody else turned? Any of my friends?

Her eyes dimmed, fluttered. He shook her a bit, and they opened again. Her lips moved. He leaned in closer, his ear against her mouth, but he could make nothing out. Perhaps she prayed.

He rose and scooted away as if she were a great spider that had clawed its way up from the earth's red heart. Her head lolled sideways, her cheek resting on the bloody ground. On the street, men and horses, raised voices.

Ford picked up her knife and saddled up and galloped away, through all the grass they could find and down roads and through yards, heading back toward Metairie.

Ford zigzagged on surface streets up toward Claiborne and back down to Rampart. He rode through alleys, past Troublers who paid him no mind, and swung wide of pickets fixed at intersections, keeping his head tucked behind Thess's neck, hoping the cover and the darkness would prevent any guard from identifying him. He rode more or less parallel to Veterans Memorial Boulevard until he veered off onto West Napoleon in Metairie, several blocks ahead of the posse, which had to hunt for him in every nook and chase every sound of echoing hoof-beats to their source. *Never knew I'd be so glad for the noisy streets*, Ford thought more than once.

He reined up and dismounted next to a crumbling building on Transcontinental between Zenith Street and West Napoleon. Taking his rifle out of its scabbard, he leaned it against the wall. Then he removed his saddle and dumped it and the scabbard several feet away. Next, Ford stripped off his bloody clothes and tossed them on the pile.

From somewhere back the way he had come, hoofbeats, shouts, someone barking orders.

He found the building's rear door, opened it, and stepped inside. Citizens seldom ventured into decaying places like this one unless they were part of a demolition crew. You never knew what might fall on your head. Such places worked well for caches.

Against one wall lay a pile of old rags big enough to bury a man. Ford picked his way through the debris on the floor and dug through the rags until he found the pack secreted there. He pulled open the drawstrings and took inventory by feel—a quart jar full of lamp oil, flint and steel, two pistols and ammo. He took out the jar, the flint, the steel. Then he retied the bag and stuffed it back under the rags. If he had to shoot anybody, he was already as good as dead, so why bother?

Outside, he unscrewed the jar and dumped the oil over the saddle, scabbard, and bloody clothes. Then he struck the steel against the flint until his belongings burst into flame with a *whumph*. The heat scorched his face, likely singed some hair. Ford rubbed his eyes.

Thess nickered. Framed against the darkness, the horse looked tall and proud. Charters's blood had dried on Thess's coat in rivulets, savage and unknowable tattoos from a time before language. The hunter rested his forehead on the horse's, their respirations and heartbeats in rhythm. A single tear on his cheek, Ford kissed Thess's nose. I'm sorry, my friend. If I had known, I would have walked.

The posse's hoofbeats came closer. Only a block or two distant, guards cajoled each other to search harder, closer.

He wiped the tear away and stepped back. Then he cut Thess's throat.

Ford turned and ran out of the alley, away from Thess, who had fallen to his knees on the street. The weight of the night and what he had done under its cover lay heavy on Ford's conscience. A cry from the guards, the sounds of their horses. As he ran, Ford prayed—for

Charters and her family; for old Thessalonians, who deserved so much better; for himself.

He headed toward his two-story brick house on York Street near Lafreniere Park. He avoided the streetlamps, running through yards and vacant lots and alleys, the pavement warm under his bare feet. He saw no one. When he reached home, he leaped the fence into the back yard and removed the lid from his water basin. He cupped his hands and rinsed the blood from his face, his body, his long hair. A baptism as false as his murderous soul. He bathed for a long time. Then he dunked his entire head into the barrel, the water cool on his hot skin.

His hair sopping and pendulous, he grabbed the water barrel and rocked it back and forth, straining hard until it tipped over. Pink water spilled onto his grass and dispersed, sank into the thirsty soil, glittered in the starlight.

Ford went inside. In the bathroom, he lit the lamp by his mirror and examined his exhausted and guilty face. Then he toweled off, leaving faint pink smudges on the white fabric, and turned out the lamp. In his bedroom, he collapsed on his mattress, hoping no one would come knocking, knowing someone would.

He waited and tried not to think of Charters's face.

They came twenty minutes later. Ford let them knock three times before he threw on his trousers and answered. Five guards stood on his porch, one holding a lantern. Ford rubbed his eyes and squinted as if he had been asleep for hours.

Sorry to disturb you, the guard with the lantern said.

Ford faked a yawn. What's goin on?

Can we come in, sir? I'm afraid we've got some disturbing news.

The man's accent was unidentifiable. The outlanders had brought with them a Babel of slang, inflections, and pronunciations. Listening to them made Ford's head hurt. Still, he led the guards into his den and lit a couple of lamps. He gestured toward the furniture. They took their seats. He did not offer them water or food, though at least one looked at the carafe on the side table and licked his lips.

You'll forgive my directness, Ford said, but it's awful early, even for me. What can I do for you?

We need your help tracking a traitor, said the lantern-bearer.

Ford tried to look surprised. What traitor?

Recently a Troubler from Jack Hobbes's zone confessed to meeting a higher-up in a resistance group.

Resistance group. You mean the Troublers?

No. A new one.

Ford arched his brows. Don't sound likely. Ain't never had that kind of problem here.

Well, you might have it now. Our contact was supposed to capture the traitor near Armstrong Park. We hung back so we wouldn't spook them.

And your agent didn't bring nobody in?

The guard looked embarrassed. We moved in, but by the time we arrived, our contact's throat had been cut. She had also been shot in the back. We found the heathen's horse in the streets just in time to watch it die. Its throat had been cut too.

Ford tensed, gritted his teeth, made fists. The gestures were pure theater, but he did not have to feign anger and grief. Troubler scum, he said. Tell me, what did this horse look like?

The lantern-bearer described Thess. Ford let his expression become more and more dismayed. Do you recognize the animal, sir?

Yes. He's mine.

Now the guard looked surprised, as did his fellows. Sir?

I rode him this evenin. I hitched him on the street when I came in. Figured I'd ride him to work tomorrow. But when I looked outside, he was gone. I thought he just got loose and I'd find him in the mornin.

The traitor must have stolen him. That takes guts, considering you could track him to the ends of the earth, if what we've heard is true.

Troublers ain't known for their brains. What else?

We think he killed your horse to slow us down. We searched the nearby alleys and found a smoldering pile of refuse. It looked like the remains of a saddle. Beyond that, the trail has run cold.

All that action, and nobody saw nothin.

That's correct, sir.

Ford started pacing. He said nothing for a minute, perhaps two. Then he turned back to the guard. You want me to try to track him.

Yes, sir.

Fine. But if he stuck to the roads and he ain't bleedin or somethin, I don't know that I'll have much to work with.

The lantern-bearer stood. The others joined him. We'd appreciate your efforts.

One more thing, said Ford. He looked at each of the guards as he spoke. If this traitor hurts any of my folks because you let him rabbit, you'll answer to me.

The guard cleared his throat as the rest of them glanced at each other. We understand, sir. We'd also appreciate a list of anyone who might be sympathetic to Troublers.

Ford had started down the hall. Now he stopped and looked back. In my territory, you mean?

Yes, sir.

Ford stared at the man until he looked away. If I knew anybody like that, you'd have their names already. Now let me get dressed.

He returned three hours later, exhausted and heartsick. Riding on a borrowed horse beside the guards, Ford had explained how the High Temple staff kept a list of known Troublers and suspects, which was true, and that he had learned no new names since the list had last been revised, which was a lie. Under Royster's definition, most Crusaders he knew would be labeled Troublers.

*It hadn't never occurred to me that lots of folks might be a little bit of both, or maybe even neither.*

The outlanders had led him to the remains of his saddle and clothes. When he saw Thess's blood all over the alley, he nearly wept again. Instead, he pretended to cast about for signs, leading the guards out of the alley, then north. Miming the body language of tracking, he took them up one street and down another, doubling back every now and then for effect, until, three miles away, he stood upright and shook his head.

What trail there was ends here, Ford said. Either this traitor got more careful, or the Troublers picked em up on horseback. All I'm gettin now is the usual wear and tear of a thoroughfare.

The guards looked at each other, probably wondering what clues he had followed this far but, after the warning back in his living room, they were too nervous to ask.

You'll keep watch and report any suspicious activity? the lantern bearer asked.

Don't ask me another question like that. Makes me think you don't trust me.

The guard mumbled an apology. The group saluted. Ford turned the unfamiliar mount toward home in the early morning light as the city came to life.

*I'm so sorry, Thess.*

Now, back in his house, Ford removed his boots. Then he walked to the den and collapsed on the couch, where he slept for three hours. When he awoke, he sat for ten minutes and thought about how he had killed someone, had run from the Crusade, had lied to its representatives, had misled them, had misused his gifts and the power of his office. Yet no nightmares had troubled his sleep.

*I reckon that's my answer. I just hope it came from You, Father God.*

At noon, Ford stopped by Audubon Park's fields of corn and beans and peas and wheat. Stalks and plants reached for the sun like supplicants. Beyond the crops, stands of trees sheltered deer, raccoon, nutria, squirrel, sometimes even alligators that wandered from their watery haunts. Ford spent more time in this park than anywhere else, but he had hardly seen it since Royster's arrival. Today, several of his subordinates had spread blankets on the ground and were eating their lunches. No one looked happy. Few talked. Ford moved among them, waving them off before they could rise and salute. Someone handed him a plate of grilled beef, shrimp, and peppers and onions sautéed in beef fat, served over white rice. If he had shown up on a different day or time, he might have gotten a po' boy or a steaming bowl of gumbo or jambalaya. His cooks were the best in the world. Today, though, he barely registered the taste.

Quintus Vacla, the foreman, had not appeared. Odd. Vacla had spent every day of his working life plowing or reaping or picking a field, stowing food in barns, trapping prey in the woods. He had never taken a sick day. His sinewy limbs and solid torso seemed crafted for outdoor work in all weathers. He had trailed behind the plow horse despite a high fever, had checked his traps while a hurricane's outer edge kissed the city. His absence gave the place a truncated look, an arm with no hand.

Carol Mellichamp passed by and saluted. Ford grabbed her sleeve. You seen Quintus today?

Her brow furrowed. No. I figured he finally took sick. Should I worry?

I hope not.

No one else had seen Vacla either.

Altogether, Ford's hunter/gatherers constituted perhaps a fifth of New Orleans's population. They fed the city, guarded the crops from scavengers and Troublers, and controlled the local animal populations. As the park's foreman, Vacla's responsibilities were enormous. He would not abandon them.

A seed of dread took root in Ford's belly.

He ran to Rachel, the black mare with gray socks. He unhitched her, mounted up, and spurred her out of the park, riding hard for Vacla's house.

The yard was a tiny patch of green fronting an unpainted wooden house. Vacla had planted tulips and gardenias and honeysuckle bushes and verbena. Green vines wound about crude rusted metal columns holding up the porch overhang. A few years back, Vacla had moved in with his bride, a woman whose name Ford could no longer remember. Vacla never spoke of her. She died of fever a year into the marriage, taking with her the unborn child that would have been their first. Vacla never remarried or showed any inclination to start another family. He lived for his memories and his crops.

The front door was wide open. Someone had broken the latch. The dusty boot print near the knob told the story.

That seed of dread began to bloom. Ford drew one of his six-guns, cocked it, and went inside.

A chair and side table lay splintered on the wood floor. Broken lamps had spilled their oil everywhere. If someone had come along and tossed a lit match through the door, the whole place would have burned down in minutes. Ford followed the destruction—kitchen implements scattered, the bathroom basin crushed to powder—until he reached Vacla's bedroom, where he found bedclothes tossed about and blood spattered on the far wall, near the door leading to thirty square feet of back yard. *Quintus keeps his rain barrel back there, a storage shed full of tools, a little grill.* Ford opened the door and went outside. The grass had been trampled, the grill overturned, half-burnt wood chips and ashes scattered from its mouth. A blood trail led around the house and onto the street. Ford dragged Rachel away from Vacla's foliage, mounted up, and followed the blood, even though he knew where it was heading.

The trail, a scattering of droplets at three- or four-foot intervals, ended a few miles later on Airline Highway, which merged nearby with the Pontchartrain Expressway and headed southeast. *Hell and damnation. I knew it. They took him across the river, probably to that interrogation center.* Ford had asked Gordy Boudreaux about the place once, and Boudreaux had only stared at him for a moment and walked away. Ford had never been sure what that meant. Boudreaux had always been the most softhearted among them. He ate mostly vegetables, accepting a steak or a chop or a fish only once or twice a week. He scooted spiders outdoors instead of stepping on them and left food for strays on his walk. His job as a deputy lord might have seemed like a contradiction if it had not been for his faith in the righteousness of their cause, the belief that the Troublers threatened God's plan and that, if no other recourse existed, their deaths were just. But in these troubled times, a man like Boudreaux might have seen, perhaps even done, something that rattled him beyond repair.

Ford took the expressway, passing the great ruined dome of the ancients and noting places where the road needed repairs, if they should live so long. Reaching the base and getting Vacla out alive seemed impossible. He could not ride in with a better-armed force like he had always done with Troublers. For all he knew, the outlanders would shoot him on sight, if he even managed to cross the river in the first place.

⚜

Starving, stinking prisoners clustered everywhere, so many that, in places, Rachel could barely pass. The bridge loomed in the distance. The sun still sailed high and would for a few more hours. Its rays sparkled on the great river's eddies and backlit the buildings across the water.

*Will it make any difference if I wait till dark?*

If he tried, he would need a place to lay low, but nothing nearby seemed promising. People occupied the houses. Most of the other buildings had been converted to food storage, bunkhouses for river workers, warehouses full of fishing equipment. Those unrestored since the old times and those flattened by hurricanes provided no cover.

*There's that place a few streets back, where we store some of our old documents. It's been repaired just enough to keep it standin. It's isolated enough so I should be able to sneak in and out easy, and I can't see any reason they'd be watchin it. Our old crop statistics shouldn't matter to Royster.*

Twenty yards away, a group of guards noticed him. One saluted. Ford returned it. Then he turned Rachel and headed toward the archive. More light bled out of the day, leaching color and texture from the world. The houses, painted white or not at all, began to lose their sharp edges. The grass, nearly midcalf high in the neighborhoods awaiting their next landscaping day, metamorphosed from bright green to a kind of purple that would soon give way to grayish black. Dogs barked at him from behind fences. Children ran to the street and waved. He kept watch on his six, looking for a tail, but saw nothing. A handful of citizens passed on their way to or from work, but because the prisoners had not reached the area yet, no guards.

*If anybody questions me about what I was doin here, I need to have a story ready.* The archive looked even more isolated and forlorn than he remembered—the paint worn away, the paved walk disintegrating, the foliage overgrown. He looked about one last time, saw no one, and tried the door. It was old and warped and crumbling, a body whose soul had departed long ago. The knob nearly pulled free from the wood.

*We should move our documents or repair this place. It's a fire waitin on a spark.*

Ford walked Rachel around the structure and hitched her to a ragged sawtooth oak that had seen one too many storms. *Hopefully she don't just rip it outta the ground and drag it down the road without me.* Perhaps, as the sun set, the shade and the building would hide her long enough. He patted her head and then circled the building again.

Inside, it smelled of dust and animal. Even the air felt dirty. It was dim, but Ford's eyes adjusted quickly.

A human shape sat on a crate ten feet away. It was small and strapped, sidearms tight against its hips. On the ground in front of it, a lumpy shape moved about.

When I seen you followin that trail, said Willa McClure, I figured you'd come here sooner or later.

The shape at her feet moved toward Ford and coalesced into Bandit the dog. Ford held out his hand. Bandit licked it and sat, scratching the back of his head.

Ford could not make out McClure's expression. You trackin me?

You rode too fast for us to catch you.

Well, why were you tryin?

You got a nice ass.

Quit it. This is serious.

Last night, we seen some Crusaders take Vacla across the bridge.

Ford rubbed his strained, sleepless eyes. I was afraid of that. Is he at the base?

Yep.

How'd you get over there without the guards seein you?

The dog rolled onto his back. McClure came over and rubbed his belly. Didn't try to get inside. Folks was moanin and screamin, so it didn't seem like a good place to visit. But it didn't matter. Just before sunrise, they carried Vacla down to the river and dumped him in.

Anger bloomed in Ford's belly. You mean they drowned him like a stray cat?

No. He was already dead.

Ford sat on a crate, the hot and dusty air scratching his throat and nose. Sorrow squeezed his chest, making it even harder to breathe. I've known Vacla most of my life. Worked beside him for years. Ate at his table.

I know.

I wonder why they took him.

When them fellas was walkin back from the river, I heard one of em talkin about a Troubler in your camp. Somebody high up.

Ford took the girl by the shoulders. What did they say *exactly*?

McClure tried to pull away. Take it easy, she said. Bandit growled, low and ominous.

I need to know, Ford said, still gripping the girl. They're takin my people and leavin me be. This is on my head.

McClure stared at him, silent. The dog stood, his hackles raised. After a moment, Ford released the child, who rubbed her shoulders. Damn, Santonio.

I'm sorry. But please. Tell me.

McClure scratched the dog's back. Bandit lay back down.

Well, one of em said, *That guy was tough. If they did to me what they just did to him, I think I would have talked, whether I was guilty or not.* And the second man said, *He must have been guilty. Clemens said he fought hard, even before he knew he was in trouble.* And the first guy said, *I guess Clemens was right. And if he isn't, I won't be the one that corrects him.* And then they passed outta range.

Ford sat on the grimy floor, legs crossed beneath him. *Vacla knew he was dead as soon as they kicked in his door. And even while they were killin him, he stayed true. How could I have ever thought about lettin folks*

*like him die, even to save my soul?* He blinked away his tears. He had no
luxury for mourning, for indulging his shame.

No use in crossin the river, he said.

I reckon not. I'm sorry about Vacla.

Let's get outta here. I'm sick of this air.

McClure clucked her tongue. Bandit shook his head and scratched
at his jawline. Then he tensed. His hackles rose again, and he growled
deep and low in his throat, looking at the door.

McClure raised a finger to her lips. Ford nodded. Bandit woofed
softly, more like a grunt than a bark.

Ford went to the door and peeped out. The darkened sky shrouded
the city. Streetlights fragmented the gloom. Candles danced in windows. He listened, slowing his breathing so not even his own body
would mask a sign of trouble, but nothing sounded out of place. He
waited and watched another five minutes. Bandit kept grunt-growling.
McClure shushed him.

Finally, Ford motioned to the girl. I don't think we can wait anymore. Get this information to LaShanda, okay?

McClure joined him, ready to move. First chance I get, she said.

They stepped outside, Ford going first, followed by Bandit and
then McClure, who eased the door closed. The night air washed over
them like a tepid shower.

Four men rushed them, two from each side of the building. One
man in each pair held a lantern high above his head. On their shoulders,
the burlap sacks they had used to hide the glow. Each man carried
sidearms. The two without lanterns had already skinned theirs and
pointed them at Ford and McClure.

Bandit barked at the men, loud and rapid-fire, standing between
them and McClure. Easy, boy, she said. Stay.

You should hide your horse better next time, the tallest man said.

One of the lantern carriers, a fat man wearing an eye patch, grinned.
And look who it is. Mister Chief Hunter hisself, plus some kid, meetin

in secret and sneakin about. Looks like we got two more Troublers, boys. Just like that skunk, Troy.

Hatless and bearing his lantern at eye level, the third Crusader shook his head. You can't trust anybody these days. Why are you sneaking around in the dark with a kid and a dog, Ford? Does your heathenism extend to perversion?

The gunman to Ford's left said nothing. His eyes were shadowed, his breathing calm.

*He's the dangerous one. The others are just blowhards.*

Me and this girl are old friends, Ford said. Where and when we talk ain't your business.

Mister Tall sneered. Envoy Royster might feel differently. Cuff em.

Ain't you a daisy, McClure said, winking at Mister Tall.

You're makin a big mistake, Ford said.

Mister Tall just laughed. Eye Patch and Hatless moved forward, while Mister Tall and Mister Silent kept watch.

Y'all were warned, McClure said.

The child drew her gun and shot Hatless twice in the head. Her third shot destroyed the lantern before Hatless's body hit the ground.

Mister Tall and Mister Silent opened fire as Ford dove sideways, drawing in the air. He hit the ground and rolled into a crouch and shot Mister Tall in the shoulder. The man cried out and fell. Eye Patch dropped his lamp and fumbled with his pistol, muttering, *Oh Lord oh Lord oh Lord* until Ford shot him in the throat. He fell to his knees, gurgling and clawing at the wound. McClure ran across the yard as Mister Silent tracked her and took aim. He opened fire, but McClure dove for cover behind Eye Patch. The bullet took Eye Patch in the back, and he fell onto McClure, who fired as she went down, knocking off Mister Silent's hat.

A shape thundered by in the dark. Rachel galloped down the road, dragging the limb to which Ford had hitched her, and disappeared into the night. *Damnation! I was afraid of that*, Ford thought.

Mister Tall sat up and shot at Ford, who evaded in a semicircle as the bullets whined past. A line of heat on his right shoulder blade—a graze. *Pay attention. Rachel can take care of herself.* He returned fire and hit Mister Tall in the mouth. Teeth, blood, brains, and bone exploded from the back of the Crusader's skull. He fell and lay still.

McClure struggled to get out from under Eye Patch as Mister Silent stood over her and cocked his gun. Say hello to the devil for me, the Crusader said. You Troubler piece of—

Bandit sailed through the air, hitting Silent in the chest. Silent's gun went flying. It hit the ground and went off, blowing a hole in the archive's wall. Bandit landed on top of Mister Silent and sunk his teeth deep into the man's throat and shook his head back and forth. The man gurgled and tried to scream and beat at Bandit's head. Ford got to his feet and stood over them. McClure shoved Eye Patch's body away and joined him. By then, Mister Silent's feet were beating a weak tattoo on the ground, his hands falling away as Bandit ripped out his arteries and a chunk of his esophagus.

Once the Crusader stopped flopping, McClure, Ford, and Bandit stood around the body, panting. Then the girl knelt and hugged the Rottweiler. The dog's tail thumped the ground. Gore dripped from his jaws.

Good boy, she said.

We better get outta here before the rest of the Crusade comes down on our heads, Ford wheezed. Will y'all be okay alone? McClure gave him a look. Sorry, he said. Hey, you heard anything from Gabe? Or about him?

No, McClure said, breathing hard. But I'm keepin my ear to the ground.

Let me know when there's news. Take care.

But the girl and her dog were already fading into the shadows, and for all his skill and experience, Ford could not even hear them.

He set off in the direction Rachel had run. If the Lord was with him, she would not have gone far.

The next day, Ford woke to pounding on his door. He sat up and rubbed sleep from his eyes. Outside, only darkness, not even the gray light before dawn. No birds sang. No crickets or frogs babbled. He reached for the glass of water he had left on the nightstand and drank, using the sheet to towel off his sweat.

*I hope I live to see cool again.*

The pounding continued.

He picked yesterday's shirt and trousers off the floor, pulling them on as he moved out of the bedroom and down the hall, through the den, to the door. When he opened it, LaShanda Long stood there, six-guns holstered. Behind her, two stone-faced outlanders carried shotguns, bandoliers crisscrossing their chests. Their horses were hitched to his post. The animals, like the men, were stolid and quiet, just shapes in the dark.

Howdy, Ford said. Did I forget an appointment?

Long turned to the Crusaders. I'll be out in a bit.

They saluted her. She strode past Ford. He closed the door and followed her and lit one of his lamps.

Water? he asked.

No. We ain't got much time.

He gestured toward the door. Who were they?

She shrugged. Folks I'm supposed to lead. They all look alike. Big, ugly, quiet, and loyal to Royster.

*So she's only a figurehead. She'll hold office till she questions an order or New Orleans floods, whichever comes first.*

So what brings you here so blasted early? he asked.

She sat and sighed, rubbing the bridge of her nose. Her eyes

were bloodshot and heavy. You, she said. Your people. Royster wants
Charters's contact, dead or alive. And they don't believe it was Quintus
Vacla.

Ford snorted. Didn't stop em from killin him, though, did it?

No. And unless we give em somebody, they'll rip your territory to
pieces.

Ford watched her, letting the moment stretch out. She held his
gaze, arms crossed, the deerskin shirt and pants clinging to her solid,
muscled frame, her hair trailing halfway down her back. *She looks tired,
but bigger somehow, more there. It's like the office made her grow. Did it do
that to Gabe back in the day? I can't remember.*

They're tearin the whole town apart, he said. Or hadn't you noticed?

She glared at him. It's my city as much as yours.

Is it?

Don't put on airs with me. You rode down Gabe just like I did.

I remember. I also recall some secret meetings. There was a woman
there. Looked a lot like you.

She looked away, whether from guilt or shame or exasperation he
could not have said. The shadows seemed to press in on them.

They'll come for you, sooner or later, she said.

You mean *you'll* come for me.

They'll kill you. Just like they killed Vacla. What are you gonna
do about it?

I reckon I'll die.

Plenty of folks in these neighborhoods ain't what you'd call innocent. Others have met in secret too.

Ford sneered. I don't aim to save my own skin by lettin em make a
rug outta somebody else's. Would you save yourself that way?

She stood, crossed the room, and got in his face, poking his chest
with her index finger. Yeah. I would. You know why? Because everybody expects us to lead em outta this mess. The Lord knew sacrifices

are necessary. He sent His own son, just like Abraham took his up that mountain. Are you better than them?

He knocked her hand away. That was different, and you know it. I won't ask somebody to die in my place.

Yes, you will. Because this city needs you. You're chief hunter because you're the best person for the job. If you die, everybody else's chances drop that much more. Would you rather sacrifice one soul or the whole lot?

Others can lead.

Not like you. Out of all the orphans who chose order as their life's work, Gabe picked you. Our people follow you because they see what he saw. If you ever cared about him, about any of us, you'll honor our faith in you. *Especially* when it's hard.

Ford looked out the window. The citizens in his charge walked by on their way to fields, woods, forges, stalls. Fisherfolk headed for the riverfront or the lake carried poles and rods and baskets. Some rode horses as lively as any mounts ever were. But all of them were already dead—shot, ripped open from crotch to sternum, drowned, starved. Long claimed only he could lead them from that path, as if when the flood came, he could part it, like Moses, or raise them above it, like Noah. That was nonsense, but LaShanda was right about some things. Troy picked him for a reason. Martyring himself seemed like folly at best, hubris at worst.

Or maybe that was his coward soul talking.

Ford passed a hand over his face. I don't know what to do.

Long put a hand on his shoulder. Pick somebody. Or I will.

We could just rise up with what we got and let the Lord sort it out.

We need more fighters and time to organize em. This buys us some.

I don't know if I can live with that.

She squeezed his shoulders. You got no choice. She sat back down in the chair, unblinking, irresistible. As if someone had carved her out of obsidian while Ford slept, rounding off the angles but leaving the edges sharp.

Maybe we can blame it on a Troubler, he said, wincing at how weak he sounded.

Long's voice softened. No. It's gotta be somebody they know we trust.

Damn all this to hell, he spat. Long said nothing. Her face was stone. *No help there, or anywhere.* There's somethin else, he said. Last night I took a walk. Got too near the river bridge. Four guards tried to arrest me.

She looked at him for a long time. These'd be the four guards we found dead this mornin.

Unless four more got killed in that part of town. He said nothing of McClure. *Let whatever happens fall on me. I owe the child that much and more.* Besides, those guards had taken pleasure in the prospect of his torture and death, as if they were hell's own executioners. He would not mourn them.

Long rubbed her eyes. Well. In time, you'll have to justify those killins before God. But I ain't Him. Right now all I'm worried about is gettin Royster off your scent.

Ford thought of Vacla. *Please, Father God. If I'm goin along because I'm a coward, strike me down. And if she's right, lift this burden from my heart.* He leaned forward, elbows on his knees. No matter what I do, he said, I feel dirty and wrong.

Me too.

Ford shook his head. More weight settled on his shoulders.

They sat in his oven of a house and talked, and with every passing moment, peace and happiness moved farther away than he had ever thought possible this side of hell. Later, they knelt together, hands clasped, their foreheads touching. They prayed silently, and then they prayed aloud, taking turns beseeching the Most High for guidance. They pleaded and despaired, wept and gnashed their teeth like the worst penitents, their immortal souls hanging over the fiery pit on gossamer strands. Ford exhausted himself and felt no better about anything. When Long rode away, taking the Crusaders with her, Ford watched them go from his porch, heat enveloping him like hellfire.

## ✤ 25 ✤

**T**roy had been living in the wilderness for close to two weeks, but he had not acclimated. As lord of order, he had always deferred to Santonio Ford as soon as brick and mortar gave way to trees and thicket and swamp. Everyone knew Troublers built houses on stilts and hummocks, that they fished and frog-gigged and trapped, that they somehow fended off disease-ridden bugs and vermin, mosquitoes you could see from ten yards, and nutria big enough to saddle and ride. He had assumed the heathens had a communication protocol—familial units, small paramilitary cells, individuals who seldom saw their nearest neighbors, larger settlements nestled deep in the wilderness, all of them planning and acting in concert—but he had seldom considered the ingenuity required to maintain it, despite the shifting waterways and soil erosion.

Since the bridge, he had learned of Troubler nests in the city, of other outposts in the woods and swamps and small towns around New Orleans, of a worldwide network moving slowly but efficiently from hamlet to town to major city to outlying swamp or wood. He now knew enough to dumbfound any lord of order, enough to understand the Troublers' true threat for the first time. The Crusader still stubbornly clinging to life inside him shuddered whenever he considered the scope and efficacy of their operation. If he had discovered it all before Dwyer, before Royster and Rook's orders and the river bridge and his own dawning horror at what the Crusade had become, would he have welcomed the chance to remove so many Troublers, his lifelong enemies, from the field at any cost? Would this knowledge have been enough to silence his conscience? Would he have let New Orleans drown?

*That's fear talkin, not righteousness,* Troy thought. *Lord, keep me on your path, even when I'm scared.*

Moving across the water, past safe houses and pickets, he had seen many familiar faces, Crusaders he had passed every day on the streets before Royster's arrival. Single men here, two or three women there, whole families bearing bags of heirlooms and bladed weapons and clubs, most of them shocked to see him, all of them happy. As if his presence eased their fears about their own souls.

They were all under guard, but they were being fed and sheltered. Better treatment than those chained wretches in the city, by far.

*They seen what was comin and ran. Didn't even have to be turned. The Crusade did the Troublers' work.*

Troy sat on the porch of the cabin they had given him after he and Stransky completed that long canoe ride through the bayous, a hip-deep slog through bogs too overgrown for boats, a mosquito-laden walk up the high hill on which the cabin sat. His right leg, still stiff, was propped in front of him, the calf and foot resting on an old, rotting chair. The shack overlooked the Irish Bayou Lagoon. Down by the water, a handful of gators sunned themselves on shore. One of them had to be ten feet long. It lay with its mouth wide open, as if waiting for some fool to come along and stick his head in. The heat felt like a malignant presence, despite the shade trees. *If a hurricane hits this place just right, them trees will smash this cabin into kindling.* But no one had asked his opinion. Since leaving the sisters', he had subsisted on tasty swamp gumbo the Troublers brought him, on fire-grilled fish, on frog legs and fried gator, on tough bird flesh gamey enough to get up and fly away, and on vegetables grown in the swamps or smuggled out of the city.

Most of the Troublers still watched him as if he might at any moment reach into his back pocket and pull out a fully armed column of raiders.

Ragtag, dirty, and courageous, they saw themselves as freedom fighters. Yet they had more in common with the typical Crusader than either side would have admitted. Except for the Crusade's higher-ups, who lived in the rarified air of their privilege, folks on both sides went to work and helped their neighbors and tried to make it through the day without getting shot. Many of these Troublers even followed a kind of Christianity, just as Stransky and Sister Sarah had claimed. They did not believe in the righteousness of Jonas Strickland or Matthew Rook or any of the Crusade leaders in between, but most believed in God and followed a code. Their long generations had lived with the kind of contradictions Troy and his people had only recently discovered. Still, it was hard not to think of them as enemies, especially the more sardonic, haughty ones who spat when they saw him. Stransky had tried to mend fences, but even she could only do so much. After all, Troy had been stalking, imprisoning, and killing Troublers for years.

Today, he and Stransky were scheduled to sneak into the city near the old St. John the Baptist airport, where some of the buildings, smashed flat or burned to cinders in the Crusade's great origin, had never been rebuilt. The streets were still pockmarked with craters, though the wrecks themselves had long since been dismantled and melted down, the burnable refuse torched. Those grounds served as the city dump, with a crumbling tower overlooking a landscape ruled by rats and carrion birds. Its circumference bulged like a glutton's waistline. Troy had planned to shift the dump into parts of the wetlands known for the heaviest Troubler activity. Poison the land, kill the vermin. He had wanted to raze the airfield and sod it and plant trees that would eventually shelter game. Now he wondered at his folly. As if every spot on God's Earth wanted only the right man to defile it. As if killing one's enemies somehow negated the ruination of what should be sacral and pure.

After reaching the cabin that day, Stransky had told him of underground caches near the dump, food and water and weapons, even a few well-stocked shelters. They needed to inspect those caches. Plus, Troubler scouts estimated the wall's builders would meet near the dump. The territory had to be scouted, a strategy hatched, yet he did not want to leave. It was peaceful here, more than anywhere he had ever been. In a place like this, a man might repudiate the life he inherited with his office. He might wash the blood from his eyes and turn them back to the Lord.

*I didn't even realize how tired I was until I stopped movin.*

Stransky was late. Perhaps she had decided to reschedule their inspection in favor of more training. The Troublers had always been guerillas, used to fighting from ambush in small pockets, and while those skills would be useful, only a larger, organized force could march on the Crusade's positions. Troy had been instructing Troubler companies and regiments on military strategy while they glared at him or looked at him in awe, their enemy standing before them in the flesh and offering his open hand. Meanwhile, Stransky had taught him more about insurgent techniques than he had ever cared to learn.

It all seemed like a dream from which he would wake at any moment, safe in his bed.

He dozed on the porch for an hour. When he awoke, he was starving, but it was too hot to stoke the fire, and he did not want cold gumbo. Besides, from the movement down by the water, he would have little time. The gators were gone, but three canoes paddled toward the little dock. Stransky sat in the lead boat. Two people rode in each canoe, the middle one paddled by the giant Stransky called Bushrod. A hooded, bound man rode behind him.

By the time Troy limped to the dock, praying he would not slip and break his neck, Stransky and her companion—a thin, dirty woman with stringy blond hair and a faded, soiled sundress—had forced their way through the low-hanging tree limbs and thick vegetation providing the dock with natural cover. As the woman tied off Stransky's boat, Bushrod plowed through the foliage by sheer force. He secured his boat and stepped onto the dock. Then he reached down and grabbed the hooded man by the arm, practically lifting him out with one hand. The third canoe was still docking as the rest of them climbed the hill.

What's this all about? asked Troy.

Stransky nodded toward the prisoner. Some of my people brung him to me last night. Found him pokin around the edge of the Refuge, lookin for any Troubler he could find. She turned to the hooded man, raising her voice. And he's goddam lucky they didn't just blow his fuckin head off.

Troy pulled off the man's hood. Norville Unger blinked in the sunlight, his hair askew, an old cloth shoved in his mouth. Troy would have been only a little more surprised if it had been Jonas Strickland himself. Seeing Unger in the bayou was like spotting a wild hog wearing a coat and necktie. Troy looked at Stransky and Bushrod and the others. When no one said anything, he removed Unger's gag.

Still squinting, Unger worked his tongue around his mouth and spat out a white effluvium that was almost solid. Lord Troy, he croaked. Is it really you?

It's me, Troy said, brushing hair from the old man's face. What are you doin here?

Unger burst into tears. Oh, praise God. We dragged the river for three days. Everybody thought you was dead.

Troy squeezed his shoulder. Well, I ain't. And I'm right glad to see you. He turned to Stransky. Untie him. Where would he run?

Stransky nodded at Bushrod, who removed Unger's bonds. The sergeant fell to his knees and grasped Troy around the legs. I can't believe it. You're really here.

Troy grimaced as Unger jostled his bad knee. Two wiry men with bad teeth and sidearms walked off the dock, the last mariners. Troy pulled Unger to his feet. Don't genuflect. I ain't God. Unger hugged him so hard that Troy thought his ribs would break.

Jesus. I think that old fella's in love, whispered one of the new arrivals.

Troy broke free of Unger and pushed through Stransky and Bushrod, ignoring the protests from his bum knee. He drew one of his pistols and struck the man across the head with the grip. The Troubler collapsed even as the other one tried to draw. Troy cocked his gun and stuck it in the man's face, mashing his nose down like putty.

Norville Unger risked his life comin here, Troy said. Show him the respect he deserves, or I'll make sure the gators eat good tonight.

The Troubler winced but said nothing. Stransky, her unnamed companion, and Bushrod had all drawn their weapons. Troy did not even look at them.

Lower that weapon, Stransky said. You done executed enough of us.

Troy increased the pressure on the man's nose and spat. Fine, he said.

But then the Troubler grinned at him, showing blackened stumps of teeth, so Troy backhanded him across the nose with the pistol barrel. A sound like a thick twig snapping. The Troubler collapsed.

Bushrod jammed his pistol into Troy's back, his voice deep and rasping. You heard what she said. Holster your weapon.

Troy gritted his teeth. Norville's been true, and he ain't never fired a shot at anybody. Does makin fun of an old-timer give all you big, bad outlaws a thrill?

Stransky grinned. Shit, Gabe. You're full of kinky notions. Spend much more time out here and you'll be talkin like me.

God forbid.

She cackled. Let's get under that net. These skeeters are eatin me alive.

Troy holstered the gun. Bushrod holstered his. Then Troy helped the old man up the hill, both of them limping and huffing in the heat. Troy's stomach grumbled.

As Unger eased into the good chair on the porch, Troy turned to Bushrod. I know it might be too much to ask of a man that needs to hogtie an elder just to keep him from jumpin out of a canoe, but you reckon you can start a cookfire and heat up that pot of gumbo?

The big man glanced at Stransky. She nodded, and he left without looking at Troy.

*There's another problem. I can't lead this rabble if every order or request needs Stransky's approval, and I can't just shoot all these ornery knuckleheads.*

Troy knelt in front of Unger, grunting as his stiff knee flexed. Unger looked alarmed. You all right?

I'll live. We got some gumbo comin. But I need you to talk. Can you do that for me?

Unger nodded, his face reddened and dripping sweat. He kept looking at the gathered Troublers as if they were black bears and he had just stumbled on their cubs. But when he spoke, his voice was steady.

It's all bad. Ever last lick.

Bad how?

Unger grimaced. That godforsaken wall's almost finished, and the whole city is paved in Troubler flesh. They're lined up from south of the river almost to the lake. They stopped at places like Robert E. Lee and Morrison. Just enough room left for the guards and the builders to move about without tramplin folks. I like to never got past em. Santonio's gotta wade hip deep in miserable wretches just to check his crops, and the wildlife that got stuck in our parks is scared half to death. Not three days ago, a handful of deer trampled three chained-up Troublers and turned about and plowed back into the forest.

So we got even less time than we thought.

A week or ten days at most. I heard that Clemens fella talkin about how there ain't but a few parties still on the way and how the wall ought to be done right after they're settled.

Troy mopped his brow with his shirtsleeve. Lord help us.

That ain't all. They house-arrested Jack Hobbes and Ernie Tetweiller. Ain't seem em since, but Santonio says they're alive. Not that I asked him. After what he done to you, I wanted to cut his throat.

Troy's flesh wounds still ached. Ford's bullets had shaved him closer than a well-stropped razor. He had tried to reflect on that day, but sometimes it was hard to think with the bugs whining all night, giving voice to the tumult in their own Troubler souls.

I reckon Santonio did what he had to do, he said. What about LaShanda?

Unger scowled again and spat. They made her the new lord. Didn't give her your office, and they don't even let her say the lord of order's prayer on Sundays. Royster does it. Attendance looks like it's gone down by half since you left. Don't know if that's because people can't stand the envoys. Maybe the outlanders put em in chains somewhere, or killed em all. Nobody tells me nothin.

Lord above. So LaShanda's doin what?

Runnin about the city supervisin Troubler transfers and tellin folks to go along, do what the outlanders say, kiss their hindquarters.

Don't be too hard on her. If she had really turned, Jack and Ernie would be dead, and so would a lot of other folks. What about Gordy?

Unger picked at a splinter on the chair, his mouth working as if the words had stuck in his throat. A tear carved a swath through the grime and dust on his face. Gordy's changed, he muttered.

Changed how?

Unger told Troy about Boudreaux's recruitment, about the trips across the river, about how the young deputy's eyes had emptied, his once expressive face frozen into a stoicism as plain as a white wall. By the time Unger finished and Bushrod appeared with a steaming bowl of gumbo, Troy feared more for Boudreaux than anyone or anything else, even the city. Buildings could be reconstructed. Gardens could be salvaged. But where lay the soil in which you could replant a good man's essence?

Unger ate the gumbo, his graying hair corkscrewing from his scalp like steam, wrinkles road-mapping his face and hands. Bushrod and the others stood around, watching the area for movement, as vigilant as any Crusader Troy had ever seen. If only discipline and vigilance were enough.

He pulled Stransky into the cabin proper. You heard Norville. We need to be ready to move in a week. Or less.

She smiled. We're good at movin fast.

I wouldn't put it past Royster to up and execute Ernie and Jack. We gotta spring em.

She was shaking her head before he finished speaking. I don't think that's a good idea.

Anger rose inside him like vomit. He scowled. They risked their necks to bust you outta the towers. Jack Hobbes took a bullet just to make it look good.

Stransky laughed. Yeah, and they did it just for me, outta the goodness of their hearts. Right?

Troy grabbed her by the throat and shoved her against the wall. I ain't negotiatin. I want my people alive and free.

There was no fear in her eyes. That's all any of us ever wanted too, and look how often you assholes gave it to us. Besides, Gabe, this act's gettin old. Grabbin my neck and talkin tough. Remember where you are? Hurt a hair on my head, and you'll never make it outta the bayou alive. Neither will that old fart. Now get your goddam hand off me before them boys out yonder pile in and gut you.

Troy squeezed her throat even tighter. She sounded like she was breathing through a tube the size of a pine needle. Her face turned red, then purple. But she never stopped smiling because she was right.

He let her go and stalked away, clenching and unclenching his fists. His knee fired bolts of red pain up his leg.

My friends are deep in the desert, he said, and I can't lead em out.

Look, Stransky rasped, rubbing her neck. You might not believe this, but I want them boys free too. Hobbes is cuter than a fuckin puppy dog, and Tetweiller's the only one of y'all without a goddam cypress trunk up his ass. Right now, though, Royster's got every reason to believe he can relax. You're dead. He's arrested your people or turned em. But if we do one damn thing before the big day, he'll know we're comin. And if we ain't got surprise, we might as well run.

Troy punched the wall. Splinters barely more than powder cascaded through the air. And what if they kill Jack before then? Or Ernie?

Better to lose two people than to paint Royster a goddam sign sayin, *Please shoot here.*

Troy sat in a decaying easy chair and leaned his head against the cushions and closed his eyes. If only he could open them in the past, back in the days when he had never heard of Jevan Dwyer and Royster had been just another name on the Crusade organizational charts and Lynn Stransky had been a ghost, a rumor, a shape in the distance about which even McClure could only hypothesize. All of them in their proper places playing their assigned roles. But time marched ever forward, the most implacable soldier in the army of some unknowable general. The decisions you made today echoed in your tomorrows and in all the days of those you loved.

He opened his eyes again. Fine, he said. We leave Ernie and Jack where they are.

Stransky laid a hand on his shoulder, squeezing it as if they were old friends, as if all the years and all the bullets between them existed in some other when, some other where.

Bushrod stuck his head in the door. He saw them touching but said nothing, and Stransky did not remove her hand. She feared nothing and apologized for less.

We got incoming, Bushrod said. One of our canoes. Three men. One bound.

Troy looked at Stransky. Now what?

She shrugged. Let's go see.

Except for the apparently famished Unger, who kept downing gumbo, everyone waited near the dock as a skinny red-haired Troubler secured the boat. Her prisoner, hooded and bound, bore on his shirt the Crusade insignia. He sat bolt upright and silent, still except for the rise and fall of his chest inside the bloodstained linsey-woolsey shirt. Behind him, a threadbare, scurvy male Troubler covered him with a rusty pistol.

They hauled the prisoner out of the boat and dragged him before Stransky. The male guard kicked the Crusader behind the knee, forcing him to kneel. Then the woman yanked the burlap hood off his head. The guard squinted.

Troy exhaled. *An outlander. I ought to be ashamed, but I'm glad he ain't somebody I know.*

Stransky crouched so she could look the guard in the eye. She reached out and smoothed his brown hair as he tried to maneuver away from her. Howdy, she said, her voice still raw. Know who I am?

The guard looked her up and down, his brown eyes defiant. Then he glanced at Troy, the others, the cabin on the hill. I'd guess you're Lynn Stransky, and the rest of you are a bunch of no-name heathens. Except for you, Troy. Everyone knows your face and your name. Aren't you supposed to be dead?

Troy shrugged. I reckon I got better.

The Crusader spat. You're going to hell with the rest of this scum, and that right soon.

Troy said nothing.

Stransky laughed. You got balls. I'll give you that. But unless you wanna know what they taste like, you're gonna tell me how the guards are deployed. And you're gonna tell me the truth.

The guard said nothing. His lips pressed into a thin line.

Bushrod cuffed him on the back of the skull. Speak when you're spoken to, boy. You wouldn't be the first Cultist we've fed to the gators a piece at a time.

That word again, *cult*, spat out like a curse. *Time was I would have killed Bushrod just for that. He's got all Stransky's venom and none of her better qualities. Wouldn't be the worst thing if he caught a stray bullet once the fightin starts.*

Bushrod cuffed the guard again. Still the man said nothing. The female Troubler stepped forward, drew her pistol, and smashed him across the temple. He fell to the ground, his eyes rolling white, half his face in the dirt.

Now the torture would start. Troy had used it as a last resort, knowing the information it produced would always be suspect. After a while, a person would say anything to stop the pain. Besides, it had always made him feel indecent, even devilish.

He put a hand on Stransky's arm. This ain't the way, he said.

She raised her eyebrows. No? You've tortured my people for years. You threatened to torture me.

I was wrong.

She pulled her arm away. Maybe so. But we ain't got time to be nice. Get behind me on this or walk away till it's done. But don't try to stop me. You're outnumbered.

Troy looked around. The Troublers scowled and gripped their weapons. Bushrod sneered.

We should be tryin to build somethin better than what we've had, Troy said.

We will, Stransky said. After all these motherfuckers are dead.

Her eyes were sharpened steel. The guard drooled blood.

*I hope you made your peace with God, son. You'll be meetin Him soon.*

Get him up, Stransky said.

Bushrod grabbed a fistful of the man's hair and yanked him to his knees. Stransky slapped him across the face once, twice, three times. Nothing. She sent Bushrod for some water. He came back with a canteen and handed it to her. She dumped it over the guard's head. His eyes fluttered open but did not focus. She poured more water on him. When he seemed more or less conscious, she knelt again.

I'm gonna ask you nice one more time, she said, her voice gentle. After that, it's gonna get bad. Now. How are they deployin y'all? How many guards on the explosives? Tell us, and maybe you'll live to lick Rook's ass another day.

The guard spat in her face.

Bushrod drew his pistol, but Stransky waved him back. She wiped the spittle away and grinned. You shouldn't have done that. Ain't nothin these folks like better than beatin one of you self-righteous fucks half to death just to see how long you'll last. Mister Bushrod, y'all take him out back.

Bushrod yanked the guard to his feet and shoved him up the hill. The other Troublers followed. Stransky stayed behind with Troy. When the others passed out of hearing, he said, This part tastes bad in my mouth.

You can stay on the porch with the old man. No need to watch.

He shook his head. If we're together, we're together. I aim to see it through.

Suit yourself.

She started up the hill. Troy followed, hoping the guard would talk quickly, knowing he would not.

Ten minutes after Bushrod tied the guard to a straight-backed chair and started beating him, the man's brown mane had turned as red as the

Nile when Aaron raised his hand over it. The guard's lips were bloated leeches, his left eye swollen shut. An egg-sized hematoma sprouted in the middle of his forehead. His chin rested on his chest. Flecks of blood spattered his clothes when he exhaled. Only the ropes held him in place.

A Troubler brought a satchel. Bushrod took out a mallet, a chisel, and a thick rope tied into a noose. He held it all up to the Crusader's good eye.

Troy leaned against the far wall, flexing his right knee. *In the by and by, I'll pay for this. Another mark on my soul, deep and jagged like the scrawlings on a prison wall tallyin up the endless days.* But he did not turn away. You had to remember. You had to carry your shame with you like stones in your pocket. If you lived long enough, maybe you could earn putting it down, one rock at a time.

Bushrod circled the guard three times, tossing the mallet into the air, catching it by the handle, tossing it again. He never missed, the sound of wood on flesh metronomic and flat. The guard's lips moved. He was praying, but for what? Deliverance? The strength to die well? He kept silent but for his labored breathing.

Stransky knelt in front of him and pushed the hair from his face, as a lover might do. It left swaths of gore, lined like brushstrokes. When she spoke, her voice was tender. Just answer the questions, and all this will stop.

The guard said nothing. Stransky shrugged and stepped away.

Bushrod tossed the mallet into the air, caught it by the handle as it was still arcing upward, and then brought it down with all his force on the guard's left shoulder. The man's banshee scream overrode the sharp crack of smashed flesh and breaking bone. The guard's head jerked upward, the cords in his neck standing out. Half a dozen startled birds flew out of a nearby tree. Stransky watched them go, her face serene. The guard grunted and moaned through clenched teeth. Nearby, two trees stood on the hill like sentries, an improbable tire swing hanging from the cedar, perhaps a gift from some Troubler father for his Troubler children. Diagonal slats of light shone through the branches, which the breeze sent swaying, the sun's rays kaleidoscoping, hypnotic. The guard's breath sounded heavy and wet, as if Bushrod had driven his clavicle straight into a lung. The arm hung lower than any arm should. The divot in the shoulder looked deep enough to hold water.

Let's try that again, honey, said Stransky. She might have been asking him inside for coffee. Remember you got a whole shitload of bones. Where are your people deployed? How many on the ordnance?

The guard watched her, his nostrils flaring like a blown horse's.

Bushrod raised the mallet with both hands and brought it down on the other shoulder. The guard fell over, chair and all, and screamed, guttural and animalistic. A deranged prophet of doom risen from time's most fetid pools. He clenched his teeth hard enough to shatter them, white flecks on the scarlet staining his shirt. Blood gushed from his mouth. Bushrod took up the chisel. He sat on the guard's upper arm, grinding the crushed bones together, and set the chisel against the man's hip. Then he brought the mallet down again and again and again, metal thudding on metal like someone staking a tent. The guard shrieked, his voice hoarsening. He tried to buck Bushrod off, but the Troubler held his seat and kept pounding, as merciless and implacable as ocean waves on rock, until the tip drove through clothes and flesh alike, blood spurting and pooling beneath them as if Bushrod had been drilling for it. By the time the hipbone shattered, the guard had already passed out.

Bushrod stood as Stransky retrieved a dipperful of water from the rain barrel. She doused the guard, who awoke sputtering and screaming as if he had never ceased. Stransky squatted and peered into his cheese-colored face. Talk, she said.

Bushrod knelt and fit the chisel against the guard's knee.

No, he said, and then he burst into tears.

Stransky turned to Bushrod and nodded. The big man got up and stepped back with the others, watching, listening. Stransky stroked the guard's bloody cheek. All right, she said. Tell me.

The guard looked as if he wanted to die. He likely did.

Pickets of twenty-five and a cache of explosives every half mile along the lakefront, he croaked. And every quarter mile on Lakeshore Drive. Same number every half mile along the river levees. Fifty guards and more explosives on the east side of the 17th Street Canal. Fifty on the Industrial Canal—twenty-five on the northeast side, where it meets the Gulf Intracoastal Waterway, twenty-five on the southeast between Florida Avenue and Claiborne. Fifty on the east side of the London Avenue Canal. Posts on street corners every three blocks. Six to a dozen troops at every one.

Do they ever stand down?

Never, the guard said, spitting blood. His teeth looked like jagged icicles. There are rumors, though.

What kind? She daubed at his lips with her shirt hem.

When the wall's done, he said. Some say Mister Royster will call us all there to witness its completion and celebrate the Lord's victory over you heathens.

Stransky looked at Troy. See? That fucker's done got cocky.

It's just a rumor, Troy said.

But it sounds like him, don't it? Dancin on our graves. She turned back to the guard. Well, honey, we're gonna have somethin to say about that.

The guard found the strength to look defiant. Just kill me, you seditious harpy. Send me to the bosom of my Lord. I need to make my apologies.

Okay, Stransky said.

She stood and drew her sidearm and shot him in his ruined face. He jerked once and lay still. Blood oozed from half a dozen wounds.

Bushrod was wiping off his instruments in the grass. The other Troublers turned away and chatted as if at a picnic.

Troy felt sick. *Everybody we ever lost, the ones who went out on patrol or walked home alone and just disappeared. How many of em ended up like this man? A brutality worse than hell itself.*

Stransky was looking at him, waiting. He supposed he had to get on with it. He had come this far. God help him.

He cleared his throat. Them canals—those are the same places that breached durin the ancients' time. In the storm they called Katrina.

Stransky holstered her weapon. Yeah. Looks like Rook knows his New Orleans history.

We didn't learn nothin here we couldn't have figured out by ourselves.

She shrugged. Had to be sure. Ain't all of us got that McClure kid workin for us.

Troy frowned. She's got nothin to do with this.

Stransky cackled. Sure, she does. You're lookin at us like we're monsters, but sendin a little kid into the lion's den all these years— you're cold, Gabe. Colder than me, and smart like a goddam rattlesnake. You been runnin the wrong outfit all along. She turned to Bushrod. Dump this dead-ass motherfucker in the bayou.

What about the inspection? Bushrod asked.

Send somebody else. I got too much to do here.

She brushed past Troy and walked through the cabin's back door. Bushrod untied the Crusader. A thick coat of blood covered the Troubler's hands, his clothes, his face. A savage from a time when the ancients were but babes. He picked up the body as if it were a child's and slung it over his shoulder, flinging blood about the yard, and then he traipsed around the cabin and down the hill.

*I could follow him to the water's edge. Gun him down, knife him in the liver and then cut his throat, bash his skull in. Be the lord of order one last time. And all it would cost me is the town I love and everybody in it.* Troy swallowed his rage yet again like the bitter pill it was and turned back toward the house, hoping that his sick stomach could hold down some gumbo. It would be a long day.

# ✦ 26 ✦

**W**hen Jack Hobbes joined the lord of order's office, Troy gave him a house on North Rampart. In ancient times, it had been a small inn, big enough for perhaps a dozen people if they shared rooms. It faced an old and crumbling vacant lot. Hobbes had always expected Troy to fill that lot someday, but he never had, perhaps because Hobbes liked the open space when the everyday burdens he bore like hundred-pound sacks of grain—all the violence, all the death—threatened to crush him. He had always dreaded Troy's resignation, retirement, or death, not only because of their friendship but also because it would likely force Hobbes to move into the lord's traditional quarters. Too much room for a man's thoughts, his guilt, to echo and distort into something even worse.

Now, Troy's home had been razed, the ashes picked through and scattered, and Royster had turned Hobbes's sanctuary into a prison. LaShanda Long was lord of order, but she had received neither the traditional Temple office nor a new lord's residence nor much actual power. What could you count on in times like these? Everything seemed made of smoke and rain.

Hobbes sat in the den, the lamp turned low, an island of light in a dark sea. Outside, nothing moved in his yard or the lot. The guards' conversations, muted and unintelligible, blended with cricket song and the deep and bellicose croaks of frogs. If Hobbes were to set foot outside, those guards would gun him down. And sometimes that seemed like a sweeter fate than boiling to death indoors, gelded and meek.

All the crews had done their jobs as well as ever. Firewood in the kitchen tinderbox. Fresh water in the barrel out back. Chamber pots emptied. Food in the cupboards. Later he would take a cool bath and then sweat himself half to death all over again. Then he would probably take another bath because what else was there to do?

Santonio Ford's people would be planting and growing and watering and tending and hunting and fishing. Hobbes had always loved to fish in his downtime, taking the occasional dip in the river to cool off. But now he could not even smell the water. He could not open the windows, for then the guards' prattle would drift in, would tempt him to dig under the floorboards and drag out his pistols and splatter brains and viscera all over the street. Such an end would be wasteful and selfish.

No matter what else happened, he had marked his guards' faces. He would send them to their rewards before he met his own.

He took up the carafe of tepid water from the side table and poured a glass, drained half of it, and set it back in the pale ring it had formed on the varnished wood. *Wonder what Ernie and Gordy's up to. And if Gabe's alive.*

Outside, an unseen guard tittered. The stars winked and glittered, as if the very universe mocked Hobbes's hopes and dreams.

# ❖ 27 ❖

Tetweiller lay on his sofa, windows thrown open to whatever breeze might come. Outside, the guards conversed about the wall's completion and how the Troublers were squeezing the city's population out of their homes. *I ought to knock their noggins together. They don't do nothin but talk, and you can only take so much jabber about that goddam wall or how bad somebody's constipated.*

He drank from a demijohn of whiskey, one shot at a time, the liquor amber and fiery in the morning sunlight. Like Hobbes, he had stored plenty of contraband under his floorboards, all of which he would have to haul like a pack mule when the fight finally started. He had also hidden enough whiskey for ten men. He did not intend to spend his confinement brooding or scratching out his memoirs with a goose quill. No, he would stay good and drunk, because once the shooting started, he might not have the chance again this side of heaven. He might catch a bullet five feet from his own door.

He set his shot glass down without draining it and closed his eyes. *Lord, watch over Gabriel and Jack. Please deliver Gordy from whatever's eatin him. And if you got any patience left for an ornery old bastard like me, help me stand tall one more time. I wanna die on my feet.* After he said his amens, he picked up the glass and drank. The whiskey settled in his gut, as hot and comfortable as ever.

Someone rapped on the door, hard and steady. He cursed, got up, and answered it, the whiskey sloshing inside him.

LaShanda Long stood on his porch, a half-dozen armed Crusaders backing her. She smiled. Hey, Ernie. Get your boots on.

Long rode beside Tetweiller, the guards flanking them. The old man had not spoken since mounting up. His worn pistols hung in their cracked holsters like wilted flowers in the buttonhole of a tattered and emaciated groom. Anger and the smell of whiskey radiated off him, but Long sensed no fear. He rode with his head high. *He heard about how I wounded Gabriel. Maybe he even hates me. But he wasn't there. He didn't see everybody watchin us. If every shot missed, then me and Santonio would be dead or stuck in our houses or out in the bayous with the Troublers.*

They reached Jack Hobbes's house and dismounted and handed their reins to the guards. The old man refused to look at her, but he followed her to the porch. She knocked, the same rapid hammering she had unleashed on Tetweiller's door.

When Hobbes answered it, he looked them over, his face noncommittal. Huh. Nice to see you, Ernie. LaShanda.

He turned and walked back into the house. They followed, Long shutting the door behind them. They sat in the stifling den. Hobbes brought them water. For a while, no one said anything.

Then Tetweiller turned on Long. You ain't told em about us. That's clear. But you shot Gabe and took his office. What the hell you playin at?

Long sighed. I didn't want any of this, Ernie.

Hobbes drank some water and put his glass on the side table. Reckon he's scared. Me too. We're leaves in the wind. For all we know, Gabe's dead.

And if he is, it's on you, Tetweiller said.

Long looked Hobbes in the eye. We all did what we had to do. Gabriel included. As for the office, Santonio turned it down, and when they gave it to me, they didn't bother to ask if I wanted it.

So you shot Gabe with love, Tetweiller scoffed. I reckon you ain't even thought about bowin down to Rook and Royster and lettin the city die.

Of course I have, she said. I'm torn up inside and scared to death. But I didn't give y'all up. Neither did Santonio. I recruited up until I couldn't go nowhere without guards. Don't that say somethin?

They sipped water and sweated and shuffled in their chairs. The heat settled onto their skins, greasy as ointment rubbed on a wound.

Private talk with traitors, Hobbes said. Must have been tough to manage.

Long smiled. They can't call me lord of order without givin me somethin.

Maybe, said Tetweiller. But I ain't sure we should trust you any further than I could throw the river bridge.

Dang it all, Ernie. You're as stubborn as a mule.

Reckon we'll need a little more than your word, said Hobbes.

She sighed. Fine. Let me tell you what Santonio and me have done and what we're about to do.

Hobbes watched her for a moment. Then he nodded. Tetweiller said nothing.

She told them everything.

Long and Tetweiller left that afternoon. The guards followed, asking no questions. The sinking sun was a blood orange on the horizon, the warm breeze refreshing after the sweat-lodge atmosphere of the house. It had smelled dank and sour, like sweaty underarms and damp crotches. Hobbes had looked twenty pounds lighter.

Tetweiller had softened. He and Hobbes still had reservations and probably would until she and Ford started gunning down Crusaders in the streets. But the three of them had found some common ground.

Long addressed the guards. Take Mr. Tetweiller home. Until he's inside, don't let him outta your sight, not even to make water.

The guards saluted. Tetweiller rode away without a word. Judging by the sun, it had to be around four o'clock, an hour before Long's meeting with Ford near Loyola. Needing to think, she let her horse amble for half an hour. Then she turned it toward the park.

She arrived twenty minutes later than she meant to, having stopped every ten feet to reassure someone of their safety. She had never noticed how much time Troy spent doffing his hat and shaking hands and listening to folks' troubles. Long had little patience for it. She was a warrior first and a diplomat second, or perhaps fifth, since she was also the chief weaponsmith and a loader of bullets and a pretty good hunter when Ford needed extra hands, just as he had worked well at her forges when she and her people fell behind.

*We've always helped each other, but so many of us don't even know anything's wrong.*

She passed Tommy Gautreaux and Laura Derosier, who were eating corn and beefsteak at a sidewalk table. She nodded. Gautreaux turned away and spat, his big belly heaving, juice dripping from his thick gray beard. Derosier saluted without getting up, the gesture almost defiant. *She's gonna slip one of her knives in my back if this goes on much longer.* For all Long knew, Mordecai Jones and Antoine Baptiste lay in wait somewhere ahead, guns already cocked, the bullets that would shatter her skull already chambered. *Them four. They've always been tight, but ever since Gabe fell, they've been joined at the hip. They'll be a real boon to us if they don't skewer my gizzard first. I wish I could tell em to be careful, but these days, they ain't like to hear anything I say.*

Ford waited in the darkening woods, looking over crops and workers. He was still riding Rachel. She held her head aloft, sniffing the air.

Long allowed Cherokee, her reddish stallion with the white star on its forehead, to saunter under the cedars and pecans. She reined up beside Ford. They watched as the workers left the fields. The sun set, the long gamboling shadows of humanity blending with the forest's shade in a great and shadowed pool. As if the people were fusing back into the land they worked.

You pick your man yet? Long asked.

Ford did not look at her. Fleming Lange. He ain't in charge of nothin but a few rows of tomatoes and okra. Good at his job. Never late, seldom absent. He ain't married, and the last of his family died in that cholera outbreak eight or nine years back.

He still a Loyalist?

Borderline. Ain't spoke of rebellion, but in the fields and around the cannin jars, he's talked of how the Crusade's plan must be one of God's own mysteries because he sure can't see a good reason to wreck this town. He's mouthed off just enough to make him a likely candidate but not so much to make him obvious. And I doubt he'd be useful in a fight. The meanest prey he ever killed was a fried green tomato.

Sounds perfect.

Perfect. Hell and damnation, LaShanda.

We've been through this. You're doin the right thing.

Ford grimaced, as if he smelled something rotten. Sure. For everybody but Fleming Lange. You ever think maybe we deserve the water?

Overhead, a bird and squirrel argued in their chattering language. The last of the workers carried their hoes and baskets and shears from the field, along with the plenty bequeathed to them by God and the rich soil.

Sometimes, Long said.

I liked it better when we were just puttin our own lives at hazard.

I know.

To the west, an orange fingernail's edge glowed like a beacon, drawing them to whatever event horizon God had formed there. They sat their horses under the trees for half an hour past dark, the woods coming to life around them, crickets and frogs and mammals that crouched a safe distance away, eyes burning in the starlight. The world coalescing and dissipating, watching them as they watched in their turn. They did not speak again until, as if in response to some signal, they nudged their horses and rode back toward the road.

Fleming Lange had no idea why they had summoned him to the dilapidated building on South Carrollton. The place was dusting back into the earth. He passed it every day but had never given it any thought. Now, according to his area supervisor, who had heard it from her foreman, who had gotten word from Santonio Ford himself, Lange had been chosen for a special duty. But what would find its genesis in such a place? The building reeked of age and weather, its boards crumbling, the brick and mortar broken as if some baleful child had gouged out the chunks with a dull knife. The long and glassless picture window, latticed with cobwebs, faced the street like a dead eye. The façade had probably been painted once, but it had faded to a no-color that disturbed him somehow. Perhaps the place's destitution explained its utility.

Lange carried no special dispensation to be about after sundown. *I shouldn't have come. But Mister Ford and my bosses have always done me right. I just hope I don't disappoint em.*

The humid night was a fist wrapped in damp cotton. A weak breeze only underscored the misery. In the distance, hoofbeats drummed the streets. Boot heels clocked the seconds. Chains clanked amid groans and muted conversations. The horde's whispers rose and hovered like the buzzing of a beehive. Nearby, the black river flowed through the moonless evening. Someone lit the streetlamps one by one. An occasional voice called for water.

Lange spat and thought about curfews and punishments.

Soon some of the footsteps grew clearer. They seemed to be heading his way.

Figures emerged from the gloom, their silhouettes bobbing together like the body of some misshapen beast. Lange stood straight, his pulse racing.

Then Santonio Ford's voice called out. Lange? That you?

He relaxed. Yes, sir. Over here.

The figures were only ten yards away when one of them lit an oil lamp and turned the wick up high, dazzling Lange, who held one hand in front of his eyes and blinked, spots playing over his vision like swamp gas floating over a bog. The figures surrounded him, pressing in, their faces like skulls in the lamplight—Ford; new Lord of Order LaShanda Long; the young deputy, Gordy Boudreaux; that hot-head envoy named Clemens; High Minister Jerold Babb; and two Crusade guards, one of whom held the lantern. Clemens and Boudreaux and the second guard had drawn their weapons and were aiming at Lange's head.

Lange blinked. What is this?

Clemens stepped forward, his voice flat. Is this the man?

That's him, said Ford. He sounded sad.

LaShanda Long approached, a pair of cuffs in her hand. Stand against the wall. Palms on the wood. Make a wrong move and they'll gun you down like the dog you are.

Lange blinked. He felt foggy, as if he had drunk whiskey and awakened on the red plains of another planet. He turned toward the wall and set his hands against it. It felt squishy. Mister Ford? What's this all about?

Shut your mouth, Troubler, Clemens said. We know your heart.

Babb tsked. I never would have figured you for treason, Fleming.

Long grabbed Lange's wrists and pulled them behind his back and shackled him.

Treason? he said. I know I broke curfew, but only because Mister Ford asked me to meet him here. Tell him, Mister Ford.

Long grabbed Lange by the shoulder and spun him around. Ford turned away. The others holstered their weapons and talked among themselves, as if Lange had already ceased to exist. His breath tore in and out of his lungs. Deep red panic fell over his vision like a caul.

You must confess, said Babb. Do not meet the Lord with a tainted soul.

Lange looked about, wild and desperate. He moved toward Ford. A guard shoved him back against the wall. Mister Ford, he shouted. *Please*. Tell em you asked me to come here. I'd be home eatin supper right now if it wasn't for you. Tell em.

Ford said nothing.

Fleming Lange burst into tears.

Babb came forward and touched Lange's forehead, tracing the sign of the cross. May the ever-generous Lord of Hosts forgive you.

Sobs erupted from Lange like foul effluvium. They watched him a moment. Then Boudreaux grabbed his arm and yanked him across the darkened street, toward the stoic and noble shapes of the horses. Lange wept like a lost child and begged to be turned loose. No one paid him any mind except Babb, who prayed aloud, speaking of forgiveness and penance and mercy and hellfire. And as Boudreaux shoved him into the saddle, Fleming Lange knew he would never see the sun again.

As Boudreaux led the prisoner's horse away, Clemens turned to Ford. Tell me again how you found him out.

Ford looked at him, annoyed. Ain't nothin changed since the last time I told you. Fleming came to me and said he heard y'all thought I was leakin information. He knew people who wanted y'all gone. If I met with him here after curfew, he'd introduce me.

Clemens studied Ford with narrowed eyes and furrowed brow. Why didn't you play along and ferret out the rest of the rebels?

After what happened to Gabe, it don't seem healthy to ride with traitors.

How did he claim to know what we suspect and what we don't?

Ford shrugged. He didn't say. Just told me I'd find out everything tonight. I knew he was lyin about y'all suspectin me. Figured he was tryin to turn me. So I came to you.

Clemens shook his head. You'd think a Troubler double agent could do better. A transparent lie like that—even a fool would have seen through it.

Ford clenched his teeth. *I'll tell you what's transparent. That you don't like me much. And I'd rather stick my privates in a bear trap than throw in with you.* Well, he said, when your best friend turns traitor and you chase him off a bridge, it tends to change your views. I reckon he just miscalculated which way it changed me.

Maybe. Boudreaux will get it out of him. Your friend's got a flair for interrogation.

Does he, now?

He does. Let's go.

Clemens mounted up and rode after Boudreaux, taking the guards with him. Ford and Long lingered. When they could no longer hear hoofbeats, Ford spoke. What we did here tonight damns us.

Long squeezed his arm. I hope the Lord sees it different. You're more important to His true work than Fleming Lange. It's one man or many.

I don't reckon choices like that should be up to us.

For a while, they listened to the prisoners' buzzing conversations, as if a plague of locusts had infested the streets. Look, Long said. Ain't no point in wishin it could have been some other way. It's this way, and that's all there is to it. Now let's go home and wash this day off our hands.

She spurred her horse and trotted away, leaving Ford alone.

Close by, the river wound across the world like a flat black string. He stood beside Rachel, patting her sides, feeling her thick muscles. A good horse, steady in a firefight. Maybe one day he could put her out to pasture. She deserved to live out her days in peace. But peace, like clear consciences, was in short supply.

Boudreaux led Lange past the outstretched arms of writhing Troublers. Unwashed flesh, human waste in festering heaps. Clemens and Babb and the two guards followed, Clemens spitting on upturned faces and laughing at shrieking children. Babb pulled his shirt over his nose and wiped his reddened eyes. Clemens drew his revolver and pointed it into the crowd, grinning when they cringed and shrieked. After that, Boudreaux refused to look at him. *I'll kill him if I do.* The streets stretched before them in ever longer and darker iterations, wrinkles on the earth's face. Finally, the riders reached the High Temple. Boudreaux saluted the gate guards. When they saw Lange bound and weeping, they scowled and spat at his horse's feet.

Boudreaux was not entirely sure Lange had done anything wrong, but what of that? He was just another damned soul. So were they all.

The prisoner's eyes were fixed on his horse's neck, as if the answer to how he had come to this sorry end were written there. Now, as they reined up at the Jesus statue and dismounted, Lange wept again, his voice low and craven.

Please, Mister Boudreaux. I ain't done nothin. I don't know why Mister Ford thinks I did, and if I gave him the wrong impression, I'm real sorry. Just let me talk to him. *Please*, sir.

Boudreaux said nothing. He helped Lange dismount without fracturing his skull or breaking an ankle and then pushed him toward the Temple.

Quiet, Clemens snarled from behind them. Or I'll shoot off your genitals.

Lange stopped talking but continued to whimper, low in his throat like a kicked puppy. They shoved him into the Temple and past the empty front desk. *Unger's gone. I ain't never seen that desk without him. It looks like a face without a nose. Did they do somethin to that poor old man?* The night guards stood at attention against the walls. Clemens's Crusaders joined them as Boudreaux, Clemens, and Babb marched Lange upstairs and found Royster's door open, the man himself standing at the stained-glass window looking onto the courtyard, the buildings across the way reduced to pure geometry and shades of dark.

Royster turned and smiled. So this is the traitor in Mister Ford's territory, eh?

No, sir, Lange blubbered. I—

Clemens pistol-whipped him across the back of the skull. Lange sank, moaning, blood dribbling from the wound.

Royster watched without expression. You will speak when prompted, or Mister Clemens will pull out your tongue. Brother Babb, has this man confessed?

No, sir. He claims innocence. His story hasn't altered a jot.

Royster shook his head and tsked. I suspected as much. Most captives turn sarcastic and indignant, but sometimes they show their cowardice. Or is this strategy? Perhaps you hope we will let you go back to your hell-bound friends if you refuse to confess. Is that it, Troubler?

No, sir, Lange whimpered.

Clemens kicked him in the ribs. Babb winced. Lange crawfished and gasped for breath, slobbering all over himself and the floor. Royster looked at Clemens, who shrugged. I figured the question was rhetorical, the deputy said.

He dragged Lange to his feet. Royster turned back to the window. Normally, we would interrogate you. But our time here grows short, and frankly, what you know or don't know matters little. This is your last chance to confess. Do it or don't.

Babb put a hand on Lange's shoulder. Fleming. I beseech you. Set your burdens down before it's too late.

Lange looked into Babb's eyes for a long time. Then his fists clenched. He set his jaw and slowed his breathing and drew himself up to his full height. It ain't me that needs absolution. You're murderin an innocent. May the Most High forgive you.

Royster laughed. Mister Boudreaux, take him out and dispose of him. You may choose the method.

Yes, sir, Boudreaux said.

Father, receive him into Your kingdom, Babb said. Your glory to behold.

Clemens grabbed Lange's elbow and yanked him toward the door. Lange held his head high. They had never uncuffed him. Boudreaux followed, his face as blank as an overcast sky.

Minutes later, Boudreaux and Lange passed the Jesus statue. The night grooms sat on one of the courtyard's benches, talking low. The horses watched the deputy lord and condemned prisoner pass and then turned back to whatever contemplations occupied their minds. Lange wept but did not speak. Boudreaux would not have heard anyway. He had burrowed deep inside, hoping to unearth the self he had once been. *I've rode to the river at least half the days of my life. I always knew the way. Now my head's all aswirl, and I've lost the light of the Lord.* Troy and Royster, the city and the Crusade—hands molded and stretched him beyond the most tangential human shape. He never smiled or laughed anymore, his mouth always the same thin line, his eyes dead. *At least Lange's cryin. He knows what's about to happen ain't deserved. When was the last time I felt so sure of anything?*

Before crossing the river. Before Kouf.

The gate guards saluted. Boudreaux ignored them. Lange wept and wept, tapping some unfathomable reservoir. Perhaps, before the end, he would reach into his guts and find his dignity again, as he had in the lord's office. But it would matter little, as nothing mattered. Lange would die. The Crusade would crush Boudreaux's closest companions or shatter itself against the Troublers' resolve. Eventually, time itself would forget the Crusade and all its deeds. Boudreaux would die, shot off his horse or run through by some scraggly Troubler, or perhaps he would grow old and become a limping shadow, like Tetweiller, a man who had once ridden into a nest of Troublers and killed them all, three with his bare hands, a man who could barely get out of bed these days. The winds and rains and searing summer heat and transitory human memory would erode every achievement, every hope and dream, leaving only bleached bones and crumbling buildings that might have housed anyone at all. What trace would linger for the next world's historians, and what would they make of the strange effluvia?

Boudreaux and Lange crossed Decatur and mounted the steps to the levee and crested and went down the other side to the water's edge. The mud smelled strong and rich, like new copper. Lange had stopped crying. He watched the river, a great snake with its mouth open to the Gulf. In that water swam catfish and bass and bream and gar and alligator and, near the mouth, bull sharks capable of ripping a man in half. In it floated the bodies of prisoners, Crusaders who stumbled into Troubler nests, small children who wandered too close to the edge, and youngsters who swam out past the easy water and foundered in undertows as strong as gravity. And of these bodies the fish would eat, and then people like Ford would catch those fish and fry them or roast them over open fires and feed them to the hungry population. Cannibalism after the fact, a circle of consumption. And in a world where such was possible, what consequences from one more death? What price the life of men like Lange, who chose wrongly once in their lives and walked the earth dead without knowing it until their fates caught up to them at last?

Boudreaux put a gentle hand on Lange's shoulder and exerted pressure. Have a seat, he said.

He expected Lange to turn and fight despite his bonds, but he did not resist. Instead, he prayed aloud—for his soul, for redemption. In that moment, Gordon Boudreaux hoped those prayers would be answered, that a bolt of lightning would burst from that overcast sky and strike him down, but nothing happened, and nothing would. God had turned His back again. Boudreaux did not blame Him. Nothing but blight here, foul excretions waiting for the cleansing waters.

Lange prayed faster and faster as if keeping time with frenetic music only he could hear. At the first pause, Boudreaux jammed his pistol against the back of Lange's head and fired. Brains and blood and chunks of skull spattered the water. Lange fell facedown into the shallows, legs on the ancient steps. His feet drummed a rhythmless tattoo for a handful of seconds and then stilled.

Boudreaux holstered his weapon and unbuckled his gun belt and set it on a higher step. Then he grabbed Lange's belt and shirt collar and towed him into the water. The cold Mississippi filled Boudreaux's boots. The mud sucked at him. He shoved the body outward. The current caught it and spun it away, just another piece of flotsam. Boudreaux turned and labored out of the water, wiping his hands on his shirt and taking up his weapons of office again. He fastened his belt and righted the weight of the guns against his hips, and then he trudged back toward Decatur. By tomorrow, everyone would know what had happened, what Lange had done, who had killed him. Boudreaux mounted up and rode home in the otherworldly dark, the chained choir's demonic moans keeping time with his hoofbeats. Later that night, he would find deep red stains on his garments. And when he saw them, he would not even weep. At least the brains and bone had washed away.

From the moment Boudreaux and Lange left the Temple, Jevan Dwyer followed, moving like a deer, flitting from shadow to shadow. He witnessed the execution and let Boudreaux pass. Then he went down and watched the body drift downriver. It would bloat and rot and fragment in the mouths of river creatures. If nothing snagged it, the trunk might reach the sea.

Then Dwyer turned and scampered after Boudreaux, following the horse's easy amble, pausing on occasion to clout a Troubler and move on before the man, woman, or child even saw him. As if the universe itself had clenched its fist and pounded them for the effrontery of living so long. And when he had watched enough and noted what there was to note, he turned back, reaching the Temple sooner than should have been possible for anyone afoot. He walked past the guards, who still refused to look at him unless they had no choice, and ascended the stairs, laughing as if their fear amused him. In Royster's office, he reported that Gordon Boudreaux had performed well, that he belonged to the Crusade, that he would, in Dwyer's considered opinion, execute his own mother if Royster ordered it.

Soon they would stand together on the wall and listen to the righteous sound of the levees and canals exploding, to the screams of the damned. They would see the Troublers of New Orleans floundering like ants swept from their hill in boiling water. And then they would go back to Washington and await the pleasure of Matthew Rook, whose judgment and purity stood second only to God's.

When Ford got home, Long waited on his walk beside her hitched horse. He dismounted and hitched up and led the new lord of order inside. Then he made two glasses of cool water with molasses. She sat in the den as he lit a single lamp and turned it low. Long watched him, sipping her drink. Ford sat in his favorite chair, the sweat in his hair glistening like goshenite. *He's thinkin about Lange and Gabe and Gordy and the people bound in the streets prayin for a Moses.* Long knew how Ford felt. The cries of the dying echoed in her dreams. New Orleans now housed the insane and the criminal alongside the true and the just, and she carried all their weight. Sometimes she wanted to shoot them all just to shut them up, to kill every Crusader for bringing them here.

*Thank you, Lord, that this is almost over.*

Tomorrow's sun would bring the culmination of all their planning and prayers. One way or another. She needed some sleep, but she could stand vigil with Ford for another half hour. Perhaps he would sleep tonight too. Perhaps he would even dream of better days, of his favorite game trails and lush crops and soil pregnant with possibility and a city without walls.

At his desk that night, Royster ate a plate of beefsteak and roasted corn, a napkin tucked into his shirt. Benn stood before him, nostrils flaring, licking his lips. The deputy envoy had not eaten all day. The aroma of the peppered, buttered steak must have been driving him mad.

*Yet he has not looked at my plate once. Admirable.*

And so the wall is done, Royster said, his mouth full.

Benn's face was unreadable, though Royster could have sworn the man's stomach growled. Yes, sir. The men have been instructed to hold the last section, as you ordered. They'll be waiting for us tomorrow at sunrise.

Royster swallowed and smiled. Almost time to solve our vermin problem.

Yes, sir.

And then we can go home.

Yes, sir. Then we can go home.

Royster smiled wider and returned to his steak. He wished he had ordered a baked potato with butter and fresh chives. He would truly miss New Orleans's food. Ford's hunters and farmers were excellent, the city's cooks peerless. Even leaving out what you could get anywhere—a pork chop or a roasted chicken—the city swam in flavors and odors, jambalayas and etouffees and gumbos and boudin balls, fried alligator and smoked fish, everything teeming with bell peppers and onions and celery, rich spices in every dish and remoulade sauce on hand for all occasions. If he could have saved anything from this festering boil of a city, Royster would have taken its food stores whole, every last head of cattle, every fish from the great river and the Gulf. He had, in fact, tasked Jevan Dwyer with copying all recipes, gathering all indigenous seeds. The river and the Gulf would endure after the city fell, and so would the cuisine of a vanished people.

He pointed his fork at Benn. What will you do when all the Troublers are dead?

Benn considered a moment. I think there will always be Troublers. Just because we've caught the ones we suspect doesn't mean we've suspected all the right people.

True, true. But still. Imagine a world where you could forever set aside your gun. Where you can trust every face you meet as a temple to the one true God. What would you do with your life?

Benn shifted a little. I've never given myself leave to imagine that world, sir. But I suppose I'd spend my days taking naps with my wife and teaching my daughters to fish. When we weren't at worship, that is.

Royster nodded and ate, sipping tea cooled in jars at the river. A wedge of lemon floated in the glass. That sounds like a lovely life. Send word to Misters Clemens, Boudreaux, and Ford. To Lord Long as well. They are to attend the fastening, the speeches, the beginning of the celebration. All guards not on duty are required to attend.

Yes, sir.

In fact, instruct the guards on the canals to come too.

Benn frowned. Do you think that's wise, sir? What if the Troublers attack?

Then the guards at the lakefront will flood the city, as God brought the Red Sea down on the Egyptians after the Israelites passed safely. The Troublers know this. Their best play is to stay in their verminous swamps and let this city drown.

But what if Troy—

Troy is dead. His friends have turned or sit captive in their ill-gotten homes. Not one true Crusader has been harmed. No, Mister Benn. Let the canal guards join us, that they may go forth afterward and spread the word of our victory.

Benn seemed on the verge of speaking again. Then he cleared his throat and said, Yes, sir.

Leave me. I have much to do.

Benn bowed and exited. Royster finished his meal, hoping that, wherever they might be, the loyal would eat well. Soon they could lay down their burdens.

On the eve of what would likely be their last stand, Stransky and Troy stayed in a cabin near the Refuge's westernmost edge. Stransky's Troublers slept on tiny hummocks or stood guard or dozed in boats of sundry sizes and shapes and material. When it was time to move out, Stransky would give a signal, which would fan outward like water rippling after a tossed stone, and they would descend on the city, killing and razing everything in their paths. They would take New Orleans from Royster or die trying. There was no third choice.

Troy lay awake, thinking of his absent friends; the citizens for whom tomorrow would seem like the cataclysm, not the cure; the many ways everything could go terribly wrong.

Outside, the sound of oars in water. A guard hailed someone.

Troy flexed his right knee. It still felt stiff, but he could walk without limping, could even run for short bursts. Across the room, Stransky sat on her cot, black hair falling over her eyes. She picked up the oil lamp from the little side table and lit it, banishing the shadows to the corners of the room. Troy stood. She gestured for him to wait and went to the door and poked her head out. Someone muttered to her, but Troy could not make out the words.

She turned to him. It's your girl and that fuckin dog. Kid better hope we don't end up in a goddam siege, or we may have to eat it.

Troy followed Stransky onto the rickety porch, where two guards armed with rifles stood vigil. Someone was carrying a lantern up the hill. The guards must have let McClure pass. How had she found them?

Soon enough, girl and dog stood before Troy and Stransky,

McClure's faced bathed in sweat, the dog panting, its pink tongue lolling.

Howdy, Troy said.

McClure wiped sweat from her forehead. Howdy. Hotter than hell out here.

Yeah, and I reckon the fish ain't bitin, Stransky said. What the hell you doin here?

McClure ignored her. Y'all was hard to find. If I hadn't heard them boys on the dock talkin about you, I might have rowed right past.

Stransky shook her head. Loudmouth assholes. I should gut em.

How are you? Troy asked. How are the others?

Everybody's alive, McClure said. Jack and Ernie are still confined to quarters. That ain't the big news, though.

The kid told them what she had heard on the streets—a meeting at dawn, the canals unguarded. When she finished, Troy fetched her a glass of water and a bowl for Bandit, while Stransky ran about, giving orders. Troublers scurried hither and yon. Soon their oars beat the waters as they moved out to spread the word.

Stransky came back, breathing hard. Gonna be a harder fight at the wall than we thought.

Don't change nothin, Troy said. We still gotta bust my people out, keep the outlanders from blowin the levees, and take the wall.

We know where Royster's gonna be. That helps.

Plus, McClure said, the ordnance crews got orders to light their fuses *after* the evacuation, if they got any choice. That gives us some time in the city.

Right, said Troy. Willa, head back and get started on your part. The more you can do, the better off we'll all be.

McClure stood. Bandit, who had been asleep on the floorboards, sat up and wagged his tail. Then the girl exited and trotted down the hill, the dog following.

Troy drank from McClure's half-full glass. With most of the guards gone, a surgical strike inside the city's better than a mass force.

Stransky spat and shook her head. Strike team ain't got much chance.

Once we free Jack and Ernie and mobilize our people, we can cut the prisoners loose street by street. I'll take a dozen troops with sidearms, plus some extra rifles and shotguns.

Nobody here's gonna follow your orders. Not till they see you're really with us. That means you go alone, or I go with you.

You need to lead the wall assault. Send Bushrod with me and tell him I'm in charge.

Bushrod can take the wall. He's better at that *we who are about to die* shit than I am. Besides, I wanna see Jack Hobbes's face when he sees who's rescuin him.

Troublers leading both prongs of the attack seemed like letting a couple of wolves guard a newborn babe, but Troy could not dictate terms. If Stransky wanted, she could order him bound, gagged, and buried to his neck in the back yard while she took her chances. And she was crazy enough to do it too.

He sighed. Fine.

For a while, they watched the furious activity in the yard and at the dock. You sure the Crusaders won't blow the levees as soon as they hear shots? Stransky asked.

Can't be sure of nothin, but they ain't known for independent thinkin. They're taught from birth to follow orders. If I was a bettin man, I'd take odds they won't light them fuses until we're about to overrun em.

She flicked her hair from her eyes and looked hard at him. So our lives depend on a guess.

Yep. But we're outta time.

Stransky grinned and slapped him on the shoulder. Then she got up and went inside.

Troy prayed for courage, for guidance, for the rightness of his cause. After he said his amens, he followed Stransky in and stretched out on his cot. Perhaps he could sleep a little before they moved out. He might never see a bed again.

he sun was a thin rind when Royster arrived at the wall on horseback and sauntered before his gathered people. Thirty yards outside the main structure, the final section awaited like New Orleans's tombstone, wanting only a steady hand to carve it. Facing the opening, Clemens and Benn stood beside their mounts, flanking Jerold Babb, who seemed to have come afoot. Boudreaux, Ford, and Long lined up behind them, their old and tattered horses grazing. *They have chosen poor mounts for the occasion. We must find them better horseflesh before they ride into Washington at my side.* On the other hand, those broken-down animals seemed in keeping with the city dump festering nearby, its stink curling upper lips and watering eyes. *I must reprimand Misters Melton and Glau for their poor planning. This is no setting for an august occasion.* The architects and more than two dozen higher-ranking guards stood behind the deputies. Beyond them, gaggles of off-duty Crusaders lined up at parade rest, their numbers stretching far back into the city.

The great segment rested on crude log rollers. Teams of horses and Troublers were yoked to it. No one guarded them. Where would they go? Seeing Royster, some of them turned aside and spat.

*Those heathens disdain my holy office. Before we flood the city, I will see them drawn and quartered by the very horses they toil beside. Even drowning is not enough to purify their souls. In hours, a day at most—as soon as the last Crusader clears the wall and the ladders have been retracted, when the guards stand ready to repel all who try to escape—corpses will pile and stack like detritus damming a swollen river. Clouds of insects and battalions of vermin will attend them. These wretches who dare spit in my presence, though—they will know the tortures of the damned.*

He smiled his shark's smile. Then he took a deep breath and shouted, My friends! Fellow servants of the Most High and His Holiness Matthew Rook! Today we etch our names in history! Today we strike down iniquity! Today we complete the wall that is part and parcel of Brother Rook's vision! Rejoice, for today, more than ever, we walk under the loving and protective gaze of God!

The faithful erupted in cheers and raised their fists. Babb spread his arms and lifted his hands to heaven, his eyes closed, his lips moving. Melton and Glau embraced and slapped each other on the back. The Troublers looked away.

Royster raised his hand in the air. Once he let it fall, the elite guards would march outside and steer the Troublers and horses to their work. And when the last section had been driven in place and sealed, Royster would issue only two more commands in New Orleans—one to begin the faithful's exodus, the other to light the fuses.

*And then we can ride from this pond full of dead scum and never look back.*

Then something struck his right shoulder.

Pain and heat shot down his arm and across his chest as he spun and fell off his horse. He landed on his back, the breath driven from his lungs in a single gush. A second later, a rifle's flat report. Crusaders cried out and ran, ducked for cover, scanned the city or the trees beyond the wall for the shooter. One of them screamed something about the forest, and those guards who were both armed and near the gap began firing. Horses reared and threw riders. Royster's own mount's forelegs smashed into the dirt only inches from his face. Troublers cheered. Panicked voices blended together. Benn was shouting for everyone to *cease fire, keep your heads, know what you're shooting at.* He, Clemens, Boudreaux, and two guards lifted Royster and carried the envoy to safety. Royster's wounded arm dangled and jounced with every footfall, fresh waves of pain washing over him. He moaned. Jerold Babb jogged alongside him, huffing with effort. Just before they ducked behind the wall, Royster saw Troublers boiling from the woods, out of the ground itself. Their leader, a man almost as big as Jevan Dwyer, paused at the lone segment and hacked at the Troublers' chains with a hatchet. Several of his fellows did the same.

Chaos everywhere—Crusaders took positions at the gap and clambered up ladders and fanned out up top. They fired, reloaded, fired again. Melton and Glau cowered nearby, their arms about their heads, Melton blubbering. Guns roared from within and without. The injured and the dying bawled and pleaded for help. A woman's body fell from the wall and landed less than ten feet from Royster. Her blood spattered him and pooled around her still-twitching limbs, her left arm bent at a right angle halfway between the shoulder and elbow. Babb prayed aloud. Every sight and sound seemed farther and farther away, the light too bright. A semicircle of faces looked down upon Royster: Babb, Clemens, Benn, Long, Ford, Boudreaux.

They're coming, Benn said, mopping sweat from his eyes. Orders, sir?

## 30

**T**roy and Stransky reentered the city before dawn, bringing with them two dozen armed troops. They used old, rusty grapples and ropes and scaled the wall between the skeleton crews manning positions along the top, Troy gritting his teeth as his injured knee throbbed. All of them carried sidearms and knives strapped to their belts or hidden in their boots. Some wore shotguns in scabbards on their backs. Inside the wall, chained and emaciated Troublers covered the streets and much of the lawns and lots, but the guards were limited to fixed positions. The usual riders and ambulators had gone to see Royster's big show. For every guard, fifty or more prisoners. *If everyone rose, they could kill these outlanders and take the city. But these folks are starved and dehydrated and half dead. Lord, let em find their spirit once they're free.* Troy's and Stransky's troops were dressed in Crusade attire. He did not want to know how they had gotten the tunics, but they worked. Beyond those who saw them come over the wall and grinned their damned grins, the prisoners barely glanced at them. The guards and the pickets nodded or waved or even saluted. No one tried to stop them. *They're lax. And why not? They've always won.*

Troy's band ducked into an alley and huddled up. It was time to separate.

Stransky laid a hand on the shoulder of the Troubler nearest her, a man with thick blond hair and a scar on his neck. Y'all goin with Troy—remember that today, an order from him's as good as one from me. Any questions?

No one had any. The Troubler with the neck scar said, Thanks for choosin me, Lynn.

Stransky waved him off. I figure all I'm doin is gettin you killed. Still, good luck. And good huntin.

Good huntin, they replied.

Stransky took her twelve troops and exited the far end of the alley. Troy looked over his group—eight men and four women, bony and dirty-faced and armed to the teeth, their expressions fierce and angry.

I know we don't like each other much, he said. But this is our principality, and ain't nobody gonna drown it while we can still fight. We gotta watch each other's backs and kill every outlander we see. But unless we get cornered, *nobody* shoots until we free my deputy. He knows who he's recruited. They'll reinforce us. Questions?

Again, no one had any. Troy motioned for them to follow him.

## 31

**S**transky's posse passed Hobbes's house once, stepping past and over and around the people in the streets. Every block or so, a single guard, two, a cluster of six sweltered in the damp heat. They were armed with handguns and shotguns. Stransky frowned. *Sheee-it. We gotta take em out fast.* Still, the numbers looked promising. Surely some of those prisoners could still fight. If her people could overwhelm the guards at one end of a block, they could confiscate weapons and use them against the next group, and if Troy came through, several waves of reinforcements would arrive. Every block they took would bring more weapons, more support.

And if Troy's troops faltered or betrayed them, at least Stransky would no longer have to tolerate the prisoners' god-awful smell.

Some guards they passed were clubbing a skinny, filthy man. The victim hung on to their ankles and pleaded for water, no matter how many times they punched him or kicked his ribs or pistol-whipped him. One guard caught Stransky's eye. He had red hair and carried what looked like a genuine cutlass on his belt. God knew where he had found it. He grinned, his front teeth missing.

*If I can find you later, I'll slit your throat for you, fucknuts. We'll see how you smile then.*

They passed sandbagged corner positions manned by jovial and inattentive guards. In the outlanders' minds, they were already home. They paid Stransky's bunch little mind.

Soon she angled across Hobbes's yard and into his driveway. Two guards at the front door, another two on either side of the house.

Probably at least two more in the back yard. The troops on the porch saluted them. Stransky saluted back.

You must have gotten your orders mixed up, said the man on the right. We're on until dark. Or the evacuation, whichever comes first.

Stransky grinned. Ain't that the goddam shit?

She drew her knife and buried it in the man's abdomen and clapped her other hand over his mouth, stifling his scream.

The second guard tried to pull his sidearm, but one of Stransky's men had already drawn his weapon and jammed it against the man's testicles. Say one fuckin word and you'll sing alto for the rest of your short-ass life, the Troubler whispered.

Someone opened the front door. They filed inside, dragging the prisoner and the dying guard with them. Stransky shut the door. *Nice and quiet. As long as the others don't wander around the house, we got a little time.* Her people cut both Crusaders' throats and left them crawfishing on the floor. Then they followed Stransky into Hobbes's den. The deputy lord sat in a straight-backed chair. He wore his boots and his good sidearms. All around him lay ripped-up floorboards and what Hobbes had hidden under them: a shotgun and rifle on shoulder straps, bandoliers of shells and a pouch of sidearm ammunition, three or four canteens, and a sack of jerky.

He stood. Bout time. Gabe alive?

Stransky peered out the nearest window. He's goin after Tetweiller. How you gonna signal your people?

Let me take care of the other guards and I'll show you. Pass this stuff out, except the pistol ammo.

As the whispering Troublers argued over who should get the guns, Stransky followed Hobbes to a bedroom with windows looking onto the side yard. The guards were visible through thin white curtains. Hobbes reached into his shirt and pulled out a pistol fitted with a long screw-on barrel.

Nice, Stransky said.

He aimed at one sentry's head and pulled the trigger. The gun barked, the sound still too loud in the quiet house. A neat round hole in the curtains, the tinkling of broken glass. Hobbes shot the other guard as the man stood over his fallen friend. It took perhaps two seconds.

He turned to her. Gotta hurry in case the others heard.

He trotted to the sliding glass doors leading to the backyard, Stransky on his heels. He unlatched them and threw them open. Two Crusaders turned their way. One managed to spot the weapons and draw his sidearm before Hobbes shot them both between the eyes. As they fell over on their backs in the ankle-deep grass, Hobbes was already moving back through the house. Stransky stopped in the living room and shushed her people.

No sound from outside.

A moment later, Hobbes burst into the room. Ain't nobody out there, he said. Must have heard us. Gonna have company soon.

He dashed down the hall.

Stransky turned to her group and shrugged. Well, okay. I reckon we'll just stay here and wait on em to shoot us then.

Hobbes returned, carrying a bag that rattled as he walked. He dragged a spool of string, playing it out on the floor.

Damn, someone said.

Shit, said Stransky. You ain't fuckin around.

Hobbes winked. It was like watching a rattlesnake walk upright. Let's make some noise, he said.

What's in the poke?

Two hatchets and a load of hacksaws.

She nodded at a Troubler, who took them from Hobbes. About ready?

Almost. He took a paper out of his back pocket and handed it to her. Here.

She opened it. He had drawn a crude map with positions throughout the city marked with a series of *X*'s. What's this?

Locations for my caches, Hobbes said. In case I get blasted.

You're too pretty to die, Stransky said.

Hobbes turned to the others. Got a fast fuse here, so hit the street shootin. Kill every Crusader you see and free as many prisoners as you can. Take any weapons you find and arm the freed folk.

A scraggly-looking man with a long black beard said, You ain't gotta tell us shit. We been waitin on this day all our lives.

All right then. Hobbes took some matches out of his pocket and struck one on his boot. He lit the fuse and backed away.

You ready? Stransky asked.

Reckon so.

Outside, they fanned out toward either end of the block, shooting and reloading. Crusaders gathered at the intersections fell to the pavement in silence or screaming and holding their guts, their throats, their shoulders. Two or three returned fire. One of Stransky's men cried out and fell on his face, his gun clattering on the street.

Stransky took the bag of blades from her man and tossed it toward the nearest captives. Free yourselves, she said. Grab the first weapon you can find and follow us.

And then, with a thunderous roar like what the ancients' city-killing bombs must have sounded like, the house blew up, raining fire and brick and burning wood into the street.

# ✤ 32 ✤

Troy's band was still approaching Tetweiller's house when the explosion rocked the city. Guards and detainees alike turned to watch the ball of fire, the smoke. Even the men stationed outside Tetweiller's front door ran to the sidewalk and pointed, arguing about what they should do. And in that moment, Troy drew his silenced weapon and shot them in the head. They fell like the two-hundred-pound sacks of meat they were and moved no more. A Troubler woman nearby raised one finger to her lips and winked. Troy trotted up the walk and opened the door, leading his little flock into the den, where they found Tetweiller prying up the floorboards with a crowbar and hauling out weapons, food, canteens, ammunition.

He looked up at them. You get the ones around the house?

No, said Troy. We just walked on in.

Tetweiller screwed a silencer on a Glock. Good to see you again, Gabe. Troy clapped him on the back and started loading down the Troublers with supplies while Tetweiller went from room to room, dispatching the guards through the windows as Hobbes had done. When he returned, he took his gun belt and favored sidearms from a Troubler. Sorry, boy. These have stood me in good stead longer than you've been walkin the earth.

Come on, Troy said. We got a lot of city between us and the lakefront.

Hang on, said the old man. He disappeared down the hall and came back with a set of burlap sacks filled with hatchets and hacksaws. He doled them out. Y'all distribute these to yonder chain gang.

Troy opened the front door, saw what was out there, and slammed it again, shouting, Duck!

He and Tetweiller hit the floor as a volley of shots splintered the door. Troy jarred his sore knee and groaned as the man behind him cried out. Blood spattered the floor, the wall. More grunts and moans. Troy looked up. The man who had been standing behind him and a bullet-riddled woman lay twitching as the rest of the Troublers crawfished into the den. Troy grabbed the dying woman's hatchet and followed, crawling over her and through her blood.

What the hell? panted Tetweiller.

They're convergin on your driveway. I reckon they saw the bodies.

Shit.

They let us bottleneck ourselves. We're lucky we lost only two.

*Stupid. Stupid.*

Everyone gathered around the wounded. The woman made a horrible gurgling sound. She had been shot in both lungs and the abdomen. Part of her jaw had been blown away. Her tongue flopped about. The man died, his jugular vein and femoral artery pumping macabre fountains. The woman passed a moment later.

The Troublers looked to Troy. What now? said a man with a sandy beard and one eye clouded in cataracts.

Troy closed the dead Troublers' eyes. The guards we passed out yonder? Some of em are probably headed this way. We gotta push through em and be gone before anybody else gets here. You bunch keep em busy while Ernie and me—

A series of explosions close by rattled the walls. A chorus of voices shrieked in pain. Troy ran to the nearest window and looked out.

The Crusaders who had formed a skirmish line on the walk now lay everywhere, some dead, others alive but shattered. It looked like one of them had erupted and taken the rest with him, along with several nearby prisoners, some of whose ruined limbs still hung, disembodied, from their chains.

What the fuck? Tetweiller said.

No idea, but we gotta move.

Ignoring his stiff knee's protests, Troy led them through the foyer and outside, guns drawn. They fanned across the yard, stepping in blood and onto bits of flesh and bone. One by one, they dispatched the wounded.

Willa McClure and Bandit sauntered out from behind a house across the street. The girl stopped in the center of the carnage and observed, thumbs hooked in her gun belt.

Where'd you come from? Troy asked.

McClure spat on a dead guard's forehead. After we reconnoitered the lake, we snuck over here and holed up in yonder house. Figured you'd come for Ernie, seein's how Stransky's taken a shine to Jack.

Troy indicated the bodies. I reckon you did this?

She reached down and rubbed Bandit's belly. The dog rolled about in the street, mindless of the gore. You reckon right. I buried a cache of grenades and such a couple blocks down. Same time y'all started hidin your own supplies. This bunch was so focused on y'all, they never seen me walk over and roll four grenades up under em. Too bad about these other folks, but I figured it was them or you.

The street was an abattoir, a sodden arabesque of war. *She just killed at least a dozen folks and wounded twice that many, but it don't faze her. I reckon that kind of coldness comes from growin up hard, with only killers for friends.* There was nothing to say, no platitude that could rekindle the girl's lost childhood, the story of which Troy himself had helped author. So he tossed his hatchet to a nearby Troubler, who began hacking away at the locks. The rest of Troy's band passed out their blades, all of which were snatched up in emaciated hands.

What do we do when we're loose? someone asked McClure.

Find a weapon and start killin, she said. Or run. Or die.

Lord, girl, Troy said.

The child wiped blood off her dog's coat. What?

Troy opened his mouth to reproach the kid, but he closed it again. On a killing field, lecturing about the virtues of compassion and empathy seemed too hypocritical even for the damned. So he turned back to the Troublers. All right. Just like we planned. And don't forget where I hid my caches. They'll help.

The group split in two and set out toward opposite ends of the street, McClure and Bandit trotting at Troy's side with half the Troublers. Tetweiller led the rest toward whatever might come.

**B**ullets struck the wall with a sound like axes falling on thick logs. Someone shoved a cloth onto Royster's wound hard enough to crack bones. He groaned and gritted his teeth as the world went gray. The cries of the injured rose like the calls of strange birds. A Crusader lay on his back fifteen yards away, a flaming arrow in his heart, his uniform and flesh sizzling like a beefsteak in a hot skillet. The acrid smoke burned the envoy's eyes and nose.

Benn and Clemens had climbed a ladder and were firing on the Conspirators from up top. Ford and Long stood on either side of the gap. Every so often, one of them would lean out and return fire, but neither seemed all that eager.

*Are they faltering or conserving ammunition?*

Melton and Glau cowered ten feet away, backs against the wall, both pale, both watching Royster with wide eyes. Jerold Babb knelt in the dirt and prayed aloud. Gordon Boudreaux watched Royster bleed, his face an inscrutable image carved in a granite cliff.

Royster grabbed the sleeve of the guard tending his wounds. How is it?

The guard's face was pale and wan. The bleeding's slowed, sir.

Help me get up.

You're liable to make it worse.

Royster shoved him away. And the Troublers are liable to overrun us. If you're not going to help me, go shoot someone. Gordon, your assistance, please.

Boudreaux hauled Royster up by his good arm, the envoy groaning and wincing and hissing through his teeth. He caught Long's eye across the way and motioned her over. She waited for a lull in the fire and then sprinted across the gap, bullets spattering the dust and grass at her feet. When she passed Ford, he fired once more and followed her.

Hear me, Lord, Babb cried. Deliver us.

Gordon, Royster said. Please scale that ladder and ask Misters Benn and Clemens to join us. Then go find my highest-ranking officer present, not counting all of you or those two weaklings over there. He nodded at Melton and Glau.

Boudreaux left without a word. Somewhere up there, Benn and Clemens crouched behind the blast barriers running four feet high on both sides of the wall. Moments later, all three men descended and gathered round. Babb said his amen and crawled over.

Highest-ranking man present, except us, is Aaron Listerall, Benn said. He's down that way, unless he's dead. He nodded to Royster's right. The envoy flapped a hand at Boudreaux, who ran off in that direction.

Very good, Royster said, wincing. For a while, no one spoke. Royster rested his good hand on Benn's shoulder and prayed.

I hate this town, Clemens said to no one in particular.

All right, Royster wheezed, looking them over. I want the four of you in town. Take no troops. You will find plenty of Crusaders willing to kill or die for you along the way. Your mission is to reach the lake. Blow the charges.

Benn's eyes widened. Do we allow our personnel to retreat, sir, and trail the fuse behind them, as we planned?

Royster groaned. Could no one think but him?

If such can be done, yes, he said. If they must choose between saving their own lives and doing God's work, their path should be clear. Either way, I want these streets flooded within the hour. Send any laggards to meet the Lord ahead of us.

Babb looked as if he had seen his mother naked. You'd let the Lord's own die with the heretics?

Benn cleared his throat. I understand your sentiment, Mister Royster, but—

Do not argue with me, Royster said. He leaned forward, his shoulder wound dribbling onto the ground and Benn's boots. We find our whole purpose here at hazard. If the Lord requires our lives today, we shall give them, and gladly. *Go.*

Benn, Clemens, Ford, and Long ran to catch their horses, leaving Royster and Babb alone. Benn kept looking over his shoulder, eyes bugging. The gunfire and explosions and death cries continued unabated, contrapuntal music from hell. Babb cringed every time someone fired, which, given the frequency, made him look like the victim of a nervous disorder.

Royster must have fainted, for he found himself sitting, his head spinning, his vision unfocused. His ears seemed to have been stuffed with cotton. Whatever energy he had found when barking his orders had departed. Babb had wandered off. He sat in the dirt some yards away, ministering to a dying man with a crushed skull. But Gordon Boudreaux knelt beside Royster, and Aaron Listerall loomed over him, calm and expressionless.

*Perhaps I should have made him a deputy. Even Mister Benn begins to doubt.*

Boudreaux did not bother to bow. Aaron Listerall, sergeant at arms from the D.C. principality, the deputy said.

Royster tried to swallow, his throat a sheet of sandpaper. Gentlemen. The godless have halted our work. We must remedy the situation.

Listerall was six feet tall and a solid two hundred pounds. He wore long blond hair and a bushy, uncombed beard, a sweat-stained hat, a leather jerkin, knee-high boots, a sidearm, and a knife big enough to gut a bull. These aren't ragtag guerillas, he said. They're well armed and strategically situated. If we go after the segment, they'll cut us to shreds.

Royster looked at Listerall until the man took off his hat and mopped his brow with the back of his hand, studying the gap, the bullets whining through it, the arrows, the fire. A Crusader plummeted, screaming, from the wall, three arrows buried in her chest. She landed on her back, dust pluming about her and blood erupting from her mouth and burst skull.

If we can't keep them out, Royster said, they'll kill us anyway.

Listerall nodded. I'll ready the men.

He moved away, sending runners to reposition the best shooters on the wall. He led the rest of the nearby Crusaders, between forty and fifty in all, to the gap. Listerall looked back at Royster one last time and raised his arm. When he let it fall, his guards boiled out of the gap, screaming at the tops of their lungs and leaping over their fellows who had already fallen dead or dying from the Troublers' initial volley.

# ✤ 34 ✤

**F**lames licked the wall's summit in half a dozen places. Crusaders smothered the fire with dirt hauled up in hats, with their drinking water. One man trying to use his own urine took an arrow in the throat. Listerall's group watched all this with their backs against the last segment. On the other side, he knew, a cluster of Troublers waited for them to make their move. The rest of the Conspirators had taken cover in the tree line, behind lone bushes and rocks and the piles of dirt and debris thrown up during construction, behind overturned Crusade wagons, behind their own horses. The Crusaders on the wall fired six-guns and revolvers and shotguns and hunting rifles and arrows and sniper rifles. Some used slingshots. Some threw grenades. Others pitched glass bottles full of oil with a flaming rag stuffed in the neck. Foliage and vehicles and people burned. Horses screamed. Blood spotted the ground.

Listerall directed most of his people to take up the abandoned ropes and shattered chains. As they made ready, he gathered his remaining seven men and five women.

Circle around this thing and clean out the Troublers on the other side, he said.

If we do, said a man carrying a shotgun and a machete, the heretics in the trees will cut us to pieces.

Yes, said a woman with brown eyes and a pistol. She stood less than five feet tall and might have weighed ninety pounds. We're all going to die. Why did we come out here?

Others in the group nodded and muttered among themselves. They kept glancing back at the wall, likely calculating their odds if they ran.

Listerall had his six-gun in hand. Now he cocked it and jammed its barrel against the woman's forehead. She gasped and moved backward. He moved with her. We're out here because Mister Royster ordered it, he said, looking at her but talking to them all. And if you don't get moving right now, I'll kill you myself.

She shook with fear, but she held his gaze. I didn't know we were so expendable.

He laughed. Of course we are. Or they wouldn't have sent us. Now choose.

Shotgun-and-Machete stepped forward, staring at Listerall with distaste. We'll move. *Sir.*

The others muttered and glared, but they filed to one end of the segment, waiting. When Listerall nodded, they charged around the corner, shooting. Screams and curses and meaty thunks, probably the machete being put to use. Listerall watched as best he could. Some of the Troublers ran for the trees. One Crusader limped past Listerall, headed for the city, a bullet lodged in his guts. Aided by snipers on the wall, the other eleven fanned out toward the tree line, picking off wounded Troublers. Two of them were shot and fell dead. The rest kept pressing forward, probably burning with battle fever. Two more fell. And three more. Everywhere on that hellish field, the dead and dying lay in pools of their own blood and viscera, limbs blown off, torsos churned into ground meat, skulls shattered, brains puddling out like vomit. Troublers dropped charging Crusaders in midstride and were in turn avenged from the wall with withering fire that ravaged trees, men, women, and horses. Hidden artillery boomed from the woods, spewing foliage onto the field. Seconds later, the shells either hit the snipers' positions, digging chunks in the wall and vaporizing flesh and bone, or sailed into the city, blowing holes in the earth and tearing horses in half. The last of Listerall's crew to charge the tree line—the tiny woman with the steady gaze—fell only yards short of the woods. The rest of his crew pulled and yanked on the chains and ropes or worked the rollers, picking them up as the segment passed over them and toting them up front. The section inched forward one tug at a time. Someone tried to bring a team of horses through the gap, but the Troublers shot the animals down and then sighted back in on Listerall's crew. The air turned sharp and deadly. Acts of great valor and courage on both sides, the kind from which ballads are born, yet none there marked those moments, for all were killing or being killed, drawing the last piece of the wall forward or arresting its progress.

Finally, Listerall retreated through the gap and knelt beside Royster, his chest heaving, blood from his bullet-grazed temple caking his dirt-smeared and gunpowder-blackened face. I'm sorry, sir, he panted. We can fight them, or we can move that thing, but we can't do both. We just don't have the hands.

Royster's face was a pale moon, his eyes bruised fruit. Pull your people back. Keep the Troublers outside the wall at any cost.

Listerall saluted and hurried away.

# ✤ **35** ✤

**G**ordon Boudreaux squatted next to Royster. The envoy licked his lips and swallowed with some difficulty. I wonder if you'd do me a service, he said.

Boudreaux's expression was blank. I reckon so.

Royster squeezed his forearm. No one has come to our aid. I fear our comrades have encountered some fell treachery. Yet if we pull any more souls from the wall, we will lose too much covering fire. Therefore, you must ride into town and gather some troops. Enough to drive back those Troublers in the woods. We must finish the wall before the waters come.

Boudreaux stood and slapped dust from his hat and put it back on. For a moment, he studied Royster, paying special mind to the wound.

Okay, he said and walked away.

He caught his horse and mounted up. Royster watched him go until he disappeared in the smoke. Only then did the envoy allow himself to sleep a little.

## 36

**B**ushrod lay on his belly, watching the gap. He estimated his losses thus far at around fifty. At least another four hundred hid in the trees and natural ditches and foxholes dug out of raw earth. Some sat their horses ten or fifteen yards back of the tree line. Bullets whined through the air in irregular volleys, probably just to keep them honest. One foolhardy bravo rode to the forest's edge, and a sniper blew him off his horse. The animal neighed and bucked and ran off, uninjured but scared half to death. More sense in the animal than the man.

*We gave better than we got. We could breach with sheer audacity and meet Lynn in the middle. I could bring her Royster's head. But Troy wants it done right here, with most everybody watchin at once, and Lynn's with him. Well, if the city floods, we ain't lost nothin. We live on the water anyway.*

Nearby a woman stood and aimed her rifle and caught a bullet between her eyes. She fell over in the dirt and lay still. More food for the insects and carrion birds, one less gun in his arsenal.

Stay down if you don't wanna get killed, you knuckleheads, Bushrod shouted.

Then he hunkered down to wait.

## 37

**L**ong, Ford, Benn, and Clemens rode down I-10. Prisoners sat on the roads unattended, their guards siphoned to one battleground or another. *We gotta play this just right,* Long thought. As they approached the causeway in Metairie, individual sounds began to separate from the city's low hum—explosions, gunfire, high-pitched screams of pain, the cacophonous and ancient voice of war. *We always come back to this. Hand to hand, knife against knife, who's the faster draw or which one brought more ammo. It's as natural as breathin, eatin, comin in outta the rain.* Lord of order *ain't right. They should have named me lord of slaughter.*

Something exploded less than a mile away. They reined up. Benn turned pale.

Clemens spat. Blast the Troublers. They don't know when to lie down and die. We better get over there.

Sounds like your people stepped in it, Ford said, shaking his head. LaShanda and me can head to the lake if y'all wanna go get bloody.

No, Benn said. You two have no authority over our guards. They're under orders not to blow those levees unless they hear from one of us or they're being overrun. Clemens, you and I have the levees. You two rally your people. We've got to carve a path through the Troublers and get out of town.

Benn and Clemens spurred their horses and rode lakeward. Ford and Long watched them go for a moment. On the streets, the chained Troublers looked toward the sounds of battle, their faces aglow for the first time in who knew how many months. Hope, or fear?

We could have just shot em right here, Long said. Like fish in a barrel.

No, Ford said. In close quarters, it could go either way.

One of us needs to hunt down whoever's leadin the fight in the city, in case Gabe and Ernie and Jack are dead. Our people won't follow Stransky.

I know.

You're the best hunter I ever knew. You take Benn and Clemens.

Ford saluted as if he had sworn fealty to her and not Gabriel Troy. *I wonder if he knows how much that tastes like ashes in my mouth. Or that I'm makin this up as I go. Is that what Gabe's done all these years?*

You be careful, Ford said. Madame Lord. Before she could reply, he galloped off.

*Chances are good I'll never see him again.*

She spurred her horse, riding toward the gunfire and the billowing smoke and the misery. They rode past hundreds and thousands of chained and ragged unfortunates—children and grown-ups, filthy and emaciated, the stink of them like something that would draw buzzards, the dead's legs still shackled to the living's, fleshy anchors that would pull you to the bottom of the floodwaters as sure as stone. Clusters of Crusaders shifted from foot to foot like puppets whose masters had left them dancing in the wind.

Soon Long turned a corner and waded into hell. Carnage in the streets and yards, on the stoops of buildings, New Orleanians and freed prisoners stabbing Crusaders with knives and improvised spears, shooting them with bows and arrows, blowing them to pieces with grenades and captured firearms, strangling them with the broken chains of bondage. The guards returned fire. Men and women alike with cut throats, torsos split from groin to sternum. Carrion birds picking at spilled entrails. Children crushing skulls with the butts of liberated pistols and hamstringing guards from underneath the very bellies of Crusader horses.

Long pulled her pistols. Some of the guards saw her coming and turned, raising their hands in a cheer. Their fists were still in the air when she shot them, trampled their bodies under her horse's hooves while the chained Troublers and free natives whooped and fell back to slaughtering like fiends loosed from the pit. Long reloaded and let her horse carry her deeper into the battle. Here and there she stopped to send runners throughout the city, there to urge the locals to rise and unchain the Troublers, to slaughter the outlanders, to save New Orleans.

# ✦ **38** ✦

**F**ord urged Rachel onward. He took side streets and alleys and yards, leaped over hedges and the heads of Troublers who ducked and covered their skulls with their arms. The Crusaders he passed looked frightened half to death. Most of them had probably never fired a shot in anger and had gotten used to dealing with starving dociles in chains. Ford could have shot half of them, but the deputy envoys took priority. And so he rode and dodged and hurdled, shouting and waving people out of his way. Finally, he rounded a corner and found Benn and Clemens only blocks from the lake.

He drew his sidearm and fired into the air, shouting their names.

Benn looked back and said something to Clemens. They reined up and half turned their horses toward him. The animals' snouts bumped each other as they stamped the road.

Ford grinned. He spurred his horse. They picked up speed.

Realization dawned on Benn's face. The deputy envoy went for his pistol.

Ford shot him in the stomach.

Benn howled and fell off his horse, his gun clattering to the ground.

Clemens's horse reared, front hooves pawing the air. Rachel plowed into its exposed belly. The outlander's mount shrieked, a high-pitched sound that was almost human, and fell backward. Clemens skittered fifteen feet across the pavement. Rachel trampled the downed horse. It screamed again, Rachel's legs tangling in its own. Ford sawed on the reins, and somehow Rachel stayed upright. He sighted in on Clemens, who was trying to regain his feet, his clothes ripped to tatters and hanging off him like a shroud.

Then a gunshot, and fire ripped across Ford's ribs. He dropped his pistol and fell. As he landed, he rolled for his gun and grabbed it, his ribs awash in hellfire.

Clemens stood, empty-handed, legs trembling, his face blank and dazed and half covered in road rash. Still, when Benn's horse fled past him, Clemens grabbed its saddle horn and swung himself onto its back.

Ford sat up on the road and aimed, but a shot careened off the pavement near his feet. Benn was sighting in on him with one hand and holding his leaking gut with the other. Ford fired three shots. Two struck Benn in the upper chest, knocking him backward. The third obliterated his throat, blood-spray fanning over the road like mist from a cataract. Benn dropped his weapon and fell onto his back. His feet twitched, and he clawed at his neck, blood geysering and coating the blacktop.

Ford struggled to stand as Clemens rode toward the lake, swaying in the saddle. *Thank God Rachel's better trained for battle than them Washington horses.* She tamped her feet nearby, unspooked. He stumbled over to her, yanked his rifle out of the scabbard, and knelt in the street, sighting in. He fired. Clemens's horse collapsed on its forelegs and somersaulted twice. The deputy envoy went flying again, flopping across the pavement. Even from the distance, Ford heard something snap like a thick branch. Clemens screamed. The horse crawfished on the road and tried to rise, legs buckling as if it were newly foaled.

*Wound's throwin me off. I aimed for the man.*

Ford mounted up and shoved the rifle into its scabbard. He reloaded his pistol and snapped the reins. Rachel broke into a run as his ribs protested. His side was slicked with blood.

Clemens managed to stand again, left arm twisted and pumping blood. Still screaming, he stumbled onward.

Sweet Father God, Ford said. He's too stubborn to die.

When Ford passed Benn's body, he spat on it. Thin red threads wove themselves through his slaver. *Don't think about it. Just ride. Just shoot.*

Clemens wobbled down the street like a drunk.

Ford passed Benn's thrashing horse and shot it in the head without stopping. Rachel's every clop on the pavement seemed to shift something inside him. *One broke rib, maybe more. Lungs filled with broke glass. Don't think about it. Just ride. Just shoot.*

Clemens looked back and saw Ford and screeched. He broke right and sprinted for the nearest house. Then he kicked in the front door and stumbled inside.

Ford dismounted near the yard and whispered to Rachel, who bobbed her head as if she understood: If I just mosey up the walk, he'll blow my head off. Gonna be hard to flank him when he can probably hear me breathin half a mile away. Don't wanna let him get you either. Two animals dead on this road, no tellin how many more out yonder where the fightin's the worst. It's how we always seem to repay you for your loyalty and love. We slaughter you and leave you to rot. I'm sorry, darlin.

He took the reins and urged Rachel through the yard at an angle, keeping her between himself and Clemens.

*He's only got the ammo he's carryin, so he might not fire until he's got a clear shot.*

As they neared the house, Rachel tossed her head. Her eyes rolled as if she could smell burning gunpowder from the shots that had not been fired yet. Ford gripped the reins hard, ignoring the pain in his left side. Still nothing from Clemens. Perhaps he had fainted or died.

Five feet from the house, Ford let go of the reins and slapped Rachel's hindquarters. He flattened himself against the outer wall as she trotted away and stopped in the street, where she turned to watch the drama play out however it would. Ford crept toward the front door. When he reached the picture window, he dropped to his belly and pulled himself along, trailing blood in the grass. His breath sawed in and out, agonizing and hot. *He can hear me. I know he can. Might shoot this wall to pieces. Don't think about it. Just move.* After clearing the window, he sat with his back to the wall and scooted along until he reached the door. From inside, Clemens groaned. Ford pulled up his shirt. The bullet had gouged a wedge-shaped chunk out of his side a few inches below the armpit and passed on. A hint of jagged rib bone peeked out. *At least the round ain't in my belly or liver. Thank the Lord. I hope I don't bleed out before I finish this.* He took a slow, deep breath, clenching his teeth against the pain, tears welling. *Forget it. Take the door. Kill the man. Then die if you must.*

That you, Ford? called Clemens. He sounded like he was talking underwater. Wherever you're shot, I hope it hurts, you devil.

*No matter what, Clemens can't reach the levees.*

The main door was open, the screen shut. Ford took another breath and held it. Then, forcing himself not to moan, he pulled off his shirt. White lights danced behind his closed lids. His left foot squished inside his gore-filled boot.

*Help me, Lord.*

He inched his way up the wall until he leaned against it, panting. When the pain subsided, he stuck the shirt on the end of his pistol barrel and thrust it in front of the screen.

## 39

**C**lemens had thrown up three times and lacked the strength to move out of his own puddle of sick. Every time he shifted, waves of nausea struck him. His left arm was bent like a bird's leg, the jagged bone protruding through his bicep. The floor was covered in his blood. As a deputy envoy, he had seen violence, had instigated it. Three years ago, he had taken a Troubler bullet to the thigh. Once, he had been slashed across the chest with a machete, costing him his right nipple. But he had never felt anything like this—the arm, the skin lost in his tumble, everything. Mixed with the pain, a deep sense of self-loathing, all of it burbling in his stomach like gas. How sloppy and prideful they had been, how sure of their own eminence and the citizens' compliance. When Ford had opened fire, Clemens saw, as in a vision, all the errors born of their hubris. The hunter had never been on their side. He had lived in New Orleans all his life, had fought beside Troy since coming of age. Put beside that, how could they have been so sure, so bloody *certain*, that anything, even the Crusade, would take precedence? Ford would go to hell for turning on them, but that would do the men at the lake about as much good as it had done Benn. Clemens had to stay conscious long enough to put down the traitorous dog. He had called to Ford and gotten no reply, but the hunter was out there somewhere, on one side of the door or the other. If he had still had two hands to reload with and enough ammo, Clemens would have perforated the whole front wall, just to be sure. But he had to wait. He—

Movement from the door, a fluttering of white stained with red. Clemens roared and fired, pulling the trigger over and over until the hammer fell on empty chambers, the dry clicks like the chirping of an insect. His ears rang. The acrid smell of gunpowder filled the room. He wiped his eyes on the back of his hand and watched the door. Nothing moved.

He laughed and laughed.

I got you, he croaked, his throat parched, his mouth filled with gun smoke. Thank the Lord. I got you.

## 40

**T**he first two shots sent Ford's shirt flying into the yard. He yanked his pistol back before a bullet could destroy it. Clemens kept firing anyway, full of panic or rage or both. Then half a dozen dry fires. A moment later Clemens laughed and whispered something. Ford could not make out the words, but they mattered little.

He stepped in front of the screen door. In the dimness, Clemens huddled against the back wall, trying to reload with one hand.

Ford shot him three times.

Clemens jerked and groaned.

Ford opened the mangled screen door and stepped inside.

Oh, no, Clemens said, high-pitched, panicked. Oh, no.

One bullet had struck the deputy envoy in the groin, another just above the belt. The third seemed to have shattered his hip. Ford could have hung his hat on the bone poking out of Clemens's arm. The Crusader threw up a mouthful of stringy bile. He looked as if he had been stampeded, his face ghostly pale.

When he saw Ford watching him, though, he clenched his teeth and slowed his breathing. His eyes were still defiant. This doesn't matter, he rasped. Our men will blow the levees anyway. You'll drown.

Ford bent and inspected the ragged hole in Clemens's groin. Looks like your manhood's shot off.

At least it wasn't my soul, Clemens said. You've damned yours today.

His breath came quicker now, blood bubbling from his mouth and nose. He smiled, as if he could see through the years and all the dimensions God ever made, as if Ford's spirit already bathed in fire and screamed for mercy.

Ford pulled his hunting knife from its scabbard. Its sharp edge glinted, even in the dim light. He spat blood on Clemens's boot. You don't serve the same God I know, Ford said. Yours knows nothin of mercy or charity or forgiveness. Only wrath and vengeance. If it was me layin there, you'd let me die slow. But I ain't that cruel. May the Father forgive us both.

Clemens grinned with reddened teeth. Get on with it. Troubler.

Ford cut his throat.

Clemens gurgled, his working hand hooked into a claw that scrabbled at the open wound. Ford sat and put pressure on his own injury, watching him die. When it was over, Clemens lay with his eyes open.

Ford watched him a moment more. The pain in the hunter's side waxed and waned with his breathing. His limbs weighed a hundred pounds each. Still, moaning, he forced himself to his knees and inched over and pulled Clemens's shirt aside. Then he cut the crucifix brand from the deputy envoy's chest. When he was done, he flung the meat away and knelt next to the body, his head spinning.

As soon as he could gather his strength, Ford shuffled outside. Rachel waited in the street. He picked up his shirt and lurched to her and dragged himself into the saddle. When he clucked his tongue, Rachel trotted toward the lake. She smelled the water and tossed her head. Ford held the reins in one hand and his tattered shirt against his wound in the other. Fishhooks yanked at his lungs, his guts. His immediate future held more galloping horses, deep breathing, smoke, gunpowder. *Father God, please don't let me sneeze or cough.* He hoped he could stay conscious long enough to finish this. If not, the troops and prisoners and horses would probably trample him where he fell.

*Or somebody from one side or the other will shoot me, and I'll wake up in heaven. I hope.*

Now the great lake stretched to the horizon like a ruffled coverlet. Rachel had not drunk since they left the house that morning, and as they got closer, she trotted faster.

*Sorry, girl. Ain't no way to get to the water around here. Storm wall's unbroken for miles and way too high to jump.*

The day seemed overly bright, and sweat stung his eyes, so he nearly missed Willa McClure sitting on a black horse in a nearby house's shadow. Bandit stretched out on the grass.

The girl met Ford in the street and looked over his blood-drenched clothes. Shit fire and save the matches, Santonio. What happened?

Rachel shifted beneath him. Ford groaned. I killed Benn and Clemens, but they didn't like it much.

McClure whistled. Can you ride?

I hope so. A few inches to the side and I'd be singin hosannas and strummin a harp. What are you up to in these parts?

She gestured toward the water. Keepin an eye on things in case none of y'all showed up. I wish you would have made your move on them deputies here. Maybe I could have helped.

Wasn't much choice.

Well, that's two less sons of bitches we gotta kill now.

We're still in it deep. Royster ordered his folks at the levees to blow their charges if the fightin gets too close.

McClure grinned. They're gonna find that harder than they think. She reached into a saddlebag with both hands and pulled out a snarl of fuses.

Ford grinned despite the pain. Good job.

McClure stuffed the fuses back. It's just a few feet from near the caches. They run all the way into the lakefront buildings. A bunch of Crusaders holed up there, but they're mostly lookin cityward, so I managed this much.

Smart, Ford said. It'll look like the fuses are still there. We'll have a while before anybody realizes they ain't gonna work.

The fighting sounded closer.

We need to tend that wound, McClure said.

When we can. So, these Crusaders. They're just sittin in them old houses.

Yep.

We'll need to go around.

I see you got your huntin knife. Good deal. But I brung you this just in case. McClure reached into her other saddlebag and pulled out two pistols fitted with suppressors. She handed one to Ford and gave him some extra clips. These should help keep them boys from realizin they're flanked, she said. For a little while anyway.

Another explosion rocked the pavement. The horses shifted and nickered. Bandit scratched his hindquarters as if nothing were amiss.

We better get to gettin, Ford said.

They spurred their horses toward the lakefront. Behind them, gunshots and explosions and screams and the great clinking of Troubler chains.

## ✦ 41 ✦

With the lakefront in sight to the north, LaShanda Long knelt by her red stallion, Cherokee. He had served her well, and in turn, she had loved him as she might have loved a child. If she could have had children. And now, as Troublers and Crusaders fought and died around them; as more Conspirator sleeper cells roared out of hiding; as they took the haughty and confident Crusaders by surprise and overwhelmed them block by block, LaShanda Long held Cherokee's head. Bullets riddled his sides. One of his eyes was a gaping red hole. Three or four blocks' worth of guards had bunched up and unleashed an enormous volley in her direction. Long had dove from the saddle, but Cherokee had nowhere to hide. So much power and grace torn to pieces. She wept as she stroked the horse's blood-soaked mane.

You did well, boy, she whispered. I love you.

She lowered Cherokee's head to the ground. He breathed deeply, good eye rolling. Long wiped away her tears. Then she unholstered her gun and shot Cherokee in the head.

When he had stilled, Long wiped his face as clean as she could manage and untangled his mane. A mother preparing her son for state. Then she stood. The rest of her horses, the lord's and deputies' entire remuda, had been assigned to their fellow Conspirators. She would make do with the first available mount.

*Lord, please lift us all in your sheltering hand.*

She walked the corpse-choked streets between shattered, fiery buildings, stepping over the dead, searching for a promising mount. A Crusader galloped toward her on a white gelding. She shot the man out of the saddle. When the horse slowed, she caught its reins. It reared, but Long held on. She threw an arm around its neck, whispered in its ear, stroked its muzzle. Then she saddled up and shot four weaponless Crusaders as they ran past.

*Ten of you for every round Cherokee took, and a passel for his life.*

She reloaded as bullets cleaved the air around her.

Everywhere, Conspirators and Troublers and Crusaders fired on each other from around corners of buildings. Clusters formed and shot each other and scattered and reformed as bodies littered the streets.

*Your mistake, Royster. You brought enough guards to handle chained and broken people, but there ain't enough of you in the world to stop us now. Our blood's boilin, and we're gonna scald you to death.*

Long's forces marched on the lake, backing the enemy toward the water. The Crusaders had no route of egress, no hope of shelter beyond the buildings and houses they could enter but not defend. They could only fight and die. Long rode down the nearest pod of guards, shooting three of them in the back as the other three broke in different directions.

And then, from the east and west and south, an enormous roaring fit to sunder the world from its moorings, the sound of voices raised in a common savage cry such as she had never heard. People surged up the street in a great wave, heading straight for her, whooping and screaming.

At their head rode Gabriel Troy on a paint with white boots, one hand gripping the reins, one pistol raised.

From the west came Jack Hobbes and Lynn Stransky, leading a column of freed prisoners who shot and hacked and ripped Crusader flesh. Mordecai Jones, Tommy Gautreaux, Laura Derosier, and Antoine Baptiste rode just behind Hobbes and Stransky, firing into the bunched Crusaders, trampling the loners under their horses' hooves. Baptiste and Derosier broke from the main force, a mob of Troublers in their wake, killing from horseback while their foot soldiers engaged the outlander guards with fists and knives. Paired bodies fell struggling to the ground and crashed through house windows and disappeared.

From the south came Tetweiller and his charges, stopping to break any chains Long's group had missed. Every freed man, woman, and child took up a gun or a knife or the nearest tree limb and attacked anyone in Crusade colors.

In an ever-decreasing semicircle, the outlanders retreated.

*None of this will do any good unless we can protect the levees. Plus, there's all them Crusaders across the river. Maybe they're already over the bridge and plannin to crush us between them and the lake, just like we're doin to their friends. I hope Ernie thought to assign lookouts.*

Someone—Hobbes? Stransky?—had sent two hundred troops to flank the retreating Crusaders, who found themselves surrounded. The Crusaders fired and slashed, even begged, but before long, they broke like walnuts in a vise.

The battle ended as if it were a candle someone had blown out. And as Troublers and former Crusaders dispatched the wounded guards and tended to friendly casualties, Long, Troy, Hobbes, Stransky, and Tetweiller met on the bloody and viscera-covered street. One by one, they dismounted. They looked at each other and at the scene, a blasted and burning wasteland superimposed on the geometric grids of what they had always called civilization. The air smelled of gunpowder and stool. Already, flies and crows and buzzards attended the dead and the dying. Carnage on a scale unimagined since the Purge, bodies piled like discarded children's toys. No one spoke for long moments.

Then Troy embraced Long, and the last two months of tension and self-doubt flowed out of her like water from a broken cistern. She smiled and hugged him back. And then they all laughed and cried and shook hands, even Stransky.

How's the arm? Troy said to Hobbes.

Hobbes grinned, looking demonic, his face covered in blood and soot. Don't bother me none to speak of. Seen Gordy?

No one had. They lapsed into silence again, awash in the sounds of distant gunfire and the lamentations of the wounded.

I don't wanna get caught between the water and the enemy, Tetweiller said. We best move on the lake, and all them folks across the river too, before they move on us.

Troy nodded. With their leaders out yonder at the wall, the southern outlanders will take a while to pick a move, but once they do, we won't have much time. Where's Santonio?

Long was worried about that too. He went after Benn and Clemens, she said.

Troy swallowed hard. All the faces around him turned somber. Well, surprise has been our best weapon. LaShanda, you and Jack and Stransky secure the lake. Me and Ernie'll take Mordecai and them and hold the outlanders at the bridge. If we can.

Tetweiller raised his eyebrows. We're really pushin our luck, dividin our forces over and over like this. Bad strategy.

Troy reloaded his pistols. We can't let Royster have the levees, and we can't afford to get hit from behind when the rest of em march north. So I don't know what else to do. LaShanda, if you ain't heard from us when you got your situation under control, come relieve us. If our part ends early, I'll leave a crew to gather the ordnance on the bridge, and we'll double-time it back here.

Take half my weaponsmiths, Long said. They can disarm the caches better than y'all.

Right. Troy paused, looking at each of them in turn. God bless every one of you.

With that, they broke apart, though Jones, Gautreaux, Baptiste, and Derosier remained behind. They approached and surrounded Long. Their faces betrayed nothing.

*If they beat me down for givin in to Royster, I won't stop em.*

Then Jones clapped her on the back. I hoped you and Santonio hadn't really turned. Gotta admit I thought about puttin a bullet in y'all's heads more than once.

It was Gabe's plan, she said, but we struggled with knowin what was right.

I reckon we all have, Derosier said. I'm glad we ain't gotta kill you.

Long smiled. I'm glad we don't gotta die.

Sweat poured down Baptiste's face. Lord, I wish this was over. I'm right tired.

Long saddled up. Me too. Seein y'all alive makes me happier than a flea in a doghouse, but we got business. May the Lord watch over you.

They all mounted up and saluted her. Then they rode after Troy.

Long turned her horse and trotted amid the refuse. Her fellow deputies and Lynn Stransky were already giving orders to their lieutenants, who sent word down the chain of command. The resistance forces numbered in the thousands, and as they moved across the city, the sound of their boots on pavement rattled windows. Long rode at the head of her column, Hobbes and Stransky flanking her, their combined masses marching shoulder to shoulder toward the lakefront.

**R**oyster felt a bit stronger, though still light-headed. Sweat poured off him, thanks to the wound and the southern weather. His shoulder throbbed with every heartbeat, but at least it had almost stopped bleeding. The firing from the wall and the woods beyond it had died down to the occasional burst, both sides waiting for the other to make a move. The levees had not broken, and Gordon Boudreaux had not returned. From the city proper, the clang and clash of steel on steel, hideous animal shrieks of pain, the guttural roar of ten thousand shouting voices. Yet he felt himself drifting.

*Let sleep come. What else is there to do here at the edge of civilization?*

Then the sound of galloping horses, dozens of them, drawing closer. Using the wall as a brace, Royster stood, his legs trembling.

In the distance, Gordon Boudreaux rode hard for the wall, leading at least a hundred men and women wearing Crusade colors, some standing in the stirrups and raising their weapons.

Praise the Most High! wailed Jerold Babb, his robes of office dirty at the knees, his face red and sweaty.

*Yes, thank you, Lord.* Boudreaux and company halted in front of Royster, the smell of the animals' sweat acrid and heavy. Royster smiled. *Gordon has again proven himself a loyal and resourceful servant of the Crusade. Now we can complete the wall.*

It's all I could find, Boudreaux said, dismounting. I count a hundred and twelve.

Babb shuffled over and clapped Boudreaux on the back. Bless you, Gordon.

Boudreaux glanced at him and said nothing.

Royster held out his hand. I would embrace you if it weren't for this wound. Instead, I give you the honor of procuring the wall's final section, with my thanks.

Boudreaux shook, his face as expressionless as ever. Then he turned to the troops. The first thirty of y'all, come with me. Give the others your guns. The rest of you, get on the wall and fire on that tree line. If so much as a squirrel sticks its head out, blow it off.

Boudreaux's thirty Crusaders gathered around him, the rest dismounting and tying their horses to whatever they could find. They climbed the ladders and crowded in beside the others, clustering around the fortified firing positions, slipping their barrels through the notches.

When they were ready, one of them signaled to Boudreaux. Let's go, the deputy lord said, spurring his horse.

He rode through the gap. The others followed.

*I pray he is up to the task.*

From above, the apocalyptic sound of all those guns firing at once, over and over, the cacophony punctuated with short pauses for reloading.

Don't use all your ammunition, Royster called. Be sure of your target.

He could not tell whether anyone heard him, but the effort took all his energy. The world swam out of focus. Sounds retreated into the distance. He slumped back down the wall, holding his wound and breathing hard. Babb sat beside him. Royster lay his head on the old minister's shoulder.

# ✦ 43 ✦

**B**oudreaux led his riders to the segment and dismounted. Then he picked up a towrope and looped it around his horse's chest, tying it off. Others did the same. The rest swatted their horses on the hindquarters, sending them back into the city, and waited near the rollers. Boudreaux and the riders urged their horses forward, the animals straining against the ropes and the chains and the weight, the enormous block moving perhaps a foot at a time. When it cleared a roller, the troops on foot heaved the log onto their shoulders and carried it to the front, where they pushed and pulled it under the ropes until it was positioned correctly. All of them watched the tree line, listened for shots, waited for the bullet that would cut them down.

Sure enough, after they managed to drag the section ten feet or so, gunfire erupted from the forest. Many of the foot soldiers cried out and fell and lay writhing, wounded in their torsos and legs and heads. Those on the wall returned fire, shredding the leaves and limbs so the Troublers must have believed the very forest had turned against them.

Boudreaux spotted Listerall on the wall and made a *come on* gesture. Listerall shouted to his guards. Some scampered down the ladders and, moments later, burst from the gap, running for the exposed rollers, humping them over the bodies of fallen comrades, placing them in front of the segment so the mounted troops could urge their straining horses forward again. The firefight continued, Crusaders falling every few feet, more coming off the wall and replacing them, the covering fire deafening. Everyone heaved and pulled until the wall could not have been more than five yards away, stretching in either direction farther than any eye could see. It would cut off New Orleans from the world for the first time since the great storm Katrina. It only broke for the levees at Lake Pontchartrain and the river, and Royster had confiscated all the boats, had mined the waterways themselves. He lacked the guards to keep people from trying to scale the wall, but most of the Troublers would not outrun the killing waters. Many would drown. Most of the others could be turned back from the high ground.

*Lord, save us. It's really gonna happen.*

Then a great heaving cry from the woods. Boudreaux turned in his saddle. Troublers burst from hiding, riding for the gap in their hundreds, shooting at the wall, at Boudreaux's troops, at the very sky in their ecstasy. A man the size of a tool shed led them, firing a shotgun one-handed. A handful of Crusaders fell bloody and lifeless around Boudreaux, while a volley from the wall took down a half dozen of the wild-eyed creatures bearing down on him.

What do we do, sir? a guard asked.

Pull, said Boudreaux. The man bent to his task, but then half his head disappeared. Blood and brain and skull spattered Boudreaux's horse. *Or die, I reckon.* He turned his horse to face the sortie.

Listerall appeared beside him, mounted, pistol in hand, square jaw set, eyes calm. Mister Royster wants you inside, he said.

Bullets cut the air around them. *He's takin me outta the field. And I don't care.*

Behind and above them, the firing intensified.

## 44

**B**ushrod watched Boudreaux take cover in the city. *Aww. Just when it looked like Troy's poor little baby might get himself shot.* The wall segment rested only feet from the structure itself, and the Crusaders were redoubling their efforts with reinforcements. *This Royster ain't no tactician. He's givin up the high ground and cover while a bigger force charges him. That's what happens when you put a goddam bureaucrat in command.* Bushrod turned his attention to the big man who had sent Boudreaux inside. *Look at that square head. If you stuck him in that gap and nailed some boards to his noggin, you'd finish the wall a lot quicker.*

The reinforcements formed a skirmish line to protect the movers. Bushrod rode for the leader. Six or eight Troublers were shot from their horses, which, hemmed in, kept running forward. Fire shot through Bushrod's left bicep. Blood flowed through a hole in his jerkin. *Right through the meat. Y'all can't aim for shit.*

The big Crusader drew his weapon and spurred forward.

Bushrod shot him in the leg and shoulder.

The Crusader fell off his horse and disappeared amid the charging Troublers as his mare smashed headlong into one of the riderless mounts to Bushrod's left. Bushrod reined up as his troops rode into the enemy's teeth, bullets thucking into flesh and shearing bone as men and women screamed and fell and clashed in single combat.

Bushrod dismounted. He squinted against the gun smoke and dust as rounds hissed by. Those running drag passed him, waving blades and guns, screaming. Dead humans and dying horses lay everywhere, limbs broken or shot off, heads crushed.

The big Crusader lay on his back in the flattened grass, his clothes tattered, his face a bloody mask. Bushrod approached and kicked his leg.

The man's eyes opened.

He grabbed Bushrod's ankles and yanked. Bushrod landed on his back, his head smacking the ground. Light exploded behind his eyelids. The Crusader rolled on top of him and sat on his chest and punched him in the mouth. A tooth broke. His lips split open. Blood filled his mouth. Another blow knocked his head sideways.

All around them, his Troublers fought hand to hand, slashed, bit, gouged, the Crusaders giving as good as they got.

*One hell of a scrap.*

The leader punched him in the nose. More fireworks behind his eyelids, his nose a circle of numbness with fiery edges, pain radiating across his face and down his neck. His enemy grinned, teeth reddened and sharp.

I'm Aaron Listerall, the man said. Glad to meet you. He punched Bushrod's injured arm. Bushrod roared. You're the biggest Troubler I've seen in these parts. Maybe I'll make a rug out of your hide.

Whoopty shit, Bushrod said, bucking as hard as he could. Listerall overbalanced and slipped forward, nearly to Bushrod's neck. As Listerall tried to keep his balance, Bushrod bit him in the crotch.

Listerall screamed, his voice rising higher and higher, and punched Bushrod in the forehead, knocking him loose. The Crusader crawled away, searching for his sidearm with one hand, holding his privates with the other.

Bushrod forced himself to stand, pulled his pistol, and shot Listerall in the back. The Crusader groaned and rolled over, hacking and choking.

Bushrod stumbled over to him. Name's Bushrod, he said. Sounds like you got somethin in your lung. Here, let me help.

He shot Listerall in the throat.

Listerall gargled and spat and crawfished. Then he lay still, his eyes open and staring.

Bushrod shot one of them out, just for fun.

Then he turned to the mobs near the wall, still locked in battle. He waded into them, shooting anyone he did not recognize.

Minutes later, the Crusade's ragged survivors ran for the city. No one relieved them. Up on the wall, the ranks had thinned, but they still fired into the Troublers.

Bushrod fired into the air six times in quick succession, and his reserves ran from the woods, hauling bundles of weapons, ammunition, water, bandages from their hidden caches.

On the wall, Crusaders shouted at each other to defend the gap.

Bushrod grinned and turned to those around him. Charge, he said, and don't stop shootin till they beg for mercy.

He ran for the city, his people roaring as they followed.

## 45

**W**hen the Troublers raised their battle cry, Babb seemed ready to vomit or cry or both. *The man is useless,* Royster thought.

Gordon, the envoy rasped. Perhaps you should help me up that ladder.

Boudreaux looked old and broken down. You could almost hear him creak. I reckon so, he said.

Royster's bandages were nearly black. That whole side of his body felt both sticky and slick. His brain had grown too big for his skull.

Boudreaux helped him to the ladder.

Over at the gap, Crusaders saw them taking the high ground and disengaged, sprinting for the other ladders.

Royster climbed, step by agonizing step, pulling with his good arm, Boudreaux pushing on his hindquarters from below.

## 46

One block from the lake, most of the Crusaders had garrisoned themselves inside houses and buildings. Some hid behind trees and hedges. Others hunkered on their knees in the open, guns shouldered.

Long wiped sweat from her eyes. *They still got all those people across the river and some at the wall. Given that probably eighty percent of our people are starvin and just outta their chains, this is gonna be close.*

Someone on the other side must have been noting the numbers. Long never heard the order to open fire, but the Crusaders' initial volley struck somewhere upward of a hundred Troublers and freed people. They fell, leaking blood and spinal fluid and brains.

Cover up! Cover up! Long shouted as she ducked into one of the old buildings, bullets thucking into the wood and brick, shrapnel spraying everywhere. Her Conspirators kicked in doors and smashed out windows and took positions inside, where they returned fire. If they had followed orders, those behind her would be seeking cover or waiting to relieve the front line, but with untrained troops, you never could tell.

Many of the Crusaders who had been standing in the open were already dead. Some had run off, terrified. Long grabbed the nearest person, a ragged Troubler with a filthy beard and clothes that seemed to have been stitched from dishrags. Go find Hobbes and Stransky, she said. You know who I mean?

The Troubler frowned. We're all familiar with your officials. What else did we have to do while sitting in the streets and starving to death?

Stransky wasn't on the streets. She's about as tall as you. Real skinny. Long, floppy dark hair. You'll know her cause she's got a big mouth and a lotta followers.

The man glared at Long and spat. We're fightin beside you because we hate those Crusade bastards, but we didn't sign up to run errands for a bootlicker who kept us in chains.

Long shook the man by his shoulders. We can blame each other later for a whole host of misdeeds. Right now, though, I can't be in three places at once. You want to kill Crusaders? This is how to make that happen.

He pulled free and looked about, seeming to consider the situation—the incoming fire, the structural integrity of the building, which seemed about to fall in. All right, he said. But I'm not doing it for you.

Tell Hobbes to fan out to the east, Stransky to the west. Another pincer movement. We gotta engage em all at once. You got it?

I'm not stupid, he said, running outside.

Long hated to put their fates in the hands of a malcontent, but she had to do something. The Crusaders were outnumbered but entrenched and determined.

*Splittin our forces a third time's like swimmin with a hungry gator. If you get away with it twice, you probably ought not to test God's patience again. But it's better than walkin this skirmish line and hopin.*

She grabbed two more Troublers, a man and a woman. To the man, she said, Run east and tell every officer you meet to be sure of their targets. If a stray shot sets off the explosives, we're all dead. Then she turned to the woman. You run west and do the same. Go on now.

She returned to her window and fired at the house across the thoroughfare. A Crusader bullet struck the wood to her left.

## 47

**F**rom their position at the storm wall's central explosives cache, Ford and McClure had watched Crusaders ducking into buildings along the street. Now the kid sat against the concrete with a sniper rifle at her feet, her six-guns holstered.

Ford knelt beside her, one hand covering his wound. They're makin their stand, he said. Some of em will come for these caches directly.

Bandit lay on his side, as peaceful as he would have been at McClure's hearth. If she had a hearth. So what do we do? the girl asked. Sit here and pick em off as they come out, or assault em from the rear?

Both. And hope LaShanda gives us some help. If she don't, we're like to get mighty wet.

McClure nodded. She took her binoculars out of her poke. She swept them back and forth. Look to the east, she said, pointing.

Someone had emerged from one of the buildings.

Ford frowned and checked his wound. He saw nothing new. I wish we hadn't had to let our horses go, he said. I can't run fast enough to do no good.

I got him, the girl said.

I'm sorry. I'll see what I can do from here.

Good luck, the kid said as she stood.

Lord be with you.

McClure left the rifle behind and ran east, Bandit pacing her. Ford turned away. Either the girl would prevail, or she would not. He had his own problems.

He grabbed ten sticks of dynamite and made a bundle with a fuse

long enough for perhaps a minute. The Conspirators were pressing
the enemy hard, keeping them too busy to think, but any time now,
more Crusaders were apt to get jumpy. He had to keep them thinking
more about their lives than their orders. Hunkering low, he crossed
the street and crept behind the nearest building, a long, low edifice
of crumbling red brick. He stood next to a window. Inside, Crusaders
shouted to each other and fired at the Conspirators to the south. Ford
took a match from his poke and struck it against the brick. Then he lit
the fuse. It burned quicker than he would have liked, but there was no
help for that. As the guns roared again, a great cacophony of blood and
murder, he smashed in the window and dropped the dynamite inside.
Then he turned and ran as fast as he could.

The Crusaders had covered all the explosives caches with tarps to
protect them from the weather. Ford and McClure had already secured
the tarp over the kegs of gunpowder and dynamite and plastique in
the central cache, so he sprinted west. When the building exploded, a
ball of fire shot into the sky and outward at least ten yards, shattering
windows along the block. A second later, a fist of hot air struck Ford,
taking his breath. He watched the caches, praying the tarps would keep
any burning debris off the ordnance long enough for him to get back
and put out the fire. Pieces of the building rained down, peppering
the road with gnarled chunks of brick, splintered and burning wood,
charred body parts. Ford dashed back to the central cache and threw
a handful of burning boards off the tarp and over the storm wall.

*Fewer sticks next time. Hell and damnation, my ribs hurt.*

He pulled his sodden, sticky shirt away from the wound, wincing.
He had no other bandage and would just have to fight with his rib
exposed. *Unless I drown in my own blood.* He spat out a thick glob of
gore and mucus. Then he pulled out his binoculars and scanned the
next several tarps in both directions. *No other fires on the caches. Thank
you, Father God.*

A handful of Crusaders burst from the building next door, which had caught fire on its eastern side. They goggled, mouths open, guns holstered. *I don't wanna shoot if I can help it. Then everybody will know I'm here.* In their shock, the Crusaders had not even registered Ford's presence. He reached into the central cache and grabbed four sticks of dynamite. He lit them one at a time and waited until the first had burned most of the way down. Then he threw that first stick as hard as he could, his whole torso afire. The dynamite arced end over end and landed on the guards' roof. He threw the other sticks, groaning. Two guards spotted him as he tossed the last one, their eyes widening as they raised their weapons. Just then, the first stick blew, obliterating much of the building and driving shrapnel through their bodies. They fell and lay still. The other sticks exploded soon after, and the building fell to pieces with several Crusaders still inside. One man lay writhing and screaming just outside the edifice. He had lost a leg, both arms, and much of his face. Another stumbled out of the building's skeleton, engulfed in flame. *Blast it.* Ford shot the flaming man to keep him away from the caches. Then he shot the dismembered guard out of mercy.

Crusaders boiled out of back doors and windows. Some saw him and pointed and raised their weapons.

*If they shoot, they'll hit the cache.*

Ford dropped his guns and held up his hands.

A Crusader two buildings down started toward him. She thumbed back the hammer of her single-shot rifle.

And then, voices raised in bloodthirsty ululations, Conspirators hit the Crusaders from the west. The outlanders standing near the buildings died first as someone mowed them down with what sounded like a Gatling gun. Misting blood hung in the air like smoke. From the south, thousands of people surged upon the Crusader positions. Royster's army emerged from back doors and windows, screaming as the Conspirators opened fire. Some were knifed. Some were beaten to death with rifle stocks or broken chains or bare fists. None got close to a cache.

Ford's world spun as his rational thoughts evaporated. He sunk to his knees and shook his head, trying to clear it.

Moving slowly, moaning with every other breath, Ford pulled off his shirt. Then he crawled to the nearest piece of burning wood. He picked it up by its unlit end, turned it this way and that to find the right angle, and then jammed the fire against his wound.

He threw his head back and screamed, dropped the board, fell and curled into the fetal position. Everything went dark for a moment. When he opened his eyes, the fighting had not yet reached him.

*Stay conscious. Don't die. Get up and fight.*

After a moment, he stood and limped east, hoping McClure was still alive.

**A**s she left Ford at the cache, McClure ignored the sounds behind her and kept sprinting. What else could she do?

A woman emerged from a building twenty yards away. McClure fired on the run. The bullet punched through the Crusader's rib cage. She pirouetted and fell, the ground beyond her painted red. She saw McClure and tried to draw her sidearm, so the girl shot her again, this time between her breasts, and she fell backward, twitching. As McClure passed her, two men emerged from the next building down, one of them glancing about, the other headed for the levee. McClure skidded to a halt and drew her other pistol, shooting the running man with her left hand and cutting down the stationary target with the right. Then she took off again, lungs burning, Bandit galloping at heel.

Up ahead, three Crusaders exited three different buildings, as if they had started on the same signal. McClure shot the first one in the shoulder. The man fell to one knee and then tried to stand and draw. Bandit veered off and leaped on him, ripping out his throat. His boot drummed the ground. The next-nearest Crusader shot at Bandit, but the bullet whined off the pavement. *Leave my dog alone, fuckface.* McClure fired, and the man dropped, clutching his chest as blood welled between his fingers. The third man sprinted for the nearest cache. Something was wrapped around his waist. A wisp of smoke curled up and disappeared.

*Oh, bloody shit. He's made a belt of dynamite and lit the fuse.*

McClure stopped and steadied her right hand on her left forearm, sighting in on the runner. She fired and was already running again as the bullet smashed the man's knee. The Crusader cried out and fell on his face. When he rose, he was ruined—nose mashed to one side, forehead sanded to the bone, a gibbering demon face. McClure shot him in the head, still sprinting, Bandit following, blood dripping from his muzzle.

Two more men emerged from a building down the way. McClure's bullets smashed into the wood near them, and they ducked back inside as she reached the dead man with the dynamite belt. The fall had jarred some of the bundles loose. The fuse had nearly burned away. The girl yanked out her knife and sliced it off. Then she cut away the rope holding the bundles to the corpse. She set off again just as two Crusaders dashed outside, guns ready. Probably the same two she had forced to retreat. McClure dragged the dynamite in one hand and fired with the other. A bullet zinged off the pavement beside the man on the right.

Shit, McClure spat.

She adjusted for distance as the Crusaders returned fire, slugs hissing all around her. Bandit dodged hither and yon, his tongue lolling, his eyes bright and wild. The Crusaders seemed scared half to death, as if her bravado had robbed them of their own. She glanced at Bandit, the best friend she had ever made. *They better not shoot you. I'll kill em all twice if they do.* Then, still running, she tripped over her own feet and hit the street rolling, coming to rest on her knees, ignoring the road rash. She shot twice, hitting one Crusader in the gut. The man doubled over as his fellow stepped forward, aiming, blasting away.

A hot poker drove through McClure's shoulder just underneath the clavicle, knocking her backward, the gun and dynamite tumbling from her hands. She landed on her back, her head barking on the road. She could not get a breath. Her left shoulder screamed fire and murder, the pain rising out of some bottomless well and bubbling to the surface one heartbeat at a time.

*Always wondered what gettin shot feels like. Big surprise. It fuckin hurts.*

Bandit stood beside her now. McClure picked up the dynamite and held it out to the dog, who looked at it, panting. Take it, the girl said. Hide. The dog looked at her for an interminable moment and then took the dynamite in his mouth. Go on now, McClure said, but still the dog watched her. Get, she cried. Bandit ran off between the buildings, the explosives trailing behind him.

*Good boy. Maybe you can live a long life full of beefsteak and bones.*

A roaring filled McClure's ears, like a storm breaking onto a beach. She stared at the sky for half a minute before she realized no one was shooting at her. She forced herself to sit up.

The Crusader who had wounded her faced the other direction, arms dangling, his pistol lying between his feet. Rushing toward him, a tide of humanity and horse, their war cry swelling. Conspirators shot and clubbed and stabbed and moved onward even as the lone Crusader dropped to his knees and held his hands to the sky, as if beseeching God for deliverance. Someone shot him. A moment later, his body was trampled underneath the horde. The earth shook with their charge. Stransky rode at their head, whooping.

McClure chuckled, then grimaced.

Stransky reined up in front of her, the army thundering past them, and dismounted. She knelt and patted McClure's good shoulder and raised her voice over the din. If Troy had fifty of you, he would have killed us all ten years ago.

McClure opened her mouth to reply and burst into tears instead. It felt odd. She had no experience with crying. A phantom horse stomped her shoulder over and over.

Stransky embraced her, minding the wound. She hid McClure's face against her gunpowder-reeking and sweat-soaked shirt. McClure blubbered away as the pain waxed and waned.

After some time, she felt herself regaining control, as if she were coming to consciousness after a long sleep. By then, the lakefront Crusaders were dead or running.

Stransky pulled away. Yonder comes Long. Reckon we ain't gonna drown today.

McClure grabbed Stransky's arm. You tell anybody I cried and I'll cut your fuckin throat while you sleep.

Stransky cackled and tousled her hair. Don't worry, child. You and me's solid.

When did I lose my goddam hat?

Stransky helped McClure to her feet. The wound sang a brittle aria. McClure gritted her teeth and allowed herself one groan.

Long rode up and dismounted. She was bleeding from a scrape on one arm and covered in sweat and grime. You're hit, she said.

McClure nodded. Cold sweat dripped down her face, her back. Ain't nothin. We gonna go after Gabe and them?

Course we are. Can you ride?

What kind of goddam question is that?

Long smiled. Then she whistled at a nearby Troubler and gestured. The man caught a riderless horse and led it to them. McClure gathered her pistols. One had been trampled. It was nicked and dented and misshapen, as if it had been struck by lightning. The other seemed fine. She holstered the good one and tossed the other.

*Nobody better hurt my dog. I hope he's got sense enough not to eat that dynamite.*

# ❦ 49 ❦

**T**roy and Tetweiller rode in the Conspirator vanguard, heading for the river. Jones, Derosier, Baptiste, and Gautreaux flanked them. Some of their troops rode captured horses, but most went afoot, carrying all manner of weapons—revolvers and pistols and hunting rifles and shotguns and clubs of all kinds and bladed weapons of every make. Those who could find nothing else carried rocks, bricks, nail-studded boards pulled from buildings. The Conspirators heard their enemy before seeing them—the low susurrus of hundreds, perhaps thousands, of voices. Soon, as the river bridge loomed closer, higher, Troy's army and the Crusaders spotted each other. Voices on both sides rose in anger.

The Crusaders waited, lined up shoulder to shoulder, their front line at the bridge's apex, the rest falling back to the south. They all seemed to be armed. At their head, Jevan Dwyer sat his horse, his long locks flowing in the wind. He was shirtless, a bandolier of shotgun shells crisscrossing his chest, the weapon itself lying across his saddle.

Troy pulled out his spyglass. The herald looked at peace, even happy. A long hunting knife was strapped to his leather belt. Whenever he shifted, his muscles rippled like water in the wind, the forearm sinews working and working as he maneuvered his string, more cat's cradles and hexagons and zigzags.

Looks like God Himself sculpted him outta marble, Tetweiller said.

Troy counted the troops. Dwyer must have held in reserve every living man and woman south of the river, and some from the north besides, at least two thousand. *We got more, but most of ours are half dead and poorly armed. I don't know how long pure spirit will last.* He turned to Tetweiller. You think we got a chance?

Tetweiller shrugged. We always got a chance. But I'd send half our number against that goddam mountain if I was you.

Troy spat. I reckon he bleeds like any other man.

He's too pretty to bleed. You might just tap milk and honey.

I aim to find out.

They halted at the bridge's base. Troy watched Dwyer, who sat like a statue, hard and unafraid.

Troy turned his horse about. His voice was already hoarse from shouting, but he did his best. I reckon you see what's before us. I aim to kill em all, startin with that Goliath up yonder. They got more guns, and they're better fed. But we got somethin they don't.

Shit pants? someone yelled.

Everyone laughed, even Troy. Some of the tension drained from the horde.

Troy took a deep breath of smoke-scented air. No. You got your spirit and your pride. It's your town they aim to flood. These streets they dumped you on? They're yours. They've taken your houses. They've chained up your families. Now they wanna take your lives. Well, I say that ain't God's plan. I say this is our city, unless we let em have it right here, right now. You gotta pick your road, hoist up your pack, and tote it for the rest of your lives. You gonna roll over and die? Or will you stand with me?

The Conspirators roared, raising their weapons over their heads. Mordecai Jones fired two shots into the air. Laura Derosier let out a war cry that might have curdled even Stransky's blood. The sound rolled over Troy and Tetweiller and up the bridge and crashed against Dwyer, who sat solid and stoic before it, as immovable as a continent. Troy turned back toward Dwyer and raised his hand in the air.

But before he could drop it and spur his horse, Dwyer raised his right arm. His string had disappeared. Instead, he held a white flag. It hung limp on the end of its short pole.

Troy turned in the saddle and held his flat palm to his troops. Their collective sigh kissed him like a breeze.

Now that ain't nice, Tetweiller said. He ruined your speech.

I reckon he's impolite.

A white flag. You think he's surrenderin?

I think he wants a parley.

What do you wanna do?

See what's on his mind. If he moves on me, ride him down to the ground.

Before Tetweiller could reply, Troy spurred his horse.

Dwyer ambled down the bridge.

Be careful, Tommy Gautreaux called.

Troy snorted. That was the most redundant piece of advice he had ever heard.

They met equidistant between the hordes. Dwyer was expression-less, as if he were watching a particularly dull children's game. Up close and shirtless, he looked bigger than ever, all muscle and jutting jaw.

Greetings, Lord Troy, he said. And congratulations. You wanted to be a Troubler. Now you're the worst traitor in the history of the Bright Crusade.

Troy spat. And your chin looks like a shovel. You got an offer, or did you just come down to flap your gums?

Dwyer grinned, his even white teeth looking strong enough to rend bone. I offer a bargain. Personal combat, just you and me. No guns. Only knives and the strength of our flesh. The loser's troops stand down. I see no sense in slaughtering your people. Only you.

Troy snorted. Behind him, the stamp of hooves, the murmur of whispered conversations. I reckon you're used to scarin people with all them muscles, but I've faced down nutria bigger than you.

Then you accept my offer.

No.

Dwyer looked puzzled. I don't understand.

Troy laughed. If you won, you'd kill everybody anyway. Maybe not with gun or knife, but with water. You want to fight me? Fine. But if you think I'm gonna tell these folks they gotta put their chains back on and die like good little sheep, you're dead wrong. And I mean *dead*, mister.

Dwyer sneered. Cowardice dressed in pretty sentiment.

In about three minutes, you'll find out exactly how scared I am.

Troy turned and rode back, expecting to hear Dwyer's hoofbeats or the shotgun blast that would kill him. But he reached his host without incident. Dwyer had ridden back to his own column. Troy grinned, ignoring the protests in his stiff knee.

How'd it go? Tetweiller asked.

I don't think he'll bring me a pie anytime soon, Troy said.

Tetweiller checked his pistols. You ready for this?

Troy looked over his shoulder and raised his hand again. On my mark, he shouted.

The Conspirators roared again. Dwyer's group answered them. Like two tribes from the world's birthing, enemies' flesh caught in their teeth.

On the bridge, Dwyer shouted to his troops.

*Should have made your speech earlier.*

Troy dropped his hand and spurred the horse, a guttural cry rising in his throat. His followers thundered after him.

The Crusaders rushed to meet them. The bridge shook and swayed as their voices echoed throughout the city.

Leading the vanguards on that red and smoking edifice of stone and metal, Troy and Dwyer collided. Their horses crashed and tumbled, throwing them. Troy and the herald flew past each other and skittered along the bridge, bowling down enemies as if they had been launched from cannons for precisely that purpose. Something ripped in Troy's left shoulder, the pain blinding. His sore knee jerked and twitched. Around him, horse smashed into horse and body into body, every individual sound swallowed in that thundering. Troy groaned and came up firing with his right hand, putting bullets through the heads of the six nearest Crusaders, others dropping as Troublers and Conspirators shot them and tackled them and slit their throats. At Troy's elbow, a withered and stinking Troubler woman leaped upon a Crusader's back and clawed the man's eyes out. He fell to his knees screaming, and she ripped his throat out with her yellowed teeth. Jones fired into the crowd and reloaded and used his horse as a battering ram. Derosier had been unhorsed and was firing with both guns, pistol-whipping Crusaders, screaming like a madperson. Gautreaux's riderless horse galloped by, blood painting its haunches. Antoine Baptiste fired with one hand and used the other to hack at a guard with a sword, the origin of which Troy could not guess. Tetweiller stood in his stirrups fifteen yards away, aiming and shooting, his face composed and serene, a single tear on his cheek. His horse straddled a corpulent body with a long gray beard bearing evidence of three or four meals in its tangles. The chambray shirt no more than rags, holsters empty where once hung two pearl-handled revolvers. The body bled from a dozen gunshot wounds and a deep gash near the heart.

*Aw, Tommy. May the Lord carry you to glory.*

A Crusader armed with a machete decapitated a half dozen skinny, filthy wretches until Baptiste shot him in the chest. Sofronio Blanco, a water bearer who lived on Troy's street, took a bullet between the eyes not ten yards away. Two Troublers were crushing a guard's skull with rifle butts when Jevan Dwyer rose behind them and smashed their heads together. They fell, brains leaking from their ears. Someone had slashed Dwyer across the chest, the wound long and red like the tail of a comet, but if it bothered him, he gave no sign. One of Tetweiller's fighters, a lamplighter named Marcelline Caron, ran at him with a hatchet. Dwyer pulled his double-barreled shotgun from the scabbard on his back and pulled both triggers. Caron flew back the way she had come, her chest and neck and face a mélange of bone and gristle.

Dwyer saw Troy and smiled.

A swarm of hornets had burrowed under the skin of Troy's shoulder, and his knee kept buckling. But he reloaded and shot a Crusader fighting next to the herald. Then he winked at Dwyer.

The herald roared, his torso running crimson, his shotgun smoking. He raised it and slammed its butt against a female Troubler's skull. She fell and lay still. Watching Troy, Dwyer stomped the back of the woman's neck. Troy did not hear her spine break, but her limbs spasmed. She might have been the same woman he had seen only a moment ago, felling Crusaders with her bare hands. Anger rose in Troy's gullet like vomit, burning his throat. A red haze descended, obscuring everything except the desire to strangle the life from Dwyer. And the herald must have sensed it, for he dropped the shotgun and motioned Troy forward.

Troy spat at Dwyer and took aim.

But before he could pull the trigger, a Crusader tackled him from the side, driving through Troy's injured arm. The pistol skittered into the crowd, through pools of blood and innards. It disappeared near the bodies of two felled and flopping horses, the animals' eyes rolling as they screamed. Troy twisted and landed on top of the Crusader. Then he jammed his thumb in the man's eye and ripped it from its socket. The Crusader shrieked, his eyeball dangling on his cheek like a wilted flower. Troy punched him in the throat, and his screams turned to hoarse cackles. The former lord of order pulled his other pistol and shot the Crusader in the face.

Something struck Troy in the jaw hard enough to make the world swim. He fell off the dead Crusader and dropped his pistol.

Jevan Dwyer stood above him, grinning without joy or mirth or compassion. And then he kicked Gabriel Troy in the face.

Troy's head cracked on the pavement. Dwyer sat on him, driving a fist into his jaw over and over, smashing his nose, his eye. Troy went for Dwyer's eyes, but the herald pummeled his hurt shoulder. Troy grunted and clenched his jaw against the next blow, but by then, Dwyer was off him and dragging him by the hair, headed for the bridge's edge. With one hand, Dwyer yanked him to a standing position, as if he intended to pull Troy's head right off his body. The ex-lord's scalp tore, spilling runnels of blood down his face.

The herald pointed to the water. Look yonder at the riverbank, he said. See how you have given your life for this city in vain. Dwyer raised his free hand over his head and waved it back and forth. Down on the banks, a man returned the gesture. Then Dwyer made a fist and held it stationary. The man fiddled with something on the levee. Dwyer pulled Troy's face close to his own. We will destroy those levees. Your city will drown. That is the beauty of the Crusade. Our people give their lives for the greater good. You and yours care only for yourselves, and that is why you fail. Why your triumphs are written in dust, why your hopes are as ephemeral as water in your hand. Watch, Lord Troy. Watch and see.

You'll die too, Troy croaked.

When you are gone, I shall sound a general retreat. My Crusaders will disengage and flee. We may suffer losses on our way to the wall, but you shall vanish from the earth.

Still fighting Dwyer's grip with one hand, Troy raised his leg and slipped his hunting knife out of his boot.

Down at the river, the Crusader darted back and forth across the levee. Then he shrugged.

Troy grinned with broken lips. Looks like your man lost somethin.

The herald's eyes were fiery coals. What did you do?

Troy's scalp felt as if someone had scoured it with acid and soothed it with pepper. So did his throat. He could not see the herald for all the blood, but he could feel the mass of the man's body in space.

I didn't do nothin, he said. But you forgot somethin important.

And what's that?

I ain't alone. For instance, you never met Willa McClure. She's good at doin odd jobs on the sly. Like slippin in while y'all fight us. Findin your ordnance. Tossin it in the river.

Dwyer dropped Troy and braced himself against the guardrail as he looked down on the riverbank. Troy struggled to his feet. Now six or eight figures stood in a circle over Dwyer's man, beating him with sticks, ax handles, the business ends of hoes and rakes. The Crusader lay as still as the grave.

Damn you to hell, Dwyer whispered.

Maybe I'll see you there.

And then Troy lunged and jammed the hunting knife in Jevan Dwyer's gut, all the way to the hilt.

Dwyer's eyes widened. His jaw clenched. Cords stood out in his neck. He grunted.

Troy grasped the knife's handle with both hands and yanked upward, despite the sunburst of agony in his shoulder joint. Amid the din, the squelch of ripping flesh. Blood gushed over Troy's hands, his forearms, his pants.

Dwyer moaned, a sound that seemed to stretch all the way to the horizon, and glared at Troy, teeth bared. Then he wrapped his hands around Troy's throat and squeezed, thumbs driving into the suprasternal notch.

The day grew faint again. Sounds faded, only Troy's own heartbeat strong and clear. He croaked and sputtered and tried to draw breath. He lost his knife. Such strength, as if Dwyer could have crushed stone. Troy fell to his knees, grasping at the herald's hands, trying to pry the fingers from his throat, but he had little strength in one arm, and his hands were slick with blood. The herald followed him down, his weight inexorable and crushing. The light was leaving the world. Troy drove his open palm into Dwyer's nose, snapping it. For a moment, the herald's grip loosened, and he swam into focus, his teeth red. Then he bore down again. Troy had spilled Dwyer's guts on the pavement, but the herald was still too strong. Troy's arms fell to his sides, dead weight.

And then a jerk, and the fingers slipped from his throat.

Troy gasped, barely able to brace himself before he fell face-first onto the bridge. He looked up.

The herald's eyes were wide, unseeing, disbelieving. More gore spouted from his neck.

Then his head tipped to the left and tumbled off his shoulders. The body collapsed onto Troy, pumping blood directly into his face. The herald's weight was like a boulder.

Throat on fire, lungs aching, Troy turned to the side and sucked in air, and then he rolled Dwyer off of him, his knee and shoulder protesting. The herald landed on his back, links of intestine dangling from the abdomen. The head lay nearby, mouth open as if surprised, tongue protruding. Troy sat up.

Ernie Tetweiller held a broadsword in both hands, its tip against the pavement, the blade dripping blood. Beyond him, men and women and children slaughtered each other, treading on the bodies of the fallen.

Troy tried to thank Tetweiller, but his croaking voice was unintelligible. Everything hurt, the accumulated trauma of the past weeks nestling in his muscles and bones. Tetweiller tossed the broadsword on top of Dwyer's body and reached into his poke. He pulled out Troy's pistols, holding them by their barrels. Troy nodded but held up one hand, palm outward—*Wait*.

He dug through the herald's pockets and found the colored string, balling it in his fist as he stood. He leaned over the side of the bridge and dropped it. The string fluttered in the air, stretching out and out as if some invisible hand were pulling it, molding it into new and alien shapes. It wafted on the breeze until it hit the river. When it disappeared, Troy turned, his body screaming with every movement, every breath.

Tetweiller appraised him. You look like hell.

Thanks, Troy croaked. He raised his eyebrows. A broadsword?

Tetweiller looked at the blade. It was almost six feet long from grip to tip. LaShanda said Dwyer loved em, the old man mused, and somebody dropped this one out yonder a piece. When I seen the herald tryin to squeeze your noggin off, it seemed like a good time to let him have it.

Troy glanced at the herald one last time and then turned his attention to the battle. Where's Mordecai and them?

Don't try to talk. Looks like he damn near crushed your voice box. Take your pistols and join the party when you get your breath.

The others, Troy said. Several bullets struck the bridge nearby. Both men ignored them.

Tetweiller sighed. Tommy Gautreaux's dead. Shot from the saddle and stabbed like he was a pincushion. The rest are still upright, as far as I know. You gonna take these, or should I hang em from my ears?

Troy accepted the guns as Tetweiller turned and shot a Crusader off her horse. You gonna take that sword? Troy asked.

You kiddin? the old man said. I damn near threw my back out swingin it once.

Tetweiller disappeared into the calamity. Troy knelt against a dead horse for what meager cover it could provide and reloaded with trembling hands. His shoulder buzzed and pulsed. His throat was misery. His knee had gone numb. Above, a sky so blue it hurt his eyes; below, the river flowed on and on, heedless and eternal. Tetweiller had looked ten years younger. Battle fever, hands and feet and eyes performing the tasks for which they had been made, better than any other restorative. Troy touched his mangled face and winced. Swelling, lacerations, deep bruising, a putty face twisted out of true. But Dwyer was dead.

*Now the rank and file. Smash em into paste or accept their surrender, but leave no threat to the city. This is your callin. Get up and answer.*

He took a deep breath through his swollen lips, not yet daring his nose. All right, he whispered.

He raised his pistols and stepped forward.

Then the pavement shook again. To the north, thousands riding and running for the bridge, LaShanda Long and Lynn Stransky and Jack Hobbes and Santonio Ford leading them, firing into the boiling maw into which Tetweiller had disappeared.

The new forces rode down the old, smashing into the Crusaders, stampeding them, splattering guts and brains with guns of every make, cutting throats and lopping off heads with blades confiscated from the dead, bludgeoning with whatever they had found—loose bricks, two-by-fours, broken handles from shovels. Royster's Crusaders found themselves with missing limbs, shattered spines, stove-in heads misshapen like pumpkins someone had stepped in, burst abdomens. Here a Troubler fell; there a Conspirator was pulled from horseback, his or her killer soon ground to paste under the mob's boot heels.

Troy leaned against the bridge's warm railing and watched.

Laura Derosier fired her scattergun, nearly cutting a Crusader in two. She brained another with the butt and executed him as he lay at her feet. A third Crusader broke off from a group and aimed at her as she reloaded, but some Troubler blew his face off with a close-range shot. Fifteen feet away, Mordecai Jones sat on a male Crusader's chest and alternated pummeling the man with his left hand and firing a revolver into the crowd with his right. Antoine Baptiste had holstered his firearms and now used a machete to hack away at a Crusader, who tried to shield himself with a shotgun until Baptiste switched angles midstroke and cut off his fingers. One vicious double-handed right-to-left stroke later and the man's head rolled down the bridge, tripping up a group of Troublers. They went down in a heap and someone's weapon discharged, hitting no one. A guard rode by and shot Baptiste in his upper thigh. He fell and rolled and struggled to his feet, grimacing. Troy shot the Crusader off the horse.

Tetweiller had mounted up again. Screaming something Troy could not hear, he led two dozen men and women armed with hatchets and axes and hoes and knives, perhaps one or two guns among them. They ran into a group of Crusaders and slashed away, blood misting above them like smoke. Tetweiller shot and reloaded and shot some more, his horse leaking from six or eight wounds, a gash across the old man's forehead spattering his chest with red droplets. Stransky and Hobbes fought back to back, one shooting while the other covered, turning and turning, bodies falling around them in concentric circles. A guard charged at Stransky mid-reload, a spear of some kind raised over his head. When they spun, Hobbes shot the man in both kneecaps. The spear clattered at their feet. Hobbes picked it up and threw it. The blade disappeared in another Crusader's back, and he screamed until Long's horse trampled him. She swept back and forth among the groups, shooting Crusaders, bashing their skulls in with a cudgel she had picked up somewhere, rallying troops into better positions. The chaos gave way to a more organized wave of bloodletting, Conspirators pushing Crusaders against the bridge's railing and killing them there or driving them over the side, where they fell screaming and were lost in the waters below. Here and there, Troy shot someone and reloaded.

In minutes, it was over.

Victors picked through the bodies, dragging their wounded or dead friends and kin back to the streets, cutting throats when they found a lingering enemy.

Long dismounted and made her way to Troy, who sat on the pavement, his weapons holstered, feeling the day's weight in every part of him.

She stroked his injured jaw with one hand. It's good to see you alive. Though you've looked better.

And you're a vision, he rasped. Thanks for comin. She unstrapped her canteen. He took it and swigged, the water burning his lips, his throat. Everybody alive? he asked.

She looked back toward the crowd. There's way too many folks to keep up with. Santonio's shot up some, but he's still on his horse. Mordecai got winged. Somebody amputated Laura Derosier's pinky toe with a paring knife.

A paring knife. In this mess?

Believe it or not.

He laughed, then groaned. Could be worse, I reckon.

Yeah. We lost some good folks today, but they lost a lot more.

For a few moments they sat together, taking in the sights, breathing the acrid air.

So what now, Madam Lord?

Long shook her head. Uh-uh. Lords serve until they die or resign. You ain't done either. I reckon even Stransky will follow you after what we did here today.

Troy considered the scene. Butchery on a scale the likes of which he had only read about. Pavement flowing with human fluid and tissue, the urine and feces of dead horses, corpses reeking in the sun. Weapons in every living hand, clasped in most dead ones. The stick-figure men, the scarecrow women, the emaciated children.

*What exactly did we do?*

We need to find Royster and finish this, he said. For New Orleans.

Long nodded. She patted him on his bad knee. He grimaced. Then she rose and went to find the leaders of the ragged force walking the bridge. The niceties—the mourning, the services, the prayers, the condolences—could wait.

Twenty minutes later, Troy sat a spotted brown on a cracked saddle. The mount seemed strong enough, but it did not know him, and he did not know it. It might have thrown its last rider as soon as the first shot was fired. But he had no time to hunt for a familiar horse. The levees and canals had been secured. The explosives caches were being disassembled under the direct supervision of Long's experts. Survivors of Dwyer's army were fleeing toward Royster's position as if it were a sanctuary instead of a killing box.

No one could rest until the city was secure.

Troy's lieutenants sat their own horses nearby—Long, Ford, Hobbes, Tetweiller. So did Lynn Stransky, her black hair like seaweed undulating in the tides. Jones's right side was sticky with dried blood. Derosier and Baptiste rode beside him, streaked with soot.

*If we're all Troublers now, we sure look the part.*

Hobbes trotted over and leaned in close, whispering. Reckon you could hang back. Look like you're about to fall outta that saddle.

Troy shook his head. This ain't the time, not with all these Troublers watchin. What we do now will set the tone for what happens afterward.

Stubborn as a mule, you and Santonio both. What else you want done before we head over yonder?

Send somebody to contact all the ordnance details. Remind em to watch their backs in case some Crusaders decide to stop runnin.

What about our own folks who think we're doin wrong?

They can live here in peace and disagree with us, or they can go. Their choice. Don't hurt nobody unless they try to hurt you.

Hobbes nodded and turned his horse, ambling toward a gaggle of men and women hauling and stacking the dead. As he gave the troops their orders and the ragged survivors trudged down the bridge, Troy gestured for everyone to follow him. Stransky grinned and winked.

## 50

**R**oyster dreamed of lying in his own bed, the window open, a breeze kissing his bare skin. His warm feather mattress enveloped him. The pillow felt cool and soft. He smelled freshly baked bread, likely from that corner stand he loved, the baguettes crusty and crunchy, the insides so gossamer you could practically see through them. His stomach rumbled. What he would not give for a plate of bread and smoked fish and hash browns. But when he sat up, his shoulder was black with blood, which stained the white sheets deep crimson. Pain struck him like a sledgehammer.

He awoke on the wall, his shoulder screaming.

The sun shone in the cloudless sky like God's own eye. Royster hacked up phlegm shot through with red tendrils. His throat felt parched. He opened his mouth to speak but only coughed. Boudreaux knelt and helped him drink from his canteen.

Many thanks, Royster said when he could find his voice. What is our situation?

Boudreaux laughed without humor. Not good.

He helped Royster stand. Around them, the sixty or seventy Crusaders still alive on the wall looked as frightened and timid as church mice. They were raising their hands in surrender, weapons at their feet. Below, a horde of Troublers watched them, weapons drawn. The leader, a blood-soaked giant with a ruined face, grinned through broken teeth.

*We are lost.*

From the city, the sounds of stamping feet, horses' hooves, the clatter of metal against metal—not just the usual din, but growing closer, louder, by the moment. Royster stared, his shoulder forgotten.

Minutes later, gaggles of Crusaders came into view, some mounted, most running. They looked over their shoulders as if certain that all the devils that ever were had risen out of perdition. And, Royster knew, such was not far from the truth.

## 51

**W**hen Royster had sent him into the city for reinforcements, Boudreaux had seen bodies piled like raked leaves. When he had come across scattered outlanders or loyalist New Orleanians, he had asked them to follow him. Some did. Others ran—where to, he could not say. But as time passed and ever more desperate stragglers appeared, he had known. *Royster's lost the levees*, he had thought as he led his company back to the wall.

Now another flock of shocked and ragged Crusaders boiled up the street, mimicking his earlier flight. They seemed not to mark the presence of the Troublers on the ground, who stepped aside and let them dash up the ladders and duck behind the wall's ramparts without incident.

As they came, Royster stood panting and wincing next to Boudreaux. Jerold Babb quivered nearby, eyes closed, praying aloud for their deliverance. Melton and Glau squatted like frogs.

And now came the rebel throng, a dark shadow stretching back and back into the city. What might he have done if he had been standing with Troy and seen such a sight? He would have drawn his guns and shot until the barrels melted, until the enemy cut him down, until Troy himself announced the victory or the surrender. Sometimes, when their posses had pursued Troublers into the bayous, Boudreaux had envisioned such a possibility, the Crusaders trapped on some hillock, surrounded, outgunned. Instead, it had come to pass in his own city, with his best friends leading the charge against his position. Nothing made sense.

His muscles ached. His head pounded. He had never felt so weary. Gordon, Royster whispered.

Boudreaux regarded the pale, withered envoy. He looked little like the man who had taken the High Temple for his own—seemingly twenty years older and shriveled, like the desiccated body of some long-dead desert animal. Boudreaux looked into the envoy's pain-reddened eyes. Yes, sir.

How long?

I'd give the first wave another five minutes at most, Boudreaux said. Then he gestured to the Crusaders on the wall. This lot ain't gonna be no help.

Lord, deliver us from thy enemies, Babb intoned for the hundredth time.

Royster swallowed hard and took a deep breath. He groaned. Make our faithful ready to bask in God's glory.

Protect us now, Father, Babb cried. We walk in the valley of the shadow.

Royster's pitiful force stood or crouched at ten-foot intervals—no discipline, no plan, no will. One man alone here, a group of six there. Two women crying on each other's shoulders even as they sharpened their knives with whetstones they had somehow retained as the city degenerated. Most weapons still lay at the Crusaders' feet. Melton and Glau looked as if they had already soiled themselves and probably would again. Babb babbled. No cover, no relief. Where was the glory? Where were the faithful? Where was God?

Still, with nothing else to do, Boudreaux moved from group to group, conveying the message to the brave and the weeping alike.

# ♣ 52 ♣

Troy, Long, Hobbes, Tetweiller, Ford, and Stransky reined up twenty yards from the wall. Their multitude milled behind and around them. No one fired. The Conspirators picked up and handed out the weapons that the Crusaders had lost or cast away.

On the wall, Gordon Boudreaux stood tall, one hand resting on his untied sidearm. Beside him, Royster swayed like a treetop in the breeze.

Jerold Babb stood near them, trembling. Blessed are the peacemakers, for they shall inherit the earth, he shouted, hands spread wide.

Shut up, Boudreaux said.

The minister's hands dropped. He looked at Boudreaux, then at Troy. This is wrong! cried Babb. Surely you know that in your hearts. Stop this devil's work. Turn your holy weapons on the enemies of God and reclaim your place in heaven.

There ain't nothin holy about weapons, Troy said. It took me all my life to learn that, but it finally got through my thick skull.

If that's so, Boudreaux said, why do you still carry them pistols?

No choice, Troy said. Not as long as other folks with weapons want to kill us. Not until we make a better world than this.

Troy turned to Hobbes and whispered, Nobody shoots Gordy or Royster. Leave five or six others alive. Pass it on.

Hobbes turned to Stransky, who turned to Bushrod—What did you do, she said to her lieutenant, run face-first into a hammer fifteen or twenty times?—and in this manner, the word spread through the ranks. The Crusaders watched the gathered New Orleanians, their expressions dark and full of loathing. A breeze kicked up, bringing with it an incongruous, almost otherworldly amalgamation of scents—the fresh smell of bougainvillea and morning glory, the sharper aromas of coppery blood and gunpowder, and the sickly sweet odor of rotting refuse. A single cloud passed overhead like a great schooner on the blue main. Someone coughed as they all waited for whatever came next.

Then Royster, leaning on Boudreaux, spoke in a thin and failing voice. Greetings, Lord Troy. I would ask how you still live, but I see those traitorous dogs at your heel.

You're the treacherous one, Ford said. They had tied him to his saddle, and he slumped forward like a drunkard, but his voice was strong. You're the one thirstin for slaughter and blamin it on God.

Troy held up a hand. Let the man have his say, Santonio. He can't hurt us now.

Royster grinned, still sharklike. You've won nothing. Matthew Rook's reach exceeds any man's, and we are but a single finger on his hand.

Troy rode out five feet beyond the others. If God's on our side, Rook don't matter. And if He ain't, your boss is the least of our problems. Either way, you'll never know.

Well, Royster said, what are you waiting for? Get it over with.

Troy smiled. First, watch this.

Countless Conspirators dropped their weapons and ran for the Crusade's supplies beyond the wall, while others rode out and yoked their horses to the last section of wall. A few minutes of beasts and humans straining and grunting, and the section fit into place perfectly, as Melton and Glau had intended. Other troops hauled over ladders and thick planks and hammered-flat scraps of metal, and they nailed and screwed the section to those on either side. They filled holes and covered the section in pitch. Carrying what they could and leaving the other tools behind, they climbed the ladders to the top. Crusaders stood aside as they pulled the ladders up and eased them down inside the wall. Then Troy and Stransky's people descended back into the city, taking all the ladders away except the one nearest Royster and Boudreaux.

The Crusaders watched it all without a word.

When it was done, Royster patted the wall and wheezed.

*He's tryin to laugh, and that's all he's got in him.*

We're takin your goddam wall, Tetweiller shouted. And your river mines. We'll use em to keep trash like you out.

Ernie, please, cried Babb.

Fuck off, Jerold. You ready, Gabe?

Troy pulled his sidearm and shot the Crusader nearest Boudreaux and Royster. The man cried out and tumbled against the outward-facing ramparts. The assembly listened to him die.

For a moment, nothing else happened. The very day seemed to hold its breath.

And then the horde opened fire.

They tore the Crusaders to pieces.

Royster fell to his knees and curled up, covering his head with his hands. Babb dropped, shrieking in fear. Boudreaux stood next to them, thumbs tucked into his belt. Bullets smashed into Crusaders and the iron bulwarks and the wall itself, splintering its wood. Bodies crumpled. Booming gunfire covered the screams and gurgles of the dying. Smoke roiled, heavy and thick like a fire made from human fat. Seeing their fellows shot down like clay targets, perhaps a dozen Crusaders, Glau among them, took their chances and jumped over the far side.

It was over in thirty seconds.

Cease fire, croaked Troy.

Jack Hobbes and Ernie Tetweiller rode up and down the line, repeating the order. The shots tapered off and finally ceased. Ford slumped in his saddle, holding his injured ribs. He holstered his pistols and tried to smile. Screams emanated from outside as the Crusaders who leaped for safety bemoaned their broken ankles or worse.

When this is over, Troy said to Stransky, let's send somebody up top. Put them wretches out yonder outta their misery.

Stransky snorted. You old softy.

On the wall, five Crusaders half crouched, their hands still in the air. They prayed aloud. Babb led them. Royster kept silent.

Don't worry, Envoy, Troy said. We're gonna let you live. Might as well get up.

Boudreaux helped Royster to his feet again. The envoy leaned on him and sneered. You have won your precious city, Royster said. But Gordon and I will stand by the Lord's side when you are judged. And when He tosses you into the pit with the rest of demonkind, we will celebrate with the longest hosanna in heaven's memory.

I got a feelin you ain't gonna have much better luck in the next world than you had here, Troy said. Now come on down. Use the ladder or jump. Either way, you're done.

Behind Troy, everyone roared in celebration. The five living guards descended, shaking like palsied elders. A brief, almost transcendent cool breeze sprung up and passed, leaving the dump's stink and the matted rats and crows slinking throughout the city even now, drawn to the putrescence that would only get worse in the damp heat. Standing beside Boudreaux, even Royster, envoy to the world's largest and bloodiest charnel house, seemed cowed. Then he turned and whispered to Boudreaux.

Troy caught Hobbes's eye. Be ready, said the lord of order.

# ✤ 53 ✤

When the last Crusaders surrendered, Royster turned to Boudreaux. I don't believe they'll let us live, the envoy said. No, they have some pageant in mind for us. A show for their Troubler comrades. But take heart. The Most High will welcome us into His everlasting arms. Here on Earth, Matthew Rook shall spread our names throughout the realm. We are martyrs. And that means we never truly die.

He's right, Gordon, Babb said, his voice a thin reed in a strong wind.

The Conspirators' thundering cheers broke into pockets of catcalls and taunts. Troublers from the swamps and bayous, former Crusaders, and frail freed people stretched back as far as Boudreaux could see, individuals merging into a composite mass covering the streets like floodwaters. Smoke and the thick smells of slaughter hung over the city. But Boudreaux registered all this with only part of himself. The rest of him studied the envoy.

*Look at all that gray hair, them wrinkles around his eyes and mouth. Like he climbed that ladder and stepped into his own future.*

Royster's blood loss had paled him, as if he were already shifting into whatever translucent form might come next. Below them, the cheers and jeers died down. Royster smiled, as he so often did, still confident in his mission, his faith. Even after all the murder. This man had forced Boudreaux to torture, to stand against his friends, to kill in cold blood.

*Except that ain't true. I always had a choice. I could have died a man of*

*God. Instead, I did what some boss asked me, just like I always have. I did it*
*for my friends and my city, but I also did it for myself, because I was scared.*
*Well, I lived. And it only cost me my soul.*

Gordon Boudreaux, former deputy lord of order, New Orleans
principality, was a husk without bone or sinew or gut, so that none
could say what it once might have held. Perhaps nothing.

He shoved Royster away.

The envoy stumbled into Babb, who fell. Royster tripped over him
and sprawled against the fortifications. The envoy's eyes widened. His
shark's grin disappeared.

Movement from behind, a form rising from underneath bodies.
Boudreaux whirled and fired. The architect, Melton, fell back onto the
dead, a hole in his forehead. Blood trickled from it and ran down his
face like tears.

Boudreaux turned back to Royster. You ain't no martyr. You lost
a whole army and made one for your enemy. You think Rook's gonna
sing your name for that?

Gordon, we can—

You keep talkin about *we*. But you wasn't never on my side. Or
God's. You're just a madman's errand boy. Well, you picked the wrong
damn city.

Royster held up his hands in surrender. Wait—

Boudreaux shot Lisander Royster in the head.

The Troublers roared again. Royster lay on the wall, fingertips
brushing the balustrade, eyes open to the sky, as if searching for a
heaven that would accept a craven, bloodthirsty piece of trash like
him. *The real shame of it is that I ain't so sure he's wrong. About heaven and*
*hell, about God, about wipin away all our stinkin blasphemy in a Purge. We*
*deserve it.* The void inside Boudreaux howled, but now, looking on the
mounds of corpses, amid the chittering rants of the mad crowd and
the smells of garbage and death, that void had spread everywhere else

too. They were all flotsam, wave- and wind-tossed, now submerged, now breaking the surface. But always and forever trash. Him most of all.

He turned to the crowd below. It fell silent, as if he had slit its collective throat. He stepped over bodies until he stood over a ladder notch and looked down at Troy.

Come on down, Gordy, said Troy.

No.

It's over.

Boudreaux sighed. He took off his hat and laid it on the nearest body. I never stopped bein your friend, he said. But you asked too much of me.

Gordon? Babb said from somewhere nearby.

Boudreaux raised his weapon and jammed the barrel under his chin.

## 54

**H**obbes fired. The bullet smashed through Boudreaux's right thigh. He dropped his pistol and fell against the far-side ramparts.

Troy spurred his mount forward. He reined in and grabbed the ladder as his people held it steady. Then the lord of order stepped from the saddle onto the rungs and pulled himself up, his body throbbing, his head fit to burst.

Up top, Boudreaux was drawing his other sidearm. Gritting his teeth against the pain, Troy hurdled Jerold Babb, who ducked and covered, and kicked Boudreaux in the jaw as hard as he could. The deputy's head rocked back, and he slumped as if boneless, the gun sliding from his grip. Troy picked it up and threw it over the side and sat next to Boudreaux, cradling the deputy's head in his lap.

He brushed the hair out of Boudreaux's face. Sorry, he said. Don't nobody get off easy today.

Hobbes and Long hauled themselves onto the wall. They picked their way over the bodies in silence, as if afraid someone might awaken. Babb got on his knees and watched them, tears on his cheeks, his old-man hands trembling.

Y'all help us down, Troy said. I feel like I could sleep for a month.

Babb crawled over and squeezed his arm. Gabriel, I—

Not now, Troy said, pushing Babb's hand away. Maybe not ever.

## 55

Sister Jewel moved about the sanctuary, setting hymnals in their racks as Troy watched from the front pew. Votives flickered on the altar as they had done since the old times. Her long and angular shadow attended her. She hummed under her breath, tuneless, the song unrecognizable. A strand of graying red hair had slipped out from beneath her habit and dangled against her cheek.

Soon the back door opened, and Sister Sarah stepped inside. Troy stood. Her habit seemed more severe than ever, more shapeless. How much did she weigh? Did she bear any scars or warts or freckles? How old was she? She might have sprung whole and clothed from the river, from stone, from the very air. She was a great mystery, like faith itself. Like love.

She approached and studied him a moment. Then she turned to Sister Jewel. You about done?

Jewel wiped her forehead with her sleeve. Well, I still need to sweep and clean up the wax on the altar, and—

Sarah cleared her throat. Surely that can wait a bit.

Troy pretended to cough.

Sure, Jewel said. Evenin, Lord Troy.

Take her easy, Troy said.

Easy ain't our way.

When she had gone, Troy and Sister Sarah sat and faced each other. I know you're hurt, Sarah said, but I've been back for two weeks. You could have come sooner.

His left arm hung in a sling. His right knee was thickly bandaged. At least his face had healed some.

Sorry, he said. Got my tail end kicked, but the other guy got worse. How about you? Any problem gettin back inside?

No. Your lookouts took care of us. It was easier than gettin out in the first place.

I'd hate to climb anywhere in that habit.

They fell silent, sweating, self-conscious. Troy sensed her gravity, the elemental yearning magnets and metal must feel before they come together. Did she feel it too?

*It's like somethin inside me has always tossed and turned, and now it's come to rest. Maybe this is what peace feels like. Or possibility.*

Lands, she said. It's hot.

Yeah, he said. So what's next?

She swept her hand from left to right, taking in the sanctuary. The Lord's work is never done. This might be the greatest evangelical opportunity since the ancients' time.

So you'll stay.

New Orleans is my home. I learned that all over again when I left. I won't abandon it again this side of the grave.

Troy nodded and looked around. How long would it take Sister Sarah to fill those pews? Some Troublers were Catholics who never could abide living under the Crusade's yoke. Those folks would probably come to Mass. Others would trickle in—the converted, the curious. The sisters might even need a bigger church.

But someone else would have to see to that.

I'm glad, he said. This town needs you.

How about you? Royster's dead. We've all got sanctuary. What now?

I've been thinkin about that. I've had a belly full of fightin. I'd like nothin better than to set these guns down and never pick em up again.

She smiled. It did not seem happy. But? she asked.

But Royster was right about one thing—nothin's really over. Rook still runs the world. I doubt he'll scrap his plans for a new Purge. Or leave us be.

So?

So we can't just sit here. Besides, Royster burned down my house, and I don't cotton to movin into the presbytère with Jerold Babb. I reckon he snores.

Sarah did not laugh. I heard you set a dozen Crusaders free so they could spread the word of what happened here. Maybe Rook will decide we ain't worth the trouble.

It was only five. And no. He'll be more determined. If others out yonder don't get in the fight, he'll settle us, sooner or later.

But you can't beat the whole Crusade. That's your pride talkin, and when you have to swallow it, you'll find it the bitterest draught you've ever tasted.

He let the quiet stretch around them for a while and took her hand. She squeezed his in return. Her sweat mixed with his, her pulse a steady thumping that matched his own heart's rhythm. A single tear slipped from her eye. He wanted to hold her, kiss her, build a life with her in the soil they were seeding here.

*I'd stay for you and let the world burn. God help me, I'd do it, if you'd only ask.*

But she never would.

He picked at a loose thread on the pew's cushion. We're makin a council. Every member with an equal voice and an equal vote. Officially, it's me, Jack, Ernie, Santonio, LaShanda, and Stransky. We'd put Gordy on it, but I don't think he'd accept.

Sarah raised one eyebrow. Stransky agreed to that?

A man can hope. We plan to offer her and her people equal seats to even out the numbers. But we need a swing vote. Somebody we can trust, somebody who loves this city and all its people, who'll always do what's best for everybody. We need you.

Sarah sighed. For a moment, she looked up at the cross. Then she shook her head. I got too much to do already.

You wouldn't have to give it up. You'd be addin to your ministry's influence.

I ain't no politician.

Me neither. But somebody's gotta lead.

It don't gotta be me.

You're the only person me and Stransky will ever agree on. Please, Sarah.

She rubbed her temples. A bit of hair slipped out from under her habit, as Jewel's had done. It looked auburn, but that might have been a trick of the light.

If Stransky agrees, I'll do it until it interferes with my work here, she said. Then I'll resign.

Troy nodded. Thank you.

You said it's *officially* you and the others. What does that mean?

He picked at a scab on the back of his hand. It was hard to look at her and say these things.

You're right about how we can't beat the whole Crusade, he said. But we can cut off its head.

Her jaw tensed. You're goin after Rook.

Troy looked her in the eye. She deserved that much, and more. Yeah. Him and his whole inner circle.

She shook her head. More violence. More death.

I don't want it. But it's them or the world.

Maybe somebody worse would take their places.

Who could be worse? They wanna kill nearly everybody on the planet. Again.

She laughed bitterly. So Gabriel Troy's gotta stop em because nobody else is up to the task. What did I say about pride?

I don't think I'm the only one who could. But nobody else is.

Her grip tightened. Nails bit into his flesh near the scab he had picked. Or maybe you're lookin for a reason to keep doin what you've always done. Ride. Shoot. Kill.

That ain't fair.

Are you sure?

Look. We've talked about it at length.

Well, now I feel better.

We're gonna go to Washington and find somebody in authority, somebody who's as horrified as we are. There has to be one. And then we'll kill everybody that outranks him. Or her.

Sister Sarah turned away. Her free hand gripped the crucifix dangling on its leather lanyard. You want to stop mass murder by committin the same sin on a smaller scale.

He let go of her hand and took her face in both of his, turning her head, gently, gently, until he could look into her eyes again. I'm tellin you *I don't want this*. I'm sick of death. But they ain't gonna stop unless somebody makes em. And me—well, I've got too much blood on my soul already. Better me than some kid who's still got a chance to see heaven.

Hundreds of miles between here and there, she said. All of em filled with Crusaders who want your head. You'll die before you reach the capital.

I reckon so. But I couldn't live with myself if I didn't try. She pulled away. He reached out, tentative, as if trying to grasp a butterfly. He laid his hand on her shoulder, just enough to feel her flesh and bone underneath the habit, the heat of pumping blood, intake of breath. Life. *I have to say it.* When he spoke again, his voice quivered.

Sarah. I meant what I just said. But if somebody I cared about— somebody I loved—was to ask me, I'd stay.

For a moment, she said nothing. When she turned back to him, tears stained her habit even darker. She stroked his cheek, her fingers wisping through his four days' beard. Sometimes, she said, I wish for you more than anything. Mother of God, forgive me. But I can't

abandon my vows to satisfy my own traitor heart. My duty is—I—I
just *can't.*

She stood and scurried across the room, her garments swishing like
quick, excited breaths. A sound lovers might make as they touched.
She put her hand on the doorknob and paused.

Sarah, Troy said. I—

My prayers ride with you. Be well.

Then she was gone.

Troy settled back against the pew. The back door was closed against
him, just as it had always been and always would be. He stood.

Goodbye, he whispered.

Then he turned on his heel and limped out. The votives flickered
in the breeze of his passing.

Before Dwyer and Royster came to town, Camp Street had mostly
belonged to the sisters, who traversed the sidewalks, market bundles
in hand, or rode one of the two horses they stabled nearby. Only the
oldest hardliners had ever complained. Troy had always told himself he
protected the sisters in the name of Christian mercy, but he had done
it mostly for Sarah. He could admit that now. He would not meet God
still lying to himself.

With Japeth hitched nearby and munching oats from his feedbag,
Troy sat on the sisters' front steps and noted the changes Royster's
coming had wrought. The Temple's officers would have their hands full
for months—filling residential requests, expanding crops, integrating
Troublers into the trades, making sure everyone had enough food and
clothing and water and shelter and peace. In anticipation, people wandered Camp in droves, sizing up empty buildings. Easily a hundred and
likely twice that number, walking to and fro, talking and laughing, all
ex-Troublers. Not so long ago, Troy would have killed them all or died

trying. Now they nodded to him as they passed, and he nodded back. They shared the city. He could only pray it lasted.

Stransky and Hobbes rode up in a mule-drawn wagon and stopped next to the curb in front of Troy. Boudreaux sat in the back, bound with rope, his leg wound bandaged. As far as Troy knew, he had not looked anyone in the face since they pulled him off the wall. Not when they visited him in the Temple's jailhouse infirmary, not when they tried to explain how everyone understood what he had done, not when they told him they believed God would understand too. Boudreaux had offered no explanations or insights. He had stared at the walls, the floors, the barred windows of the cell where they protected him against himself. But the prison was no place for a man like him. If he sought death, he would find a way, and if he wanted to live, he could not do it in lockup.

Stransky and Hobbes climbed into the back of the wagon and helped Boudreaux up and out. Troy went to him and put one hand on his shoulder.

Gordy, Troy said. Look at me. Troy patted Boudreaux's cheek and nudged his head upward. The deputy's eyes were haunted and blood-shot. Listen, said Troy. There's somethin I gotta do outside the city. I'll be gone a while. Maybe forever, because it's dangerous. I need somebody I trust to watch over the city.

Boudreaux looked away again. Task Jack. Leave me be.

Jack's comin with me. So are the others. I need you.

Nobody needs me.

Again, Troy took Boudreaux's face in his hands and made the young man look at him. You're wrong. Everybody needs you. Especially me. I can't do what needs doin knowin Sarah's in peril. I need a good man to keep her safe.

I ain't a good man.

Only a good man could go through what you did and still come down on the side of what's right. I don't know a better man than you.

Boudreaux's face was a study in despair, painted in darkened hues of blood and anguish. *God won't never forgive me for what I did.*

*God will forgive anything if you ask Him. Have you?*

*I ain't got no right to speak to Him.*

*Everybody's got that right. And you won't find a better place to call on Him than here. Take care of this place, Gordy. Take care of* her. *Please. I'll beg you if I gotta.*

Boudreaux looked at Troy a moment longer. The deputy trembled, as if the war inside him might spill out and leave a heap of muscle and sinew torn asunder. Then he sighed, as if breathing exhausted him. *I reckon so,* he said.

Troy patted his shoulder. *Thank you, my good friend. Jack, let's get rid of these ropes.*

Hobbes pulled out his hunting knife. A moment later, the bonds lay about Boudreaux's feet. Troy stuck out his hand. Boudreaux shook it. Troy embraced him.

When Troy let go, Hobbes shouldered his way in and hugged Boudreaux, who grunted. *Missed you, son,* Hobbes said, grinning. *Let's get you inside. Comin, boss?*

*No,* said Troy. *There's some things I can't do twice.*

Hobbes nodded. Then he put his hand on the small of Boudreaux's back and guided the younger man toward the doors.

Troy turned to Stransky. *Now. Let's talk about what comes next.*

Corpse-disposal crews had been working day and night since the battle, sometimes hampered by angry citizens wanting to hang dead Crusaders from lampposts or dump them in the river. New Orleanians who had stayed loyal to the Crusade, or who could not abide seeing so many of God's temples desecrated, confronted those crowds. Only Troy and Stransky's unity staved off violence. Many had been disappointed to hear Royster's troops would receive a proper Christian burial outside the city, only consoling themselves with knowing that the Crusaders would fertilize the land with their own decay. Others, reticent to repudiate long-held beliefs, grumbled that Troy had overstepped by taking arms against God's chosen. Crusader and Troubler clashed with words, deeds, and, on a few small-scale occasions, fists. *Seems like the savagery we found inside ourselves won't go back in,* Troy thought as he and Stransky passed a crew stacking flyblown bodies into a wagon. The detail wore bandanas over their noses. *We've gotta find a way, though. The Bible says there's a time to kill and a time to heal. There's nobody left to hurt but each other, and we've done enough of that.*

The lord of order's office had been stripped clean of Royster's belongings. Now Troy sat at his old desk and looked at Stransky across its bare, distressed surface. She grinned. The last time she had sat in that chair, she had been in chains.

We need to fortify the waterways, she said. They're the Cult's best chance to get inside. Raise the levee walls, buttress the river positions, map Royster's mines.

Troy sighed. I wish you wouldn't call it a cult. It's still my religion.

Her smile disappeared. I ain't talkin about your beliefs. I'm talkin about the organization. A Crusader might be good, but the Crusade has been rotten from the start.

I can't defend the Purge or what Rook tried to do here, but the Crusade did good too. It brought peace. It didn't care about who you were or where you came from or what you looked like, as long as you loved God.

You mean, as long as you loved Jonas Strickland.

I'm sittin here with you. Don't that show what I really mean?

Maybe.

You've blamed us for everything bad that's ever happened and ignored the good. We did the same to you. I bet that's how it's always been. Just folks tryin to get by and rammin up against each other like two addled horses. But now we know each other.

She watched him, her eyes sparkling with cunning. But any system built on genocide needs killin. You know that, or you wouldn't be plannin what you're plannin. The question is how far you're willin to go.

Troy laughed, humorless and flat. You want me to wipe out every Crusader because one leader lost his way. How is that different from genocide?

It's self-defense.

How do you figure?

The Crusade's way has always been *kill anybody that don't think like us.*

You're sayin that to me when we just left the sisters'?

I am. You ain't in love with nobody from my bayou.

We just fought beside you. You're sharin the city and the leadership. I'm goin to Washington to kill Rook. What else do you want from me?

To know you're all in. That you'll walk over anybody who gets in our way. That you ain't gonna balk when Rook's in your sights.

I didn't balk with Royster.

No. But Rook's bigger than that. He's more important and less personal.

When we march on Washington, we'll kill Rook and his inner circle. Their families and friends. Their lieutenants. Their generals. The whole leadership. Even their pets. Ain't that enough?

She sat back and pondered a moment. Then she shrugged. I reckon we'll see.

Troy tapped his fingers on the desk. Stransky would never change. As long as she lived, she would poke and prod him. Well, he said, before we can worry about Washington, we gotta figure out how to keep this city from eatin itself when we're gone.

Her long hair hung in her face. She peeked at him from behind its curtain. For starters, no second-class citizens.

Nobody's gonna be persecuted for worshippin God their own way. Your people will get the same courtesy mine do, and Sarah's.

We're all one people now.

Exactly. Nobody's knifin each other. Everybody's eatin. Everybody's workin.

She nodded at his guns. What about weapons?

We keep em in the armories until they're needed.

But who decides when to distribute and how?

The council.

Stransky looked at him for a long time. He looked back at her, holding her gaze, neither of them blinking. Finally she nodded. I can live with that. Though I can imagine there'll be times when folks ain't got time to wait on a vote if what they need is a gun.

He got up and poured them glasses of ice water. She drank half of hers. He sat back down. I'd like to name you a deputy lord, just like Jack and Gordy. All of us accountable to the new council.

Stransky burst out laughing. I ain't no deputy.

It's just symbolic. Shows we're together. Besides, I won't even be here. It's likely I'll never come back.

For my people, it'll be symbolic I've rolled over. That's just touchin a match to a fuse.

Troy folded his hands and thought a while. He had not wanted to say what would come next. It tasted like dirt in his mouth. But New Orleans needed it.

All right, he said. Co-lord.

Stransky laughed again. Well, if this don't beat all.

This way everybody will know you'll never stop talkin in my blasted ear. No one person with too much power.

She shook her head, grinning. Never would have guessed this day would come in a million years.

Me neither.

All right. We got a bare-bones idea of what to do with New Orleans. Now all we gotta do is save the rest of the world.

Troy sipped his water. It soothed his raw throat. He leaned over and took her hand. She almost jerked away but did not.

I aim to take Jack, Ernie, Santonio, and LaShanda with me, he said. We're already pickin proxies for our duties and the council. They'll raise the crops and work the forges and keep the peace until we get back.

Who's got your proxy?

Mordecai Jones.

And what about my folks?

We'll divvy up duties. Water, security, sanitation, housin, a hundred other things. You'll get equal representation on the council. As for you, I could use you on the road. I've studied the maps and picked a route, but your contacts would make us twice as likely to get there alive. Maybe even get back. Or you could keep your seat on the council and be co-lord with Mordecai. Your choice.

She got up and walked to the stained-glass window and leaned her forehead against it. Troy followed and stood beside her.

I ain't never known nothin but New Orleans, she said. But I don't let others fight my battles. I'll come.

Will your proxy work with Mordecai and treat my people right?

He will, or I'll cut his throat myself. She had never looked so serious, not even when torturing that guard in the swamp. Nobody ever had the balls to take out the Supreme Crusader, she said. Maybe we're just throwin rocks at the moon, but if you're gonna try, I've gotta be part of it.

He put a hand on her shoulder. I'm glad you're ready for some *We who are about to die* moves after all. You and me, we've got a lot to make up for.

Think we can pull it off?

He looked at her for a moment. Then he shrugged. I don't have the slightest idea.

She laughed. It's crazy. Probably stupid. I love it.

This time Troy laughed with her. They stood in silence for a while, watching night take the river, the courtyard and statue, the street where Crusaders and Troublers alike whooped and ran like children playing games in the sunniest, most peaceful meadow God had ever grown.

When Stransky reached Jesus's statue, the crews were lighting the streetlamps. Ex-Troublers and ex-Crusaders danced and sang songs sacred and bawdy. The evening was filled with the scents of roasting meats and vegetables, spices, wood smoke. Despite the scattered squabbles, the city was mostly at peace.

Jack Hobbes leaned against the statue, holding her horse's reins.

She tried to look serious. What did you do to get busted all the way down to groom?

Hobbes handed her the reins. Reckon Gabe told you what he's got in mind.

Stransky climbed into her saddle. Topple the Cult in its greatest fortress, with nothin but a half dozen guns to back his play? Yeah, he told me.

What do you think?

She laughed. I think he's crazier than anybody I've ever known. I also think he's right. Ain't nobody safe while Rook and his kind run the world.

Figured out we're likely to die?

She turned to the sky. Look at them stars. So far away, and they look so small, but every one bright enough to reach us.

Don't know what that means.

It means I'd rather get my ass shot off out yonder than sit here scared half to death every time somethin outside that wall steps on a twig.

Hobbes glanced toward the Temple. Stransky imagined he felt

relieved that Troy was back in the office. But everything had changed. The city's geography, its population, the foundations of Hobbes's faith. *Shit,* she thought. *That ain't the half of it. Jacky's always been an officer and a killer. Now he's gotta figure out how to be a man.* Her horse shifted, stamped, trembled. It wanted to gallop, the wind in its mane. She knew how it felt.

Finally Hobbes cleared his throat. He seemed downright nervous. Comin with us?

She tossed hair out of her eyes. Yep.

He exhaled, but in relief, or dread? Once we go over the wall, you can't back out. Try it and I'll shoot you myself.

Stransky slapped her knee. Jacky, you gotta learn how to talk to a lady, or you ain't never gonna get past first base. Now, if you don't mind, I'm gonna get some of that food I smell.

She turned the horse and walked it toward the gate. He would have no idea what the metaphor meant. Neither did she. The reference had been lost to history, as dead as the old times and the old people. But it would make him blush. That pleased her, even if she could not see it in the dark.

Then, his voice. Stay with me. Gonna have plenty of food at the meetin tonight.

She reined up and turned back. His shape blended with the statue's, as if the stone itself were speaking to her. Why, Jacky. If you ain't a sweetheart.

Shut up and wait while I get my horse.

# ✦ 57 ✦

**L**ong stood in her back yard, washing off the day's grit, when a man on horseback rounded the corner. She was naked, her skin glistening in the moonlight. When she saw him, she uttered a little cry and grabbed her filthy smock off the ground and held it over her body. But when she recognized Santonio Ford, she laughed and let it drop. They had washed together after many battles. As he got closer, his sweet scent, like lavender, told her he had already made his ablutions.

She picked up an old piece of sacking and toweled off. On your way to the Temple?

He dismounted and leaned against her poplar tree. His horse rolled in the grass. Yeah. Gotta say, after the last couple months, I wish Gabriel had let us be for one night.

She splashed a handful of water on her face and scrubbed with her bare hands. I reckon he don't intend to wait long. You still goin?

Course I am. And so are you. It ain't even a question.

So what's wrong?

Ford cleared his throat. Long picked up her grimy clothes. Inside, she had left a few lamps burning—one by the door, one in the den, one in her bedroom. She led him into the den. Ford sat in a chair and waited while she walked to the bedroom and put on a fresh shirt, pants, socks, boots. When she returned, he was kneeling in prayer. She hung back in the doorway and let him finish.

When he rose, he smiled, though his eyes looked sad. I've spent half my time in prayer lately, he said. I can't get past what I did, no matter how I spin it in my mind.

She sat on the couch and patted the seat next to her. He took it, and she grasped his hand in both of hers. His slumped shoulders, his tone of voice, his eyes—they told a story of guilt and sleeplessness.

You're thinkin about what all we did to save our lives, she said.

Ford nodded. Not so much what happened after the shootin started. Everybody knew what they were gettin into. But the deceit. Charters and Lange—innocents goin out like garbage. I don't care what the reasons were. We did wrong. *I* did wrong.

From outside, the shouts of children running through the streets. I feel it too, she said. I reckon we all do. We'll lose some of our treasures in heaven.

If we get there at all. I feel like Judas, with my own life the thirty pieces of silver. My future the potter's field.

Long knew what he meant. Her inner aches made the celebrations outside seem farcical. I reckon that's why Gordy wanted to die, she said. He walked through more muck than we did. I wish we could stay with him. Or take him.

Me too. But we gotta march, and he ain't ready. Gabe's right about that.

That would be their reward for deeds both good and ill. To leave the city they had saved. To sleep on the ground and eat what they could kill and fight for their lives every step of the way.

It's a quest, she said. Our purification.

Yeah.

She got up, crossed to her window, and pulled the curtains. It all made sense. They would march on Washington to balance the scales with the Lord, whose will they had done through devilish misdeeds. They would march for atonement with no more mendacity about where they stood.

She stayed at the window a while longer. Then she walked back to the couch and sat beside Ford, whose head was bowed in prayer again. They sweltered in the heat and drank water and spoke to God. Soon enough they would mount their horses and ride through the streets, pretending to be as happy as most everyone else.

**T**he Temple personnel had pushed Troy's desk against the wall and stacked his straight-backed chairs on top of it. They had brought in dining chairs and tables, most of which were covered in platters of roast beef and chicken, fried pork, corn and beans and rice and peas, crawfish etouffee, smoked sausage and duck jambalaya. A cook hauled in pitchers of water and cups. Someone had set the dinner table. Tonight they would feast. Tomorrow they would start preparations for the journey. Troy intended to go over the wall in one week. They would enter unknown country and ride through it, walk it, sleep in it. Probably die in it, like Moses. A bitter cup that would not pass from them.

They sat together as staff scurried about, filling cups, taking away dirty dishes and replacing them with clean plates and utensils. Everyone ate as if they had starved for years, and though Troy had enjoyed the gumbos and such the Troublers had fed him, he had missed the city's food.

As he helped himself to fire-grilled steak and oven-baked potatoes, he pondered those around him.

Lynn Stransky, her hair washed and combed back from her forehead, talked through mouthfuls of food and elbowed Jack Hobbes every time she told an off-color joke. Hobbes, clean and groomed, sat at his ease beside her. Something about them, the way they leaned in to share a word, the glances when one passed a dish. *Good for y'all.* What would Sarah's hair look like, falling loose past her shoulders or wafting in a breeze? Jack Hobbes or Lynn Stransky or both might die out there. What would happen if one survived the other?

Ernie Tetweiller wore his usual three days' growth of white beard, now clotted with the fatty drippings of roast duck. *He still serves four or five days out of seven.* The old man could have spent all his time drinking his precious whiskey and eating fatty meats and cursing, but he had stood with Troy, and now he planned to ride with the rest of them. At his age, and given the nature of their enterprise, he would likely never see his city again, even if the rest of them somehow made it back. And so, whenever Troy could catch the old man's eye, he raised his glass and smiled. And Tetweiller smiled back, meat caught in his teeth.

Santonio Ford had been quiet much of the night. The recent campaign had required much of him, as devout a servant of God as ever there was. In his future lay even more weight for his conscience. *I hope you can find your peace again, my friend.*

LaShanda Long sat opposite Ford and joined in the revelry as much as anyone, but it was clear she struggled with her own heavy heart. Much of the populace might never trust her. Perhaps they would remember her years of loyal service and the strength and plentitude of the weapons she had provided. Or perhaps they would not.

Willa McClure had chosen a seat between Ford and Tetweiller, Bandit lounging under the table and snapping up the scraps people dropped for him. The girl had brushed off Troy's suggestions that she and Bandit stay and help the proxies run the city, saying, *You ain't got nobody else that can do what I do. Santonio's quiet, but he's bigger.* Troy could not argue with that, but he kept picturing McClure lying dead in a ditch.

*She deserves better. Lord, please watch over this child. Bring her home, even if the rest of us die hard. Your will be done.*

Was it even right to call her *girl*? She had been through as much as most people Tetweiller's age. What was the precise measure of a woman?

Jerold Babb sat apart from the others, silent and meek and blushing.

His place at the table stemmed from respect for his office, not because the man belonged in their company. He had sided with Royster and, in the city's eyes, was party to all those deaths, to all that would have come with the flood. He moved like an even older man. Had he scourged himself? Or did guilt have weight?

*You followed your heart and the teachins of your church. I just hope you'll help Mordecai and them keep the peace.*

And their absent friends—Gordy Boudreaux and his injured mind, his sickened spirit. Sister Sarah, wrapped in the arms of the Lord as surely as her body was wrapped in the habit. What would happen to them?

Troy blinked away the tears that wanted to come. As always, he had to be strong, the rock all the world's waters could not wear away, the oak no lightning could split or burn. He was the lord of order. No matter how tired, he would lead them forward until they won or died. There was no third choice. Not in this world.

When Norville Unger slipped into the room, Troy stood. All right, y'all, he said. It's time. Norville?

Unger held up a sheaf of paper and a quill pen. He sat and smoothed the paper on a corner of Troy's desk and dipped the pen into an inkwell. One by one the rest of them stood.

Troy went first, saluting his fellows. I, Gabriel Troy, Lord of Order of the New Orleans Principality, name Mordecai Jones my proxy. May he serve long and well.

So say we all, said everyone, even Stransky.

And so it went around the table. Lynn Stransky named Bushrod, ignoring Troy's dark looks. Ernie Tetweiller named Ruth Longfellow, a woman steadfast and true, a butcher by trade who had ridden in many posses. Even Stransky recognized the name. She had probably seen Longfellow through a rifle scope.

Jack Hobbes named Loudon Grimm, a steelsmith who had likewise fought Troublers in streets and swamps. Grimm stood nearly six and a half feet tall and could heft an anvil on his shoulders. Troy wished he had sent Grimm after Jevan Dwyer. His own face would have fared the better for it.

In Boudreaux's stead, Hobbes and Tetweiller named Cecily Fitzhugh, a fisherwoman with a head for figures and a draw as quick as anyone's. She also helped in the markets, making sure everyone's belly was full, their shelters sound. It was understood among those at the table that Fitzhugh would serve while Boudreaux remained with the sisters. If he ever chose, he could take his rightful place.

Santonio Ford named Liv Tetweiller, a cousin of Ernie's who had distinguished herself as a hunter.

LaShanda Long named Benson Ruddiger, her best metallurgist. The man had no leadership experience, but she believed he could learn on the job.

Willa McClure controlled neither territory nor trade, so she named no proxy. And in any event, who could replace her? She sat and listened, feeding Bandit under the table, keeping her own counsel.

Jerold Babb would hold no council seat. If he retained a fifth of his former congregation and his title, even for a few months, it would seem a minor miracle.

Derosier and Baptiste had removed their names from consideration but had agreed to serve as special liaisons to the population, solving disputes between former enemies, enacting the council's decisions, and the like.

Stransky announced the names of the former Troublers who would co-chair the trades and serve on the council. Their own lieutenants' incorporation would be another task for the council and the city. Troy knew none of them, but he had agreed to trust Stransky and could not gainsay her first decision. No one else objected.

The proxies and new members so named, everyone sat, awaiting dessert. Norville Unger slipped out, his sheaf of paper in hand. He would return to his desk, where he would craft and copy the official proclamation. And in one week, most everyone at the table would quit the city. Outlawed and hunted and persecuted like the Christians of old. Some had never traveled farther than the nearby bayous. As old as he was, even Ernie Tetweiller had never seen the Gulf, had never ridden as far as Jackson. Who knew for certain they could even find Washington?

The staff brought in half a dozen pies, apple and blueberry and pecan, cherry and peach and huckleberry. The desserts were sliced and passed around. Everyone ate and laughed. Though weary and wounded, they had made their stand. And, for this night at least, they could celebrate, toasting each other with their bellies full.

For just a moment, everyone fell quiet. All eyes turned to Troy, who sat at their head, his plate cleared, his bruised and battered face solemn. Saluting their bravery and their sacrifice, Troy raised his water glass one last time. They drank, and then Troy led them in prayer. When he was done, they sat for a long time, letting the night stretch out and out, reluctant to break the circle and move into the rest of their lives.

# EPILOGUE: THE CEMETERY

The day workers had long since left. The man's voice had degraded into a hoarse croak. Half a dozen times during the telling, he had snapped his fingers at one child or the other, their glazed look suggesting minds that had drifted. Each time he had backtracked five minutes, reminding them of their obligations to the generations yet unborn. Nearby, the great monument stood sentinel. Their jerky was nearly gone, their water low.

When the man fell silent, the boy cleared his throat. What happened next? he asked.

Next? the man rasped. Why, they went over the wall and sought their destinies.

Yes, but what *happened*? the girl asked. Did Gordy get better? Did they make it to Washington? What about Willa and Bandit?

The children had never seemed so young.

They found what they were seeking, the man said. Their place in God's plan.

Yes, but what *happened*? the boy demanded. You can't just tell part of a story.

The man stared at his son until the demanding, insolent look left the boy's face and he turned away.

That isn't how this works, the man said. Those men and women—and, yes, the girl and her dog—took their journey in stages. It wasn't always clear when one stage ended and another began. And that is how we tell their story. One piece at a time.

But that's not fair, the girl insisted.

Fair? Those people had to learn patience and humility and honor and sacrifice so we might live in a world free of terror. A world free of any one person who stands above us all, wielding authority like a hammer that knocks us all to pieces. You must learn those same qualities so you may be worthy.

Of what? the boy said.

Of what has been given to you. Of leading the world farther up the path. Of God's love.

The last light bled from the day. From everywhere, crickets and cicadas and birdsong.

So how do we learn those things? the boy asked.

The man stood, wincing as his joints popped. You gather our things and follow me home. Speak no more of these matters. Not to me, not to each other. If you can manage that, then in one year's time, we will return to this place and continue the story.

But what if we can't wait?

Then your weakness will fulfill its own prophecy, and you shall never find your answers. The choice is yours. No one can make it for you.

His throat felt as if he had swallowed fire. He limped, the blood needling through his legs and feet. The children's frustration washed against him like gentle waves. He had reacted much the same when their grandfather left him alone in the cemetery to gather the blanket and the empty canteens. But he had spoken true. They had to decide for themselves, as everyone must, and each choice would alter the course of the world, even if no one noticed but God. Such was the way of things.

Soon enough, he heard them moving, the rustling of the blanket as they folded it, the clank of the canteens as someone shouldered them. He thanked God for laying His hand on the children, troubling the waters of their souls, teaching them the value of the tale and of their own wills. And then the man, the father, the tale-teller walked through the gloaming toward the wagon and mules waiting for him to take up the reins and set everything in motion once more.

# ACKNOWLEDGMENTS

Thanks, as always, to Kalene Westmoreland—my first reader, my partner, my love.

Thanks to Shauna, John, Brendan, Maya, Nova, Luna, Cookie, Nilla, and Tora for bringing me so much joy. When the night is darkest, I think of you.

Thanks to Vicki Adang, editor extraordinaire, for making the book better and for indulging so many of my stylistic eccentricities.

Thanks to Mark Sedenquist, Megan Edwards, and everyone at Imbrifex Books for all the stellar work.

Thanks to God, for everything. Forgive us for the wrongs we so often do in Your name.

And thanks to you, reader, whoever you are. I hope we cross paths again before our lights leave the world.